A fourth-generation grazier, Nicole Alexander returned to her family's property in the early 1990s. She is currently the business manager there. Nicole has a Master of Letters in creative writing and her novels, poetry, travel and genealogy articles have been published in Australia, Germany, America and Singapore.

She is the author of five previous novels: *The Bark Cutters*, *A Changing Land*, *Absolution Creek*, *Sunset Ridge* and *The Great Plains*.

T0359222

Also by Nicole Alexander

NICOLE ALEXANDER

Wild Lands

BANTAM
SYDNEY • AUCKLAND • TORONTO • NEW YORK • LONDON

A Bantam book
Published by Random House Australia Pty Ltd
Level 3, 100 Pacific Highway, North Sydney NSW 2060
www.randomhouse.com.au

Penguin
Random House
Australia

First published by Bantam in 2015
This edition published in 2016

Random House Books is part of the Penguin Random House group of companies whose addresses can be found at global.penguinrandomhouse.com.

National Library of Australia
Cataloguing-in-Publication entry

Alexander, Nicole L., author.
Wild lands/Nicole Alexander.

ISBN 978 1 74275 989 0 (paperback)

Pioneers – New South Wales – Fiction.
Frontier and pioneer life – Fiction.
Historical fiction.
Love stories.
New South Wales – History – Fiction.

A823.4

Cover design by Luke Causby/Blue Cork
Cover photos: landscape © Philip Lee Harvey/Corbis, woman © Demurez Cover Arts
Internal design and typesetting by Midland Typesetters, Australia
Printed in Australia by Griffin Press, an accredited ISO AS/NZS 14001:2004
Environmental Management System printer

Random House Australia uses papers that are natural, renewable and recyclable products and made from wood grown in sustainable forests. The logging and manufacturing processes are expected to conform to the environmental regulations of the country of origin.

≪ Author's Note ≫

In the history of many civilisations, the subjugation of a native people by others intent on land ownership ultimately leads to bloodshed and dispossession. It was no different in Australia. This, then, is the background to *Wild Lands*, the story of a woman in an untamed land, one that is rife with grievances between black and white.

Although this is a work of fiction, many of the major incidents in the narrative are based on historical accounts, as are the prevailing attitudes of the period. Although, in my role as storyteller, not all of the confrontations in the novel may have occurred in the locations used.

I have endeavoured to portray both black and white perspectives in the narrative, and to that extent I am most grateful to Mr Ted Stubbins for his careful reading of the manuscript and thoughtful opinion regarding the portrayal of Australia's first peoples in the novel. I am also indebted to the following: the University of New England and Regional Archives (UNERA), Armidale, whose collection of early manuscripts proved invaluable; The Inverell Pioneer Village; Ashford Local Aboriginal Land Council Cultural Centre, Keeping Place & Art Gallery; Bingara District Historical Society & Museum. Thanks also to the very generous time given to me by volunteers at Old Government House Parramatta and the Parramatta Visitor's Research Centre. As always, I have made use of the Alexander family archives.

With four generations of farming blood in my veins, land management practices past and present intrigue me. It was fascinating to learn of Australia's first peoples' attitude to the land, and the changes to Australia's landscape that occurred after the arrival of white settlers. I may well be white, but the land sings for me too.

Wild Lands's narrative covers the time period of the documented Aboriginal massacres at both Waterloo Creek (Slaughterhouse Creek) and Myall Creek. The Myall Creek Massacre near Bingara in northern New South Wales involved the killing of 28 unarmed Indigenous Australians by colonists on 10 June 1838. Seven colonists were found guilty of murder and hanged. Although these massacres are not covered in detail and do not form the main narrative of the story, I mention their inclusion for those Indigenous Australian readers who may find their depiction distressing.

Thank you as always to David and my family and friends who have supported me throughout the writing of this novel. To Penguin Random House, my publisher Beverley Cousins, managing editor Brandon VanOver, publicist Erin Seymour and my agent Tara Wynne – thank you for your professionalism, guidance and friendship. Farewell to Brett Osmond, former head of marketing at Penguin Random House. From a writer's perspective, having Brett in your corner made you feel you could take on the world. Thank you, Brett.

Lastly, to the many libraries and booksellers here and abroad, my friends and readers, old and new, thank you.

I am indebted to the following texts and recommend them for further reading:

Australian Frontier Wars, 1788–1838 by John Connor

Forgotten War by Henry Reynolds

Bush tucker, Boomerangs & Bandages, compiled by Michelle McKemey and Harry White

Sticks and Stones, compiled by Tony Sonter and Harry White

Massacre at Myall Creek by Laurie Barber

Waterloo Creek: The Australia Day Massacre of 1838. George Gipps and the British Conquest of NSW by Roger Milliss

The Biggest Estate on Earth: How Aborigines made Australia by Bill Gammage

Bingara 1827–1937 by J.T. Wearne

Blood on the Wattle: Massacres and Maltreatment of Aboriginal Australians Since 1788 by Bruce Elder

A Million Wild Acres by Eric Rolls

Pioneers of the North West Plains, compiled by Kath Mahaffey

A Short History of Australia by Manning Clark

Australians: Origins to Eureka by Thomas Keneally

A History of Bathurst, Volume 1: The Early Settlement to 1862 by Theo Barker

Parramatta: A Past Revealed by Terry Kass, Carol Liston and John McClymont

Wind & Watermills in Old Parramatta by Olga Tatrai

The Squatters by Geoffry Dutton

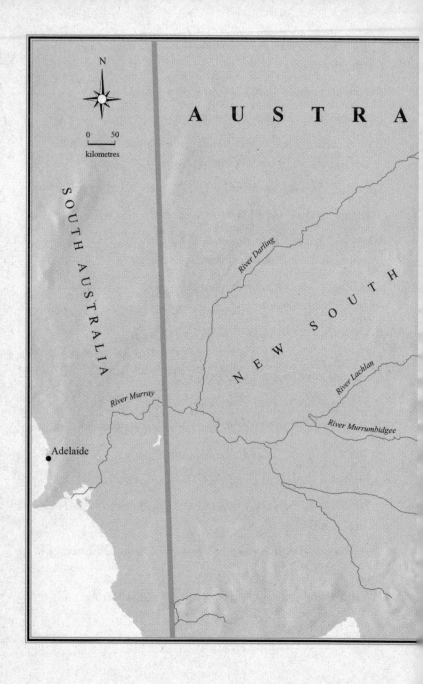

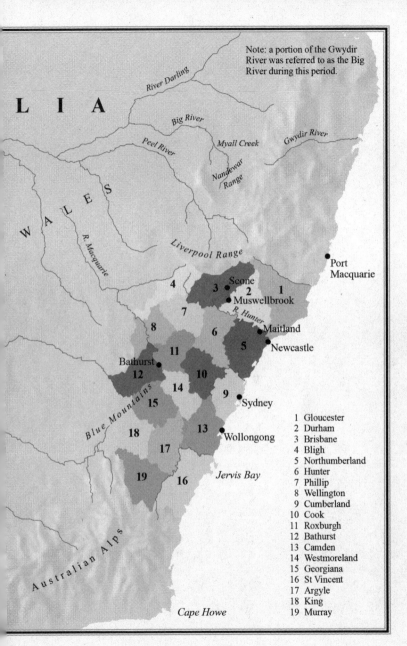

Note: a portion of the Gwydir River was referred to as the Big River during this period.

L I A

River Darling

Big River

Peel River

Myall Creek

Gwydir River

Nandewar Range

W A L E S

R. Macquarie

Liverpool Range

Port Macquarie

4

3 Scone

2

1

Muswellbrook

7

R. Hunter

8

6

Maitland

11

5

Newcastle

Bathurst

12

10

14

9

15

Sydney

18

13

17

Wollongong

19

16

Jervis Bay

Blue Mountains

Australian Alps

Cape Howe

1	Gloucester
2	Durham
3	Brisbane
4	Bligh
5	Northumberland
6	Hunter
7	Phillip
8	Wellington
9	Cumberland
10	Cook
11	Roxburgh
12	Bathurst
13	Camden
14	Westmoreland
15	Georgiana
16	St Vincent
17	Argyle
18	King
19	Murray

Australia *c.*1837

⋘ Prologue ⋙

1817 – The Mountain

Florence pushed open the bark door of the humpy. Outside she sensed movement in the dense scrub. Black against black beneath a late-rising moon. She stood motionless, waiting for the man to show himself. He finally appeared from the tangle of scrub to stand on a rock on the far bank of the creek. The black was a barrel-chested man with spindly legs and a long spear, which he leaned on while watching the humpy. He peered across a slice of moonlit land, the trees threw shadows, the creek glittered. Florence tugged at the shawl hugging her shoulders and turned to check on her son. The six-year-old remained sleeping.

The black had appeared after her man's leaving. She had no musket for protection, only a sturdy branch resting near the door, which had been used to smash snakes and spiders but not a savage. It was strange but she was becoming used to seeing the black perched on the opposite side of the narrow creek. He came around midnight when the countryside was so still the slightest of sounds seemed inordinately loud. It was usually at the same time that the fire in the humpy dwindled and the ache in the small of Florence's back made her rise from the chill of the dirt floor. Now the nights had turned cold her boy, Adam, was fractious. He was constantly hungry and in his sleep he kicked and plied at her body as though a mewling puppy seeking the teat.

Scrubby trees framed the grassy clearing and the flat-topped rock that the black had claimed as his own. He remained motionless. Alone. Watching her watching him. He too must have been feeling the bite of the weather for tonight his dark torso was covered by an animal hide. The cloak was decorated with strange patterns and accentuated his thin, angular legs.

Florence wiped at her runny nose. For four nights she'd confronted this wild man, who stalked her from a distance, and every night, as now, she pulled the ill-fitting bark door closed on him, her heart a lump of fear.

Adam was now sitting upright, rubbing his eyes, complaining of the cold, of being hungry. She shushed the boy back to sleep with the promise of Tom's return and stoked the fire until it burnt good and hot. It was impossible not to imagine the worst. She'd heard the stories of whites being speared, of friendly natives turning into murderers. The colonials had the law on their side and the Governor was quick with retribution, but she and Tom and the boy had no-one. Her hand rose to the necklace about her throat. She'd fossicked for the shells on the beach when looking after Captain Harbison's children and had strung them on a piece of twine. It was the only thing of value she'd ever owned and it reminded her of her old life.

The next morning Florence watched as Adam, sitting on the floor of the hut, selected one of two white pebbles and transferred it to a neighbouring pile. There were six pebbles in the week's pile.

'Tomorrow's Sunday.'

'Yes, it is.' In truth, Florence had no idea what day it was. With difficulty she levered her aching body up from the ground and, opening the door of the humpy, peered outside.

Across the creek a large lizard was sunning itself on the stone. Adam rushed past her before she could stop him and was soon at the water's edge, throwing sticks. Behind their dwelling, which had been erected against the width of a gnarly barked tree, the bush was quiet.

The morning was brittle with cold. It was not the bone-chilling misery of the Mother Country but it was cold enough to feel the stiffening of joints and to wish for warmer days. Florence felt cramped by the smallness of this place that they inhabited yet scared by what lay beyond the fringes of their world. The sheltered clearing, which had been their home for the last month, was marked by two stretches of narrow grass split by the water and bound by the scrub on either side. It had taken two weeks of bashing through the scrub, across deep and rocky gullies, to reach the spot, during which time she, Tom and the boy had often found it easier to wade along the water's edge than try to penetrate the dense bush. Exhaustion made them stop here. It seemed as good a place as any to wait out the winter.

As Florence's stomach growled, she thought of the dwindling stores piled in a corner of the humpy; two potatoes, a pound of flour, a bit of tea and a twist of sugar. She'd existed on less. When Tom had escaped and begged her and her boy to run away with him, they had spent a week on the fringes of the settlement, holed up beneath a rock ledge. Each day they'd sucked on a strip of salted mutton and sipped sparingly at the water dripping from the overhang into the quart pot. And each day Adam had been happy to be part of a great adventure, but it had gone on for too long. Tom had swapped one gaol for another. Out here, an unknown land kept them all in bondage.

'Ma, Ma.'

Florence shushed her son to quietness, pointing at the bush

that loomed around them. The boy frowned and pursed his lips, kicking at the ground. He was slight for his age, brown-haired, with the beginnings of a determined streak. He had his father's bearing. Captain Harbison had looked after his female convicts but he expected repayment. For months Florence had endured a quick rutting in the pantry at midnight, her face pressed against a sack of wheat. And although the Captain never looked her in the eye, if the truth be told Florence didn't mind his attentions one bit. But then Tom Fossey had arrived on the farm. Oh, he was a fine man to gaze upon. Too fine to be a convict like her. She was like a fly attracted to a bowl of dripping and so they'd run away and in the doing given no thought to the consequences. Adam had begun to call to her again. She lifted a hand in warning, threatening to smack him. If they found her she would be flogged to within an inch of her life, and Tom would be placed in irons and at the very least sent to a chain gang.

Florence walked back and forth along the creek bank, examining the objects Adam brought to her: shiny pebbles, a tuft of grass, handfuls of sludgy creek sand.

'How long do we have to stay here?' asked Adam for the hundredth time.

'Until Tom comes back.' The man had asked her to run away with him, hadn't he? So why did Florence have this niggling doubt that maybe he'd abandoned them? *One night*, he'd told her. *Back before you know it*, he'd promised. 'You know he's gone to find food.' Keeping the boy quietly occupied consumed her, especially now with a black keeping watch from across the water. Over the last couple of days Florence had taken to scanning her surrounds on a regular basis. She would look over her shoulder convinced someone was watching them, only to be faced with a scuttling creature, while a flurry of birdsong accompanied her very worst thoughts.

'But, what if he doesn't come back?'

'He will,' Florence replied abruptly, wondering who she was trying to convince. Anything might have happened to him. At this very moment he could be lying in a ditch with his head split open. Or maybe the blacks had got him. Florence swallowed.

Stirring the outside camp fire to life, Florence gathered twigs and branches and watched as the flames grew and a white-grey smoke rose into the air. Adam gathered his own pile of kindling and intermittently fed the fire.

'We should go home.' Adam poked at the flames with a thin stick.

Florence sat the quart pot on the fire. Last week's tea-leaves bubbled in the water.

Adam's memories were of a warm place to sleep, of bits of bread in fat. He wouldn't remember the rest – the floggings, the hours of toil, the hardship. Florence thought of her past life often, for the wildness of this place made a person wish for what they'd run from. She looked to the bend in the trees where she'd last seen Tom, as Adam helped her mix flour and water together on a piece of bark. They moulded the mixture around two sticks and when the timber was encased in the dough, Florence rested them on the fire. The concoction cooked quickly in the embers and they picked the sticks clean, finishing their meal with the stewed tea shared from a pannikin, before washing up in the creek.

The black was behind them when they turned. He stood between the fire and the humpy and in his hand held their remaining twist of sugar. Florence clasped Adam to her. The black held his ground. Behind him a spear leant against the side of the humpy. Up close the man was of medium height, with a spreading nose and thick lips. Florence guessed he was aged in his late twenties. The space around his dark eyes was whiter than white and his stare remained unbroken as he extended a hand and dropped a chunk of meat onto the fire. Florence examined the sizzling flesh, keeping a cautious eye on the black as he gathered his weapon and quietly merged back into the bush.

Adam struggled to be set free and ran off after him.

'What are you doing?' Florence yelled, following him. 'You'll get lost if you set one foot in there.'

Adam halted at the edge of the wickerwork of trees. Florence tugged harshly at the boy's ear and he howled loudly, his thin voice echoing. 'Shush up.' She glanced nervously in the direction the black had gone. 'What if there's more of them out there, eh? And here you are whining like a dog. Telling all and sundry we're here.'

The boy quietened. 'What if Tom doesn't come back, Ma?'

'Now why wouldn't he, eh? Here' – she took the string of shells from her neck and wound them around the child's wrist – 'they're special to me, they are, Adam, so you look after them.'

They stood on the edge of the scrub, their worn shoes straddling the border between the known and the unknown.

Mother and child carefully backed away.

The meat smelt strong, like mutton almost past the point of eating. Florence didn't want to touch it. She wanted to throw it in the dirt and stamp on it. Instead she walked into the hut and checked their few remaining possessions. He'd only taken a bit of sugar and reluctantly Florence admitted to herself that it was more than a fair trade. They sat on the ground by the fire and prodded the roasting meat with a stick.

Florence had taken the knife from the humpy and she unrolled it from the piece of cloth, revealing its fine bone handle. She'd snitched it from the Harbisons on the way out the door. The meat was tough and stringy, but the knife hacked through the flesh, marking the bark plate with interlacing cuts. They ate hungrily, grinning at each other as the juices ran down their chins.

That night Florence lay on her back inside the humpy, the boy by her side. Her head hurt and her limbs shivered and ached and she worried that the black had poisoned them. She lay a hand on Adam's brow. Her son was fine, sleeping peacefully. Thank the heavens for that mercy. The sickness had started that afternoon, followed by a fever that set her body trembling. She wished now for a bit of sugar to suck, for Tom to return. She even wished for the old days, before Tom had caught her eye. Some time in the early hours of the morning, the sickness lessened. Florence crawled outside to see if the black was watching, but the moon had risen late and he couldn't be seen among the shadows. Even he had left them.

She laughed bitterly and returned to her hollow in the dirt. Overhead, the smoke from the fire drifted upwards and out through the opening in the bark roof. Florence was tired of the brightness of the moon, of the stars that she'd never grown to love. She curled herself into a ball and waited for the morning.

By daylight the world had been obliterated, replaced by a dense fog that masked the creek and wrapped the land in a shroud of wispy whiteness. She could hear noises, speech of some sort, but the fog distorted the sounds and it was impossible to know from which direction they came or how far away they were. It could only be blacks. The thought caused her stomach to tighten, but she inspected the hazy surrounds gratefully. For the moment the fog kept the humpy safe from view. Carefully retreating into the hut, Florence closed the door, tied the shawl tightly about her shoulders and placed the thick branch Tom had left for protection by her side. She could only hope that the fog would shield them long enough for the blacks to move on.

Inside, Adam quickly grew restless. 'Who's out there?'

'Blacks.' Florence roasted one of their precious potatoes to keep him quiet, but too soon the boy had gulped down the food and was on his knees peering through the ill-fitting pieces of bark.

'I can't see nothing.' He slumped down on the dirt. 'I wanna go out.'

'Shush up, boy.' It was then she thought of the fire. Even if they couldn't see the humpy, whoever roamed outside would smell the smoke and pick up the scent of Adam's meal.

'Ma, what's out there?'

The thud of something being thrown against the wall of the hut stilled Adam's tongue. The noise sounded again, and again.

'You stay here,' Florence warned softly. 'Go over there.' She pointed to the corner. 'Keep the fire between you and the door, alright?'

Adam moved to the far wall, the strand of shells clutched in his small hand. Reaching for the stick, Florence took a deep breath and went outside.

Five blacks waited in the lifting fog. Of mixed age, they had pot bellies and matted hair. Each held a spear or a club while one had a dead kangaroo draped over a shoulder. The leader spoke to her brusquely, waving a hand at Florence as if she'd committed some offence. She held her ground, the thick branch clasped before her as the other men's voices were raised in annoyance, each man revealing a mouth with the front teeth missing.

'Get out,' she yelled, 'get off with you!' She raised the thick branch as if she were shooing away chickens. 'Go away.'

One of the men rushed forward and hit her with a club. Florence staggered and fell. There was something sticky on the side of her face and for a moment her eyes dulled. Dazed, she heaved herself up onto her elbows and began to crawl towards the humpy. She pushed at the door as a wave of dizziness came over her. Florence looked at the far wall. A piece of bark had been removed from the rear of the hut.

Adam was gone.

❖

The blacks rummaged through the humpy, stepped over Florence and walked towards the creek. With her remaining strength she rolled onto her side and watched as her attackers disappeared into the bush. They carried blankets and the quart pot, but there was no sign of the boy. The creek gurgled and gushed. She didn't know how long she'd been lying in the dirt, but the morning was now sunny and bright. Florence thought for the first time how beautiful this place was, how quiet. The ground grew warm, as though ready to embrace her.

The canoe appeared like an apparition. It slid into her field of vision, gliding along the creek soundlessly, carried by unknown forces. There was a black sitting in it. The black from the rock, who had brought the meat. He looked at her.

Behind him a white child, a boy, reached out his hand and called to her.

Florence closed her eyes.

*We are at war with them: they look upon us
as enemies – as invaders – as their oppressors
and persecutors – they resist our invasion. They
have never been subdued, therefore are they not
rebellious subjects, but an injured nation, defending
in their own way, their rightful possessions, which
have been torn from them by force.*

Attributed to James Erskine Calder, settler, 1831

≪ Chapter 1 ≫

Ten years later
1827 June — eight miles west of Sydney

A cooling draft wafted in through the shuttered window, bringing with it the sweet scent of rain. Ten-year-old Kate Carter lay listening to the sound on the roof and the moaning howl of a dingo. It was the third time she'd heard the wild dog in as many nights and she wondered if he too felt lonely as she did. On her left, one of the two older women in the cramped room coughed and muttered in her sleep. Pushing aside the coarse blanket, Kate shuffled her way to the end of the bed. The tampered dirt floor was cold underfoot as her palm slid across the surface of the roughly mortared wall, bits of protruding oyster shells grazing her hand. She moved soundlessly to the end of the room and reached the window, which looked out across the rear of the garden. The room that adjoined the kitchen smelt of cooked mutton and a full chamber pot but the open door allowed the heat from the fire to take the chill from the air, and Kate was comforted by the wan light that the embers produced.

At the window she pushed the shutters open and rested her arms on the sill. At the end of the garden a fig tree glistened in the patchy moonlight, its green leaves glossy with moisture. The great woody plant reached up into the heavens, the uppermost branches appearing to caress the stars. The tree was dense with leaves but from the highest branch there was a good view of the countryside. The Reverend's farm, where Kate lived, was surrounded by other farms in an area thick with natives and highwaymen. Only last year one of the fanciest homes in the area, Burwood House, had been robbed and the men responsible were captured and hung by their necks. The two women she now shared space with had been sent with the rest of the convicts to be reminded of the grisly end such actions caused, but the women had thought it a fine outing, one that spared them a few hours of work.

Kate drew her thoughts from images of taut ropes and kicking feet and pretended she was atop the fig tree. If she looked westward to Parramatta she imagined she could see the cemetery where her father lay buried. In the topmost branches, surrounded by birds and leaves, she spoke to him, telling him of the small things that filled her days. Of course she never told anyone of these conversations, not even her mother. She'd promised her father that this would be their secret and Kate was proud that there was something special that only she and her father shared.

Yesterday she'd told him about the cabbage-tree hat that she was learning to make. The Reverend employed convict women to weave the palm leaves together to form the flat-brimmed hats nearly everyone wore. Her mother said he made a good shilling supplying free settlers and convicts but that wasn't his main occupation. The Reverend was a farmer as well. The convicts sniggered that he was a Presbyterian pastor with trade inclinations, although why everyone in his household called him Reverend, Kate didn't know.

With the darkening sky Kate couldn't see the thick roots that sprawled out from the fig tree's base like legs, but it was not difficult to imagine the hollow at the rear of the tree where she sat, once she climbed down from the boughs above. It would be cold at the base of the tree tonight, cold and wet. It seemed to Kate that there were now only two places of her very own in the world. The fig tree and the pallet that lay next to Madge's. When her father was alive she'd had her own room in a little stone house with a bark roof. His passing had changed everything.

On the floor behind her the cook, Lambeth, and the scullery maid, Madge, snored and muttered in their sleep. Kate leant out the window. Rain peppered her face and arms. Tilting her head towards the sky, droplets pricked her skin and outstretched tongue. She licked her lips and smiled as the air grew thick with the cloying smell of damp earth. A flash of creamy whiteness, a ghostly owl, flew past the window to land on the nearby woodpile, and as the rain grew heavier a gust of wind blew the shutters closed with a bang.

'What you doing then?' In the dark room Lambeth's voice was harsh. 'Get away from there before we all get the sickness, or worse.'

The shutters rattled violently as the storm grew heavier. Kate slid the latch across firmly and muttered an apology.

Madge, a girl of eighteen, was out of bed quickly. She grabbed Kate by the ear and led her back to the pallet.

'Ouch,' Kate whimpered.

'I told you she gets up and about of a-night,' Madge said harshly. 'Pokes around the place, she does, sticks that fine nose of hers into a person's business, probably tells on us to the Reverend. Stay there.' The older girl gave Kate a shove and she fell onto the pallet. 'Think yer better than us, don't cha?' Madge grabbed Kate's blanket. 'Give it.'

'I wasn't doing anything wrong,' Kate argued, rubbing her ear.

'How many times have I told you to keep the blooming shutters closed?' Lambeth said with frustration. 'Anyone could crawl through that window, robbers and such-like.'

Madge gave a chuckle. 'Well, if some handsome highwayman jumps through that window, he's mine.'

'You're as bad as the youngin,' the cook complained. 'Now get to sleep the both of you.'

Kate brushed away tears. It was best not to answer. To do so usually led to a slap across the face or a cuff behind the ear, and her mother had enough to fret over without worrying about Kate. Although Kate did her best to hide the truth of things in their new home, occasionally the line between her mother's eyes deepened and she would give her daughter a disbelieving stare. Kate guessed that there were only so many trees you could climb and keep falling from. She turned on her side, bringing her knees to her chest.

Lambeth and Madge often talked about Kate and her mother, Lesley, and at these times they were not of a mind to worry if Kate was in earshot or not. It seemed they knew everyone's story. It didn't matter if you were the Governor or a soldier's wife or a free settler, the two convicts who ran the kitchen knew all about everyone and they knew more about Kate than Kate.

They reminded Kate regularly that her mother's parents had been among the first free settlers in the colony, while her convict father had been pardoned. For Lambeth and Madge, this meant that as Kate and her mother were free and native born that they thought themselves high and mighty. Far better than everyone else working on the Reverend's farm who were convicts toiling fourteen or more hours a day. It was best, Kate's mother advised, not to say anything, even though it was true that convicts were beneath them, especially mealy-mouthed London women of questionable reputation assigned to the colony. It was a matter of hierarchy, her mother explained. Kate still didn't know what the word meant.

The room soon grew chilly. Kate reached tentatively for the stolen blanket but Madge had cocooned herself within the material and, although asleep, clutched at it with both hands. There was nothing to do but lie where she was and shiver to warm herself by the kitchen fire. Kate snuck from her bed, picking up Lambeth's shawl, which had slipped to the floor from the woman's bedding.

6

Careful not to fall over the sacks of wheat that lined the wall, she went next door to the kitchen, wrapping the shawl about her shoulders. The embers glowed in the large hearth and the few cut lengths of wood she placed on the smouldering coals from the wood box caught fire quickly.

Kate sat cross-legged on Lambeth's shawl, watching the dancing firelight, tiny red-gold figures of licking flame moving haphazardly along the burning timber. If her father were there he'd tell Kate to cheer up and be grateful for the roof over her head and food to eat. At the thought of him she felt a little better and she found herself staring at the stone fireplace that was large enough for her to walk into. Its internal ledges held clothes irons ready for heating, kettles and pans, while overhead, large iron arms could be swung back and forth to hold pots over flames. Lambeth may not have been the nicest of people, but she prepared delicious chunky stews of birds, kangaroo and possum. Miraculous concoctions of potatoes and flesh were made rich with gravy, her speciality a lavish braised liver sauce. Even the Reverend remarked that the cook's clear soup of boiled bones was not to be sniffed at.

The smoke curled through the hole in the bark ceiling above the fire as rain fell. Kate's sleeplessness had come a few weeks after her father's death. At first it was her mother's tears that woke her in the middle of the night and then Lesley's frequent pacing in the small parlour, which had been her pride. Whatever the reason, Kate had grown used to waking when the household was asleep and because her movements were strictly supervised by Lambeth during the day, she enjoyed her nightly wanderings. Wrapping Lambeth's shawl about her shoulders, she opened the kitchen door. The slab stone step was freezing underfoot and the rain had intensified. Mud splattered her feet as large droplets splashed the dirt of the narrow track that led to the cottage. The building was out of bounds to everyone except those who were assigned specific tasks, such as cleaning and the serving of meals and tending to the fire. This rule was especially difficult for Kate, whose own mother slept in the cottage's second bedroom.

Wiping rain from her cheeks, Kate ran between the two dwellings, mud squelching between her toes. She wondered if her mother would be awake. On previous occasions when she'd snuck into the cottage there'd often be a light beneath her door, but she didn't dare disturb her. It was enough to sit outside her mother's room, to remember what it was like to be a family, until sleepiness overcame her and Kate was ready to return to bed. The front door handle turned easily. Kate wiped one foot over the other and stepped into the austere parlour. The room was in semi-darkness. She shut the door quietly and waited, listening, then tip-toed across to the fire. Kate could tell that the Reverend had only recently gone to bed. The stink of a slush lamp hung in the air, an open bible sat on a table and the Reverend's coat was folded carefully over the back of a two-seater sofa.

Outside a rumble of thunder was accompanied by a flash of lightning. Kate flinched, watching as the brightness lit the white-washed walls, emphasising the plainness of the room and the musket sitting on brackets above the mantelpiece. Droplets of moisture sprinkled the timber floor as Kate lay the shawl across a chair to dry and then warmed her hands by the fire. She knew she would be in dreadful trouble if she were caught in the cottage, but she couldn't help it. Kate didn't see much of her mother. She was always busy penning the sermons the Reverend dictated and running his household. Lambeth said it was just plain wrong for Lesley Carter to sleep under the same roof as the Reverend, but it didn't really bother Kate, except that there was no room for her.

A light still shone from beneath her mother's door. Kate placed her palm on the timber frame as thunder rattled overhead. In between the sounds of the storm Kate was sure she heard a rustle from within and the murmur of voices. Perhaps her mama had taken to saying prayers, as it was said the Reverend did so day

8

and night. But then it was two voices she could hear, a man and a woman's, her mother's and . . . The keyhole was cold against her skin. Kate pressed hard against the lock, straining to see within, and under her weight the door partially opened. The breath caught in her throat, but the movement went unnoticed as the storm raged on.

Her mother sat on the edge of the bed. One by one a length of blackness fell to her shoulders as she unpinned her hair and placed the pins on the bedcover. A slush lamp silhouetted her with a weak yellow light and for a moment Kate thought her beautiful mother looked how she imagined an angel would. On the grey blanket next to her was the hairbrush Kate had used to brush out her mother's hair before they had arrived at the Reverend's. Kate often thought about sneaking into the room. It would be like the old days, when her father was still alive. She remembered kneeling behind her mother brushing her hair, as her father smoked his pipe and told them about the wool yield he hoped for or when rain was needed for the newly planted wheat. One hundred strokes. Her mother counted each stroke aloud and Kate would repeat the numbers. She'd learnt to count that way.

Her mother ran long fingers through her hair, and stretched her neck from one side to the other. Outside, the wind blew forcefully. Surely her mother would let her stay for the night, let Kate cuddle next to her. Hadn't she done everything her mother asked of her since their arrival? Hadn't she been seen and not heard as the Reverend demanded? Kate was about to walk into the bedchamber when a white blaze of lightning illuminated the room. A man's cough followed the thud of a lightning strike. Kate's eyes widened as she cautiously peered around the door.

'Always remember the consolations of religion, my dear.' The Reverend observed her mother from the other side of the room, a spluttering candlestick in one hand. 'The demands of the Lord must be accepted for only through his work can we show the true way to the light.' He held his palm above the flame, wincing in pain before drawing it away. 'Think of our meeting place, of our little church. It may only be of mud brick, with a thatched roof and plank seats, but the faithful come every Sunday to hear God's words, words that you help compose. Now think of that same space as a school. A school for the children of settlers and convicts alike, a school you would be mistress of.'

Kate pressed her shoulders against the wall and looked anxiously across the parlour. If she ran now it was possible that no-one would notice her. If she ran now the whistling wind and rain would conceal her footsteps, muffle the click of the door. If she ran now, she'd not be accused of spying, of sneaking into the cottage when she shouldn't be here, of being blamed for some missing item, and then who knew what would happen.

'Plain education will be the hallmark of our school. In our small way we will be instrumental in stimulating a sense of moral and religious duty so that the impoverished will grow up to be faithful servants while ensuring they remain within the bounds of the lower status that they were born into.'

'A charitable institution?' Lesley asked.

'For the children of convicts, yes, for free settlers some payment must be expected. But enough of this. You see the task before us. In our darkest hour, God will come to us and save us, but we must be ready, we must be prepared.'

The man walked around the narrow bed and gestured for her mother to stand. 'Come now. You know what we talked of, Lesley. You join me in service to God.'

Lesley studied her hands and then slowly, almost reluctantly, lifted her eyes to the man who stared down at her. 'And my daughter?' She rose from the bed, the movement spilling the hairpins to the floor. The slush lamp revealed the soft curves of her mother's body, bare beneath the thin material of the shift. Why did she not reach for a shawl to conceal her nakedness? For if Kate could see her mother's body, then so could the Reverend. Lifting the candlestick he held it close to Kate's mother's face. The light flickered across olive skin and clear, bright eyes. Lesley Carter raised a dimpled chin.

'You are quite unafraid.' His questioning tone was a mix of surprise and delight. 'I wonder if it is your beauty that gives you such strength. If that be so then remember, my dear, you will fade like a wilted flower one fine summer's day. You would do best to remember that there is only one quality in a woman truly appreciated by man – dutiful obedience. You must work on that quality. You must pray to God for guidance, for stubbornness will not be rewarded on earth or in God's Kingdom. Stubbornness, disobedience and outspokenness are unacceptable, indeed quite at odds with the fragile female mind. Such behaviour may well send you into a state of flux from which there is no recovery.' He rubbed at a front tooth, licked his lips. 'You would do well to be more pliable, more grateful.' He ran his fingers up and down her bare arm. 'After all, it was you who begged me to take Kate in. And as we both know I have little need of a child, nor another servant. I have quite enough to contend with already with the convict class.'

'We are free born,' Lesley reminded the Reverend politely, 'and am I not of service to you in your work? Have I not done all you have asked of me in my dual capacity as secretary and house-keeper?' She paused. 'Have I not done everything required to fulfil my duty, and more?'

The Reverend nodded as if calculating the shrewdness of the woman opposite. 'Why Kate will live with us, of course.' He agreed as if this had always been his intention. Kate bit her knuckles in excitement.

'In this very room with you,' he assured. 'And at those times you're required,' he cleared his throat, 'you will of course come to me as God intends.'

'But you won't marry me?' Lesley probed.

11

Kate couldn't believe what she was hearing. Did her mother really want this tall, thin man with his flat nose and scraggly whiskers to take the place of her father?

'Have we not discussed this? Have I not told you of the impediments that prevent such a union? I would have thought you would be on your knees praying to God for the light that has been shone on you and yours, thanking our Great Almighty for the bountiful benefits that have been heaped upon you since you and your daughter found yourselves alone in the world, without kin, without the providing hand of a husband, bereft of a home.' His voice rose and he held a hand in the air as if he were preaching in the wattle and daub hut that was for making cabbage-tree hats during the week and for sermons on Sundays.

'You hope for a better match?' Lesley Carter raised a questioning eyebrow. 'Surely I deserve some assurance that my reputation, the reputation of my daughter, remains absolute? Surely you do not propose my ruination, for such a dismal state will occur with such an arrangement.'

'I beseech you, Lord, assist this woman in understanding that she has been led to me to help in your work. If she refuses what I offer, after providing her with hearth and home, then I in turn must refuse her and her daughter.' He paused and levelled his gaze. 'Consider this an arrangement of mutual advantage.' The Reverend walked towards Lesley and touched her breast beneath the cotton shift. 'It is not to say that I may not change my mind,' he enticed. 'Besides, you want what I offer. I see it in your eyes, Lesley. I see how you enjoy running this household, how the idea of a school appeals.' He cupped her breast. 'I see how you enjoy the life I provide and you are adept at the tasks I give you.'

His hand lifted the material of her mother's shift. As it disappeared beneath a ruffle of cotton, Lesley grasped the Reverend's shoulder, leaning towards him.

Kate's eyes widened.

'And there are other things you want, the base cravings of a woman that can only be satisfied through a servant of God.' His voice grew hoarse. 'See how you want this union. Enter it in the knowledge that you are serving God through serving me.'

Shocked, Kate watched as her mother lifted the flimsy material of the shift over her head. It fell to the floor. 'I will care for you and your daughter. Is that not what you want?' The Reverend tipped the candlestick. Hot wax dripped on her mother's breast and she moaned. She moaned as she had moaned with Kate's father, loudly. Loud enough for Kate to hear her parents through the thin walls of their old home. But she'd never seen them together. Not like this.

The Reverend blew out the candle and sat it on the dresser next to the slush lamp and began to undress. He told Lesley how blessed she was and then pushed her onto the bed.

Her mother waited, her arms extended above her head as if a cat stretching in the sun. The Reverend lay the pistol he wore at his waist on the bed and, dropping his trousers, slowly lowered himself onto her body. Kate was sure that he would squash her mother flat but instead she lifted her legs and the Reverend began to move backwards and forwards, like Kate had seen two of the convicts do when they thought no-one was watching. As Kate began to back away her mother turned her head sideways and looked into her eyes. Kate blinked and ran. She ran through the parlour and out into the rain and back to the warmth of the kitchen, where she curled up before the fire and cried herself to sleep.

⪥ Chapter 2 ⪥

1827 June – eight miles west of Sydney

Kate kept busy in the kitchen until their noon meal – soup and bread for her, Lambeth and Madge, roasted kangaroo with potatoes and sage stuffing for the Reverend and her mother, followed by a plate of native fruits and nuts. The cook was in a bad mood, one minute weepy and maudlin, the next sharp-tongued, with not a kind word to be said for anybody, particularly Kate. Apparently the Reverend was very angry with Lambeth, although Kate had no idea why. Kate chewed the tough bread, watching the puddles drying through the door, aware of the two women staring at her. She could tell they wanted to say something. They broke their bread into pieces and poked the dough in their bowls, all the while exchanging glances as if urging the other to speak.

Through the open door the day was clear and bright. The view from atop the fig tree would have been wonderful, but for the first time since her arrival in this place Kate didn't feel like climbing the tree, nor speaking to her father. She knew what she'd seen last night in her mother's bedroom was wrong and for some reason she found herself hating the Reverend. The bread was a hard wad in the side of her cheek.

Lambeth spooned the remnants of the soup into her bowl instead of sharing it equally, as was the custom. The cook sniffed as she ladled the thin broth while Madge's lips quivered. Kate had seen that look before.

'You're a wicked, evil thing you are, Kate,' Madge told her.

Kate concentrated on the bits of kangaroo floating in her bowl. Madge had been calling her a wicked evil thing ever since the cook had been scolded by the Reverend that morning. Kate knew she should answer her, but whatever she said would only cause more trouble, and Kate had no idea what she'd done wrong. She was usually in trouble for dawdling, and then the pots and pans had to be scrubbed twice over; and if she was caught wandering about outside, her meals were cut in half. This was a particular favourite as it meant Madge and Lambeth ate more. Kate wiped her nose on the back of her hand and lifting the bowl slurped up the soup. The women were still staring at her but Kate was beginning to think about other things, white fleshy things, things she couldn't easily wipe from her mind.

Finally Madge paused in her eating, one hand knuckle-deep in the soup as the bread she held grew soggy in the meat-flavoured water. Her head tilted sideways and with the movement Madge's curly hair poked out from beneath the mob cap.

'You went in there, didn't you, Kate? Nicked Mrs Lambeth's shawl and then left it in the Reverend's parlour so he'd think she was out to steal something.'

'Madge,' the cook cautioned, 'remember who she is.'

'I never,' Kate retorted; she felt her cheeks turn red.

'Caught, you are, good and caught. But you know it won't do no good what I say, or anyone else, 'cause you're her daughter and she's with 'im. Oh yeah, we know all about it. Your mother lays with him, she does. The God-fearing man what calls 'imself the

Reverend. *Reverend*!' Madge spat on the dirt floor. 'And your pretty mother opens her legs for 'im and says Amen.'

'She does not,' Kate cried.

'Lambeth 'ere will be punished for your doings. She'll be sent to the Female Factory in Parramatta with the rest of the sluts and the whores who've done wrong and they'll shave her head if she even points her little finger in the wrong direction. She'll spend her days making rope and carded wool. Isn't that right, Mrs Lambeth?'

The cook's eyes grew wide with fear. 'I thought them women did sewing and the like there now?'

'Sleep on piles of wool she will, eat slops that a pig wouldn't touch. I always said you'd get us into trouble, you with your native-born ways, sneaking about, thinking you can go anywhere and do anything.'

'I never,' Kate replied, shrinking back from Madge's anger.

'Maybe if *she* said something,' Lambeth began thoughtfully, her gaze resting on Kate. Her lower eyelids drooped so that the red inner part of the eyeball revealed itself. 'Her mother has the ear of the Reverend, like you say.'

'She's got a lot more than an earful,' Madge replied knowingly. 'Turn a trick that woman can. And who would have thought it? Native born, better than us, eh? I don't think so. Lesley Carter's no different to the rest of us. In the end the only thing a woman has that's worth a spit is what's between her legs.'

The two women stared at Kate from across the table. The room was stuffy with the heat from the fire. Sweat dripped from Kate's hairline and ran down her cheek. She wanted to tell these women that they were wrong. That her mother wasn't like them, that she would never be like them because Lesley Carter was free-born.

'Look what you've done, Madge, you've made her cry,' Lambeth tutted.

'Go on. You could say something, you know.' Madge's voice grew soft and wheedling. 'Help Mrs Lambeth out. She does feed you and care for you in her own way.'

'Yeah, in me own way.' The cook leant across the table, reached out a crinkly skinned arm.

Kate pulled away from the woman's touch.

Madge's cracked smile revealed a line of broken teeth. 'We could all be friends then, eh? You show us you're willing to help one of us and we'll be more kindly towards you, won't we, Mrs Lambeth?'

'Yes, yes, of course.' The cook stacked the chipped bowls and wiped the table of crumbs, tipping them into the pot bubbling over the fire.

'You being so pretty and all,' Madge continued, 'well, how could the Reverend say no to you?' She turned to the cook. 'Spitting image of her mother. Ain't she the spitting image of her mother? That long dark hair and them big eyes.'

Dipping the bowls in a basin of water, the cook wiped them disinterestedly with her apron and sat them on the table. 'I've said it before, haven't I, the very same words. It's a boon it is to be a woman and to be pretty. Men will do anything for a pretty face. They can't 'elp 'emselves. Why, if you were a convict lined up with the rest of the prettiest girls ready for the choosing, some fancy soldier would drop his hanky in front of you and you'd not be desperate like the rest of us to pick it up. No, there'd be a better one for you, young Kate. There'll be a better proposal of marriage for you in the offing.'

'Plenty better,' Madge agreed.

Kate thought of what she'd seen last night. If that's what men and women did she was never getting married. She would die an old maid with two cats for company.

'You, Lambeth,' the Reverend commanded from the door. 'Get your things and come out.'

The cook turned white. 'Please, sir, I didn't do it. I was asleep in my bed, I swear, just like I told you. Ask her, ask young Kate. She gets sleepless at nights she does, sir, and wanders about, not meaning anything of it of course, sir, and she gets cold, sir, so she took me shawl, not that I mind, sir. But it wasn't me, sir. Please, sir, I've done me best for you, never done nothing wrong, served you loyal I have these three years, I swear. I've only got a year to go, sir, please, sir, a year to go.' Mrs Lambeth pressed her squat body into the far corner of the kitchen, between barrels of preserved fruit and bags of salt and sugar.

Madge and Kate moved to stand before the hearth, their faces downcast.

The Reverend gave Madge a hard look and then turned to Kate. 'Is what Lambeth says true? Did you take her shawl and enter the cottage last night without permission?'

Kate licked at the sweat on her upper lip. Behind the man in the dark cloth suit were two soldiers wearing the distinctive red tunics of the British Infantry.

'If you are lying, God will strike you down in your sleep. You know that, don't you, Kate?'

It was an accident. She'd only borrowed the shawl and then left it there by mistake when she'd run away. Surely God forgave mistakes.

'Kate!'

She flinched.

'So you've nothing to say?'

What could she say? If Kate told the truth the Reverend would certainly punish her, perhaps send her away, and if she told the truth he might guess that she'd spied on him and her mother and that seemed worse than taking Mrs Lambeth's shawl and sneaking into the cottage. Kate felt bad for Mrs Lambeth, but she pressed her lips together and said nothing. The Reverend gave her a stony stare. Kate swallowed. If God didn't forgive her Kate figured she would be a lot worse off than Lambeth.

The cook rushed at Kate, lifted a bowl from the stack on the table and hit her on the forehead.

'Take her,' the Reverend said disinterestedly, as Kate fell to the floor.

Mrs Lambeth screamed and begged and wailed but the soldiers grabbed her and dragged the older woman through the kitchen.

'I'll get your things,' Madge called out above the din, running into their room and reappearing with a few items of clothing bundled into a ball. 'Take 'em and God bless.' She pushed the bunch into the cook's hands.

When the soldiers and their noisy charge finally departed, the Reverend mopped his brow with a handkerchief. 'Well, tend to her,' he said to Madge.

The kitchen was moving in a circle. Pots and pans spun. Kate put her palms to the floor to steady herself as Madge dampened a cloth and squatted next to her.

'It's a bad cut.' She pressed the wad of material to the side of Kate's head. 'She needs a doctor.'

'Clean it, bandage it and put her to bed. She's young, she'll survive.'

Kate woke lying on the pallet in the room next to the kitchen. Her right eye was blurry and her head pained awfully. It had been three days since Lambeth had attacked her. Her mother had made soup and tied a bandage around her head that she changed once a day, but the cut was slow to heal. Her head spun as she sat up and took a sip of water. On the dirt floor lay a mirror, which her mother had left. Unwrapping the bloodstained bandage, Kate looked at the cut. The edges of the wound were an angry red.

'There you are. You'll be up and about in no time.' Madge passed her a piece of bread, grimacing at the injury. 'Nasty that is, real nasty. Lucky your mother had some skill with the bandage. I'm not much good with things like that. You'll have a fine scar, something to remember old Lambeth by, eh?'

'I still can't see properly from this eye, Madge.'

'Well, the way the world is today a person is better suited to only seeing half of it anyway.' She sat cross-legged on the pallet next to Kate's and leant forward conspiratorially. 'The Reverend was called away this morning. It seems one of the wives has got uppity. Mrs Markham, what used to oversee the hat makers –'

'I remember her.'

'Will you let a person tell a story? So, it seems her husband had enough of her shenanigans and was keen to be rid of her so he put a rope around her neck and tried to sell her at the markets. Seems she didn't get one bid, she didn't. Anyways, on account of that, Mr Markham called for the Reverend and that's where he went to this morning, to their farm to give her a good thrashing.'

'That's awful,' Kate exclaimed.

'Aye, the poor man. They've been married for years, so you can imagine what she would have cost him in food and not one bid.'

'Madge?' the Reverend called.

The girl moved quickly. Quicker than Kate thought possible. The Reverend waited in the kitchen, pressing a handkerchief to his brow before folding the square of material and placing it carefully in his trouser pocket.

'Yes, Reverend, sir, I was just checking on Kate. She's coming along she is, sir.'

'I've decided you're to have Mrs Lambeth's position.'

Madge gave a little curtsey. 'Thank you, Reverend.'

'Kate.' He moved to the doorway, avoiding her gaze. 'You're to get up and start moving about. You'll not heal yourself lying about all the day and I've not the space for invalids. And you're to move into your mother's room. Tonight. That's not to say that you're to stop your daily tasks. In the morning you will help Madge prepare

20

the midday meal and tend the vegetable garden. In the afternoons you will work with the women making cabbage-tree hats. And you'll continue to eat here in the kitchen.' He pointed a stubby finger. 'Children should be seen and not heard. And if there have been any unlawful wanderings as has been suggested, I would imagine that your recent injury will stymie such future thoughts.' He turned to Madge. 'I'm partial to potato soup and we'll have the kangaroo cold this evening with a mustard sauce, and don't forget the oysters. The household deals with Wills' Groceries and Fine Produce, as you know. We've a standing order and he'll also be expecting his weekly supply of hats for the store as well. Mr Wills' man will be at Burwood Farm at three of the afternoon. He is known for trading with the natives but we can't condemn the man for that if he provides us with sustenance to do the Lord's work. Take six hats with you and don't dally, girl, and you best take one of the convict women from the lean-to for safety's sake. Mind you choose one who's already filled her quota of hats.' He turned to leave. 'And in future you will discuss the week's menu with Mrs Carter.'

'Yes, sir,' Madge replied.

When the two girls were alone again Madge rejoined Kate, watching the young girl as she wound the length of cotton around her head. Madge tied the ends of the material together, her tongue poking out between her lips in concentration. 'Fell on your feet, didn't you?' she commented, not unkindly. 'Well we both did, so we're even, for now.'

'Will Mrs Lambeth get a flogging?'

'Maybe, it depends on what the Reverend says. But that would be fitting, blood deserves blood. Come on now. Let's get you up for a bit.'

Kate allowed Madge to pull her up from the pallet. In the kitchen she sat down quickly, her head throbbing.

'With Lambeth gone, you and I will be feasting from now on.' Taking a bubbling pot from the fire, Madge stirred the gluggy contents. 'Today it's kangaroo, bread and potato.' Ladling a small amount of the stew into a bowl, she pushed the serving across the table. 'Eat it slowly, mind, you've only been on soup.' Removing her apron, Madge selected a straw hat from the peg on the wall. 'Well, I'm off for the oysters. You best chop four potatoes and put them in water to boil. Add a pinch of salt and sit the pot in the embers. And no wandering off leaving the fire unattended.'

After Madge left, Kate selected some potatoes from the shelf and, placing them in the centre of the table, crossed her arms and stared at them. One of the spuds had a black spot on its dirt-crusted skin, which appeared to move up and down as if winking at her. Kate held a hand over her weak eye and the spot stopped moving. She couldn't believe that she was finally going to be able to sleep in the same room as her mother. That they would be together once again. But now she didn't want to go. Kate was angry with her mother and she hated the Reverend. She thought of what Madge and Mrs Lambeth had said and of the night Kate had seen the Reverend and her mother together. Sitting at the table she began to pick at the black spot on the potato with a knife. If God was truly going to strike her down he may as well do it while she slept in the pallet beside rag-doll-haired Madge, than in the bed her mother and the Reverend Horsley had lain on.

After supper Kate went to her mother's room. Lesley sat on the bed wearing a plain beige cotton dress that fell in soft gathers from her bust. Lesley smiled and patted the coverlet.

'I'm so pleased to see you up and out of bed, Kate.' She fingered the bandage, straightening it a little and tucked a length of matted hair behind Kate's ear. 'We daren't wash your hair until the wound is dry. Tomorrow we'll sit you in the sun for a bit. That will help.' She held out a bone-handled hairbrush. 'I would have come to see you more often but you know how demanding the Reverend is.'

Kate held onto the wooden bedstead for balance. 'Madge said I should have had a doctor.'

'Come now, sit on the bed and brush my hair and we'll talk like mothers and daughters should. One day you will be doing this very thing with your own daughter, Kate, and probably in this gown.' She fingered the material. The dress was slightly worn in places but had been carefully looked after. 'I have always loved this dress of my mother's. Of course it's really verging on the unfashionable, even with all the alterations. One only has to walk down the street to see that the high bustlines are slowly dropping downwards.' She sat the hairbrush on the bed and unwrapped a package, unfolding a thick swathe of material. 'Look, cotton and muslin.' Lifting the gauzy fabric, her mother pressed it to her face with obvious delight. 'And,' a card held a length of wide cream lace, 'imagine, a lace hem and collar.'

'Is it for a wedding dress?' Kate asked.

Her mother folded the lengths of material, a line forming between her eyes. 'No. It's for a day-dress.'

'Oh.' She wanted to say 'good', that she didn't want the Reverend for a father, instead Kate brushed the front of her own cotton dress. It was smeared with dirt from tree-climbing, blood from the cut on her head and patched with marks from the greasy washing-up water that she tossed outside after the dishes were done.

'It's for church. And for other occasions. The Reverend is a particular friend of Reverend Lang, who built the Scots Church of St Andrew's in Sydney. I imagine there will be various gatherings we'll have to attend.'

'He's not really a Reverend, you know.'

'Who told you that?'

'Everyone knows it,' Kate replied, secretly pleased at the deepening scowl forming on her mother's brow. 'They say he left England with nothing but a bible. That he read it and then set himself up to be a Reverend.'

'Busybodies and mischief-makers, that's who told you.' Her mother placed the material on the plain wooden dresser. 'A person who ministers to his congregation is a Reverend. Come now, Kate, be a good daughter and sit by my side.'

Kate couldn't understand why her mother would pretend that everything was as it had always been. Ignoring the outstretched hand, she moved to the opposite side of the room to gaze out the window. Dusk made the trees shadowy, the sky a pinkish red. One of the women who worked on the Reverend's farm waddled out of the hut she shared with the other female convicts and tossed a bucket of dirty water into the dirt.

'Well, I suppose you're a little old for brushing your mother's hair.'

Kate decided that once her head was mended that she would climb out the window every night if she wanted, blanket in hand, and sleep among the comforting roots of the fig tree. She would have to wait until it grew dark of course, and everyone slept, but if it got cold she could always lie down in front of the kitchen fire. A floorboard creaked. Her mother's hands were light but insistent on her shoulders.

'One day, Kate, you will know what it is to be a woman in a man's world. You will understand that sometimes it is necessary to succumb to less than we deserve simply in order to survive. Your father and I had a good life, a wonderful life together. It was not filled with material things, a superior house, tasteful furnishings nor fine gowns for me or a tutor for you, my darling, but it was filled with love. Love, that most wondrous of qualities. Only love truly nurtures.'

Kate wriggled her shoulders. Lesley released her grip, but remained close.

'Do you love the Reverend?' Kate concentrated on the convicts as the men and women sat outside the two huts, spending their free time grinding their grain ration into flour, smoking pipes and talking. The Reverend locked the men and women inside every night. And although everyone knew it was to stop them from running away, he said it was for their safety. And there were fights between women, between men, between men and women, Kate had seen them. One woman had been belted unconscious for sleeping with another man.

'No, but he provides . . . things. Things for me, for us.'

One of the male convicts began to play a wooden pipe. The homemade instrument produced a whistling sound. Sitting on a tree stump he tapped his foot in time to the music and soon a woman began to sing about a long voyage and lost love.

'Those men and women are being made to do much needed work for the colony, for the Reverend. But things may get better for some of them. One day they may be pardoned, like your father was, and grow successful through hard work and thriftiness. Their lives may change as ours have changed. From good to bad, bad to liveable. Governors come and go, new roads are built, children are born and men die. We are beyond controlling every part of our lives, which means that we too must change. Do you understand?'

'No.' Kate folded her arms across her chest.

'The Reverend is a good man, Kate. And one mustn't deny the consolation that the Lord's word gives to the humblest among us. I have received great solace from the Almighty these past months. He has helped me come to terms with your father's death.'

'So you've found religion too, like the Reverend?' Kate pursed her lips and spat the words out like Madge would.

Her mother grasped her shoulder, turning Kate to face her. The action made her head throb terribly. 'Listen to me. Not everything I do for us to survive in this world will be perfect and not everything that you do will be right either. Three days ago you chose between yourself and Mrs Lambeth. Mrs Lambeth knew that you had done her wrong and she has paid for your lie.'

Kate kicked at the gappy boards underfoot. As she hadn't been struck down three days ago, the Reverend and her mother could say what they liked about religion.

'I'm sorry, Kate. I know things are difficult for you and that you've had to grow up too fast since your father died, but he's been buried many months. It's time to stop your wanderings. It's time to behave for the good of both of us.'

'I don't like it here.'

Her mother knelt at her feet and took her hands in hers. 'We need a home, food, protection. The Reverend provides all this and more.'

'You were just meant to be his housekeeper.'

'He has agreed that you may sleep with me in this room. And I am to start a school in the building where we gather to worship God.'

'I don't like him.'

Her mother lifted a finger to her lips. 'Shush. I wasn't sure of him either to begin with, but he has his ways, and I have mine. Together we have an agreement. One which benefits all of us. You see that, don't you, Kate? For if there is another man you know of, a man of means who would take us in immediately, without hesitation, then certainly I would listen to your suggestion.' She waited patiently for a response. 'You see then, we must be happy with our lot.'

Kate brushed away a tear. 'If Father had not got sick . . .'

'Come now. Let us pretend that everything is perfect. Your father wouldn't want to see you sad.' Her mother returned to sit on the bed and held out the hairbrush.

Begrudgingly, Kate climbed up onto the bed and, sitting behind her mother, began to unpin her long hair.

A few minutes later her mother gave a little cough. 'Sometimes the Reverend might want to visit me at night.'

Kate dropped the hairpins onto the bed. 'What for?'

'Oh, to talk, things like that. When he does I'll let you know, and then you'll have to go back to your old pallet for the night. But I know you won't mind because the Reverend is being very kind letting you share this room with me.' She began to hum.

Kate brushed her mother's hair with long, slow strokes and did her best to stop the tears from running down her cheeks. She wanted to tell her mother that she'd seen her and the Reverend together and that Madge had called her mother a whore, and Kate knew that was very bad but the words wouldn't come. Instead, Kate thought of her father. She just knew he wouldn't be happy either.

'Everything will be fine, Kate. You'll see. Things will get better. One hundred strokes,' Lesley reminded her daughter. 'Ouch, careful. You've grown careless.'

Pressing her lips together, Kate untangled hand and hair and began to brush. The dark lengths soon grew soft and shiny beneath the bristles and as Kate worked she noticed her mother's breathing begin to slow and her shoulders droop. Her father would be angry at her for pulling her mother's hair. He would remind Kate that they were alone now, that they only had each other left in the world, as he had on his deathbed. 'My two little women forced to fend for themselves.'

Lesley reached out and stilled her daughter's hand, squeezing it tightly. A single tear traced Kate's cheek. Maybe everything would be all right. Maybe her mother was right.

'I think it best that you sleep with Madge while you're still healing. Besides, tonight I think I will want this room to myself.'

Kate's grip tightened on the bone-handled brush.

≪ Chapter 3 ≫

Ten years later
1837 July — eight miles west of Sydney

Kate looked up into the sheltering foliage of the fig tree and wished she were ten years old again. If she were ten she would change the way she had behaved, she would have been nicer to her mother. Kate would have forgiven her for staying with the Reverend Horsley, for living in sin, and she may have tried, just a little, to please the Reverend. She even would have excused Madge and the other convicts for their knowing looks and snide remarks. But she had done none of those things and in the not doing, she and her mother had slowly drifted apart.

Last night, after they had said prayers for Lesley Carter, when the finality of her mother's illness had become apparent, Kate had eaten for the very first time with the Reverend at his round table. She'd had little appetite but there was leftover burnt parrot pie, fresh fruit and a cordial made from tart lemons and too much sugar. Madge's skill had never quite matched Lambeth's, and Kate's life had never changed the way her mother hinted it might.

28

The Reverend had been guarded in conversation. He spoke of the cost of funerals, of the simplicity required of God's creatures in both life and death, of the good fortune granted to Kate since her arrival in his household and how compassion was not infinite, charity not to be considered a right. For her part, Kate said very little. Her relationship with the Reverend had been one of feigned politeness. The man, her provider these many years, had every right to throw her out. The thought made Kate ill with worry. Her mother was dying. Very soon she would be alone in the world.

As their conversation waned the Reverend turned his attention to the windowsill and the single leech that lay motionless in the bottom of a water-filled bottle, a piece of rag over the opening. There will be a frost in the morning, he'd stated, tapping the base of the phial. The leech didn't stir. The bloodsucker was the household's indicator for all matters pertaining to the weather. The day before the creature had moved continuously in its watery confines, only to stop immediately just before a southerly wind began to blow. If only God had made man with such intuition, the Reverend had remarked.

Kate had excused herself from the table and returned to her bed, the pallet next to Madge's. Last night she'd dreamt that she was the leech, bottled-up for all eternity, with the Reverend tapping at the glass trying to get in.

The smudge of grey light changed slowly to a frosty pink. Kate blew on the tips of her fingers as the first warming rays of a wintery sun struck her face. Frost layered the ground, it latticed the grass with ice and spun a cobweb stretched across the woodpile into a line of pure white.

A group of Aboriginals walked across the far edge of the wheat field. Fear seizing her, Kate quickly hid behind the tree. The line of men draped in animal hides against the chill moved purposefully. Kate often saw men, women and children, the original inhabitants of this land. All knew to be wary of them and the continuing reports of attacks on outlying farms made everyone fearful.

Everyone except the Reverend. It was said that he'd sat down with the warriors that walked across his farm and treated with them. His neighbours laughed, calling such attempts a folly, but they'd never had a person attacked, and although their crops were plundered regularly, they never wiped the farm's stocks out. The Reverend had kept peace with the Aboriginals by allowing them to come and go as they pleased, and by giving them grain on a monthly basis. When he saw them the man bowed, often sinking to his knees in prayer, although his pistol was always at the ready. Other larger farms had not been so fortunate in their interactions. Shepherds were occasionally speared and livestock stolen.

Out of habit Kate now watched the warriors until they merged with the green-brown tangle of bushland, finally disappearing. Only then did her sense of unease depart.

One of the convicts appeared to collect wood for the fire. He was an old man, with perpetually watery eyes who'd been pardoned some years prior, but with nowhere to go he'd stayed on at the Reverend's small holding in exchange for food and a roof over his head. A piece of old leather made a strap for the musket he carried and he hefted the rifle across bony shoulders. On seeing Kate he lifted a hand to his cap in acknowledgment, pausing as if he wanted to say something to her. He couldn't. Barely a word of English passed the Welshman's lips. The moment was broken by the crunch of icy grass.

'He wanted to say he was sorry for your mother.' Madge hugged a blanket around her shoulders, her breath appearing as a puff of whiteness in the air. 'Didn't you?'

His convict woman, who'd helped in the kitchen, had died a few years earlier. Both Kate and her mother had tried their best to nurse her back to health. It had been a messy business. The woman had been ill until there was nothing left to sick up. Then the runs had begun.

The convict nodded, shifted the wood from one arm to the other, and then left the two women alone.

'The natives just came through.'

Madge shivered. 'But they're gone now?' She relaxed a little when Kate informed her they'd moved on. 'How is she then?' Madge had grown skinny and coarse of skin with age. 'None of us thought she would last the night.'

Kate thought of her own sleepless night as she looked through the row of stout orange and lemon trees to where children began to arrive and play near the little church-cum-schoolhouse. 'Neither did I,' she finally replied. The timber walls of the building had been well-sealed with mud, but it would be cold inside without the sun's warmth.

'Will you be moving then? Into the room, you know, after your mother —'

'No. I would never,' Kate replied quickly.

'No need to get crotchety,' Madge answered, equally blunt.

'I hadn't thought about it,' Kate admitted, then frowned. 'I hadn't thought about what would happen next.' She lifted a finger to her lips and nibbled on a fingernail.

Madge grabbed her arm and studied the nail-bitten hand before freeing her. 'Sure you have. No point pretending otherwise, Kate. I know you as well as the next person here, probably better than your own mother. It's me that's been snoring next to you these many years.'

'Don't I know it.' A brief smile touched Kate's lips.

Madge laughed. 'So take a bit of advice from this old maid then, Kate Carter. I know you've had it hard compared to your mother. Don't give me one of your uppity stares, your mother got the best of the arrangement, everyone knows it and that's fair. The woman kept you housed and fed these many years in the best way she could, but now it's your turn.' Madge had never been a considerate person, but she touched Kate's arm briefly. 'This is your opportunity. You have to look after yourself, do what's best for you, that's what your mother did and there are worse places than here. Think on it. There's no need for hand-wringing and nailbiting.'

'We've never got on, he and I. You know that, Madge.'

'But you ate with him last night. It's a beginning.'

'Yes, and he told me that a person couldn't expect charity.'

The cook's expression barely changed. 'But who will run the school, his house?'

'Maybe he's found someone else already?'

A screech broke their conversation. Madge pointed to the group of children. Three of the boys were arguing and a fight quickly followed. 'You best settle them before the Reverend gives 'em all a belting,' she suggested, as one of the boys was pushed to the ground. 'As for me, I've got a bag of wheat as big as old Lambeth to grind, and a sheep's tongue to boil and toast for the master's midday feed.' She sniffed, walking back through the wet grass towards the kitchen.

Kate lifted her skirts and moved quickly towards her charges. The fight had ended with a punch and a bawling child. At her approach the children formed a half-circle around the fallen boy, who was now sitting upright in the wet grass, tentatively probing his face. They were a mixed lot. The convict children were bedraggled and bare-footed; while the sons and daughters of free settlers and emancipated convicts-made-good were neatly dressed with leather shoes.

'Get inside, the lot of you,' Kate chastised, 'before the Reverend takes to all of you with the stick.' A baker's dozen of girls and boys ran towards the building as Kate dusted off the injured seven-year-old Thomas, pressing the underside of her skirt to his bleeding lip. 'There, no harm done,' she said gently, brushing his clothes free of grass and leaves. His short pants were soaked through from the wet ground. She turned to a young girl who was weeping beside them. 'What are you crying for, Lizzy? Were you in the fight too?'

The girl twisted her skirt between her hands. 'I'm hungry.'

Kate had tried in the past to entice the Reverend to give the children a piece of bread and water mid-morning but he'd countered her arguments with the cost of such an endeavour and the impossibility of getting coin from convict parents. 'Well, then, the sooner we start our lessons, the sooner you will be able to go home and eat.' Lizzy wiped her runny nose and opened her mouth to protest. 'Go with Thomas now. I'll be in directly.'

The boy dawdled. He was bow-legged with a large boil capped with pus on his neck. 'Don't you want to know what we was fighting about, miss?'

'No, Thomas, not this morning, I don't.'

'But Mrs Carter always does.'

'Well, I'm not Mrs Carter. Go inside now.'

'But Fred said that the teacher would die. If she dies I'll have to go with the rest of them who've convicts for parents and learn a trade. They take you away, they do, to some big building, then when the learning is done they send you out to work. Them that you work for own you, they do. My ma and pa they had an awful fight about me getting lessoned by the Reverend. My pa was against it 'cause there's no food or bed and me mother got a black eye. I got me lessons. But if the Missus dies, and there ain't no school, me pa will send me out, he will. She won't die, will she?'

Kate didn't want to talk about what would happen when her mother died. It was taking every ounce of her strength just to get through the morning. 'There'll always be a teacher here, Thomas,' Kate replied. 'Haven't I been teaching you these past few months? Now go inside and tell the others to start finishing the hats we were making.'

The boy couldn't look more pleased. He ran off towards the schoolhouse chanting, 'I was right, I was right.'

Although partially obscured by the fruit trees and the spreading branches of the large fig, the Reverend's cottage appeared almost quaint. Inside, in the room that looked directly across to the convicts' huts, her mother lay on a bed, waxen-faced. Kate often thought of the woman Lesley Carter had once been. The image that came most often to her now was of her holding Kate's father's hand and giggling. Giggling. Such laughter seemed to have crumbled forever. Her mother had never worn the white gown with the lace collar and cuffs to any grand receptions, but in the ten years they'd lived here she'd slept each night in a warm bed that was off the ground and never once went hungry. Kate took a deep breath. Her heart was beating too quickly. It wasn't fair. Her mother was only thirty-eight years of age.

Smoke was streaming from the cottage chimney, twirling into a sky grown clear and bright with the rising sun. The Reverend had done well for himself. He now had a lucrative farming enterprise of four hundred acres. Fields were planted to wheat and corn every year, and there were cattle and sheep. The cabbage-tree hat business was ongoing, with the schoolhouse providing a new source of labour, a boon with the decreasing number of convicts available as workers. The Reverend was not a wealthy man, but he wanted for nothing. And Kate and her mother had also been provided for. Kate wished she'd been a better daughter, a more loving child, for Madge was right – Lesley had done her best for the both of them.

Reverend Horsley came to Kate in the schoolhouse as lessons ended. She assumed the worst, however his attention went immediately to the pile of cabbage-tree hats stacked on a rear bench. He lifted each finished item and checked the quality of the work. Small fingers made for intricate weaving of the palm fronds. The

Reverend's charitable school of plain education aligned itself nicely with Governor Macquarie's original model, for the children's lessons also included the learning of useful industry.

The children ran past Reverend Horsley as he approached, a sword jingling at his side, his pistol obvious against the black cloth of his suit. 'She lingers,' he explained to Kate, allaying her fears. He clasped the King James Bible to his chest. 'But I am not here to talk about the dying. I am here to discuss your future.'

Kate's throat went dry. She was not ready for this. Surely he would give her a week's grace to think on her situation, especially as her mother was yet to depart this world.

'You are to be complimented on your willingness to assume Mrs Carter's role as schoolmistress at my humble institution. You seem capable of handling the duties required of the position.'

'I have been assisting my mother these many years,' Kate answered carefully.

Crumbs littered his whiskers. They hung amidst the coarse hairs as if being stored for future meals. 'Yes, and the free education you received at her side during that time has been of great benefit to you. You are skilled with the pen. I thought perhaps you would undertake the writing of my sermons as dictated by me, as your mother did.'

Kate felt a surge of relief followed by awkwardness. Carefully closing the book that she'd been reading aloud from during lessons, she placed it on the table that was used as a pulpit on Sundays. 'I don't share my mother's religious inclinations,' Kate replied. 'But, if you would spare me that role I would be pleased to stay on as teacher here. The children are quite advanced for their age and –'

'You are a non-believer?' His nose twitched. 'But you attend our services, you have prayed side by side with your mother.' His voice rose. 'By these actions you have professed to be a good Christian soul.'

'I have professed nothing, Reverend. I simply do as I am told and try to live my life honestly,' her gaze met his, 'as expected.' Kate could tell by the expression on his face that her answer had not pleased him, but it was the truth.

The Reverend placed the bible carefully next to a bundle of birch sticks on the table. The swatch stung the skin painfully when applied with some enthusiasm. Kate had never used it, although her mother had been quite fond of the punishment. 'I did not realise that temptation was rife within our household. I am remiss, my child. I have done you a disservice.'

'Not at all. I believe that there is a right way and a wrong way to live one's life, but I don't believe in an all-knowing God and I certainly don't believe in your church's beliefs. What is the point, after all?' asked Kate.

The Reverend grasped the edge of the table, his knuckles turning white.

'God did not save my father from an early death,' Kate continued. 'Nor it appears will he intercede on my mother's behalf. We only have ourselves to rely on, Reverend. The insubstantial will not feed us or clothe us or care for us when we are ill, no matter how glorious you make him sound, no matter how terrifying. I do believe that for some the idea of such a figure may be a comfort, and I certainly agree that the reciting of words at burial must be done, if only to bid farewell to our loved ones and offer our respect. But if your perception of a good Christian soul is reliant on your beliefs then I am certainly not a member of your flock and I never professed to be one.'

'I understand entirely, Kate.' His tone grew silky. 'You have your mother's enquiring mind and with regard to her own gradual understanding and acceptance of the faith she herself required tutorship. We spent many an hour together in fellowship.'

'I have no doubt,' Kate replied sarcastically.

'One's faith is extraordinarily important.' He edged slowly around the table. 'The Great Almighty offers guidance, hope, salvation. I am the way,' he said loudly, 'the truth and the light.'

The children playing at the rear of the building paused briefly in their game to look at the two adults.

'I can help you. You must let me help you.' The Reverend held her gaze, the intensity of which was quite mesmerising. He clasped Kate's hands between his. 'I have great admiration for you, Kate. You are your mother's daughter, strong-willed, bright, but sensible enough to know your place in the world, to understand your shortcomings, to know where you belong.' He paused, tightening his grip. 'I have always favoured a woman's obedience and duty. These characteristics are so much more attractive than fleeting beauty. And I see in you a strength that your mother didn't possess. A strength that would allow you to sit with me and talk of our Lord with an open mind.'

Kate pulled her hands free of his clammy grip.

'But such instruction is for another time. For now we have other matters to attend to.' The Reverend cleared his throat. 'In short I am delighted to offer you the positions of schoolmistress, housekeeper and your mother's room in my household. And all that that entails,' he finished bluntly, wetting his lips.

'My mother is not yet dead.'

The Reverend tilted his neck skyward to the bark ceiling. 'God's will be done.' Above them a large furry spider scurried along a wooden beam. 'In truth I have for some time found her bed cold.'

Kate's fingernails bit into the palms of her hands. 'I am not –'

'Miss, Miss Carter.' Young Thomas Prescott was grim-faced as he ran down the aisle.

'Think on this, Kate. Where else will you go? Who will take you in?'

'There are black kids outside, miss. See?' A grubby finger pointed through the open shutters, to where two young Aboriginals sat cross-legged in the grass. The pair were close enough to hear lessons. 'They're not allowed to do learning, are they? Not with us.'

'We are not up-country, Thomas,' Kate reprimanded. 'We call them natives or Aboriginals, remember?'

'Well, my pa will tan me hide if I go schooling with blacks.' Thomas wiped a ragged shirtsleeve across a runny nose. 'Please, miss, send them blacks away.'

The Reverend clasped the boy's shoulder. 'Your parents are convicts, Thomas. It is not up to you to tell your betters who can or can't be schooled here.'

'Well, blacks is blacks.'

Reaching for the swatch of birch, the Reverend thrashed the boy's bare legs. 'Then don't come back.'

'Reverend Horsley,' Kate complained.

Thomas kicked the Reverend's shin and ran out the door. Kate lifted a hand to her mouth, hiding the smile on her lips.

'You are too soft on them,' he replied, wiping a sheen of moisture from his brow, although the exertion appeared to have invigorated him. 'The lower classes need to be kept in their place if there is to be any semblance of normal society. England is dependent on us to ensure that this colony retains the dignity and societal norms that are expected in the civilised world. You'd do well to remember that, Kate, for you yourself carry the stain of convict association.'

Kate's jaw tightened. 'I have no interest in your offer,' she replied brusquely.

'Don't be ridiculous.'

'How could you expect me to accept it, after the way you have lived with my mother? You, who profess your Godliness, you, who tell me that I carry the stain, as if you were better than me, than my mother.' The breath caught in her throat. Kate thought he would strike her for the Reverend's hand lifted and then just as quickly he lowered it to his side. Kate had been witness to his beltings before. The man was not averse to hitting woman or child. She had no idea where she would go, but she wasn't staying with this man a moment longer.

'Your mother has been well cared for.'

'My mother only decided to stay in your employ because she was scared. Scared to go out alone with a young child to fend for. Do you think that I would agree to live as my mother has lived? My mother's family were free settlers, my father, although convicted for forgery, a crime he did not commit, rose to become a respected farmer in his own right. Do you think I would allow myself to –'

'Our arrangement was not uncommon. You know that, Kate,' he placated.

'Have you forgotten how my mother slaved for you these past ten years? She has assisted in the writing of your sermons, has been your housekeeper and run the school, for which she received no more benefit than a new dress every two years. And you who depended on her for so much could not go so far as to give her your name.'

'You have grown disrespectful, Kate,' he responded. 'I think it best if you go indoors and attend to your mother. Perhaps in her final hours she will remind you of your good fortune . . .' He hesitated. 'Your mother was not the virtuous creature you speak of, my girl, or did you think she was faithful to your father's memory between his passing and your arrival on my doorstep?'

Kate's mouth opened and closed. She didn't believe it.

'Her doings were not unknown to me, and still I provided for her and you. And you accuse me of not taking her as my wife? Beauty is a curse, your mother traded on hers. So be it.' The Reverend lifted the prayer book to his chest, his collar yellow where it rubbed against the folded skin of his neck. 'I will leave this matter to another time, when you are not so overwrought, when common sense has returned. Go to your mother,' he urged, 'stay with her until the end. Forget your duties until she slips from this world to the next. But while you sit by her side, ask her, for both our sakes, if her time here has been happy. She will answer yes.'

'Kate . . . Kate?'

Madge was breathless. The woman halted abruptly on seeing the Reverend and stood rooted to the spot in the dim light of the schoolhouse. 'I beg your leave, Reverend sir, but I've news. It's your mother, Kate,' she faltered. 'She's gone.' Madge moved towards them, twisting a dirty apron between her hands. 'I would have come for you but there was no time. I only went in to see if she wanted a little water. She was awake, so I propped up the pillows, but her eyes never opened, not even to blink. But she asked for you, she did, said a few words and then the breath left her.' Madge let out a little puff of air. 'Just like that and she was gone.'

A band of tightness circled Kate's chest.

'Kate, did you hear what Madge said?' the Reverend spoke loudly. 'Your mother is dead, may she rest in peace.'

'What, what did she say?' asked Kate breathlessly.

Madge pressed her mouth together, rolling the skin until her lips all but disappeared. 'She said to tell you that she was sorry.'

An air of expectation seeped from the Reverend. Flicking through the pages of the bible, he placed the book in Kate's hand. 'John, chapter five, verses 24 to 26. "Verily, verily, I say unto you, He that heareth my word, and believeth on him that sent me, hath everlasting life, and shall not come into condemnation; but is passed from death unto life."

'*Shall not come into condemnation*, think on it, Kate.' The bible was swiftly removed and the Reverend strode down the aisle. 'I'll make the necessary arrangements, however the body will need to be washed and, Madge, you will, from this moment onwards, speak to Miss Carter with regards to all meals.'

Kate sat heavily on one of the benches. She felt as if all the air had left her body, that she would never breathe again. The older woman approached silently, an eyebrow lifted. 'Well, that's that then. At least she went quiet. Not a whimper.'

It was difficult to believe that her mother was dead. 'I should have been with her.'

'Rubbish. You sat with her last night and the night before that. And besides, Lesley Carter wasn't the type to put up with mollycoddling. She was a survivor, your mother.' Madge sniffed. 'Well, a woman has to be. But in the end when your time's up I reckon it makes no difference if there's someone holding your hand or not. Once you're on the way to the boneyard there's no stopping the journey.'

Kate didn't agree. No matter what Madge said she knew the comfort that could be given by the touch of a hand. She'd seen it in her father's eyes. 'Do you think my mother was happy here, Madge?'

The cook turned up her nose. 'Happy? What's happy? For some it may be a good meal, others a place to sleep, for meself any year without a thrashing is a boon. You'll be right. Set yourself up in the cottage. Do as he says. There are worse places than this. You'll see things will turn out like a good baked loaf.'

Kate waited until Madge had left and then sank to the ground and began to sob.

To where 'neath glorious clustered stars
The dreamy plains expand –
My home lies wide a thousand miles
In the Never-Never Land.

'The Never-Never Country'
by Henry Lawson, 1906

✤ Chapter 4 ✤

1837 July – on the western side
of the Blue Mountains

The two men stood on the sloping earth where the dense trees rose from low ground between grassy hills. The land below was damp from recent rain and would be hard to burn, so they concentrated on the hill, knowing that the southerly wind would drive the flames into the grass and towards the scrub some distance beyond. The area had not been burnt since this time last year and Bidjia was keen to entice new growth in the spring. His people needed food and the fire would encourage the leaves and grasses to sprout. The tender young plants would attract animals and increase hunting opportunities, as well as stimulating yams and other food sources.

Forming a nest of dry grass, Bidjia sat cross-legged on the ground. In his hands he held a stick, which he began rotating into a notch cut into a piece of softwood. The stick twirled quickly between his palms. He held it close to the nest and the heat borne of his handiwork caused a dark fleck to fall on the dry grass. His son, Jardi, picked up the smouldering pile and waved the grass gently through the air. A flame appeared.

'Where is your brother?' Bidjia asked his son.

Bronzewing had only returned to them last night and already he was disrupting the day. Two of their clan waited on the edge of the scrub some distance away. Once the grass was fired, the game would rush to escape it and head straight for the hunters.

And once smoke appeared, the whites would know where they were.

The younger man shrugged and pointed to the thick trees behind them.

'Find him.' Bidjia watched as his son walked swiftly away, he was in no mood for delays. The white settlers were a half-day's walk away, but with their horses they could travel quickly over the land. It was as it had been on the great waterhole side of the blue hills. The strangers came slowly at first, but once the road across the mountains was built by the men in chains, the whites came in great numbers, claiming land, building dwellings and disrupting the old ways.

The Lycetts, the ones who had come to build their hut near Bidjia's clan in the folds of the hills, were friendly enough, but they brought sheep with them and Bidjia had already been warned many times that a firing of the grasses would not be tolerated. Such disrespect was unknown to him. The whites did not own this land and the sheep fouled up the waterways for man and beast alike, ate the grass to the ground and stomped the rest to dust.

Jardi's white brother darted through the trees, circled him swiftly and dived, cuffing an ankle so that they both fell to the ground. 'I thought I had missed you.' Jardi accepted the older man's hand and was pulled to his feet. 'Now I'm not so sure.'

Bronzewing laughed. 'So then, have you found yourself a woman yet?'

'Have you?' Jardi countered, as they began to walk back towards Bidjia. 'You've been gone a year.'

'Nothing took my fancy,' he admitted.

'And the business, it went well? You were too busy arguing with my father last night to share all your stories.'

'There isn't much else to tell.' Bronzewing had crossed the mountains back to Parramatta last year with Mr Lycett and assisted in taking his wool to market. With a good price obtained, he'd then joined a party of settlers intent on journeying south-west towards the Murrumbidgee River. He'd not travelled to that part of the colony before and although he was employed to act as intermediary with the various clans and tribes along the route, he was, more importantly, an extra white man with an extra musket. The trip had been eventful. The wife of one of the settlers had given birth along the way and lost the child; they'd had sheep rushed and speared. Bronzewing had not always been successful dealing with this land's first people. His knowledge of the different languages was slight, but he knew their ways and he did his best to reassure both black and white in the hope of avoiding attacks, by either party. In his absence, however, relations between Bidjia's clan and the Lycetts had deteriorated.

Ahead, Bidjia waited, his brow wrinkled tightly. 'Late,' he accused.

'Must you burn here?' Bronzewing complained. This is what they'd quarrelled about last night. 'Surely we could go a mile or so further west. Jardi has told me how angry Mr Lycett is with the clan for burning his land. Do you really want to make things worse?'

'You have spent too much time with the whites.'

Bronzewing adjusted the spear in his hand. It felt good to have the familiar weapon back in his grasp.

'Go,' the older man told them.

Bidjia waited as the two young men detoured around the slope of the hill so as not to disturb the animals. Spears in hand, the sinewy frame of Jardi matched the longer stride of his white brother. Although Bronzewing was a foot taller and well-muscled for his age, he'd had to train hard to match Jardi's natural ability. The boy

47

Bidjia had taken from the humpy those many years ago was now a man, brought up in the ways of Bidjia's people and schooled by the well-meaning Archibald Lycett, who'd tried to entice the boy back to an unknown God and the life he'd lost.

When the boys were out of sight, Bidjia lit the grass. The flames caught quickly, fanning across the ground and gathering pace. A line of smoke rose into the sky as the fire grew in intensity, fed by the wind. Bidjia skirted the edge of the burnt ground. In the distance he could see a small group of wallabies racing away from the fire towards the waiting hunters. They would eat well tonight.

By the time Bidjia reached the scrub, one of the animals had already been speared. Colby and Darel, the other men of his clan, were talking to Bronzewing and his son and were in a hurry to leave. They stood engulfed by the smoke, their eyes streaming, the wallaby lying on the ground between them.

'Lycett,' Colby stated, explaining that one of the settler's men was riding nearby on horseback.

'Let's go,' Bidjia told them.

Bronzewing led Bidjia and Jardi westward through the dense bush. They followed a different path to that of the other two men in case the whites gave chase, weaving through thick trees gnarled with age. Their route back to the camp was not direct but if they were lucky, Lycett wouldn't be able to prove that it was them who had lit the fire, although the man would guess at the truth.

'You can go to Lycett and make the peace if it is needed,' Bidjia told Bronzewing. The white boy had formed a bond with the settler over the years and was friends with Lycett's eldest, a stragglylimbed youth named Winston, who spent most of his time drawing shapes on paper. It was a strange occupation for a man.

They ran at a steady pace in single file, startling the odd kangaroo and wallaby. Through the trees ahead they could see sheep grazing and, close to the animals, a shepherd. Bidjia was quick to change their path. They crossed a dry gully and were nearly out of sight of the shepherd when a musket shot rang out. They halted immediately, fearing the worst.

'It is some distance from us,' Bronzewing advised, 'and with the wind as it is the sound could have travelled much further.'

Bidjia wasn't convinced but they kept moving. The boy was usually right. Most of the settlers in the area knew Bronzewing, although they called him by his white name, Adam. As a child he'd been known as the bush-boy, a description that had allowed him to move relatively freely between blacks and whites, but with age came mistrust. There were some on both sides who questioned his loyalty and treated him warily. But Bidjia was glad to have taken Bronzewing from the hut near the water on the other side of the mountain. A man could never have too many strong sons. Had he been a weakling he would have abandoned him, but the boy was quick to learn and begrudgingly his clan accepted him.

When Bidjia had first come across the humpy, the day of the white man's leaving, he knew from the beginning that the boy's mother would not survive if her man did not return. Instead of spending the days usefully, making things or foraging like women should, she moved like a mouse and gave fright at the slightest sound. In contrast, the boy was bright-eyed and curious and the darkness of his hair, which shone a burnished copper in the light, reminded Bidjia of a Bronzewing pigeon. The day the warriors from another tribe came through, his clan had decided to cross the mountains and escape the encroaching white settlers. It was by chance that he'd approached the place of the white woman and child and seen the warriors. The mountain people were aggressive. He'd guessed that they would kill her. While many of his people were confused by the whites' use of the land and the brutality that they directed against their own people, others were angry with them and sought vengeance for the changes forced upon their way of life. Bidjia didn't even think of saving the woman, he only wanted the boy.

So he had taken him and, with the few remaining clan members, they had walked away from their country, following the ancient pathways through the mountains and down the valley to the plains. The scuffling between two ancestral creator spirits, the giant eel-like Gurangatch, and the large native cat, Mirragan, had scratched out the features of the terrain, the rivers and hills, and it was the story of this unknown territory and the description created that helped to direct them to new lands. Bidjia would never have imagined that the whites would cross the mountains as well.

They reached the camp some hours later. A wisp of smoke and the scent of roasting meat meandered through the trees, leading them to a shady clearing where two bark humpies sat among the timber. Colby and Darel had arrived some time before them.

'We saw no-one,' Colby told them as the men sat around the camp fire. After Bidjia, he was the eldest of the clan. 'But my spear was ready.'

'As was mine,' Darel said enthusiastically.

'We saw a shepherd in the distance and heard musket fire, but that was it,' Bronzewing told them. 'And just as well, fighting is the last thing you want, if you wish to stay here.'

'And how would you know what is best for us?' Colby asked. 'You have been gone from here many months and you come back and tell us whether we should fight or not?' He stared at Bronzewing from across the fire. 'I think you would put the white Lycett first. He is your colour, and you are not of ours.'

'Enough,' Bidjia warned. Drinking water from a kangaroo skin bag he passed it around the group. The wallaby smelt nearly done. It had been cooked whole in the fire pit and unskinned to retain its goodness.

'One of Lycett's men came here when we were hunting,' Colby advised the group. 'Merindah spoke to him.'

Colby's woman, Annie, approached the men in Merindah's place. Merindah was heavily pregnant with Bidjia's child and kept her distance from the men now her time was drawing close. Annie pointed at Bronzewing. 'Lycett wanted to know if you had returned. I said nothing.'

Bronzewing nodded.

She backed away quickly to wait near one of the shelters with Bidjia's woman and the clan's three surviving children, a young boy and girl belonging to Annie, and a sick one-year-old, who was Merindah and Bidjia's child.

'He knows it was us.' Jardi tugged the wallaby from the fire pit and began to cut pieces of cooked meat from the carcass, before pulling out the heart, liver and kidneys.

Bidjia accepted the organs and divided them up between himself and Colby. The other men received a square of bark with chunks of meat on it and began to eat. Wooden bowls held the wild nuts and berries the women had prepared. 'When the moon grows fat and lazy we will burn the adjoining ridge.' Reaching for a kidney, he chewed on the tender flesh, the juices running down his chin. 'If the rains come the grasses will grow thick and fast.'

'There is plenty of game here, to hunt and trap.' Colby ate hungrily. 'It will be a good season for us.'

'What about Lycett? Maybe we should go to another place further away,' Jardi suggested.

'This is another place.' His father reached for the fresh water, took a sip and then stuck his finger into a bag of sugar and sucked at the sweetness. The sugar was a ration, along with blankets, provided to the clan by the Lycetts in exchange for occasional work, such as barking trees. 'Our tribal lands are on the other side of the blue hills where the mullet run and the lilies grow. Within those lands is the place where my mother took the afterbirth when I was born and buried it in the ground. That is where my mother laid me down. That is my land. Do you expect us to keep moving forever?'

The men ate silently. It was difficult to argue with Bidjia.

'You who are born of this land may go to your sacred place, the place of your totem and perform the rituals that make this land grow and flourish. You have this right. I do not. I cannot go to the place of the yam and do the ceremony to make the yam plentiful. I cannot ensure the release of the life force to which I am connected. I am stolen from my land.'

The men finished eating, the truth of Bidjia's words reminding each of them how he suffered.

'You saved your clan, Bidjia.'

The Elder of the tribe looked at Bronzewing. 'Only some,' he muttered.

They sat by the flames, the sadness dissipating as birds settled in the trees around them and night creatures began to forage.

As darkness began to send its wispy shadows across the clearing, one by one they moved slightly away from the campfire. Bronzewing stretched out his legs and rubbed his shoulders against the bark of the tree behind him. A few feet away Bidjia rested his aching muscles by lying flat in the dirt on his back.

With the men's leaving, Annie served up meat for the children and herself, and then carried nuts and fruits to Merindah. Bronzewing shouldn't have been surprised to return home and find Merindah with child again, the second in two years, however she'd been unhappy here since her arrival and a year had not improved her countenance. She was a pretty girl, whose young body had attracted envious glances from both Darel and Colby, but she was clearly miserable. Her sick child lay on a piece of bark while Annie's two children ate and played.

'How is the baby?' Bronzewing asked Bidjia while following Annie's movements as she went to check on the infant.

Bidjia shook his head and closed his eyes. The men's bellies were full and they were tired from the day's work. A short distance away Darel and Colby talked quietly, Jardi had disappeared. With the lengthening shadows Bronzewing sought out Merindah. She had her own fire behind a bark lean-to and the sick child lay close to the warmth of the flames. The girl started at his approach, drawing a blanket across her swollen belly.

Bronzewing squatted opposite her and asked after the child, noticing that the foods brought to her remained untouched.

The young woman touched the baby's chest gently. She had swabbed the child every day for three days with an infusion made from the leaves of the paperbark, which could help with aches and pains, but there had been no change.

'How long is it now?' Bronzewing asked the girl.

Merindah poked at berries cupped in her palm. 'Four days, he grows weaker. He will not suckle. The milk is good, but if he does not drink ...'

Her words hung. In the firelight the child looked starved. His tiny rib cage stuck out and the cheeks were sunken. It was only a matter of a day or so at most. Perhaps there may have been a chance if the child had been taken to Mrs Lycett – there still may be – but Bidjia's approval was needed and in his current mind-frame such consent would be unlikely. 'You're still unhappy here? But are you not looked after? You have enough food?'

Merindah stroked the child's face. The young girl had come from another tribe two years ago, the agreement brokered by Bidjia when his last woman had died in childbirth. This was the fifth woman of Bidjia's that Bronzewing could remember. It seemed with the death of each previous one, whether through sickness, childbirth or accident – his first woman had been bitten by a snake – that each subsequent woman had even less time to walk the earth. The continuation of the clan was vital and most of the women who came into their group fitted in easily but it was different with Merindah. She was open to understanding the ways of the white settlers, and she'd been quick to pick up the English Bronzewing taught her, but she was also very young compared to her husband. The loss of the child would not help things. 'I'll talk to Bidjia.'

Merindah's dark eyes grew luminous beneath a rising moon. He felt the lightness of her touch on his arm as he made to leave. 'I work for the Lycetts.'

'You can't, Merindah. You belong to Bidjia.'

'I would wear the woman's clothes, I would learn their ways to keep my children healthy.'

'Sometimes not even white medicine will help, you know this, and who is to say your child does not have a white's illness?'

The girl ignored this. 'You see, I have this.' From beneath a blanket she pulled out a ball of material, unravelling it to reveal a woman's dress.

'Where did you get that from?'

The girl snatched it away.

He glanced over his shoulder. 'I won't say anything, but keep it hidden.' He wondered where the dress had come from. Who had given it to her? 'Merindah, you are with Bidjia now, you can't leave here, you know that.'

'I would be your woman, Bronzewing.'

He thought of what it would be like to lie next to her. To feel the warmth of another's body, the companionship of sharing more than just a piece of the earth. It had been nearly eleven months since he'd bedded the girl at the hostelry the night Lycett's wool had been sold. Bronzewing had treated himself to a good meal and a nip of rum sitting out on the verandah, the small dining room being full, and later found himself with company that wasn't bad looking. It had been a long year since that night, but he didn't look back as he walked away.

He found Jardi by following the noise of metal against stone. The young Aboriginal was sitting in a patch of tall grass a short distance from the camp. A cold wind rustled the pasture so that the surface of the land appeared to be rippling outwards, much like the ocean.

The grass grew golden in the moon's light and in the centre of this halo sat Jardi. He was sharpening a knife on a flat rock, spitting on the shiny surface, scraping the edge of the blade in a circular motion. Bronzewing had gifted the blade to him some years prior.

'You make the noise of two kangaroos,' Jardi muttered, remaining absorbed in his task, not lifting his head.

'And I see you no longer hug the fire at night.'

'Was it not you who told me that the night spirits wouldn't drag me away? Some things I listen to.'

Bronzewing looked over his shoulder. The camp fire burnt brightly. Jardi never strayed too far from the fire's protection. 'I have spoken to Merindah.' He sat down in the long grass, broke a stem and chewed on the sweetness.

'She is close to her time, Bronzewing,' he rebuked.

He wanted to tell Jardi about the dress Merindah concealed but the garment suggested that the girl had had recent contact with the whites. She would be punished. 'I know, but I wanted to see her and the child. It's probably too late but I could take the baby to the Lycetts in the morning. They may well have some treatment that could help. Mrs Lycett is a kindly woman and –'

'They have already sent enough of us to the spirit world with their sicknesses, even their own people weaken and die. Their medicine is not so strong.' Jardi lifted the knife to inspect his handiwork, the fine edge of the blade glinting in the moonlight. 'Anyway, my father would not allow it.'

'The child won't survive,' Bronzewing stated flatly. 'Surely that must be a consideration.'

'We managed to look after our own long before the whites came.'

'I know but they bring their illnesses to the clan and they may have the knowledge that can heal them.'

Jardi sighed. 'There are some things that must be left alone, Bronzewing. You should respect our ways. You have lived with us these many years.'

'You and the tribe have always had my respect, you know this to be true, but we speak now of a child's life. To do nothing, to simply wait until the baby dies, is wrong.'

'The sick will be replaced with the new. Merindah will soon birth another.'

At times the customs of the tribe gnawed at Bronzewing's conscience, yet the ultimate goal with every decision made always led back to the overall wellbeing of the clan and their survival. It was difficult to argue with such thinking although Bronzewing knew that were it not for the strained relationship between Bidjia's people and the Lycetts, his wish to take Merindah's baby to Mrs Lycett may have been considered and consent begrudgingly given.

'You have always been the hopeful one, my friend.' Jardi dropped a length of grass across the knife blade. The sharp edge sent two halves falling to the ground. 'And I know that you do not understand us at times. My father says that things were simpler once, that life was better. I understand this from the stories he has shared. Life for my people is not as it should be. Nothing is right. Between one place and the next, this land has no sense of itself.'

'Things will get worse before they get better,' Bronzewing agreed.

'Do you believe that? That things will get better?' Jardi stabbed the knife in the dirt at his feet. 'What will you tell Lycett when he asks you about the burning? And what will he do when we burn again? My father will not be stopped and I fear there will be trouble.'

Bronzewing spat out the soggy grass stem. 'I know.'

≪ Chapter 5 ≫

1837 August – en route to Parramatta

'Told her not to go I did, but these young things never listen. Do you listen, dear? It's important to listen to your elders.'

Kate nodded politely to the talkative woman, one of five travelling companions since joining the Sydney coach at Ashfield, and held onto the timber surround that was all that separated her and Mrs Allen from the road below. Dust spun up from beneath the carriage wheels, the grit clouding the stone road as it grew small in the distance. At any minute Kate expected to be jolted from the rear outside seat to land with a thud on the road. The wide stone thoroughfare of Parramatta Road may have been considered quicker than taking a boat down the safer Parramatta River but it had been a rough journey.

'You'll be right, love,' one of the male travellers called from the carriage roof where he was perched between baggage.

Kate was unsure whether he alluded to the roughness of the journey or the chance of attack by either natives, highwaymen or both. Apparently such incidents happened frequently, a fact that was confirmed by the driver who'd warned them to keep an eye out. The man who'd called to her kept a musket in hand. Kate had spent most of the trip looking at the thick bush they passed through, her stomach knotted by nerves.

'So I says to her,' Mrs Allen continued, 'you go then. Pack yourself up and head to Sydney Town, but if you end up with some down-at-heel soldier or sailor with nothing to show for himself except a toothy smile and a mile of promises, don't come running back to me. Looked at me, she did. Told me to mind me own business. My own daughter. She'll end up with a bastard, she will, and the poor little blighter will be found on the streets wandering with the rest of the homeless urchins and be taken to one of them orphanages.' Mrs Allen blew her nose loudly into a handkerchief, and then coughed up a mess of something from the back of her throat and spat the globule over the side of the moving carriage.

Apart from a few other drays and wagons, the majority of the traffic was confined to the hostelries located at intervals along the Sydney to Parramatta road. These rest stops serviced many travellers, but with spring soon to arrive, shorn wool was already being brought to market. Kate was intrigued by the many settlers with drayloads of wool, who were talking animatedly to buyers on the side of the road. One such merchant cut a slash in a bale as Kate's carriage rolled past and, pulling free a handful of wool, examined it carefully then spoke animatedly to the man next to him. The settler frowned, shook his head and made a show of moving on.

A row of timber cottages, each with a waft of chimney smoke lingering in the sky, suggested they neared their destination. Drays of cut wood and carts of lime fought for space with those walking; men, women and children, convicts and free settlers. Those with horses, well-to-do settlers and the military skirted past the traffic, giving little time for people to move aside. A gang of convicts were repairing part of the road, carrying stones back and forth under the watchful gaze of the military. None of the men looked up when the carriage rolled past.

'Parramatta!' the driver yelled, stringing the word out so that all could hear.

'Home at last.' Mrs Allen nudged Kate in the arm and pointed to the north. A glimpse of the town appeared through the trees. Open land, pretty in its gentle undulations, folded inwards to Parramatta proper, with its carefully laid-out streets and the spires of a church. 'Mr Howell's wind and watermill. I always feel better when I see them sails.'

The wind and watermill featured picturesquely in the foreground, the four long arms of the windmill rising up from the banks of the Parramatta River as if standing protectively over the town.

'I've heard it on good authority that Mrs Elizabeth Howell is involved in the business. A woman, with a family to rear and all. She helped birth my Margery's boy, she did.'

The horses slowed and the carriage came to a rolling stop. Kate stepped stiffly down. For a moment it was as if she still moved and she leant against the coach for balance, as her travelling companion bustled past.

'You'll get your land legs soon enough, lass,' the older woman called. 'Parched, I am, and in need of a feed. They keep a good table inside. Come join me.'

'Thank you but I'm not hungry,' Kate lied. Tugging at her bonnet, she watched the woman enter the inn and then sheltered from the morning sun beneath the bark-roofed verandah. Kate was wind-blown, her bottom hurt from the hard seat and her skin felt tight from the sun, but she refused to show her discomfort as the Reverend stepped from the interior of the carriage. An extra shilling to travel inside was not forthcoming for her journey. He dusted off his clothes and, barely acknowledging her presence, waited as travelling trunks and bags were unloaded. The postman exchanged the brown leather pouch slung over his shoulders for a bag of mail for Sydney with his Parramatta counterpart and then joined the other passengers inside the inn.

Return passengers for Sydney were already milling about the staging post as horses were unhitched and led away to be watered and four fresh ones brought forward. Sweat from both man and beast mingled in the air as the Reverend waited some ten feet from where Kate stood. She would have dearly loved something cool to drink and a tasty bite to eat, but with no coin to her name she contented herself with the chunk of bread Madge had pressed into her hand on leaving. She bit into the hard dough, chewing slowly. There was barely enough spittle in her mouth to moisten the bread but she was grateful for it. Kate had not looked behind as the rickety dray trundled away from the Reverend's farm, even though they'd lined up to see her leaving; Madge, the new girl in the kitchen and the old Welsh gardener.

Wiping crumbs from her face, Kate rewrapped the portion of bread and tucked it into her mother's empty drawstring bag. Lesley Carter had been dead this past month, however Kate's decision to leave the Reverend was made the day following her burial. At times her resolve had weakened. To throw away the known for the unknown, to tempt the fates was a steadying thought. For his part the Reverend, having expressed his anger, simply stopped talking to her. The school was closed. He sent the children to plead with her. Young Thomas Prescott gave her a hangman's stare. The lad was to be sent away to learn a trade, indentured to a wheel-wright. Even Madge expressed her disbelief at Kate's decision, growing sullen and bitter as the departure date grew nearer. Better the devil you know, were her words of advice.

Kate hadn't known a person's heart could hurt so much. Although she and her mother had grown apart, her death had struck her forcibly. Kate missed her with every breath she took. In the grief that stalked the hours following her mother's death, she did consider staying with the Reverend, in putting the children's needs before her own, in assuming her mother's role. Yet Kate only saw two roads that could be taken: abide by her decision to leave and start a new life, whatever that may be, or remain where she was and live as a hypocrite, an impossibility after all she'd said and thought about her mother's arrangement with Reverend Horsley. And yet as she waited outside the inn, with strangers milling about, Kate felt more than uneasy. Had she made the right decision?

'Be on yer guard all of youse travelling to Syd-e-ney. We might be in this fancy carriage but there are bushrangers and natives on the Parramatta Road and they're not afraid of showing themselves, if you know what I mean.' The driver hitched his trousers up. 'We'll be leaving in thirty minutes. So look sharp, the lot of you.'

A dray pulled up behind the carriage and the driver, a narrow-headed man with a thick beard and bandy legs, scanned the people outside the inn before picking the Reverend out of the crowd. He jumped from the dray. 'You be 'im that's going to Mr Kable's farm then, Father?' His Irish accent was thick and rough.

'I am not a priest, I'm Reverend Horsley, but yes, my companion and I are –'

'Well then, let's get you loaded. They don't normally send a dray but considering it's the likes of you, Father.'

Kate took one look at the Reverend's sour face and did her best not to laugh.

The Reverend sighed, beckoned to Kate and soon they were sitting on a hard bench seat behind the driver, Kate's grandmother's travelling trunk and the Reverend's bag stored in the rear of the dray.

'I'll take you the scenic route, Father. I'd be appreciative if you keep that pistol of yours at the ready.'

The Reverend rested the flintlock on his thigh.

The dray passed a roadside inn where a group of men stood in a ring, cheering partially dressed Aboriginals. The dark men weaved about the circle, their legs unsteady, clearly drunk. Two of them were fighting, and the men were taking bets and enjoying the sport. The men called out *coo-ee*, one making a lurid remark about what he could do for her if Kate had a mind for a bit of sport. Her eyes grew to the size of organ stops, and she blushed and turned away. The Reverend, his knobbly knees bumping against hers, too close for comfort, clucked his tongue disapprovingly. The two-seater dray, seemingly springless, with a pair of headstrong horses that were a poor substitute for the set of four Cleveland Bays who'd pulled them so efficiently to Parramatta, clattered across the road and then veered right.

Around the curve of the road the white walls of the Governor's residence gradually appeared. The building rose from atop a hill, its symmetrical lines softened by the surrounding manicured grounds. Kate watched the ruling seat of the colony until timber obscured its beauty. Far from feeling she was in the centre of life, the further they travelled from Parramatta, the more ill at ease she became.

The Reverend's cottage may have been isolated but at least there she'd been between Sydney and Parramatta. This road they travelled led them away from the bustle of civilisation, towards the mountains and lands she'd never seen. Kate thought of Mrs Allen, of her daughter Margery and the windmill and bakery. Maybe she should have enquired as to the possibility of work in Parramatta. Maybe Mrs Allen could have helped her. The dray bumped and jolted them at every step. A chill afternoon breeze wound down from the distant mountains.

'Stop fidgeting, Kate,' the Reverend complained.

'It's the bumps,' she told him, noting that he seemed intent on sitting right in the middle of the seat. 'Could you move over a little please?' She could feel her hipbone growing bruised where it lodged against the dray's timber side.

'You can always get out and walk,' the driver called over his shoulder. 'Four miles to go.'

The Reverend patted his whiskers. 'A little late to be complaining now, Kate.'

At one stage Kate thought it possible that the Reverend may well throw her out on the street, when she finally and most adamantly refused his offer of employment. Instead he'd come to her with the offer of finding Kate suitable employ. It was quite unexpected and even Madge expressed wonderment. Nonetheless theirs was not an amicable parting, although Kate was grateful for the lengths the Reverend had gone to in finding her a suitable position. There were few alternatives available to a single, educated young woman. Marriage remained the only other option but it was an unappealing alternative. She still remembered the night she'd seen her mother and the Reverend together. To be with a man, in such a way, well, she didn't think herself possible of ever forming such a union, nor marrying, and she would never do either without love. So here she was, in a quaking dray, nervously awaiting the moment when she'd meet her new employer.

Apprehension grew as the miles increased. Kate's life had been restricted to the cottage and the schoolhouse, and the weekly trip to the markets with her mother, only six miles' walk from where they lived. Hers was the life of a fringe dweller, forever perched on the outskirts of Sydney, and though she lived in an area surrounded by bush, the Reverend's holding was still far removed from the wilds that spread out to and over the blue hills beyond. This was a new world where great expanses of grassland were punctuated by towering trees and scant houses. 'Is there a village over there?' Smoke was visible in the distance.

'That be Toongabbe,' the Irishman was quick to answer. 'The settlers are doing well for themselves over there. There's water-a-plenty in the crick there, some say too much. It can flood something terrible further up. Three miles to go.'

The dray trundled roughly over the ground. They were at least a mile from the last dwelling they'd seen and still the carriage headed inland. The wheels clanked and squeaked continuously. Kate grasped the worn edge of the timber seat as the driver somehow managed to hit every hole and crack that lay in their path. She tucked at the hair which had fallen loose from the cap beneath her hat and rubbed at grit-filled eyes.

'Two miles to go, miss,' the driver encouraged. 'I'll be thinking you'll be pleased to stretch your legs after today.' Lifting a flask he took a long gulp. The smell of rum grew strong. 'What about you, Father? A swig to warm you from your head to your toes? Makes a man hearty, it does.'

'No, thank you.' The Reverend sat stiff-backed, his black garb contrasting with pale skin and much attended to whiskers running down the length of his face. Kate could smell sweat mixed with the stink of pipe smoke. Indeed the Reverend's odour came closer to surpassing that of the rum-belching driver.

The dray turned from the road and followed a path rutted by wheel tracks. The boning in the seams of her bodice pinched at her sides and waist as Kate blotted out the scene in the schoolhouse the day of her mother's passing. Even now she caught the Reverend glaring at her at times. There was dislike in his hard stare, undisguised annoyance, but often-times Kate also glimpsed familiarity in the tilt of his head, in the way he addressed her. It reminded Kate of the way he'd been with her mother.

'It is a pity you have made this choice, Kate. The world is a harsh place for a single woman.'

'I thank you for the efforts you have gone to on my behalf, Reverend.'

'You are fortunate. Mr Jonas Kable is one of the leading men of the colony.'

It was not surprising that the Reverend had gone to the trouble of escorting her personally to the Kable farm. He'd told Kate that Mr Kable had grown rich on the back of supplying wheat to the colony, and sheep and cattle added to an already handsome income. Reverend Horsley was one for making the best of his connections and a cousin of the Kables had been instrumental in obtaining a place for Kate in their household. She gathered the Reverend now hoped for continued association, an endowment perhaps, for his place of worship was in much need of repairs. Kate imagined a yearly stipend to add to his earnings would do much to ensure his continuing comfort.

'You are learned enough to fulfil the role of companion to Mrs Kable, although I fear your musical accomplishments are somewhat lacking.'

'Less than a mile now.' The driver pointed to a tree. The bark was marked by deep scarring, which extended some eight feet in length, its width reaching across the breadth of the trunk.

'A native canoe, I would imagine,' the Reverend explained.

Kate's eyes widened. 'Natives here?'

'Well, of course. What did you think, that we'd wiped them out? Yes, well your mother was prone to such moments of female ignorance. May her soul rest in peace. Amen.'

Kate looked to the hills. The building of a road across the range had been completed over twenty years ago. During that time settlers had moved further westward, and the local Aboriginals fought and had apparently been brought to heel. 'I thought most had moved further out beyond the mountains.'

'A people should know when they're conquered,' was the Reverend's oblique reply. 'Count yourself lucky, Kate. The mountains are a buffer from the vast wilds on the other side.'

The thought of all that immeasurable space stretching towards a setting sun intrigued Kate. 'What's out there?'

'Natives, escaped convicts, bushrangers. I pity a man who must travel to the beyonds.'

Kate could only be grateful that the Kable farm lay within the boundaries of civilised society.

They crossed a narrow gully at a snail's pace. A trickle of water ran across a pile of smooth rocks, which jolted the dray sideways, nearly throwing Kate to the floor. The Reverend tutted as Kate straightened her skirts. The queasy sensation in her stomach grew. She was beginning to feel short of breath. Ten years had passed since her father's death and now her life was to be changed yet again, and always it was death that so utterly altered the threads of her life.

The dray bounced dangerously from left to right before resuming a steady gait. A number of timber buildings were visible through the trees, houses for convicts, a farrier's workshop and, beyond this clutch of outbuildings, the dome of a smokehouse. The white-washed walls of a sturdy home appeared amidst scattered trees. Smoke curled from the stone chimney and cattle and sheep were scattered about the park-like surrounds. There were shepherds tending to the livestock and further afield wheat swayed beneath a winter breeze. The Kables, as free settlers, had been assigned numerous convicts and as the carriage mounted the slight hill these men became more distinctive in their waistcoats of yellow and grey cloth, coarse woollen jackets and pants.

'Mr Jonas Kable keeps a fine table. I believe Governor Macquarie was a guest in the early days. Of course since then any person of import seeks to break bread with the family although Mrs Kable is more inclined to entertainments in their Sydney residence.'

As they grew closer a separate kitchen with an adjoining covered walkway could be seen on the western side of the house and two young children were running through a grove of lemon and orange trees, a servant in attendance. Kate kept a smile from forming on her lips. This was simply the grandest place she'd ever been to.

The Reverend brushed the dust of their travels from his clothing and rubbed a forefinger briskly across his teeth.

Considering everything that had passed between them, the Reverend had done right by her in the end. Perhaps it was in deference to the regard in which he held her mother. Or had Kate underestimated the man's propensity for goodness? Whatever the reason, Kate thanked the man opposite her with genuine gratitude. The dray jolted to a stop.

'Perhaps you may grow to have your mother's qualities,' Reverend Horsley replied, stepping down from the cart and placing a hand briefly to his lower back. 'Obedience and humility are the virtues expected of the fairer sex, Kate.' He extended a hand to her. 'Either way I am sure your new role will be an enlightening experience.'

Kate took his arm and set foot on the grounds of her new home. The Reverend kept her hand in his, the pressure of his grip increasing. 'I notice you are wearing one of your mother's gowns. One of a number I gave her. It becomes you.'

'You're hurting me.'

'Am I?' He released her immediately. 'How careless.'

Kate rubbed at the red mark on her wrist. She would be pleased to see the last of him.

Before them stood a fine colonial bungalow of red brick washed with lime. There were French doors in place of windows, deep timber verandahs with fine lattice-work and a trailing vine at the western end. The building had the symmetrical qualities of the Governor's residence and a low-pitched roof of the type said to be favoured in India. There was no doubt in Kate's mind that she was entering the world of the rich and the progressive.

The driver dragged Kate's trunk from the rear of the dray. Everything she owned, including the few possessions of her mother's, landed with a thud on the ground. The front door swung open. A pointy-nosed convict stood on the threshold. The woman, aged in her thirties, was scarred by the pox, but it was the servant's tapping foot that caught Kate's attention. 'You be the Reverend Horsley and the new girl.' Her expression never altered as she turned her attention to the Irish driver, giving the man a withering look. 'You should have come round the back.' The woman stuck her hands on her hips.

'I brought the Father with me, I did,' he argued. 'What's a person to do? Drop one at the front and the other out back? One stop at either end was the instruction, girl, and that's what I done.'

Ignoring the driver's remarks, the maid beckoned to them. 'Well, come on then. The Missus is expecting you.' She looked Kate up and down. 'And you're a half-hour late.'

Kate trailed the Reverend into the entrance hall. There was just enough time given for hats and travelling cloaks to be removed and no time to study the oil portraits of the three members of the English gentry who lined the passageway, although Kate was aware of their querying gaze. No dirt or hewn timber met her heeled leather shoes. Instead the timber boards were covered with thick canvas, painted in black and cream squares to resemble a marble floor. There were two doors on either side of the hall and a line of servant bells, each differing in size and tone according to room, were suspended from one side of the hall. One began to tinkle.

The maid knocked once on a door and announced them.

Kate found herself standing in the grandest room possible. The walls were pale yellow, the windows hung with striking floral material with bright contrasts of blue, orange, green and red and the furniture was simply exquisite. Twin rosewood sofas were positioned near a brightly woven rug opposite a large fireplace. There were a number of fine pieces of furniture, sideboards, a sewing table and chairs, while a large vase of native flowers and grasses was arranged on the breakfast table, which was placed close to the French window and the natural light.

'So then, Jelly-belly, they have arrived, very good. You can serve tea.' Mrs Kable closed the sheet music and, having dismissed the maid, turned from where she sat before a small piano. She studied them both, one at a time, slowly. It was a practised gesture. Kate imagined their hostess counting to ten, but although Kate was savvy to the older woman's intent towards causing discomfort, it had the desired effect.

'Reverend Horsley, welcome.' The piano was quite unadorned except for a large panel of scarlet material above the keys, which was gathered prettily to meet in the middle at a rosette. In contrast, on rising, Mrs Kable quite outshone her surrounds. Aged in her early forties her pale skin, brown hair and short stature were emphasised by a mustard gown with sloping shoulders and a narrow waist that tapered to a small point at the front before layers of skirts and petticoats floated over full hips. Every feminine curve was accentuated by the cut and cream lace trim.

'And you must be Miss Carter,' Mrs Kable said politely. 'Do sit, my dear, I am only too aware how tiring that journey can be. You experienced no problems, I hope. We never know when the natives may appear but thankfully this area is becoming more settled and their numbers have been dwindling. And you, Reverend Horsley, having to return in the morning, you will be quite exhausted.'

The Reverend's smile, one much used for widows at funerals, was replaced by a pulpit glare. Sitting stiffly on one of the sofas, he crossed his legs. By the size of his travelling bag it was clear that he'd expected to be invited to stay for at least a few days. In the awkward silence the carriage clock on the mantelpiece chimed. They were interrupted by the maid, who sat a tea-tray before them on a table. The porcelain china rattled noisily and the girl apologised profusely and curtsied before leaving the room.

'Convicts,' sighed Mrs Kable as she poured tea and offered both sugar and milk. 'They can be wearing at times. Jelly-belly does her best, but, well . . . We've two new girls from the Female Factory at Parramatta, one of them has markedly fine needlepoint.' She took a sip of her tea. 'You must sit with her, Miss Carter, and observe. She is a woman of sour disposition but her talent is quite remarkable.'

Kate looked at the creamy coloured tea, sipping it carefully. The flavour was wonderful and she savoured each mouthful. This was a home of import. Even the Reverend didn't serve milk as milking cows were a rarity. 'I wanted to thank you, Mrs Kable.'

The woman shook her head, causing the movement of numerous ringlets. 'It is my husband's doing. Initially I was not in agreement, it's the responsibility, I'm sure you understand. You will be a long way from the Reverend, and a young woman such as yourself, well, to be blunt, I consider it strange that you would wish to venture so far afield.'

Admittedly it had been somewhat of a journey to the Kable farm, however Kate was more than pleased to be here. 'Sometimes one must travel in order to reach the appropriate end,' she answered, copying Mrs Kable's formality.

Mrs Kable peered over the rim of her cup. 'She is quite schooled, isn't she?'

The Reverend merely nodded.

'You should be seeking a suitable husband, raising a family. That is a woman's duty, after all, is it not?'

Kate bristled, her personal situation was not something that she considered to be for public discussion. 'Some would say so.'

'Some?' Their hostess gave a mock cough, held a handkerchief to her lips. 'All would say so, my dear. Whomever has suggested otherwise is quite at odds with the way of the world. Such things can be unlearnt, can't they, Reverend Horsley?'

'Indeed, Mrs Kable. All things are possible.' He turned in Kate's direction. 'With time.'

'Well, to the matter at hand. You are here in search of employ and although I am at odds with your acceptance of the role, I must think of my own family's needs at this time.'

Kate was at a loss at this comment. Did Mrs Kable believe her above the position of companion? If so, this was an auspicious start. She straightened her shoulders a little more. The Reverend dropped his gaze to the woven matting at his feet.

'I more than most understand the benefit of companionship. And you, Miss Carter, are obviously a gentlewoman in spite of certain, shall we say, limitations.'

'Limitations?' Kate repeated.

The woman ignored her. 'The Reverend says you are a willing participant in this venture in spite of his offer to retain you in his employ.' Mrs Kable paused, as if seeking confirmation.

'Most willing, yes,' Kate agreed, taking a sip of the hot drink and then gently placing the cup soundlessly on the saucer. Her mother would be proud.

Mrs Kable observed her carefully and made a clucking sound with her tongue. 'Very well. As long as you are aware that if the situation does not suit you, Miss Carter, that it may be a good year, indeed longer, before you have the opportunity to leave. There is the question of travel and of course the difficulty of trying to obtain someone to replace you.'

The Reverend remarked on the weather and a brief discussion ensued as to the lack of rain.

'Now, if we've finished . . .' The older woman moved to a corner of the room and tugged at the bell pull.

Kate glanced at the partially consumed tea, took a sip and then another before reluctantly sitting the cup and saucer on the table. If milk were to be served up every day, she would be happy indeed.

'Jelly-belly will show you to your rooms. Tea is at six sharp.' Their hostess waved a hand in farewell as the pointy-nosed maid reappeared.

Kate waited in the hallway while the maid escorted the Reverend to his bedchamber. It was an airy space and the portraits lining the walls were of two men and a woman, all suitably smug in the way that only the high-born can appear. On the maid's return, she led Kate to the rear verandah, past a trellis covered in vine, which Kate guessed provided a pretty aspect during the warmer months for those occupants fortunate enough to be sitting at the breakfast table. A French door fed into another passageway and then to a small room. Plainly decorated, Kate wondered if this was to be her personal domain for the bedchamber had a narrow wardrobe, washstand and mirror but no desk or chair. From the curtained window above the bed there was, however, a fine view of the mountains. They sat like a smudge of pale blue ink against a washed out sky while in the foreground the green wheat fields, which she'd seen on their arrival, swayed gently in the breeze.

As Kate surveyed the cold room, the maid hovering behind her, heavy footsteps announced the arrival of her trunk. Two convict men dumped the chest in her room and left without a word.

'Mrs Kable mentioned tea was to be served at six. Might I have water to wash, please?'

The maid looked at the water pitcher on the washstand. 'I'll have some brought directly, but Mrs Kable said you're to have tea in your room on account of your journey.' The maid lowered her voice. 'They've got guests and the Missus keeps a first class table, she does. They're good people and fair, if you know your place.' The maid pressed her lips together, aware she'd been outspoken.

'Your name isn't really Jelly-belly, is it?'

'You don't know much about how big houses run, do you, miss?' The question hung. 'I'm the head maid, every one of us has been called that,' she announced. 'They can't be expected to remember our names. If you don't mind me saying so, I think you're terribly brave, miss.'

Kate smiled. 'Brave? I'm probably the least brave of anyone I know. Besides, I can't see how being employed in the capacity of companion to Mrs Kable could be anything other than pleasurable. I'm yet to be acquainted with her in full, although she seems like a charming lady.'

The maid's brow knitted together. 'I'll get you that water, miss. But I'll not be waiting on you while you're here.'

'I wouldn't expect you to.'

With the rules of their relationship established, Jelly-belly gave a satisfied nod and left.

Kate opened her trunk. From it she retrieved her mother's bone-handled hairbrush and cream woollen shawl. Pressing the bristles against her palm, she placed it on the beige coverlet of the sagging bed, then, shawl in hand, Kate walked along the hall and onto a rear porch, open to the elements. Wrapping the stole about her shoulders, she stepped from the verandah out into the garden. The area at the rear of the house held an extensive vegetable garden behind which sat grapevines. A convict woman was bucketing water onto rose bushes, rubbing at the small of her back and straightening as she moved to the next plant, while another rushed in the direction of the kitchen carrying a basket filled with herbs.

The sun hung low above the mountains, turning the pallid sky bright as it crested the tops of the hills in a white halo. Kate had always been in the kitchen with Madge at this hour. It had been many years since there'd been a quiet moment to watch the day merge into night, and with myriad chores to attend to, the arrival of night had become an almost insignificant event. But now the moment held Kate transfixed. You're becoming sentimental, she mused, as the landscape softened under lengthening shadows. Prettiness was never a word she'd used to describe her surrounds, the bush was changeable, mysterious. But here in this place Kate witnessed what could be created with money and labour. And all of it sat beneath the gaze of the blue hills and a softening sun.

It was the quietness that surprised her. There were no convicts talking or arguing, no children fighting, no Madge busily ordering her about, no Reverend with his demands. The hush was both strange and pleasant for a late afternoon. Sheep were calling to each other as convict men converged uphill to their barracks. There was birdsong and the chopping of firewood and the sounds of a household readying for darkness, but everything was muted, ordered. Beyond that it was as if the very countryside watched and waited. For what, she had little idea.

'You'd notice the quiet, coming from Syd-e-ney and all.' A man stepped out from behind a tree. He carried a musket and wore a brace of pistols at his hips. 'You'd be Miss Kate Carter.' He tipped his hat. 'We've heard all about you.' He walked towards her and was slow in running his eyes across her body. 'You're a little thing. I expected a big bonny lass.'

'You have the advantage, sir.'

'George Southerland.' He was tall and lean, with a thick, ragged beard. There was a distinct smell about him. Pipe smoke and rum and wet earth mixed with the scent of a body long past bathing. He was not averse to staring and beneath his gaze Kate found her fingers tightening on the shawl. 'They say you've not been married. It's a wonder, out here, looking the way you do.' He rubbed at the mat growing from his chin. 'You came with the Reverend.' It was a statement. 'He keep you under lock and key, did he?'

Kate stiffened. 'Of course not.'

He chuckled, and began to scratch at his beard, and kept on scratching until he'd circumnavigated his chin like some ancient explorer. 'Best we get on, miss, don't you think, seeing as you'll be depending on me over the coming weeks. And don't be a-feared, I have no liking for skin and bones with attitude, no matter if it comes with a pretty face. Out here a man wants something to hold onto at night. I'd just as likely squash you flat.'

Kate clutched at the shawl and turned to leave. She hadn't travelled all this way to be spoken to so brazenly by a rough stranger.

'Don't stalk off on my account. I mean no harm. I've lost some of me niceties on account of being out bush for so long, but we'll get on, you and I, as long as you follow the rules once we get under way.'

'Under way?' Kate faced the man. 'I think you have me confused with another, Mr Southerland.'

'Not if you're to be a companion to Mr Kable's cousin's wife, Sarah.'

'Cousin?' Kate repeated. She didn't understand.

'She's a fine woman, Sarah Hardy is. Tougher than most. She'll be pleased to see you, lass. Female company is less than scarce.'

Kate had seen no other dwelling nearby.

'We thought to leave within the next few days so you best be prepared. Mr Hardy is waiting on a load of stores.' He cocked his head. 'I wonder at your going. Still, you can be grateful we're not herding 1500 Saxon ewes and rams up-country, let alone the twenty head of cattle and two drays that were part of the initial expedition.' He looked briefly skyward. 'The weather's holding. Best we make the most of the fine days, although I doubt there will be a break in the season just yet.' He looked her up and down for a second time. 'You best be prepared for there'll be weeks of hard travel along rutted tracks, creeks and rivers to cross, mud and sand to get bogged in and broken axles to mend. It's a distance and there's not much between here and there apart from shanties and bush-rangers and blacks.'

'I think there must be some confusion,' Kate began but Mr Southerland had already taken his leave of her without a backward glance. She wrung her hands. If indeed it was Mr Jonas Kable's intent for her to be sent elsewhere, Kate had a right to know where. Voices carried from the front of the house along with the familiar noise of horses on gravel. Kate wanted to see who the visitors were but she was neither maid nor guest. It occurred to her that with her new position she didn't quite fit in on either side of the household. And now she wasn't even sure who she was to work for.

Jelly-belly reappeared and called her indoors. 'Mrs Kable says you're to dress for dinner on account of Mr Kable wanting everyone present. The Missus is none too pleased so if I was you, miss, I'd be as quick as you can and quiet as a mouse once the dining begins.'

Sitting a jug of water on the washstand near a large blue and white porcelain bowl, she handed Kate a candle. 'If you've got a decent gown, now is the time for it. As for me I've me own problems what with Mrs Ovens having two extra at table and Molly not being presentable enough yet to serve. That's the worst of them factory girls, they're always stirring up trouble. Had her head shaved she did for nicking outside after dark. Heavens, miss, I still think you're terribly brave.'

Kate was still digesting George Southerland's revelation as she lifted each layer of clothing inside the chest. Eventually her fingers touched the creamy cotton, lace and muslin her mother had shown her so excitedly all those years ago. The gown had been altered over time. The cream bodice with lace collar was now boned in the seams and the gauzy muslin fell prettily from the waistline. It was true it lacked the quantity of material in the skirt and sleeves that the current styles favoured, but it was still of fine quality, albeit slightly old-fashioned.

Stripping off her clothes, Kate washed her face and hands with a cloth and a sliver of soap, then proceeded to sponge the remainder of her body. She turned once or twice during these ablutions to glance out the window towards the hills. She had the strangest sensation that she was being watched, and finally she drew the curtain against the failing light.

Stepping into her drawers, Kate pulled the two separate leg pieces over damp skin and tied the cord at her waist then tugged a shift over her head. Once dressed in her mother's gown, only then did she remove the cloth cap covering her hair. The oval mirror reflected wide almond-shaped eyes and dark hair, which she quickly smoothed into a bun at the nape of her neck. Three ringlets, slightly droopy from the day's travel, framed either side of her face. Wetting her fingers Kate coaxed the messy curls into more uniform spirals, patting the ones on her right temple in an attempt to hide the scar. The old injury was now a reddish blemish, which curved like a question mark from above her eyebrow around her eye. By day the cloth cap she wore beneath her straw hat helped to conceal the wound, but it was impossible to hide otherwise. Her mother had suggested a little flour would lessen the slight discolouration but there was no disguising the jagged edge of Lambeth's fury.

'This will have to do.'

Kate didn't have the looks of the 'currency children', those born to convicts. Most of the native born were tall, slender and fair. Instead she resembled her mother. Of middling height, with a lithe figure, she bore the mark of a Scottish heritage that Lesley once told her was mixed with Spanish blood.

A clock chimed from somewhere within the house. Kate heard muffled footsteps, conversation and laughter and the irritable whine of a child. This was a busy household and by the brief attention granted her and the Reverend on arrival, its mistress ran it efficiently. It would not do to be late. Kate took a final look in the mirror, smoothed the tightly fitted bodice and, with a steadying breath, thought of what lay before her. The truth of the position that the Reverend had so *kindly* sought on her behalf.

❧ Chapter 6 ❧

1837 August — on the western side of the Blue Mountains

Winston Lycett was sitting in his usual spot, a flat rock at the base of a tree split in half by a lightning strike. The branch on the ground angled down to a narrow trickling creek and on the other side of the gully was a patch of grass frequented by kangaroos. Bronzewing moved through the timber silently. It was already late. Having spent the morning hours searching for the light wooded trees that were used for spear-making, the sun had overtaken him and no shadow trailed his progress. He'd not seen his old friend since he'd left with Archibald Lycett last year and he'd missed his company. Winston was usually drawing at this time, his sandy head tilted to one side, lank hair falling across his brow, a piece of charcoal hovering over paper. Still some distance away from his friend, Bronzewing lifted a hand to yell *coo-ee* in greeting, but halted. Today there was no scatter of drawing materials. Instead the usual artist supplies were stacked to one side.

There was an Aboriginal with him, a woman. Winston had been fond of girls from an early age. The Codbolts with their three daughters, who lived ten miles away, had all appealed. Although they were hard to look at with their round, bland faces and overly large foreheads, Winston was not put off. All three girls had shown interest in Winston, a fact that he delightedly announced shouldn't be dismissed in a place where women were scarce – and were also willing if it meant there was a chance to snare a good husband. Clearly nothing had changed in Bronzewing's absence.

The girl sat side on. Winston lifted the woman's breast in a hand and lowering his head began to suckle like a baby. The young woman rested her hands on the ground, arching her back and drawing him closer. Finally Winston lifted his head, wiping his mouth with the back of his hand. The girl laughed and offered him the other nipple, which he groped at enthusiastically.

Bronzewing's approach startled a mob of kangaroos. Raising their heads from the herbage they'd been nibbling, their ears pricked. The movement alerted the girl. She turned towards the narrow creek and then, jumping up, ran through the timber. He was too far away to see the girl's face properly, but not so distant to recognise the movement of a man buttoning up his trousers. Winston, having dressed himself, leant back against the tree and feigned sleep.

'*Coo-ee.*' Bronzewing lifted a hand in greeting and the kangaroos hopped away.

Winston yawned. 'Back to give my work another one of your negative assessments?' he replied. There was a musket and canvas waterbag at his side.

'Should it be negative?' The only thing recognisable in Winston's pictures were trees. 'You should come hunting with me, Winston. You'll grow dull spending all your time here.'

'Stay where you are, Adam. I'm ill.'

Bronzewing took a hesitant step forward, the sound of his white name always jarred.

'I'm serious.'

'What is it this time?' He doubted there was much wrong with Winston other than the usual array of ailments that beset him, and his desire to keep his meeting with the girl secret. He wandered along the trickle of water that awaited replenishing from the spring rains that were yet to arrive, finally squatting opposite Winston beneath a spreading tree, the narrow waterway between them.

Winston scowled and then tapped his head – once, twice – against the knobbly bark. 'The pox, the sickness that comes to your lungs or head, who knows?' He coughed heavily, the action wracking his long, thin body. He wiped at his mouth. 'One of the ticket-of-leave men came down with it a week ago. He's bedridden now. One minute freezing, the next burning up. It started with a cough. And yes, my mother has forced a number of preparations down my throat. None of which have helped.' He coughed again, and stretched out his legs. 'But you're not here to visit me. Father's at the house. I expected you here sooner. It's been a year. We knew you'd returned.'

'The warmer weather will help what ails you,' Adam responded. 'The winter's been cold.'

'Father says I shouldn't complain. That London is bitter cold, with a dank fog that covers the city like a shroud. Well, the cold is bad enough here. It takes hold of your bones and won't let go.' He began mounding the leaf-litter at his side, piling small twigs and leaves. 'You shouldn't have fired the grass you know.'

'And you and your family should have stayed on the other side of the mountain,' Adam countered.

Winston gave a weak smile. 'Then who would have dragged you to the bench under the tree so you could be educated instead of remaining a heathen?'

'Sometimes I think your mother suffered more than me.'

Winston sat a little straighter and, pulling his knees up, wrapped his arms around them. 'There is more to learn, you know. There are many books to read, countries to understand, theories to unravel.'

His face grew animated. 'Like how far the land extends to the west, whether there is a great inland sea. Don't you wonder what lies out there, in all that undiscovered vastness? What people are there, what riches, what opportunities?'

The silhouettes of the timber surrounding them lengthened across the ground. 'More of the same, I hope. Although Bidjia says that those tribes that roam in the direction of the setting sun speak of lands that are flat and dry.'

'That's hardly a description.'

Adam shrugged. 'Actually I thought it pretty accurate.'

'So, tell me where you've been this last year. Father said you joined an expedition of settlers a month or so after the wool was delivered to market. What was the country like? Did the natives attack? Is it better land than here?'

Adam jumped the gully between them and squatted some feet from where his friend sat. 'Similar, yes, and in places.'

Winston frowned. 'I envy the explorers. What makes them, do you think? How does a person come to be born with such grit while others are rendered useless by overbearing fathers and familial duty?'

'Chance perhaps?'

'Then it is a bitter pill knowing that life is so random. Sorry, I'm sounding positively maudlin.' He slumped back against the tree trunk. 'I would do better in Sydney.'

'A scholar's life?' Adam suggested.

'We both know it would suit me. But Father has other plans and my opinion counts for nought.'

'You could have come with us, Winston, at least to Parramatta.'

'I know my father, Adam,' he replied matter-of-factly. 'He is one for choosing favoured company,' he said pointedly, 'and for making the best use of a person's abilities. He did entrust his wife and land to me in his absence so that is one point in my favour I suppose. Besides, while you were away I took the time to study the ledgers.

There is money to be made out here, there is no doubt of that. My father makes a great fuss of a person needing to be hands-on, but he has done the hard yards. You only need to oversee the running of these holdings, for there are convicts to do the work.' He gave his friend a warm smile. 'I will bide my time until his is over and then I will take my place as his heir. Anyway, I'm glad you're back. There's no-one to argue with, at least about anything worthwhile. Did you know that a German astronomer named Bessel has managed to measure the distance from the sun to another star? Isn't that the most marvellous thing? I wondered about it myself, you know. He did it using two different lines of sight and measured the angle between the two lines. Don't look at me like that. You used to be interested in these things.'

'And I still am, but I should say my respects to your father.'

'Another day then. I do miss our time together, as does my mother.'

Adam rolled his eyes theatrically. Mrs Georgina Lycett was a kind woman who would have been prepared to raise him as one of her own, if Adam had been so inclined. 'Reading, writing and arithmetic – I don't have much use for such learning now.'

'You will,' Winston assured him. 'One day you will. All the things you find so trifling now will one day become vitally important. You will need your signature to sign the deed to the land you will one day own, and your sums will help you count your coin, while the skills we learnt in map reading could lead you to your wife, if you remember the King's English, or should I say Queen's, and don't scare her off with your Godless ways.' He chuckled quietly at his own humour, while waggling a chastising finger. 'Eventually you will marry and have children and settle down. It is what all men want. Oh, we may come and go from the house we provide for them, but women are the hinge on which life exists. You are no different. Heathen or not. And even your blessed clan can't exist without a pretty smile.' His voice had tightened.

'You are full of advice today, my friend.' In spite of Winston's kindly intentions such talk meant little to Adam. The stars were his ceiling, the warm earth his bed and he was subject to no-one. The bush was his natural home. And although he both enjoyed and appreciated the learning that he'd been favoured with, the Lycetts could not draw him further into their world. Learning the extent of England's power, the breadth of her colonies or the many commodities transacted by the East India Trading Company would not keep him alive in this world.

Winston sighed. 'I offer it while I can and hope it's not disregarded.'

Adam never had been partial to his friend's melancholy moods. 'Your life is your own, old friend, I'll see you married yet and before me.'

'I've no doubt of that, but I know I will not make old bones so do me the courtesy of not arguing with what I know to be true. None on my father's side has lived past fifty-five years.'

'Well, if you keep talking he'll be dead before I see him.'

'Don't cross my father, Adam. He's a fair man, it's true, but we both know that when it comes to his business and the care of his family anything and anyone else is secondary. None of us have forgotten 1824.'

Adam well recalled the attempt by the Wiradjuri to expel the whites from their sacred sites and hunting grounds. The ongoing struggle had led to increased hostilities from Mount York to Bathurst and beyond, with deaths on both sides. 'I hardly think the presence of Bidjia's clan warrants martial law.'

Winston had the disinterested appearance of someone who had already moved on from that topic. 'Will you do something for me? Deliver a message?'

'To whom?'

His friend began to re-pile the mound of leaves by his side. 'I've a penchant for women, as you know, but I must break ties with this one.'

'Out of your depth, are you?'

'Yes and no,' Winston wavered. 'It's Merindah.'

'Merindah? Bidjia's woman?'

Winston picked at the leaves on the ground. 'I promised her things,' he said awkwardly, 'things that were not mine to promise. I would not like her to think ill of me.'

Adam was stunned. 'She does not belong to you.'

Winston's eyes grew in size. 'I was only talking about helping her, but frankly, she doesn't belong to Bidjia either. They are not married and she is desperately unhappy. Besides, the blacks trade women like we trade wool at the markets. I hardly think Bidjia has the right to any fuss.'

'As far as their customs are concerned, they are married.'

'I see why my father would do you the courtesy of speaking to you first rather than hunting down the natives that fired our land. You're like him. You would put your ways and your native family first before your friends, before your true life. It is a misplaced loyalty.'

'Merindah belongs to another.'

'Until she is traded or passed on.' The comment hung. 'I see by your hesitation, Adam, that some things don't sit so easily with you.' Winston flicked at the leaf litter he'd been piling by his side. 'Why do you stay with them?'

'You mean why do I return to them? I have been away this past year.' Adam hunched his shoulders. 'I am used to the life, their ways. I doubt that I would be suited to any other.'

'Really? Look at you with your blucher boots and palm-leaf hat, your hair tied back like a dandy.' Winston slumped back against the rough bark of the tree.

'I've chosen a life that suits me, Winston. Anyway, I best go and listen to your father lecture me.'

Lifting a sketch pad and charcoal, Winston studied the blank sheet. 'Lecture? It's our livelihood. Your blacks are burning our land.'

Adam trudged the half-mile to the Lycett farmhouse, an unwanted image of Merindah in Winston's arms ruining the day – he could only assume it had been her. This was a problem he'd never foreseen; his friend with Bidjia's woman. If there was more than friendship between them and the relationship was discovered, the tribe would only have one form of revenge. Such a liaison could never be revealed.

The homestead was situated amidst the undulating countryside that rolled westwards toward the Bathurst Plains. The house was a squat building of timber and bark with a low-slung verandah situated close to sheltering trees on the western side, while to the east the great divider between the inland and the coastal areas, a range of blue-tinged mountains, loomed down at the isolated farm. The positioning ensured some relief from the summer sun and also shaded a vegetable plot, which showed tufts of green sprouting up from the damp earth.

Georgina Lycett, a grey-flecked, brown-haired woman with the type of overly joyful disposition that at times rang untrue, was sewing beneath the schooling tree, as he and Winston had named it, a basket of threads on the bench. She looked up on his approach and waved. 'Adam, at last. We have all missed you. Winston especially has bemoaned your long absence. You must save us from his morbid mutterings and eat with us.'

Adam waved back. 'He is ill?'

'A fever, we have all had it, although admittedly Winston has experienced the worst of it.'

On the verandah, a suspended cage held a rainbow lorikeet. The head of the bird was a deep blue, the rest of the body a mixture of green, red and yellow. The parrot was talkative today and had clearly been enjoying a diet rich in nectar from the early spring flowers Mrs Lycett picked, for there was bird droppings splattered all through the cage, on the timber boards of the verandah and the wall opposite. Winston's father sat nearby, reading.

'Adam, good morning to you.'

'Mr Lycett.' Adam leant on one of the verandah's wooden pillars. A vacant chair rested against the wall of the verandah. It was not offered.

Grey of hair, serious, with a face creased like woven matting and immaculately dressed, Mr Lycett was akin to a coiled spring ready to bounce at a moment's notice. 'You've been with Winston? No doubt he's been regaling you with Bessel's achievements. I'm glad you're back. It will give us all something different to talk about.' His mental faculties were on a par with his son's but he had a driven quality about him and Archibald Lycett knew the difference between the educated mind and idleness, a trait that he often ridiculed Winston for. 'A letter from London. My sister.' He folded it carefully, ensuring the original creases were matched and lay the letter on the table, beneath a hinged box which held a pistol.

'I can come back when you've finished reading?'

Removing round reading glasses, Archibald wrapped them in a length of cotton and placed them in a wooden case. 'Not at all. I've read it a half-dozen times already. She writes with a fine pen. I can almost see the River Thames . . . the vendors.' He gave a sigh, tucking the letter in his coat pocket. 'Such a distance away. It means nothing to you, I know, such is the loss to the native born. You know why I wanted to see you?'

'I have some idea.'

'I don't wish to accuse as I have no evidence, except a shepherd's word. There has been another fire. The second in as many weeks.'

'The hot weather comes,' Adam replied cautiously. 'Lightning strikes are of concern to all.'

'Do you think me a fool, sir? Two natives were seen in the vicinity.' Winston's father rubbed a weathered cheek. 'Can you not explain to them, Adam, that my sheep need grass to survive?'

'You have been here twenty years, Mr Lycett. Have you not seen a change in the landscape since the arrival of your sheep? Was the kangaroo grass not up to the stirrup irons on your horse on arrival? Was the winter herbage not abundant, the earth covered by a variety of plants?'

'Archibald, I told Adam he must stay and eat with us.' Mrs Lycett stooped to collect a roll of thread that spilt from her basket as she headed towards them.

'You must have noticed that the tall grasses that once thrived in this area have been eaten out or trampled by your livestock, only to be replaced by inferior ones,' Adam continued. 'Once you could stick your finger in the ground and the dirt was ashy and soft, now it grows hard. Not only do your sheep wander in search of better pastures but so do the animals, kangaroos and wallabies. While you worry about feed for your sheep, the Aboriginals fear starvation.'

'So they try to burn us out?' Mr Lycett responded tightly.

'Firing the land entices new growth. It always has. This is not some new venture done on your arrival. It is a long-held practice, the benefits of which can be seen if one looks.'

The older man shook his head. 'I would rebuke you for your impertinence were it not for our friendship.'

Mrs Lycett had stopped again to pick wild flowers: small yellow-headed pinpricks of colour.

'I will forgive your lecturing tone and simply say that you always tell me this, Adam. Sometimes I think the blacks have put you under a spell making you believe such a thing. You owe Bidjia your life, this much I understand, but you are fighting a battle you cannot win by choosing to support their methods, by turning an eye to the atrocities that the natives commit. You of all people must realise that assimilation is the only way.'

'But how can we all live together if we're not prepared to see another's point of view?'

'Adam, people think of the Aboriginals as an annoyance at best, others see them as a blot, a blight, a stain that should be wiped away. You and I both know that if there is to be assimilation it will be under British terms.' The older man leant back in his chair and drummed his fingers on the desk. 'I know of not one settler who thinks this fire-stick farming is done with a positive result in mind. You must be able to see this yourself, Adam. If you burn land, you kill the grasses and the trees. We must then wait months for regrowth of any kind. And in this country, well, New South Wales is not England. I could sooner learn to dance on my head than predict the weather. If the blacks burn a patch of ground, in all likelihood I will not see feed for many months. If there is no feed for my sheep, then my livelihood starts to be affected and in turn my family.'

'But there are long-term benefits. Decrease your sheep numbers,' Adam argued. 'Move your stock as the Aboriginals move the native animals, from one patch of feed to another. Regrowth comes naturally.'

'Have I the acreage to do such a thing?'

'Are we all not equal in the eyes of God?' Mrs Lycett stepped up onto the verandah. 'And if that be the case then surely there can be lessons learnt here that may go some way to easing the problems you discuss.' Removing a wide-brimmed hat, she dabbed at the beads of moisture on her brow. 'It is too fine a day for ill-humour. You two must agree to disagree for Adam strides two worlds while we sit safely within ours.'

'Perhaps you would fetch us some water, my dear. Our conversation has made us thirsty.'

Mrs Lycett swapped the hat from one hand to another, the barest sign of annoyance, although her smile remained constant. 'Of course.'

'My sheep are my livelihood, Adam,' Mr Lycett continued once they were alone again. 'And let me tell you, they cost me a huge sum of money, along with the numerous supplies needed when I embarked on this enterprise. I have sunk my life savings into this place and I refuse to see my business decline because of a handful of blacks. Especially now that wool has overtaken whale products as the colony's major export earner. Prices are beyond my expectations and have been for a number of years. I'm reaping the benefits of my breeding program and my sheep numbers are such that it's time to expand.' He rose, placed a confident hand on Adam's shoulder. 'I want you to come with me to look at a holding closer to Bathurst. I'm told it is a fine stretch of country. A pretty wooded landscape, with good grasses and a scarcity of trees with a grand view across the plains. It only needs a home and a manager,' he finished pointedly.

It was as great an offer as Adam could hope to be given. 'And what of Winston?'

'My son does not possess the fortitude required for such a role. You know this.' He dropped his arm.

'To be fair, he has not been tested. I can't be of assistance to you, Mr Lycett.' He lifted a boot and rubbed the top of it against his trousers. 'Winston and I –'

'Are friends, yes, yes,' the old man interrupted dismissively, 'and business is business. Think on it. There are many who would be keen for such a position and Winston will be content with my decision. He is aware of his shortcomings.'

'My friendship with your son is not the only reason that I can't accept your offer.'

Archibald spent some moments contemplating the parrot in the cage. The bird tilted its head under the man's scrutiny. 'My son tells me that you call them your people. Well, you can tell *your people* that I am tired of the burning of my land, of my sheep being rushed, of having them stolen. Two years ago one of my shepherds was speared, as you well know. I did not retaliate as was my right and as many other landholders would have. I have hoped for understanding, for peace.'

'On your terms.'

'What terms?' Mr Lycett's boots scraped the boards beneath. 'I own this land and the sheep on it. There is no place for terms, it is a simple case of land ownership.'

'And there lies your problem, for Bidjia's people were here before you.' He was pleased Winston wasn't present for a line had been crossed with his father.

'You best take your leave, Adam.'

Mrs Lycett appeared from the house with two glasses of water. 'Adam, wouldn't you like some water before you go?'

'Leave him,' her husband said curtly, accepting the water as Adam walked away without answering.

Husband and wife waited until Adam's figure merged with the distant trees.

'He must give thought to where his loyalties lie.' Draining the glass Archibald sat it on the table.

Georgina dabbed at the perspiration on her neck. 'He is wasted out here. Adam should be seeking a commission or at least entering some trade where he can eventually purchase land and a home of his own. He is intelligent and mannered when he's inclined. He should be marrying, settling down, and starting a family.'

'He's the bastard child of a dead convict, my dear. Who knows the mix of blood that runs through his veins? We have done our best to guide him, but I think perhaps the wildness of his nature will never be tamed.'

'Why do you say that?'

Archibald poked at the caged bird and was rewarded with a screech. 'I just offered him the management of the holding near Bathurst if I decided to purchase it and he dismissed me out of hand.'

'He did not countenance it at all?' Georgina took a sip of the tepid water that was stained by the stringy-bark roof to the colour of tea. 'But it is such an opportunity for him.'

'One that my own son is incapable of involvement in.'

'You forget, husband, he is my son too. I am very fond of Adam but you must stop comparing the two of them. You have made much of Adam's abilities, while limiting the opportunities for Winston to prove his.'

Archibald gave his wife a sidelong glance. 'He has a female's tendency to weakness.'

Georgina threw the remnants from the glass over the edge of the verandah. 'I think I may rest this afternoon. The day draws hotter as we speak.'

'I want you to keep close to the house for the time being. No wandering off on one of your walks.'

Georgina looked across the pale green grass that spread out to an edging of tall trees, their branches gently swaying in the breeze. 'Do you ever think of home, of England?'

'Of course, but we are prospering here, Georgina. We've money in the bank and the sum grows yearly.'

Her husband came to stand by her side. 'At night I look up at the brightest of stars but it is not the sky my mother looks at.'

Archibald squeezed her hand. 'I miss our old world as well, Georgina, but we came here for the opportunities that New South Wales offered and all my expectations have been met.'

She nodded dutifully. 'I am glad for you, for what you have achieved.'

'For us, Georgina. I did it for us.'

'Of course. Do you recall when the constellations of our youth were replaced by this new southern one as our ship steered south?'

'It is not something a person would soon forget.'

'It was like saying goodbye to my friends and family, my life, all over again. Now I have an upside-down kite hanging above me, instead of the Great Bear.'

Archibald kissed his wife on the cheek. 'You will stay close to the house?'

'You expect trouble?' Georgina sniffed.

'Look where we live, my dear. I always expect trouble.'

❧ Chapter 7 ❧

1837 August – the Kable farm

The dining room was large and elegant, but far more austere compared to Mrs Kable's reception room. This was an area that spoke of sparseness, of the military, and Kate supposed Mr Kable may have had such a background. The table was set for eight people, although Kate was sure it could have easily sat twelve, and it was laid for four courses. A fine meal. Two portraits hung about the walls and an oval mirror reflected a mahogany sideboard displaying fine silverware and cut-crystal decanters. But it was the glow from the candelabra scattered about the room and along the centre of the table that gave the space such a decadent feel. Kate could have pinched herself.

At the far end of the room Mrs Kable was talking to two young British officers while the Reverend was pontificating in front of the substantial fireplace, his audience a rather bemused older gentleman. The man in question turned in Kate's direction and she knew immediately by the oil painting above the mantelpiece that this was Mr Jonas Kable.

'Miss Carter, a pleasure.' He drew her towards their intimate grouping, his wife nodding a polite if restrained greeting. Mr Kable was a large man with fashionable whiskers and a paunch. He introduced her to the two young officers, Lieutenant Wilson and Captain Gage, and Kate quickly found herself at the centre of the soldiers' conversation. The men were recently returned from duty over the range and the rum on their breath and in their glasses heightened the enthusiasm of their talk. It appeared they had taken part in a number of ad hoc duties, which included protecting bullock drays carrying essential supplies to Bathurst and then carrying out sweeps further west to intimidate 'uppity blacks'.

'Of course, in some regions we have equal problems with bush-rangers, convicts and natives,' Captain Gage replied in answer to their host's query regarding hostilities. Kate didn't know if it were possible for a man to stand any straighter. 'The violence of the previous decade has all but disappeared on this side of the hills, although it's true the killing of livestock still goes on and the odd spearing of shepherds occurs.'

'The native numbers have been much depleted in this area, mind you, Captain. It has taken since settlement of this fair land to gain the upper hand.' Mr Kable offered Kate a glass of brandy and water, which she couldn't help but sniff with interest. 'There are still some of us who suffer, however, and the monetary loss to those settlers affected cannot be underestimated.'

'Especially for those on the fringes of the settled districts,' the Captain continued. 'For those who have journeyed further out, the conflict persists. The colonists are spread too wide now for our small numbers to be of assistance to them. They must learn to band together and fight their own battles. More mounted police are the solution, for certainly by the time regiments of Her Majesty's At Foot march through an area, the blacks have seen us coming. We move too slowly and the red of our jackets shines like

94

a beacon. I am sure they simply avoid us and direct their destruction to another area.'

'And what do *you* think of the ongoing problem with the natives, Miss Carter?' her host enquired.

Kate, in the midst of taking a sip of the drink, coughed at the tartness. Mr Kable gave a chuckle, offering her a handkerchief as she lifted the back of her hand to wipe her lips. 'Thank you,' she replied self-consciously, dabbing her mouth.

'No, keep it,' her host replied kindly.

Lieutenant Wilson had been staring at Kate since their introduction. Pale-skinned with the ruddy cheeks of sunburn, he had bright, intelligent eyes. 'What do you think, Miss Carter, about the natives?'

'I, I have little experience in that area, sir,' she stammered nervously. 'Although I believe education of the children may help.'

Captain Gage patted a thin moustache. 'I'd rather see sterner measures. The natives are at worst a danger and at the very least a nuisance. Their numbers may be much reduced around Sydney proper, however there are still some intent on laying claim to land that is not theirs. Considering the supposed land mass to the west that is yet to be surveyed, one would wonder why they simply all don't move on.'

'It is a pity such animosity exists,' Lieutenant Wilson finally spoke, 'for it is my understanding that these natives live off the bounty of the waterways and eat what native animals can be found as well as fruits and nuts. They seem to be a quiet, harmless people, unless antagonised.'

'Lieutenant Wilson is only recently arrived this year,' Captain Gage said condescendingly. 'Although we have tried to educate him in the history of the colony he is one for witnessing events before passing judgement. So far he has seen but one of the natives' gatherings, a corroboree, listened to disgruntled settlers and chased a number of bushrangers.' He turned to Wilson. 'Oh, and he has come across a speared cow and given chase to the killers, if my memory serves me correctly.'

The Lieutenant frowned.

'Miss Carter.' Mrs Kable beckoned her towards the fire, subtly placing herself between the soldiers and the Reverend and drawing her husband to her side. The Reverend gave Kate an unmistakeable look of annoyance. 'I did suggest you would prefer your rest and would not be used to our gatherings, however Mr Kable insisted.'

'Well, of course I did. It is a rare thing to be graced with the company of two of the fairer sex, but I also must admit to some curiosity, firstly that some young gentleman has not already snatched you up,' he said with appreciation, 'and secondly that in your present state of singledom, Miss Carter, that you are actually prepared to go beyond the outer limits. It is unusual to say the least, most unusual. It takes a sturdy character to elect to go into the wilds.'

The Reverend, having positioned himself directly behind their host, gave Kate a simpering smile.

'The outer limits,' Kate repeated. She had no idea what he meant.

'But I have spoken with her, my husband,' Mrs Kable began. 'Miss Carter is convinced in her course of action.' The older woman shrugged. 'It is not for us to query a decision made, although I find her choice to go so far from civilisation surprising.'

'Surely not,' Lieutenant Wilson responded. 'Begging your pardon, miss, but did I hear correctly? Are you to be travelling to the outer limits?'

'Beyond them,' their host confirmed, pouring more wine for himself.

Kate felt as if the four walls of the room were closing in on her.

Even the Captain looked askance. He approached with renewed interest. 'It is most ill-advised. A single woman travelling through the wilds to the further edges of the colony. Why, I have it on report that clashes occur daily and many a settler gives thanks to see their home still standing when they return at day's end.'

It was then that Kate understood that she'd not been forgiven for turning down the Reverend's advances. She took another sip of the brandy, grateful for its restorative powers as the man observed her with a quiet smugness.

'And you are decided in this matter?' Captain Gage persisted.

The room waited for a response. Kate thought quickly. She would say no; that the Reverend had misled her; that she had no intention of journeying to the outer limits. But what would she do if there was no other position available within the extended Kable family? Where would she go?

'You'll be with us then, I presume, Miss Carter,' Lieutenant Wilson broke the expectant silence, 'as part of Mr Southerland's expedition, for we also have orders to travel up-country and will therefore serve as your escort for part of the journey.'

The question of how to reply was delayed by Mrs Kable's entreaty for everyone to be seated. Kate found herself on her host's left, opposite a vacant seat, which apparently awaited the arrival of a Major James Shaw. Lieutenant Wilson was at her side, immediately enquiring if Kate was quite well, where she'd journeyed from, remarking on the roughness of the roads, if he might escort her along the verandah following dinner. Answers weren't required for the Lieutenant was quite adept at having a conversation without her responding. Kate was grateful, for a cold lump had settled in her stomach and she did not think she was capable of replying.

Potato and sage soup was served. Kate glanced at the selection of cutlery laid out on either side of the bowl and hesitated. The spoon at least was an easy choice for this course. Jelly-belly stood against the far wall, as all at the table looked to their hostess to begin the meal.

'What of Major Shaw?' Mrs Kable enquired. 'And the gentleman, Mr Southerland?'

'Both men are your guides, my dear,' Mr Kable informed Kate. 'I can't confirm Mr Southerland's attendance, Mrs Kable, however I'm sure the Major will be here directly.'

'He is quite tenacious in his duties, our Major Shaw,' his wife responded. 'On request from an old friend of ours in London he procured a savage's head and had it duly shipped home.'

'The scientific study of race and the gradations of the *Homo sapiens* is an interest of my own,' Mr Kable explained to his guests, 'and these natives are splendid examples, once one goes beyond the towns. Well, we cannot wait for the Major.' He raised a glass. 'There is nothing quite like Her Majesty's At Foot for protection. To Queen Victoria.'

'Queen Victoria,' all replied.

'It is barely three months since the young queen ascended the throne.' Mrs Kable took a sip of her punch. 'Such responsibility for a young woman, and to think four kings have preceded her reign.'

'Let us hope she marries soon and delivers a male heir.' The Reverend held his glass aloft and Jelly-belly re-filled it. 'Now, let us bless the evening meal?' Placing his glass carefully on the table, Reverend Horsley folded his hands. 'Oh Lord, we thank you for the bountiful benefits we are about to receive, for the wellbeing of these good people seated at this table and for all those that come under their care and we ask that –'

'Good evening.' Major Shaw begged apologies for his lateness, oblivious to the look of annoyance on the Reverend's face. Broad shouldered and deeply tanned with blond hair tied at the nape of his neck, he had the bluest of eyes. The two junior officers rose in greeting. Kate caught a whiff of horse and saddle-grease as he sat opposite her, and on their introduction his gaze lingered. She couldn't recall having ever been looked at that way before. It made her quite uncomfortable and she lowered her eyes. She guessed him to be aged in his late twenties, as he explained away George Southerland's absence.

Conversation turned to the current state of the wool industry. It seemed that pastoral expansion was increasing at a rapid rate and it was solely due to sheep.

'Well, the British Parliament had to lower the tariff, Major. The quality of the wool grown in the colony is such that they had no choice but to recognise our ability to take part on the world stage. And here we are,' Mr Kable took a slurp of soup, 'colonial woolgrowers competing with their European rivals despite high production costs and the enormous distance to the British market.'

'Indeed the colony is now producing at international levels, but regretfully burgeoning markets can have serious consequences,' Major Shaw replied. A soft Scottish lilt was overlayed by a clipped English pronunciation.

'Such discouraging dining talk, Major.'

'My apologies, Mrs Kable, I did not come here to bore you with such matters, especially in such elegant surrounds.'

Over the years Kate had heard many a story as to the rewards that could come to the determined settler, but she'd not realised until her arrival at the Kables' holding how lucrative an enterprise fine Saxon wool could be.

'Certainly our wool is much sought after,' Mr Kable enthused. 'The climate seems to have an extraordinary effect on the weight and quality of the fleeces. I hear the softness is often remarked upon by manufacturers. But I see there is something troubling you, Major.' He nodded to Jelly-belly, who'd been busy clearing the soup bowls and pouring pale wine from a carafe. Mr Kable waited until his glass was filled and then, having ensured the Major's glass was also topped up, gestured for him to continue.

'No more than usual, however, I do have unwelcome news. The Australian Agricultural Company lost two shepherds to the blacks last month. My apologies, Mrs Kable.' Major Shaw took a sip of wine and offered his compliments. 'I would not bring such a subject up before the fairer sex,' he turned to his host, 'but with our departure imminent this has bearing on your cousin's requirements. It seems two of his promised convicts are to be reassigned to the Company.'

'Nine men. That will leave him with nine men on the farm.' Mr Kable placed his glass on the table with a thud as Jelly-belly began to transfer plates of stewed fish with wine sauce from the sideboard to the table. There was a salad of boiled spinach to accompany the entrée.

Kate noted the knife and fork Lieutenant Wilson selected, and followed suit.

'There is nothing to be done, particularly at such short notice.'

'I know that. I can hardly fight a company founded through an Act of the British Parliament.'

'It also reduces the numbers of the party once they leave Maitland, although George Southerland has agreed to stay on your cousin's run for a period of twelve months until something can be done about labour.'

'Dare I say it, but I am sorry the Colonial Secretary approved Samuel's application to lease the holding.' Mrs Kable frowned at the fish. 'Although as they have been squatting on that land for the past twelve months or more I suppose one must be pleased that their tenacity has been rewarded.'

'Our holding,' her husband gently reminded her. 'We have a part share in the enterprise.'

'The Secretary would hardly say no, Mrs Kable,' Major Shaw spoke politely. 'Samuel Hardy is of good repute, with the financial backing required.' He acknowledged Mr Kable with the slightest tilt of his head. 'Southerland paid the annual lease of ten pounds on Mr Hardy's behalf.'

'Well at least the lease is settled.' Their host drummed his fingers on the table. 'And how much does Mr Southerland want? For I've heard stories of men with Southerland's abilities expecting upwards of one hundred and fifty pounds to work on the frontier.'

'That is the figure he requested,' Major Shaw admitted. 'Souther-land is much respected and he comes with his own native tracker and guide. If there is a man to get your cousin's provisions and convicts safely northwards a second time, one prepared to stay on and manage the sheep, then it is he. Besides which, the first clip was delivered safely to market and although the wool was a little coarse and could have done with a more thorough washing, the monies are in the bank.' The Major gave Kate a sidelong glance. 'And of course, most importantly, he knows the way north. Mr Southerland did help select the holding.'

'A man of skill, I agree, but the sum requested is exorbitant.' Mr Kable looked down the length of the table to his wife. 'I suspect Samuel will complain that I have agreed to this princely sum of money on his behalf, however we must have someone up there who knows what they're doing.' He directed his conversation back to the Major. 'Apart from my own advice and that of the esteemed Mr Southerland, my adventurous cousin departed my roof after a scant three months with a copy of the *Australian Settlers Guide*. Such a pamphlet promotes the farmer over the pastoralist, a most ludicrous concept where he has settled. There is a push to make all our farms self-sufficient, to follow the Yankee model in the hope of becoming a great power. Grow barley for beer, tan leather for shoes? I can just imagine Sarah the cobbler, Samuel the brewer.' He gave a huff of disgust. 'New South Wales has grown powerful through trade and land, we buy what we need and sell what we produce and that's how it should be.'

'And yet they have survived and delivered their first wool clip,' the Major stated.

Mr Kable frowned in disapproval. 'A timely sale considering the monies already spent, and the need for more provisions.'

'And are they well-established?' the lady of the house enquired. 'Do they have a decent dwelling? For the letter that accompa-nied Mr Southerland's return painted a most forlorn picture. The loss of a child. The constant threat of the natives. Sarah sleeps with a pistol under her pillow, and they are so remote. And why is Mr Southerland not here in person to tell us of my husband's cousin's situation?'

'He is not one for company, Mrs Kable,' the Major replied. 'He tells me they have a house built and a sturdy cellar cut into the side of a hill in which to store their provisions.'

'The side of a *hill*?' Kate had not meant to speak aloud, but the image in her head was stark and desolate.

Even Jelly-belly, who was busily clearing the remains of the over-cooked fish, started at her surprised tone.

Lieutenant Wilson took a sip of wine, his fingers twirling the stem of the glass as he replaced it on the table. 'Miss Carter, you do know where you journey to?'

The diners at the table turned as one in Kate's direction. She didn't know what to say or where to look.

Jelly-belly took the Major's plate, the cutlery rattling, as he looked across the table with some disbelief. 'So *you* are the one to be making this trip? I must say I was not expecting a . . . a woman such as you.' His gaze strayed to the scar near Kate's eye. For the second time she dropped her chin under his scrutiny.

'We have tried our best to dissuade her,' Mr Kable answered.

'Surely there would be something more appropriate, miss, some other option that would be far more suitable than leaving hearth and home for the wilds.' When Kate didn't reply the Major looked to the far end of the table for support, however Mrs Kable was demanding to know why the meat course was delayed and the fish entrée overcooked. Jelly-belly was all muted apology as she left the dining room.

'Let me acquaint you with your chosen destination, miss. You are travelling northwards, across the range and the settled districts, to lands beyond.' Major Shaw turned to his host. 'I think, sir, that there would be some benefit to be gained in showing Miss Carter a map.

102

She may well change her mind when she understands the extent of the journey before her, the dangers and mishaps possible, let alone what lies ahead on arrival. I must say it is no place for a woman, any woman. Quite frankly I am surprised that any female would give consideration to such a position. And then of course there is the risk Miss Carter's presence places on the expedition, on those of us who will undoubtedly be drawn from our duties in her protection.'

Kate's head spun at the Major's words. *No place for a woman, any woman.*

'And yet Samuel's wife is already there,' Mrs Kable reminded everyone, 'enduring the hardships of settlement and in need of female companionship.'

'There are a great many women settling on the further reaches of the frontier,' the Reverend argued.

It was as if Kate were not even seated at the table. She fiddled with the linen napkin on her lap, aware of the Reverend looking at her. She willed herself not to meet his eyes. Not to see the triumphant, upturned lips that waited for Kate's acknowledgment.

'Not where Sarah is,' Mrs Kable responded sharply. 'We are not talking west of the mountains. Why it is positively civilised across the Bathurst plains, but in comparison –'

'It is fact,' Mr Kable stated, 'that when we first came here that you, Mrs Kable, were in a similar position. We too built our home, cleared the land and forged a place for ourselves in a most precarious new world. Much has changed since then. The settlements may be further afield but the obstacles and opportunities remain the same. One cannot begrudge Samuel the same chance to partake in the production and growth of fine wool. And besides, where the settlers go, the law soon follows.'

'It is no place for a woman of Sarah's sensibilities,' his wife said flatly.

'Give them time, my dear. The rigours of their early life will be but a memory in the years to come. Wool is a valuable commodity, the very backbone of the colony, and it has already been proven that the drier inlands mean sheep are less vulnerable to diseases, both internal and external. With Mr Southerland's guidance I hope Samuel will soon turn his dreams of cropping to the more lucrative benefit of sheep. Why, the successful settlers of New South Wales make the Old Testament patriarchs seem like beggars. In any case, Miss Carter,' their host barely drew breath, 'I would have thought the Reverend gave a full account of the location of my cousin's holding.'

Once again those seated around the table waited patiently for her response as Jelly-belly sat a leg of roasted lamb on the sideboard and began to carve the meat. A younger servant brought in potatoes and long lean beans, and a plate of roasted ground-birds.

'The Reverend,' Kate began haltingly, 'led me to believe that I was to be Mrs Jonas Kable's companion. It was only after my arrival that I realised this was not to be the case.' There, she had said it. She stared defiantly at the Reverend.

'You thought you were to be stationed here?' Mrs Kable waved away the claret jug and requested water as the meal was served. 'Unfortunately, Miss Carter, I have no need of a companion.'

'Indeed you do not,' the Reverend agreed. 'I apologise for Miss Carter, she is led astray by the freedom of thought so endemic in the native born.'

The meat placed before her was well-cooked, the potatoes crisp and the beans had retained their colour, but with the Reverend's comment Kate instantly lost her appetite. She poked at the plump little bird, the corners of her mouth falling. Those of her ilk may have built this colony from the ground up, but Kate was seated with the top layer of society, free settlers of means, and while she guessed that her hosts, particularly Mrs Kable, were well aware of her birthright, Kate knew it was certainly not a subject to be mentioned in the company of these fine people. She sensed it immediately in the quiet that descended, in the intentness given to the roasted meat. Had she looked up from her own plate she guessed the Kables would be at cross-purposes, for their hostess had not been pleased to have Kate present this evening.

Across the table the Major was studying her as a watery gravy was spooned across the thick slices of roast meat on her plate. A cruet stand, each silver dish containing pepper and salt, some sauce or mustard or oil, was passed around the table. Kate declined any extra condiment, convinced her discomfort would show itself in a shaking hand and some embarrassing spillage on the pristine table cloth. If it had been polite, she would have excused herself and left the room, but Kate knew she had to stay. She had to show that she was an equal, if only in resilience.

'So you are native born,' Lieutenant Wilson stated politely. 'Immigrants?'

The meat lodged in Kate's throat. She swallowed the half-chewed mass. 'My father was assigned. My grandparents on my mother's side came from Scotland.'

'The Highlands?' The Major leant forward, his elbows resting on the edge of the table. 'My own ancestors were originally from Fort William near Ben Nevis.'

'No, the Lowlands,' Kate admitted.

'Ah.' He sat back in his chair, his attention directed to the tasty meat and the sweep of mustard that he layered with some precision across his forkful.

'So then, you were landowners?' the Lieutenant enquired almost hopefully.

'Yes, yes we were,' Kate answered with some pride.

The occupants at the table concentrated on their food.

When the Australian Agricultural Company was granted one million acres in the Port Stephens hinterland, Kate still recalled the weighty conversation between her parents and the anger that they felt. The Government were purposely depriving emancipists and their children of the best lands, giving it to the very people she now broke bread with, rather than those who had laboured in its service and were now free and entitled to see their contribution rewarded.

As Kate thought of what her parents had endured, her fury grew. 'Is it not true,' she ventured, 'that many of the free men and women who have come to this colony have done so because they did not succeed in the Mother Country?' The words came out in a rush.

Mr Kable turned to her. 'In some cases.' His reply was stilted.

'People unable to maintain the standard of living once enjoyed by their aristocratic families,' she continued, 'and yet they look down on those –'

A racking cough gripped their host. Mr Kable spluttered and, waving his hand about, made a fuss of asking for water. Opposite, the Major caught Kate's eye and gave an imperceptible shake of his head.

'You have had a tiring day, Miss Carter,' Mrs Kable said pointedly as her husband quenched his thirst.

Kate moved slices of meat around the plate. The meal was cold and Jelly-belly was hovering behind her chair, waiting to clear the dish.

'There is no art or literature in the colony,' Mrs Kable began, 'no great scenery, even the simplest of things, the wildflowers for example, are hardy, mundane blooms. I fear the very sameness of this land, the general flatness that I have read extends out beyond the mountains, can never entice the poet or artist to great works.'

The guests were quick to agree.

'My wife has the heart of a novelist.'

'And yet there is great truth in her words.' The Reverend dabbed his mouth with a linen napkin. 'We of the cloth have long feared that the very lack of civilisation here is the reason why the imbibing of food and rum and the concentration on the making of money is quite overtaking society.'

106

'My dear wife will agree with you, Reverend.' Mr Kable picked at a piece of meat between his teeth. 'For at table she often bemoans that our conversation eventually returns to the running of the farm and of production and ultimately of costs. But then isn't this as it should be? I still recall my own arrival. The sublime solitude of this place, the verdant hills and plains as yet untouched by flocks of sheep. This colony is now seen by all across the world as a place of infinite possibility. We are, all of us, at business and we are here to grow and prosper.' Squeezing the meat between his fingers, Mr Kable turned his attention to Kate. 'But we are amiss.' He popped the gristle in his mouth. 'Here we are discussing the virtues and disadvantages of this great land, New South Wales, and we have quite skated over your own place in the world. If you have been misinformed,' his gaze flickered briefly towards the Reverend, 'or if you misunderstood the nature of the employ offered, then please know, Miss Carter, that you are under no obligation.'

From the far end of the table came a deep sigh. Mrs Kable's attention was directed at the sideboard with its gleaming silverware.

'No obligation at all,' he reiterated. 'I would not send any young woman out to the wilds if she does not wish to go. And as the Major says, my cousin's farm is a great distance to the north. You must say no if you do not wish to go.'

Kate looked at the wobbly custard that was set before her. There was a scent of cinnamon and a mound of currant jelly beginning to slide from the warmth of the pudding.

'Mrs Ovens prides herself on this particular dessert,' Mrs Kable interrupted with a forced smile.

'May I suggest Miss Carter think on it, sir? We are a day from leaving, time enough for a decision and there is further business that needs our attention tonight,' said Major Shaw, clearly impatient for the meal to be over.

'Please do not rush, there is compote of fruit to finish.' Mrs Kable ensured more wine was poured.

When the evening meal was over and the conversation had turned from lack of rain to politics, Kate wondered if she could now excuse herself. Her back and shoulders pained from the day's long journey, but there was far more on her mind than the aches snaking through her body.

When Mrs Kable finally announced that the women would retire, Kate was quick to leave the table. Without a backward glance she followed the older woman out into the hallway as the men laughed and chairs were dragged across the timber floor.

Once ensconced in the parlour, Mrs Kable lost a little of what affability remained. 'I will forget your recent outburst, Miss Carter, but while you are under my roof you will refrain from any further outspokenness. Agreed?'

Kate gave a slight nod. The anger that had welled up within her was only just beginning to recede.

'Now to the matter at hand. Is it true that the Reverend led you here under false pretence? And if so, one must ask what occurred? There is no need for a response, men do what they wish and leave their women-folk to make the best of things. It is more important perhaps to ask if you have other means of support, a parent perhaps, or a relative?'

When Kate was not immediately forthcoming, Mrs Kable directed her to sit in one of the sofas near the fire. The room was comfortably warm. The effects of the food and brandy made her sleepy.

'You are of marriageable age, Kate. Any number of young men would be quite willing for your hand. Lieutenant Wilson is certainly enamoured.'

'I had not thought of marriage,' stated Kate, sitting stiffly erect, her hands folded in her lap.

Mrs Kable seated herself on the opposite sofa. 'We of the weaker sex must seize upon an opportunity when it presents itself. Someone in your position –'

'Marriage is not something I have considered,' Kate repeated. Her personal state was none of this woman's business, and she was beginning to resent her dictatorial manner.

'My dear, an assumption on your part has led you down a path that it now appears you do not wish to take.' She rose to stand before the fire. From the direction of the kitchen came a crashing sound and then a loud shriek. 'Heavens! I am off to Sydney at week's end, but my travel is sullied knowing I leave my household in the grip of servants.'

A condemning voice quickly stilled the ruckus from the kitchen and Mrs Kable returned to her seat, rearranging her skirts. 'Now, I can understand your reluctance to travel inland. My husband's cousin has selected land beyond the boundaries of the colony. Such an ungodly place to raise a family. We have two of their younger children here, out of harm's way, while the boys are safely returned to England this past year for education. But there is one child with them and our old cook, whom my husband forced upon them. The woman is partially blind so if you do accept the position, be wary of the ingredients she uses.'

The older woman wrung her hands together. In the firelight the creases that fanned from her eyes were etched deeply into fine skin. 'They should never have gone, at least Sarah, Samuel's wife, shouldn't have. She is at risk simply by virtue of her sex and yet she would not leave his side. Samuel, though his qualities are many, is an adventurer of means, the worst sort of husband. They would have been better to have remained in England, but I admit that to exist on two hundred pounds a year in London would be a sorry life. Perhaps he will be lucky, perhaps he will amass a great sheep holding and breed blood horses and create a seat in the north equal to his family's lineage in London, faded though it may be. Of course he could have sent a manager or an agent to establish the farm, as my dear husband suggested, but Samuel is all for taking the lead, and five thousand pounds is an outlay that demands attention.' Mrs Kable took a breath. 'I should tell you that I have heard the most dreadful of tales – of homes made out of sticks, of starvation and attacks by the Aboriginals. I think now of Governor Macquarie. I had such time for him and his good wife and their attempts at cultivating a relationship with the natives, but even here I feel the danger of uppity emancipists, wayward convicts and the Aboriginals. It will be far worse up-country for there will not be another living white soul within some miles. If I were you I would not go, but then I have already waved Sarah off. It would certainly reassure me if you were to journey northwards and provide her with the feminine companionship she must so sorely be in need of.'

The fire was beginning to die down. 'May I think on it?' Kate said, rising, although it was more statement than question. Her hostess frowned and Kate realised that she'd not been given permission to take her leave. There was a reason free settlers such as the Kables were known as *Exclusives*, but her hostess was forgetting that Kate's mother's grandparents were of similar stock, albeit not as wealthy.

'Of course,' Mrs Kable agreed, somewhat reluctantly. 'And should you not want to journey forth I am sure that we can find a suitable husband for you. Native born or not, there will be a gentleman out there grateful for one such as you and I am sure we could find you a very good match, one that would not have been afforded to you had you been in England. Even with your background and that slight scar marking you as it does, the dearth of women in the colony makes even the most unappealing of our sex of high value, as I am sure you well know.'

'And if I have no wish for marriage?' Kate wondered if Mrs Kable had any other thoughts on a woman's role. She doubted it.

'Every woman wishes for marriage, Kate. We have three stages in our lives: daughter, wife and mother. There is nothing else to aspire to. You are simply in a state of flux and have clearly not had the exposure to young gentlemen, which is as it should be, although a good marriage could have been arranged some years ago. Think on Lieutenant Wilson.' She halted briefly for emphasis. 'It is, however, the immediate future that we must consider. If you decline the current position offered, you would require housing and suitable employ. There are a number of large establishments seeking the services of a housekeeper. I myself could use you, however knowing your background, well, it is one thing to be native born and under the care of the Reverend Horsley, quite another for your mother to have lived in his household for many years in the capacity of husband and wife. I am only too aware that such understandings are far from uncommon in the colony but I, for one, cannot countenance such immoral behaviour.' Mrs Kable produced a lace handkerchief from the sleeve of her gown. 'It quite ruined your arrival,' she sniffed, 'especially having only lately discovered that following your mother's passing you have continued to live there without a chaperone. You do understand how such an arrangement appears. But there are others, others more, shall we say, more avant-garde where such matters are concerned. But of course should you join Mr and Mrs Hardy up-country,' she continued brightly, 'one can make a new life and a new reputation.'

Kate walked to the door, lifted her hand to the brass knob and then, changing her mind, faced her condemner. 'My mother is dead, Mrs Kable, and their "arrangement", as you put it, was all that was available to her following my father's passing. On his death our land was sold off to pay our debts following his illness, leaving my mother to care for me. We uppity descendants of emancipists and free settlers have had our difficulties, but I'll not be condemned, nor my mother before me, when the Reverend Horsley sought her out and offered his home without the sanctity of marriage. I would add as well that as the Reverend was complicit in the very action that has so damned me and my mother in your eyes, that I wonder you had the temerity to let him break bread with you.'

111

Mrs Kable's lips trembled with barely suppressed indignation.

Kate left the parlour quickly, the creamy cotton and muslin of her skirts swishing as she selected a candlestick from the hallway table. Pinching the wick with the metal snuffer to ensure the candle's brightness, she lit it from one left burning and walked back towards her room.

≪ Chapter 8 ≫

1837 July — on the western side
of the Blue Mountains

The sun was dipping towards the horizon. Streaks of red-gold merged with the haze in the west, dappling the dull greens and browns of the land with a brightness that heralded a warming in the weather. Adam jogged rhythmically, his line of sight focused in the direction of the tribe's camp, his gait never varying. Song did not come to him as it did with Bidjia and the others when they travelled long distances, their minds turning inwards. Instead he concentrated on the passing world. Native plants were beginning to sprout. Male birds, intent on finding partners, displayed their plumage, strutting across the ground before attentive females. Soon the cold earth would warm. The chilly nights would be a memory and the welcoming breath of the female sun would entice.

At this midpoint between the Lycett home and the tribe it was easy to forget the world of man. All Adam need do was turn north or south. Both directions would lead him away from the current problems that he'd found himself in the middle of. He yearned to leave them to their fights and their folly but it was simply not in him to desert the man who'd saved him and the other who'd taught him something of the world from which he'd come.

In a couple of hours it would be dark and the tribe would be settling for the night. The anger he'd felt had subsided a mile or so ago but it was a rage that stemmed from the intolerance displayed by Mr Lycett and the tribe. Neither would give way to the other, even just a little. What was to become of Bidjia and what remained of his clan if he stuck so stubbornly to the old ways? And how did the Lycetts expect to exist and flourish in this land if they were not considerate of those whose understanding and use of the country went beyond monetary concerns? Both parties were trying to manage the land and live off it in very different ways. There were lessons to be learnt that could benefit everyone, but Bidjia and Archibald Lycett were like two old rams butting heads. The former was unable to grasp the invasion of their land and the settlers' use of it; and the latter was a product of Britain's great class hierarchy, desperate to create a prosperous business, indifferent to the plight of the colony's original inhabitants and supported by the Crown.

Surely this was enough to fill his head without the added concern of Winston's friendship with Merindah.

Winston.

He was as fixed in his attitude and ideas as one of the many stars he was so entranced with. But Winston's moodiness and his tendency towards inflexibility were unwelcome traits made worse by an unforgiving nature, all of which had attributed to the fractious relationship with his father. These same characteristics made friendship with Winston difficult at times and despite the length of their association, Adam knew that as adults their relationship survived only because they no longer saw each other often.

'Father says you're to be schooled with me,' Winston, aged six, *waited eagerly beside his mother.*

'It's alright, Adam, I have spoken to Bidjia. He has agreed to this.'

114

'He should stay with us, Archibald, not with them.' Mrs Lycett gestured to where two Aboriginals retreated into the bush.

'First things first, Georgina. Now, Adam, why don't you go with Winston and sit on that bench under the tree? See, over there. Mrs Lycett will be there directly. Today she's going to teach you about England and the King and the great dominions he rules over, including this colony.'

'Where is Bidjia?'

'Shush, lad. Bidjia is a good man for he found you and cared for you, but you are not one of them, Adam. You are one of us. You must learn your place in the world. He has agreed to this and in return I have agreed that we will send you back to him in the evenings.' Mr Lycett met his wife's gaze. 'For the time being.'

'My name's not Adam. It's Bronzewing,' he remembered saying, eager to be gone. He didn't understand everything these people said. Bidjia had promised to show him how to use a throwing stick and the kindly Mr Lycett, with his owl-ringed reading glasses and wooden pipe, was keeping him from practising with it.

Mrs Lycett grew impatient. The books she held were moved from one arm to the other. 'It is not a proper name, Adam. It is the name of a bird, a pigeon. Bidjia said that you told him your name when he found you. That name was Adam.'

'I like birds,' Bronzewing replied, his toes curling in the dirt. He watched as Winston ran to the verandah of the Lycett house. Dragging a chair to the hanging birdcage, he returned with the cane enclosure within which was a small brightly coloured bird.

'I like birds too,' Winston grinned.

Later that afternoon the two boys freed it, but when Mr Lycett asked who was responsible, Winston blamed Bronzewing.

Jardi was waiting for Adam a half-mile from the camp. He was sharpening a stick with a knife, the slender shavings falling on the long trousers he wore. Though his feet and torso were bare, Jardi liked wearing white man's clothes, especially during the cooler months.

'You have been gone a long time. You have missed the hunt. Bidjia thinks that one day you will go back to the world you came from and not return.' He sheathed the blade and the pointy stick quickly, securing both at his waist and then picked up the spear lying on the ground.

'I had some thinking to do, and anyway I'm not particularly welcome in the white world at the moment,' Adam admitted.

'Your time with Lycett did not go well?'

Together they walked through the timber as the sun's rays lengthened. 'No, it didn't.' He noticed splats of blood on the man's trousers. 'Do we eat tonight?'

Jardi was slow to answer. 'Sheep. It was wandering alone when we came across it and there was no-one about,' he explained quickly.

'Damn. I suppose it belongs to Lycett?'

The younger man shrugged. 'It doesn't matter. No-one will know.'

'They always know and if they don't, they guess.'

'It is a pity to waste such a skin. It would be good when the days grow short and the earth cold.'

'You kept the hide? You can't. You must bury it.'

Jardi reached out an arm and stopped Adam from walking further. 'The child died and Merindah has given birth to another. It is early, by two moons, but Annie says it should survive.'

He nodded. 'So it's healthy?'

'It is best that you see for yourself,' Jardi said cautiously.

'Why? What's wrong with it?'

At the camp half a sheep roasted on the fire. The scent of the meat was strong and gamey in the still air. Adam knew they would have left the rest of the unwanted carcass lying in the grass where it had been killed. They only ever took what they needed. The smell of the cooking meat was enticing but if the wind picked up, a person would be able to smell it half a mile away. The skin lay in the dirt, ants crawling over it. Annie looked up from where she'd been stoking the coals. 'You too late,' she said bluntly. 'Bidjia gone. The others go find him.'

'What do you mean he's gone?' He turned to Jardi. 'Where did he go to?'

The woman exchanged a brief glance with the younger man but said nothing.

'Bury the skin,' Adam told her.

The woman didn't move.

'Annie, you must bury it or there will be trouble.'

'I know trouble. Trouble come when whitefella come to our place.' She spat in the dirt and turned back to the fire.

Adam tossed the skin behind a log beyond the campsite. It was too quiet. There was no sign of the other children. 'Are you going to tell me what happened, Jardi?'

The younger man shadowed his steps as Adam walked the thirty feet to where Merindah lay on her side by a humpy. There was blood on the ground where she'd cut herself in her grief for the dead child and a pile of sickness where she'd brought up the little she'd consumed that day.

On seeing Adam, Merindah sat up weakly. Her right eye was swollen and a cut to her lip was caked with dried blood and dirt. Jagged bloody welts on her chest and arms and a blood-edged tomahawk in the dirt showed the girl's pain had been etched for eternity. Adam squatted near her, Jardi lingered some feet behind him. The question that needed to be asked caught in his throat. Had Bidjia learnt of Merindah's relationship with Winston? Had he gone to see his friend? On the ground was the dress she'd shown him earlier. It was shredded.

'How long ago did Bidjia leave?' At best there was a chance that Bidjia might use this insult to negotiate the tribe's movement across the Lycett farm, to reach an understanding on their continued use of the disputed land. Such bargaining was rare, but Bidjia and Jardi had grown to understand white ways.

'Show him,' Jardi said roughly. 'Show Bronzewing the child.'

The girl's tear-rimmed eyes were glazed but she retrieved the small bundle from the shadows of the hut, laying the child on the ground and unwrapping the blanket. The movement woke the baby. The child was tiny, its face pinched, but it moved its arms and legs with weak determination and let out a mewling noise. As Merindah leant forward to pick the baby up, Adam turned to Jardi.

'Bidjia cannot forget such a thing,' Jardi said curtly.

Adam looked back at mother and child. One dark-skinned, the colour of polished ebony, the other neither white nor black, but somewhere in between. 'Whose is it?' asked Adam, although even as he asked the question he knew Winston was responsible. Who else could it be?

'There is nothing you can do.' Jardi placed a hand on his shoulder.

Bidjia had been wronged. There would be retribution.

'So he knows who the father is?' Adam asked hesitantly.

'I not tell, but . . .' The girl's voice faded. It was clear that Bidjia had thrashed the truth from her. She leant forward in the dirt. 'Help him, Bronzewing, he's your friend,' she sobbed.

'Damn.'

'Now you are back you can come with me.' Jardi snatched the baby from Merindah's arms. The girl screamed.

'I can't be part of this,' Adam argued. 'It's not right. It's not the child's fault.' He ran his fingers roughly through his hair. 'Give the baby back, Jardi. Do it now.'

'No.' He pressed the tiny bundle to his shoulder. 'It is the mother's place to rid the child, but as she will not,' Jardi turned angrily to the weeping young woman, 'then it falls to another.'

'Bloody hell.' Even if Jardi did leave the baby alone, one of the other clan members would return to abandon the half-caste child in the bush. 'I have to go after the others,' Adam decided.

'You can't follow Bidjia. You must leave my father alone. Retribution is his by right. Come.'

'I've got to stop him. If he hurts Winston . . .'

'And what if Bidjia is wounded? Colby or Darel?' Jardi retaliated. 'Or do you place your bond with the white above that of the tribe?'

'If a white is killed, Jardi, the police will come after the whole clan,' Adam stated. 'Is that what you want, to be hunted down like a dog? All for the sake of a woman?'

'My *father's* woman.' Jardi turned on his heel and vanished into the scrub with the baby.

Merindah's screams haunted Adam as, musket in hand, he ran off in the direction of the Lycett farm. From afar came the dull but unmistakeable thud of a shot being fired.

The sun was at its lowest point on the horizon by the time Adam reached the creek and the lightning-struck tree. There'd been rain somewhere in the mountains for the small bubbles that raced along the water's surface spoke of it rising, enough to freshen the waterway. He drank thirstily, leaning over to cup the cool liquid with one hand. At the base of the woody plant, he examined the area for any signs of blood. Winston's sketch pad and charcoal lay discarded in the dirt. There were footprints, mixed with the marks made by his friend's boots, but no blood. By the impressions on the ground and the direction the prints went it appeared that Winston had run off towards the homestead on Bidjia's approach, and that Colby and Darel had followed the men some time later.

A second shot sounded.

Adam got to his feet and ran like the wind. Leaping over stubby bushes and weaving through the trees, his heart pounded within a tightening chest. There was no birdsong, no kangaroos or emus scattering at his approach. There was nothing. When the high-pitched woman's scream began and went on and on, eventually fading into the silent void that the surrounding bush had become,

Adam knew it was all over. His knuckles grasping the musket turned white. He was too late.

He approached the house cautiously. The bench beneath the schooling tree was empty, the contents of Mrs Lycett's needlework basket strewn across the ground. The parrot still hung in its cage on the verandah and squawked agitatedly, the chatty bird fluttering at the cane sides of its enclosure, desperate to get out. The desk and chair were overturned. Movement in the doorway of the house caught Adam's attention. He dropped to his knees and waited.

Georgina Lycett walked out onto the verandah. Lifting her hands she looked intently at them before wiping them together, slowly at first then faster and more roughly as if she would never remove what was on them. Just as abruptly, she stopped, lowered her hands to her sides and looked out across the spring grasses that extended in a half circle to the sparse timber where Adam waited.

Finally she stepped from the verandah. Her brown dress had wet patches on the skirt and bodice and as she moved closer Adam recognised the glistening stains as blood. He stood slowly, hoping not to frighten her, extended a hand towards her, but it was as if he were not there for the woman gave no sign of recognition, said not a word. Dull of eye, Mrs Lycett walked straight past him, veered to the left and began to walk towards the hills in the east.

'Mrs Lycett?' He spoke quietly. 'Mrs Lycett?' Winston's mother kept on walking into the scrub.

Running carefully towards the house, Adam stopped where a pool of blood was congealing in the dirt. Swarming flies rose into the air as he squatted and touched the sticky puddle. The dark mass foretold of a fatal wounding. There were footprints and the imprint of leather-soled boots. The boot marks led back to the house. The footprints stopped where the blood had gathered. By the scuff marks, the injured man, one of the tribe, had fallen face down and then been lifted and carried away. The man's borne weight showed in the deeper depressions that led away from the killing site around the side of the Lycett home. A member of the clan had returned for the wounded man. Adam's stomach tightened. Regardless of whether one of the Lycett men were dead or injured, which he dearly hoped was not the case, with the death of one of Bidjia's own, there would only be more bloodshed. Payback was fundamental to the native way of life, and to white law.

The vegetable garden on the eastern side of the house was partially trampled. Beyond the flapping bird in the cage, the lack of noise was unsettling. Then he heard it – the unmistakeable buzz of flies. Moving cautiously towards the verandah, the sound of insects grew louder. There was another pool of dark blood near the open door and the insects, hundreds of them, rose and settled in a dark wave. Mrs Lycett's small footprints were traced in the sticky darkness. Someone had been dragged down the hall towards a bedroom. A musket had been dropped and left in the narrow space. There was no sign of Bidjia or the others.

Inside the house, Adam ducked his head beneath the low ceiling of the narrow hall and listened. There was no wind. The house was cold. The passageway, plastered with old newspapers and coated with a thin layer of mud, led down to the kitchen at the rear of the house, the sound of the crackling fire almost drowning out the flies. On the left there was a tiny room, a parlour of sorts where the family read and ate their evening meals. The room next to it stored extra supplies and held a narrow cot for visitors. It had been here that Adam slept on a handful of occasions years earlier. On the opposite side of the hallway were the two bedchambers, one belonging to Winston and the other, his parents. It was into this room that someone had been dragged, the passage of the body marked by a sweep of blood. The doorknob was sticky to the touch.

Winston was sitting on his parents' bed, cradling his father. There was a messy wound on the older man's chest. Blood had seeped from the injury along the sleeve of his cream shirt and dripped steadily from his fingertips onto the timber floor. Winston looked up, clearly dazed. He appeared uninjured, but his cheeks were wet with tears.

'What happened?'

'Adam?' He sounded confused.

'Winston, what on God's earth happened?' The boards creaked as he moved closer. Winston's father was a waxy grey. There was a hole in Archibald's chest and the blood splatter suggested death had been instantaneous. Such an injury was not made by a spear and neither Bidjia, Colby nor Darel owned a musket. He laid a hand on the man's brow and gently closed Archibald Lycett's eyelids. 'Who did this?'

Winston looked vacantly around the room, at the dressing table with its ivory hair combs and cut glass scent bottle, the sturdy chest of drawers and a curved backed chair. On the wall was a framed oval painting of a man and a woman. Three young girls were standing dutifully around their parents. One girl with cherub cheeks and a radiant smile was clearly Georgina Lycett.

'Mother tried to stop the blood, but –'

Bidjia had trained him from his earliest years in the art of tracking man and beast but there was no sign of an intruder inside the house. No sign of a fight. No footprints save those of the immediate family in their leather-soled shoes. 'Winston, what happened? You must tell me for the law must be called and your mother found.'

His friend gradually refocused, his usually placid features darkening. 'They came for me,' his voice was low, 'like you knew they would when you told those blacks about Merindah.'

'I said nothing.'

'Don't lie. You know it's true. You told them about us.'

'I swear I said nothing.' Adam thought of the baby abandoned in the bush to die. 'I didn't have to.'

'They came and attacked us,' Winston began haltingly, as if slowly remembering. 'I made it to the house. Mother and I, we locked ourselves in, but Father was outside. He fought with the black. I, I thought he was dead. I thought Mother was mistaken. I didn't know . . .' Winston faltered.

'Didn't know what?'

'I had the gun. I didn't know that Father was standing outside the door. It happened so quickly.'

Adam couldn't believe what he was hearing. '*You* shot him? You shot your father?'

'I thought he was Bidjia.' Winston drew the dead man to his chest. 'So I opened the door and I shot him.' He looked at the man in his arms. 'He was better than all of us, better than you or me.'

'It was an accident, Winston. You didn't mean to do it.'

'Get out. Get out!' Winston yelled. 'It's your fault that this has happened. My father helped you, treated you as one of the family. Treated you as a son. The son he wanted,' he choked. 'The son he didn't get. He told me he wanted you to be manager of the new holding at Bathurst. Father never even thought of me. But you turned him down. '

'Winston, listen to me.'

Winston hugged the dead man to his chest. 'You couldn't even let me have Merindah, could you? You had to tell them about us. You told them and because of you my father's dead.'

'That's not true,' Adam argued. 'How could you even think that?'

'I thought you were my friend, but you'll never be friends with the likes of us, you're one of them, a bloody black!'

Adam backed out of the room. In the hall beside the fallen musket was a leather pouch of paper charges for the rifle. Digging his hand inside, he pulled out a quantity and topped up his supply.

Winston's sobbing followed him into the encroaching shadows of twilight. Outside, a convict, one of the Lycetts' shepherds, was running in from the bush, a musket in hand.

'I wounded one of them godless heathens. Thank the saints I was ready for 'em, but they clubbed Donaldson, they did, and the man fell dead to the ground.' He took one look at Adam, noted the musket he held and drew up a few feet from the verandah, instantly suspicious. 'Are you with us or them?' His Irish words were thick and breathy.

'Mr Lycett's dead, his wife's run off. Winston's inside, unharmed.'

'Mr Lycett? But how? I saw him. He shot the black, Mr Lycett did.' His eyes flickered to the spot on the ground where blood had been spilt. 'Saw the black I did, left him lying there . . .' His eyes fell on Adam's musket.

'It was an accident,' explained Adam. 'Winston shot his father. He thought he was Bidjia.'

But the look of suspicion on the convict's face was obvious. Lifting the spear, the Irishman skirted around him. 'Mr Lycett's boy mistaking a black for his own father?' Pointing the weapon, the man moved towards the doorway. 'Best you get out of here, until I know what's what. Go on,' he made a thrusting move, 'I can make a good enough hole in you to make your innards come out.'

'The police need to be informed and Mrs Lycett –'

'Mr Winston, sir, can you hear me?' the convict called loudly. 'It's Chaffy Hall. That bush man is here.'

'Get him off our land now!' Winston yelled.

'You heard 'im, get.'

'I don't want any trouble,' Adam told him.

'Then get,' the convict grunted. 'Get away with you.' He went inside and slammed the door.

The parrot was screeching in its cage. In a nearby tree a single rainbow lorikeet answered from a high branch. Adam listened as something heavy was dragged against the doorway, then he reached up and opened the cage. The bird scrambled to the door, squeezed its way out through the opening and flew off to join its mate.

Adam hesitated. He wanted to go back indoors but the grief and fury etched on Winston's face told him that it would be best to lay low until Winston's sanity was restored. Overhead, the parrots flew from the tree, outstretched wings gliding on the air currents as they skimmed the tops of the distant trees.

He too fled into the bush.

Shadows gave way to a dense blackness as stars swathed the sky in a shimmering veil. The emptiness within Adam altered and grew, forming roots that he feared would be impossible to remove. What had been done could not be undone.

The wailing threaded through the murky landscape like a serpent. It traced each step he took, pulling Adam onwards to the source of the grief. It seemed as if the land suffered as well, for the bush was intensely silent, forced into submission by the terrible sound that only a human could make. In the gloom the trees grew thick and unwelcoming. The hairs on his arms bristled as he changed route, turning away from a well-known path towards the woman and her anguish. Other voices joined in, men's voices with heavy hearts. It was pitch black, but the deep moaning drew him over the uneven ground, leading Adam towards a speck of brightness that grew in size and number. It was as if he were a moth heading for light. With the sight of red-gold flames leaping into the air, he increased his pace. Fiery sparks shot out from the burning fires, a cascade of sparkling brilliance quickly engulfed by darkness. He slowed as he drew near. The fires silhouetted a ring of trees, the thickness of their trunks signifying age beyond under-standing. This was an ancient place. This area was not the tribe's camp but a burial ground.

Adam stepped carefully into the rim of light. There were children, men and women, interred here in the soft soil, kinfolk to Bidjia; those that had followed the Elder over the mountains when the settlers had finally driven them out. Adam recalled the little ones who'd died. He'd played with them, learnt to fish and

125

hunt with them, had stood within the circle of life drawn in the dirt and been initiated with the other boys his age. The leaving of childhood and the throwing away of his old life for the new, the path towards understanding his spiritual identity, was marked by a series of scars on his chest that would remain with him until the earth claimed him.

Bidjia, Colby and Jardi sat around a deep pit, their bodies coated with white ash. Darel sat upright within the damp earth, motionless, surrounded by his possessions: a kangaroo cloak, spear and throwing stick, his face pointed towards the east. They barely acknowledged Adam in their grief as he took up his place, sitting cross-legged beside Jardi. The younger man passed him a woven basket and, dipping his fingers within, he marked his forehead and cheeks with ash. Further away Annie's keening never varied. It was constant, repetitive, comforting. Her sadness spoke for him as the men of the tribe sang in unison of the land, their mother. Adam joined the chorus of voices as they sang of their spiritual connection with Mother Earth and of the deceased's spirit, who was born of their land and who would return to it in death.

Colby placed green leaves on a small fire and as the plants began to smoulder the smoke drifted across the burial, filling the air with a pungent scent. A slight breeze twirled and fanned the smoke, enveloping them in the cleansing fumes while warding off bad spirits. Bidjia began to call out to the spirits of the dead to let them know that they were here as family and friends. The grief of the tribe would last many weeks, but out of respect Darel's name would not be mentioned again.

Adam thought of the square stone remembrances that stood so cold and lonely in the cemeteries of Sydney and its surrounds. He knew where he'd rather be. This resting place, ringed and guarded by ancient trees, would protect against summer's hot breath. Frost would layer the earth's membrane and tiny shoots would angle their way through the soil to daylight with the arrival of spring. The animals would follow to lay undisturbed in the shade of the tree's canopies, to nibble lush herbage and raise their young. This was a place of beginnings, not endings. To be cradled in the bosom of Mother Earth away from the chiselled words and fenced-off portions of a regimented society was a fine end to a good life. He would wish for such an honour.

Picking up an axe head, Bidjia made a series of cuts in an already scarred forearm. Colby and Jardi followed suit and then the stone was passed to Adam. He too cut himself, once, twice, wincing at the pain as blood welled from the jagged marks on his arm. With their grief made manifest, Annie began to sob.

≪ Chapter 9 ≫

1837 August — the Kable farm

Having been left to amuse herself since the breaking of the night's fast, with bread and sugary black tea served to her room, Kate spent the morning walking around the farm. Her mind had been in a whirl since dawn with thoughts of distant lands, as well as money, marriage and the life she knew. It was better to think on these things than wonder at the Reverend's spitefulness, for his deception was beyond imagining. Hatred was the word that came to mind when she thought of him. Kate held onto the flat-brimmed hat she'd made some years ago as the wind stirred the air. The breeze strengthened, winding up the slight rise towards her. She'd kept to the areas suggested by one of the maids, where shepherds and other assigned workers were in close proximity. The open country was interspersed with dense timber but through the trees convict shepherds could be seen tending sheep, and a windmill turned squeakily, busily driving the grain grinder.

Kate detoured through the orchard and lingered beneath the shade of a lemon tree. Small buds were beginning to form on the orchard's trees and here and there early sprays of blossom showed themselves as small white flowers. There were two female servants, one white, the other Aboriginal, collecting the last of the season's fallen fruit from the ground. The women carried a sack apiece, the contents of which were tipped into a wheel-barrow at the end of the row. The barrow held a tiny mound of mottled oranges and lemons. The cook would be kept busy making preserves from the bruised fruit to be stored away until needed.

In such a place Kate found it difficult to believe Mrs Kable's descriptions of the lands beyond the range. Surely it couldn't be that inhospitable, for over the years hundreds had already made their homes on the other side of the mountains and newspaper reports spoke of fertile lands and boundless opportunity. Certainly stories of hostile Aboriginals abounded and dangerous bushrangers mingled with those of escaped convicts, however many settlers never suffered any form of attack. The settlement and exploration of the outer areas continued apace with little prospect of slowing and it only stood to reason that the civilising of the vast area beyond the mountains would continue to grow. So how terrible would it be if she did travel up-country? Certainly there were dangers but were they much different to the possibility of being run down by a carriage in the street or being accosted by a drunken Aboriginal or runaway convict? Such things happened, but infrequently. It was more likely death would come in the chill of winter, when contagions embedded themselves among the poor, feeding on the weak, before spreading through the colony.

Kate looked at the piled fruit. The skins were slightly bruised in places, but the bad bits could be cut away, leaving the remainder of the fruit edible. In this place, the difficulties of life in the colony and beyond were hard to imagine, for the Kables had carved themselves a cultured and productive niche, the envy of many. It was not unreasonable to assume, Kate mused, that although Samuel Hardy was a very recent settler, within a year or so he too would have the beginnings of an estate similar to this. Mrs Kable had mentioned the extraordinary sum of five thousand pounds to set up their venture and there were still funds left over to pay Mr Southerland a most exorbitant wage. The Hardys were moneyed, a not unattractive reason for Kate to align herself with them, and it would be something of an adventure to be involved in such an enterprise from the very beginning. The prospect of being a companion to a landed lady was far more appealing than Mrs Kable's suggestions – that of housekeeper or wife – but did she have the fortitude to agree to such an undertaking? And did she really want to go out into the unknown?

The white maidservant was clearly bored by the morning's duty. She loitered beneath each tree singing an unfamiliar tune. The girl appeared more interested in telling the young Aboriginal to hurry up and move faster. Apparently the native was slovenly and not worth feeding, for the maidservant repeated the words at various intervals, although Kate saw that the girl moved quickly and effortlessly and appeared to take pleasure from her task. The convict should be reported but Kate had no interest in being implicated in domestic concerns and it did not appear that the white servant cared what people thought about her treatment of the native girl, which suggested neither would the Kables.

The younger woman was making her way steadily towards Kate. On seeing that she was being observed she gave a coy smile. Kate responded in kind. She commented on the diligence the girl showed towards her allotted task and was rewarded with a toothy smile.

'Missus.' The girl bobbed a curtsey. 'Me work big house.'

'Someday I imagine you will.'

The native glanced towards the older servant and, digging into the sack on her shoulder, selected an orange and gifted it to Kate.

'Thank you.' It was a simple gesture, but Kate was warmed by it.

The girl gave a shy smile and resumed collecting fruit. Leaving them to their task, Kate walked beneath the avenue of trees.

The light through the branches turned the grass to various shades of brown and beige. It striped her dress with dappled light and enticed large black and white birds to glide on the breeze beneath the canopy of trees.

Kate wondered if Mrs Kable was right in her assumption that this land would never produce any great art or literature, for surely there was beauty to be seen in everything, even if it was just the play of sunlight through leafy boughs. From what Kate had learnt the previous evening, the combination of sheep and men made mythic dreams possible. She was still young, Kate reasoned, only twenty. She need only stay a few years. It was not a life's sentence. Her father had endured much worse and on her return to Sydney there would be coin in her pocket.

A piercing scream broke the quiet. The white servant dropped her sack, and as oranges and lemons tumbled onto the ground, the woman leapt over the rolling fruit. 'Run, miss, run!' she yelled to Kate, lifting her skirt and racing towards the homestead. Her white cap was whipped from her hair by a low-hanging branch, revealing a head roughly shaved. Still the woman kept screaming as if the devil himself gave chase.

Kate began to run as well as the woman's cries drew menfolk from the rear of the house. Curiosity made her look over her shoulder, and through the orchard Kate saw a flash of black limbs and heard a frightened plea for help. There were Aboriginals running from the screen of bush that led in the direction of the river. They were young men, scantily clothed and fast-moving, and they weaved deftly between the trees. One man grabbed the native girl, another hit her on the head with a club of some sort, and as her slight body slumped, the men half-lifted and half-dragged her away. Kate stopped running and stared as the pale skirt of the native girl disappeared into the bush. A warning noise, akin to clashing metal, sounded from the house.

'Are you alright, miss?' Major Shaw was at her side.

The gifted orange Kate held fell to the ground. Her breath came hard and fast. 'T-they took one of the servants.'

'Who did?' Lieutenant Wilson took Kate's elbow as if she would faint. Mr Kable arrived red-faced and out of breath, Captain Gage with him.

'Aboriginals,' Kate replied, regaining her breath and extricating herself from the Lieutenant's grasp. 'They were picking fruit and they just grabbed her and carried her through the trees.' Kate pointed in the direction the men had run.

'Which one did they take?' Mr Kable enquired.

'The young Aboriginal.' Kate couldn't believe what she'd just witnessed.

Major Shaw turned to Mr Kable and the two officers who'd dined with them the previous night. 'You have a native in your employ? How long has she been with you?'

A number of male convicts, alerted by the clanging alarm from the house, were running through the trees towards them while at the front of the farmhouse the entire household, including Mrs Kable and the two children, stood huddled waiting for news.

'Some two months and we've had no trouble before this. The girl has had some teaching at the Parramatta School and is most obedient.'

Major Shaw digested this information and addressed his men. 'Saddle the horses and be quick about it. And, Miss Carter' – the senior officer frowned as if she were partially responsible for the attack – 'you best return to the safety of the house.' The Major took her arm, his grip firm and insistent.

'Wait.' Kate picked up the fallen orange as the officer began to steer her brusquely towards the homestead. 'Will she be alright? Will they come back?'

'Off you go, Miss Carter,' Mr Kable said more kindly. 'We'll take care of this and do tell Mrs Kable not to worry but it's probably best if the household remains indoors until we have an end to this matter.' He turned to the waiting convicts, ordering them to keep an eye out and to go about their tasks in pairs. The men looked warily around the orchard, mumbling between themselves about not being armed.

The pressure of the Major's grasp did not decrease as he led her away. Finally Kate drew her arm free. 'You didn't answer my question.'

The junior officers were a distance ahead moving towards the stables. The Major stopped mid-stride and turned to her. 'If they wanted a white woman I doubt you'd be here talking to us, Miss Carter.'

His words made her pale. The Major observed her carefully and then, without a word, left her to make the short journey to the house.

Kate didn't join the women on the verandah immediately, although Mrs Kable's demanding voice clearly suggested that that was what was expected. Instead she loitered a hundred yards from the house where there were few trees in the immediate vicinity and a clear view of some of the convict shepherds and other workmen. She needed to calm down. Kate had never witnessed anything like that before, and her heart was still pounding. Mr Kable had been quick to send a runner out to the other men in the fields, and as the first man was informed of the attack, he then set off to warn another. Kate scanned the orchard and the outlying trees into which the girl had been taken. The land was quiet. It was as if the surrounding bush had simply engulfed the girl and her attackers. Horses whinnied to her left. The thud of hooves and the sound of raised voices were quickly followed by the appearance of the soldiers. Lieutenant Wilson glanced in her direction as they rode away at a smart pace. They cut through the orchard and veered into the timber. There was a flash of red coats through the foliage then an eerie quiet.

The servant who'd run off earlier reappeared with two male

convicts. They walked tentatively toward the orchard, looking left and right, before the woman ran to where her cap lay. Quickly covering her baldness and the ugly scabs from the barber's shears, she returned to dawdle near Kate.

'She shouldn't have been here anyway.' The servant called to the two male convicts to grab the barrow and be quick about it. 'Them blacks cause trouble. They're godless heathens, they is.' She spoke loudly without specifically addressing Kate. 'A body shouldn't be expected to work with them, useless slovenly types that they are.'

In the orchard one man pushed the cart across the uneven ground, not stopping to pick up the fruit that spilt over the sides though the barrow only held the tiniest quantity. The other man kept watch, grasping a hoe as a weapon.

'Miss Carter.'

Mrs Kable was now alone on the rear verandah. With deliberate slowness Kate walked back towards the building, stopping to brush imaginary grass from the hem of her gown.

'If you've a tendency to wandering in the bush, then let this be a lesson.' The older woman pursed her lips as Kate joined her. 'Any number of things could befall you.'

Kate ignored her. 'Mr Kable advised –'

'Yes, indoors we will stay, for the moment, as all gentlewomen should in times of trouble. You would do well to take the example of others who know better.'

'I did not grow up in the streets of Sydney, Mrs Kable. The Reverend's farm –'

She waved away Kate's words with a dismissive hand. 'You saw it happen?'

Kate followed her hostess inside. 'Yes, to be snatched away like that in broad daylight . . .'

'It could have been far worse. As it is the girl is a loss but it's probably best she returns to her kind. We've only had problems since she joined us.' Holding out her hand she took the orange from Kate and placed it on the hall table. 'It was my husband's decision to bring her here, however the other servants have never taken to her. Indeed both Jelly-belly and Mrs Ovens have complained about her on numerous occasions, while the others have put up a right fuss about eating and sleeping with her. Of course, in the old days I simply would have reported them for creating a ruckus, but with Governor Bourke having seen fit to restrict the use of the whip to fifty strokes, it's hardly a deterrent. And I'm loath to lose a domestic; it's so hard to find a good replacement. Still, I did send two off to the Female Factory. Three months there will steady them somewhat on their return.'

'She seemed eager to please,' Kate argued.

'Who? The native child?' Turning to the oval mirror above the hall table, Mrs Kable adjusted the deep lace collar on her lilac gown. 'The problem is you can't treat them like the others. And you can't expect the others to put up with them.' She tilted her head, twisting a curl around her finger. 'It is all very well to have some desire to adhere to the missionary inclinations of others, but it is totally impossible to attempt assimilation, for the natives are a breed apart, half-formed things. And although my husband may argue to the contrary, and you, Miss Carter, may be easily deceived, the truth remains that the natives themselves are not comfortable with us. For all our attempts, the girl would probably prefer to be curled up outdoors on a mat. After all, they are born under the trees.'

'I thought her quite well-adapted to her new position. She was friendly and her English was –'

Mrs Kable raised an eyebrow. 'A few weeks at the native school does not prepare a native child for our life. You can't expect it to.'

'I only meant that –'

'I am sure you mean many things. The directness of your character was made most plain to me last night.' Mrs Kable rang the brass bell, which sat on the hall stand. 'After this morning maybe it is best for all if you don't join the party when they travel northwards. You could put lives at risk by your wanderings. Had anything happened to you while you were out strolling aimlessly on the farm, then our men would have been placed in danger searching for you. As it is, the Major and his men have given chase to the attackers. One can only hope for their safe return.'

'I apologise, I certainly didn't mean to cause a problem of any sort.' Perhaps it was just as well she was not to be this woman's companion. Kate's dislike of Mrs Kable was growing by the hour.

'And your misguided notions towards the natives could be more than a hindrance to the proper functioning of the Hardy farm.'

'Yes, Missus?' The pointy-nosed maid, Jelly-belly, appeared. 'Is there news?'

'I would take my midday meal in my room. And after Miss Carter speaks to the Reverend, please take her to the kitchen and see her settled with a' – she paused for emphasis – 'consuming task.'

'Of course, Mrs Kable.' The maid gave a half-hearted curtsey and left the women alone.

'Reverend Horsley is due to leave today and has consented, once again, to take you into service. I thought it a kind and generous offer, considering the inconvenience you have caused him, and others.'

'I did not mean to inconvenience anyone,' Kate began, 'and I certainly have no intention of –'

'Considering your current situation,' Mrs Kable interrupted, 'and in the absence of any other relatives, I have agreed to the Reverend's most generous proposal. It is on condition that you are accommodated according to your position.'

'You have agreed?' Kate couldn't believe what she was hearing. 'So you would send me back there, to the Reverend's cottage, under his care, after all that you spoke of last night?' It seemed that Mrs Kable's moral compass could change as quickly as the wind.

The older woman chose to ignore this comment. 'The Reverend assures me that there is a suitable room adjoining the kitchen

136

and that this room is not attached to his own abode. He has been gracious enough to offer you the position of teacher, a role he tells me your mother held until her passing. His school is closed on account of your leaving. I wonder at your ability to desert the lower classes when they are surely in need of an education. You of all people should recognise the importance of such schooling.'

Mrs Kable opened the door to the parlour, shooing Kate into the room. The Reverend stood on her entry, folding the newspaper he held. 'I'll have the dray brought around after noon.'

The door was firmly shut behind her.

The Reverend gestured to a straight-backed chair. Only yesterday Kate thought she'd been on the brink of a new life here in this very house, but she would not let this man see her dismay. Kate refused to give the Reverend that satisfaction. 'Reverend Horsley, I have no wish to live in your household, whether it be in the manner of domestic or not.'

'My dear, you are overwrought by the events of the morning.'

Kate began to pace the room. Of course she was upset.

Resting an elbow on the mantelpiece the Reverend grasped the lapel of his black coat. 'Mr Kable has offered patronage in recognition of the humble work I do in the Lord's service,' he began, a smile settling on his lips. 'It is something of a relief to have my ministrations noticed and rewarded for it means we may well have funds for the building of a dedicated church, as well as retaining the school.'

'And does Mrs Kable share her husband's generous spirit?' asked Kate dryly, stopping by the window.

The Reverend ran his tongue over his lips several times. 'I have no doubt that with this news and having discovered the location of your potential employers, that you may be inclined to reconsider that discussion that we had some weeks ago.'

'My mind is quite made up, Reverend. I would not have travelled here if it were not.'

He gestured for Kate to sit and they took up position before the smoky fire. 'I admit to misleading you. I am only a man,' he extended his hands, palms up, 'and selfish in my needs. However, I thought it necessary for you to understand the limited opportunities available to you. Indeed, I am aware of that stubbornness of character that may well make it difficult for you to change your mind. You are, after all, your mother's daughter. I would certainly not find it intemperate of you were you to reconsider your situation in light of my good fortune.' The Reverend raised an eyebrow. 'You do know the hardships, the very dangers that may befall you should you journey elsewhere. The world is not a kindly place for a single young woman.'

'There are other alternatives,' Kate replied, trying to keep all emotion from her voice.

Scratching his whiskers the Reverend leant forward on the sofa. 'So I've been informed. As a housekeeper in one of the lesser houses, a limited position, unlike my own offer, with no chance of rising above your station, something that we both know your mother would have wanted for you. To see you reinstated into society proper following the loss of your small holding would have given her pleasure. But then, considering the blood that runs in your veins, you may feel that such a role is more appropriate.' The Reverend hoped to pique a response, but when one was not forthcoming he persevered. 'Then there is the question of marriage. Mrs Kable suggests the pasty-faced young Lieutenant as a possible husband. But one has to wonder how long you would be happy to live with the other wives in the barracks before his term of service expired. Would the land granted him be productive? Is he capable of turning his hand to farming? Would he be promoted?' He shrugged, as if such a possibility were unlikely. 'Would such a union satisfy you? For we both know you are proud and have every hope for advancement in this world, an unlikely aspiration for a woman of your standing.' A fly settled on his knee and he swatted at it irritably. 'In deference to your mother I will ask you one more time if you will not reconsider.'

Kate formed her words carefully. 'But surely now that you have found such favour with the Kables your need for my services has become somewhat redundant. A teacher will be found for your school,' Kate answered sweetly, 'and I believe I would make an excellent lady's companion, a role that you cannot offer me.'

'You are a most stubborn woman.' The Reverend rose and paced in front of the fireplace, scuffing the coloured rug until he tripped on a corner. 'Are you quite sure that you will not return with me? I leave after the noon meal and journey to Parramatta tonight and then onwards to home, your home these past ten years.'

'I wish you safe passage.'

The Reverend took a step towards her. 'This is silly, my child. You have a comfortable home, with me.'

'I have the memory of what it was like to live there with my mother, and for that I must be grateful.' Rising, Kate excused herself and left the room. Softly closing the door, she rested against the cool architrave. The Reverend Horsley offered hearth and home, comfort and safety; everything that a woman required, but at what cost?

Mrs Ovens was not pleased to have Kate in her domain. Placing her at the far end of the long wooden table, opposite the wide stone fireplace, the large woman studied her, one lace-up shoe tapping the flagstone floor, a wooden spoon clutched in her hand. Kate expected to have her cotton cap struck off her head at any moment, but the cook soon lost interest when Kate said nothing, and returned to measuring out flour. The kitchen was similar to the Reverend's but more than twice the size, with herb racks on the wall, cupboards, pots, and a heady aroma that emanated from a cast-iron pot in which a large veal pie kept warm.

'Is that your trunk?' Jelly-belly, waiting for the meal to be served, opened the window and leant out.

'What?' Kate joined her and together they observed the two convicts carrying her chest, another the Reverend's travelling bag, around the side of the house. Kate couldn't believe it. Someone had packed her belongings. They were literally throwing her out.

'Looks like you're leaving.'

Kate lifted a finger to her mouth and began to bite the nail.

'Perhaps it's for the best. I wouldn't go out there, no fear.'

Returning to her seat, Kate sat heavily. The pie was served up with fried potatoes and set on a tray with a glass of lemon cordial, a single white rose from the garden, silver cutlery and a linen napkin. Jelly-belly waited for the serving to be done and then lifted her mistress's luncheon tray. Mr Kable had already been served three courses in the dining room. 'Well then, they won't make themselves.' She nodded at the racks of rose petals that had been dried near the fire and placed in front of Kate, a cool blast of air entering the room as she left.

'And don't go talking your head off.' Mrs Ovens turned her wide girth to the bread box. Hunched over the deep bin she finished mixing the ingredients and then expertly formed the loaf with two wooden paddles, before lifting the lid on the adjoining compartment and placing the bread inside to prove. 'But I will say I don't like the look of him, that Reverend of yours. Mean-spirited they all are, those types. Telling us what to do and how to do it. I'm not a believer and I don't mind saying so. It's just another way of keeping us down at heel.'

'Neither am I,' Kate agreed.

The cook gave a single determined nod as if there were some goodness in the world after all and cut Kate a wedge of the pie.

'You gobble it down now, lass, before that Jelly-legged English girl comes back. It's soup and bread for her.'

Kate mumbled her thanks, eating appreciatively, before turning her attention to the racks before her. After dusting the petals with powdered cloves and cinnamon, she placed quantities of them in small rose-satin sachets edged with coffee-coloured lace and then began to sew up the ends. It was difficult to concentrate. The soldiers were yet to return, the dray would soon arrive and here she was fiddling with rose petals while her mother's trunk sat out in the sun. If only she'd not been so outspoken last night, then perhaps Mrs Kable wouldn't now be forcing her out the door.

'Leave with him if you must.' The cook had also been thinking on the matter for she sat opposite Kate, two bulbous elbows perched on the table on either side of a bowl of soup. 'Don't be thinking you can't look after yourself, not yet. If things get real bad use those looks of yours. Plenty of women have had their bellies filled by fouler means. But I doubt if it will come to that.' Lifting the bowl she took a long drink from it. 'You've got the look of a tom-cat, easily riled and hard to temper, but smart.' She wiped her mouth with the back of her hand. 'Go where you can make a start for yourself, go where you'll be needed, but keep that uppity look from your eyes. You ain't nothing to anybody unless you can prove your worth.'

'And how do I do that?'

'Don't weep or cry out or faint, unless it serves a purpose, or it's before a man with coin. Do what's asked of you quickly and well and never ever complain or speak down to your betters. Be capable, but not too capable.' Mrs Ovens tapped her temple where a lock of grey hair poked from beneath her cap. 'And don't marry no man unless there's money enough, and even if there is, never marry for love. That's the surest way to get yourself into trouble. For the man is always right, no matter if he's wrong.' She wiped a stubby finger around the bowl and licked it.

'When you get to Parramatta,' Mrs Ovens continued, 'beg old MacIntosh to take you a bit further down the Parramatta Road to the Square and Compass. Gwen Winters owns it with that layabout man of hers. She's a good woman, Gwen. Came out on the same creaking scurvy-ridden hulk as me. Made a pact we'd help each other when we could. She owes me so tell her I sent you. The place is well-known to the wool trade – you'll be safe enough and you can work off your board and food while you decide what's next.'

Kate smiled in gratitude but frankly she couldn't think of anything worse than working in a hostelry. Serving and cleaning after drunks and finicky travellers was not a role she aspired to.

'They're coming, the soldiers are coming.' Jelly-belly entered the kitchen, dropping the tray on the table with a clatter, and moved to the window. Kate ran outdoors to the verandah. A flicker of movement caught her attention. The bush beyond the orchard appeared to be still, but a horse nickered from that very direction and then patches of red appeared, weaving through the trees. The indistinguishable figures spread out to ride three abreast, Major Shaw riding point, as if heading into action. The young Aboriginal girl was not with them.

The men rode straight up to the house at a fast trot. Dirt and grit eddied across the ground as the horses came to an abrupt stop and the men dismounted. They handed their mount's reins to a convict who'd come running, Major Shaw pulling his mare's ears affectionately before stamping his dusty boots free of dirt. Lieutenant Wilson caught Kate's eye. There was a smear of blood on his britches and his ready gaze was marred. The Major glanced at the trunk and bag sitting in the dirt and, without acknowledging her, led the solemn procession inside.

Kate hesitated, and then after a few minutes quietly followed the men indoors. The parlour door was ajar and, within, Mr Kable's profile was intent as he listened to the Major, the Reverend also in attendance. Kate waited in the hallway fearing being accused an eaves-dropper, but keen to know the fate of the young girl. She took a step closer to the door. The men's voices were barely audible.

'There was nothing to be done for her,' Major Shaw replied in conclusion, his voice rising as he drew to the end of a succinct explanation.

A decanter was opened, liquid sloshed. Kate looked down the hallway and, hearing nothing, edged a little nearer to the door.

'A pity,' Mr Kable replied.

'Indeed. Whether it was her people or another mob of blacks, it is a timely reminder of the pitfalls of befriending the natives.'

Jelly-belly tiptoed along the hallway to stand near Kate. Kate frowned at the girl and the convict scowled back.

'Many may have become debauched by their addiction to our drink in these parts.' It was the Major who spoke. 'And there are others who wish us ill. Blacks who choose to assimilate into an enlightened society are clearly in mortal danger from their own kind.'

'It is a sorry situation,' Mr Kable replied.

'We have no idea of their ways,' Lieutenant Wilson entered the conversation haltingly. 'Who is to say that the girl had not done some wrong? Or perhaps she was an innocent victim and those responsible happened upon her by chance?'

'That we will never know,' the Reverend agreed.

The conversation paused as the squeak of a wagon carried from outside.

Mr Kable turned towards the door. 'Miss Carter,' he called, 'I did not see you there.'

Kate reluctantly moved to the doorway as Jelly-belly slunk away to open the front door.

'It were best if you made your presence known, miss,' the Major accused lightly, 'this is not for the ears of women.' He drained his glass and sat it on the table before the fire then turned his attention back to his host. 'We leave in the morning. Mr Southerland is ready to depart, as you know, and the sooner I reach Maitland with the relieving troopers, the sooner my men and I can return to our duties in Parramatta.'

Kate hovered in the doorway.

Jelly-belly walked back down the passageway. 'Begging your pardon, Mr Kable, sir, but the dray is waiting for the Reverend and Miss Carter.' She curtsied and left, nodding gravely at Kate as she passed.

'I gather I need not call on you before daybreak, Miss Carter?' the Major stated.

'You're leaving, Miss Carter?' Lieutenant Wilson was at Kate's elbow, steering her along the hallway where goodbyes were being made to the Reverend.

Kate admitted that at this stage it seemed likely that she would only travel as far as Parramatta. The young man seemed to be buoyed by this remark for he squeezed her elbow ever so slightly. 'Where might I find you?' he asked quietly.

'At the Square and Compass.' The Lieutenant gave a broad smile, giving him the air of a schoolboy. With dismay Kate realised she'd given the young man a sense of hope, which was not what she'd intended. 'But I have no idea how long I'll be there for.'

'Leave a forwarding address,' he whispered.

'Lieutenant,' the Major directed, 'fetch the horses.' The two younger officers walked outside and headed towards the stables, while Mr Kable offered Kate his best wishes before returning to the parlour.

'So you're leaving with the Reverend?' Major Shaw accompanied Kate to the verandah as the Reverend's travel bag was dropped onto the rear of a dray. The driver, MacIntosh, was petting his horse between the ears and talking animatedly to the animal. The horse kept its head low and pawed at the dirt. 'You have made the right decision.'

Kate noted the slight condescension to his words. 'Really?'

'Well, no-one should expect the weaker sex to embark on such an expedition. It is bad enough that husbands drag their wives out into the wilds but a defenceless single woman?' He shook his head. 'You will do better here. In more suitable surrounds and occupations.'

What he spoke of held some truth, and Kate knew by the earnestness of the Major's tone that the words were well-intentioned. Nonetheless, they were also predictable and ultimately spoke of curtailment; the restriction of a woman's life through roles deemed suitable by society. 'As a wife no doubt, or a housekeeper, or perhaps a teacher?'

The Major frowned. 'Whatever you wish. I for one am grateful for your choice.'

'Yes, I am sure my presence would have been an unnecessary burden to you and your men.' Kate tried to keep her tone polite, but there was an unmistakeable curtness to her words. The Major's face remained impassive although the vein in his neck grew blue and thick.

'Come, Kate.' The Reverend treated her to a rare smile. 'Get your bonnet and travelling cloak and we'll be homeward bound.' He extended his hand to her. 'Our good driver informs me that we are to stay at the Square and Compass tonight and that the food is markedly fine.'

Kate's stomach turned. Was she never to be rid of this man? As Major Shaw wished her a safe journey, the convicts deposited her trunk in the rear of the dray.

The Reverend's hand remained outstretched. 'I have offered Miss Carter the role of housekeeper and teacher, Major. Positions which, although she has to date refused, will undoubtedly be agreed to. Miss Carter doesn't lack for good sense, a quality that she shared with her mother, may the Lord bless her soul. Amen.'

'A most excellent option,' the Major agreed, 'and most generous of you, sir.'

'Yes,' Kate answered tightly, 'excellent.' It was clear by the Reverend's self-satisfied expression that he was most impressed by his manipulations.

With the dray loaded, the shorter of the two convicts approached Kate. 'If that be all then, miss?' He nodded to the driver, when she gave a hesitant yes, who in turn glanced skyward at the sun and then at Kate, who was clearly delaying their leaving. The Reverend was rubbing his hands together.

Kate cleared her throat. 'I will not be travelling with the Reverend.'

The grumbling convicts looked from left to right and then, at Kate's insistence, begrudgingly carried her trunk back to the verandah, the Reverend complaining heartily.

'Please go ahead,' Kate told the bemused driver, who stood with a foot resting on one of the timber wheel spokes, a stick between his teeth.

The man waited a moment, expecting one or another to change their mind. 'The lass is still shook up from yesterday's journey,' MacIntosh said to no-one in particular. 'I don't blame her. Me own bones are fairly jolted out of their sockets every time I get in this contraption.'

'Go,' she repeated.

The driver shrugged and advised the Reverend to climb up and hang on.

'Kate, what are you doing?' he complained. 'Don't be foolish.'

'They be good nags, but you never know when they'll get spooked and take off across the flat. Best if your Holiness keep a firm grip, least you come to grief 'tween here and Parramatta. There ain't no-one to say Hail Marys out here.'

'I am not of the Catholic faith,' the Reverend stated bluntly.

'Well then, you do have it all ahead of you, your Holiness.'

'You are a most stubborn young woman,' the Reverend told Kate, once he'd assumed position in the seat behind the driver. 'You will

146

regret this, Kate. Don't come to me when you are destitute, poorer than poor with not a scrap of food nor a roof above your head to give you comfort. I will not forgive you, nor ask for forgiveness on your behalf. Who would intercede for a woman of your ilk? Who –'

The driver called out giddy-up. There was a screech of leather and timber and the raspy breath of a well-worked horse. The dray jolted forward and the Reverend was flung back and forth. He grasped the timber sides, eyes bulging, his skin turning puce. 'The Lord will frown upon you.' The dray moved off quickly, following the track that led out of the farm.

The Major turned to her. The dray was gathering pace, it had already passed the orchard, the Reverend's straight back in contrast to the slump-shouldered driver. 'Miss Carter, are you quite sure you know what you are doing? Perhaps you are overcome by the events of the morning. Would you like to sit?'

'No, no I don't wish to sit, thank you.' What would her father do? Kate imagined she was high among the branches of the fig tree again. The air was cool and clear and –

'Miss Carter?'

She was quickly jolted back to the present. 'I couldn't go with him, Major. The Reverend is not a kind man.'

Major Shaw looked askance. 'He has harmed you in some way?'

'N-no,' she stammered.

There were two rattan chairs at the end of the verandah, a matching table between them. The officer took Kate's arm, a gentle but firm escort. He led them towards the end of the porch where, having seated her, he finally replied, 'Well, then I don't understand.'

How could a man such as this ever comprehend her situation? 'Can we not talk of it, I beg of you. You would not begin to understand.'

'I should fetch Mrs Kable.'

Kate waved both hands. 'No, please don't. That woman will be of no help to me.'

If the officer was shocked by her tone, he did not betray it. Instead, the Major stood somewhat awkwardly a few feet from where Kate sat, a red-coated sentry with the chiselled profile of a Roman bust. A number of times he made the slightest of movements, as if speech were almost possible. She too felt the need to say something, to bridge the uneasiness between them. Once, twice their gaze met and just as swiftly both parties looked away.

'If I can be of service?' he asked, finally.

'I am quite alright. Thank you,' Kate mumbled.

And still the man waited as the sun grew warm and insects darted about them. Kate tried not to think of the Major's solid presence. A decision was needed. She did not want to live the rest of her days by the leave of another. Kate needed a roof over her head and a way to make money. It was money that gave people choices, gave them their freedom, allowed the bestowing of equality and respect. If she'd not realised the importance of it before, these new surroundings combined with the difficulties presented had quickly reinforced the benefit of it. Kate thought of the amount of money George Southerland was being paid.

The Major cleared his throat. 'I must apologise if I have caused offence.'

'What? Oh, not at all,' Kate replied quickly. She'd been lost in her thoughts, again.

'I simply . . . well, your circumstances cause me concern.' He stopped abruptly as if embarrassed by his words. 'You are, well, that is to say, it does not seem right for a person such as yourself to be placed in such a difficult situation, Miss Carter.'

Kate felt her cheeks redden under his scrutiny. 'Life throws all manner of difficulties in our path.'

'Indeed.' Major Shaw cleared his throat again and, clasping his hands behind his back, spent some time studying the orchard.

There was no need for the Major to remain but Kate was comforted by his presence.

'If I can be of no further assistance, I will leave you then.' He turned on his heel.

Kate took a breath. 'I will be going up-country, Major.' The abruptness of these words made him stop mid-step. 'But firstly I have to seek suitable terms of employment.'

The man looked at her as if she'd taken leave of her senses. 'A woman seeking terms of employment?'

'I know what is before me. You need not fear on my account, Major. I will not be of trouble to you.' She looked out at the country-side warming beneath a mild afternoon sun. Right or wrong, it was a relief to have made a decision.

'But you can't be serious?'

'I am indeed. I don't see why I should be paid any less than the next body who risks their person in the service of another beyond the outer limits. I am sure Mr Kable would agree.'

The officer shook his head as if trying to fathom their con-versation. They turned to watch the dray as it slowed in the distance to navigate a slight rise. When the Reverend finally slipped from their view, she felt the Major's gaze upon her. Kate saw it then, the man within the uniform. Beyond the starchy exterior he was undoubtedly trying to comprehend the thoughts of a young woman who would give up a generous and comfort-able offer, from a man of the cloth no less, to venture into the unknown.

'Even after this morning,' the Major confirmed, 'you are intent on this direction?'

Lieutenant Wilson and Captain Gage reappeared with horses in tow, stopping a short distance from the verandah to check the tightness of girth straps and place firearms in the holsters attached to their saddles. The Lieutenant, interested to see that Kate was still among them, took every opportunity to catch her eye as he readied his mount and then the Major's.

'I must caution you, Miss Carter, as a single woman you will

149

find the outer limits most inhospitable. In fact I think it ludicrous that you would even consider such a thing.'

'Is New South Wales not a new land, a young society filled with possibility?' Kate questioned.

'Yes, of course.'

What would her father think if he knew his only child had done no better in life than if she'd been born in England? The younger officers were mounted and awaiting their Major. The horses snuffled impatiently.

'If you'll allow me.' The Major retrieved a map from his breast pocket. Unfolding it carefully he spread the linen paper on a table. The colony of New South Wales was shaded in pink. It hugged the coast and extended from below Port Macquarie in the north to Bateman's Bay in the south. Westward there were few place names except for the inland rivers such as the Darling. 'We are here.' A saddle-greasy nail marked Sydney Cove and then their current position. 'And this is where Samuel Hardy has made his selection.' With deliberate slowness he dragged a finger northwards, over the mountain range and further still. The Major's route was crisscrossed by rivers and hills, bordered by areas of marshland, timbered country and open plains, a journey which passed through a number of counties. To the east lay the vast ocean, to the west and north, beyond the nineteen settled counties, unsurveyed lands.

Kate observed the increasing distance with growing discomfort. The further north he progressed the greater the expanses of white on the map. Finally he crossed a river. 'The Gwydir,' he announced, looking at her as if he'd just shared the details of a risky military campaign. Kate gave a wan smile. Surely here his finger would stop. An inch or so further northwards, it did.

'Samuel has gone beyond the settled counties,' he concluded.

Kate wet her lips. She already knew this. 'But why? Why has he journeyed so far?'

'Settlers are being forced to go further afield every year in search of land. They have been pushed afar by the sheer number of colonists, and organisations such as the Australian Agricultural Company, who in taking up huge swathes of arable land have pushed illegal squatters further out.'

'And yet he must lease this land, isn't that what was talked of last night? It seems a great journey to embark upon, to start a farm on land that he does not own.'

'Insecure it is, but the colonial powers have finally decided to try to regulate squatters beyond the settled areas. They hope it will restrain the corrupt, without disrupting honest folk such as the Hardys.' The Major folded the map. 'If the enterprise proves successful Samuel will purchase, eventually, when the opportunity arises.'

A pleasant breeze did not stop the perspiration forming on her brow. Kate knew this military man meant to dissuade her, although his tone had grown kinder. In fact, Kate felt quite relaxed in his presence.

'Do you understand where you venture to?'

Kate assured the Major that she did, although it was not until this very moment that she understood the extent of the distance involved and the frontier awaiting only the most courageous, or desperate.

'Think on this, Miss Carter,' he replied. 'Surely there are other avenues available to you? I would advise –'

Kate shut her mind to the Major's words. Everyone was convinced they knew what was best for her but the simple truth lay in the obvious. If Mrs Hardy could build a home in the wilds with her family, then Kate was quite able to travel forth and be her companion.

'Please, Major, my mind is quite made up.' Kate didn't want to argue any longer, especially with Major Shaw, for at least he'd been honest with her. She changed the course of their conversation.

'I gather the Aboriginal girl has run away. Perhaps it's for the best. Certainly the other servants were unkindly towards her although I witnessed a diligent worker, one –'

'Run away?' The blueness of the Major's eyes reminded Kate of the willow-patterned china that they'd dined on the previous evening. 'She is dead.' He left her sitting in the rattan chair and, at his horse's side, patted the animal fondly. The mare nickered in anticipation and proceeded to move as he launched himself up into the saddle. 'We found her body not a mile from here. She was hacked to death.'

Kate recalled the young girl and the gift of the orange. 'Dead, but how? Why?'

'Who knows the mind of these savages?' He nodded politely. 'We leave before day-break. Be ready.'

All three men looked at her, then they turned their horses and galloped away.

Kate walked out onto the rutted track and, lifting a hand to shield her face from the glare of the sun, looked out in the direction that the dray had taken. There was not even a puff of dust to mark its progress. The dray and the Reverend were gone.

⫷ Chapter 10 ⫸

1837 July − on the western side of the Blue Mountains

The musket slipped, grazing the slashes on Adam's arm. He grimaced with the sting, and continued walking steadily back towards the camp. He'd been up since the first blush of predawn light, circumnavigating the sheltered clearing where the clan rested following last night's burial. His self-imposed sentry duty led him to within a mile of the Lycett farm and back again, each consecutive sweep disturbing a variety of creatures; from the lizards and mice scattering through the grass, through to emus running helter-skelter, heads down through the scrub. Although he doubted anyone would be tracking them so soon, Adam could not afford the possibility of the clan being attacked without warning. There were police in the village of Hartley to the east and Bathurst to the west and the constabularies were not averse to journeying through the night, with the aid of a black tracker.

Archibald Lycett was dead. The loss of the man who'd figured so prominently in Adam's life was something he'd been unprepared for and the circumstances still made him reel. But from the tribe's viewpoint there was one consolation. Winston was not the adventurous man his father was, so would surely have waited until daybreak before he set out on horseback. And only if his mother had returned safely home first.

The tribe had mourned much of the night and through the early hours of the morning. The children could be heard answering their mother, Annie, and as he drew closer it became obvious that the group was packing up and leaving. It was not unexpected. Bidjia, Colby and Jardi turned at his approach and then noting he was alone resumed their conversation. They still bore the remnants of the powdery ash and the blood from the self-inflicted injuries they'd sustained but Colby was further wounded. A deep gash to his thigh seeped blood and the contents of a gluey poultice from beneath a bandage of woven grass. The injury was a token from yesterday's fight. Flies buzzed about, crawling across the dank moisture that leaked down his leg.

The camp fire still smouldered but the men had collected their spears, throwing sticks, stone axes and other assorted weapons. Annie moved back and forth between a pile of grinding stones, fishing nets and a few bark utensils, hiding them behind a fallen log on the rim of the camp in case any of the members should return to the spot in the future.

As Elder, Bidjia was custodian of all sacred objects. He handed the fire-making stick to Colby. 'You take.' He urged further when it was refused. 'You have your woman and children, and we must move quickly. Forge an alliance with the next tribe south. You will be safe there. Some of us must survive so that our people go on.'

Jardi left the eldest members of the clan and joined Adam. 'What did you see?'

'Nothing except the land as it should be.' Adam thought he may have stumbled across the abandoned baby, but what would he have done with the child if he had?

'I knew you would be out there, waiting for them.' Yesterday's disagreement between them was all but forgotten. 'The sorry business means we can no longer stay here.'

There had been no opportunity to speak of events last night. It was not appropriate. 'I thought as much. Archibald Lycett is dead, killed accidently by his son, and Mrs Lycett's gone walkabout.'

Jardi barely moved his head in acknowledgment. 'This is my country, but now I am like my father, for it is stolen from me as well.'

Having returned from hiding their few possessions, Annie and her two children waited patiently for Colby to say his goodbyes. The young'uns squatted in the dirt and trickled sand through their fingers while their mother stood red-eyed and puffy from grieving, glowering at Adam with unrestrained hatred.

'Merindah has run away,' Jardi informed him. 'She was gone when I came back to camp. This is good.'

Adam hoped the girl would find her baby and with luck gain acceptance with another tribe.

Taking up his spear, club and throwing stick, Colby led his family into the bush. He limped badly. Such wounds could be deadly, more than once in the past a nasty cut had festered on one of the clan, with fever and death the end result. Adam had known Colby ever since Bidjia had brought him into the tribe. He was a proud warrior, the next in line as Elder, but Colby had never truly accepted Adam's presence and with the forced breakup of the remnants of their clan, he knew they parted enemies. The man's silence and stony glare was testament to the fact. Annie hissed at him as she pushed the naked children after their father.

'He won't talk about it,' Jardi warned Adam with a steadying hand as he tried to approach Bidjia. The older man waited until Colby and his family were out of sight. They felt his sadness. It was unlikely that the two men would meet again. 'This sorry business must be left behind. It is today and tomorrow that we think on.'

'Is his vengeance satisfied?' Adam asked quietly. 'Is one death enough?'

'For now. The son still lives but there are still enough moons left for my father to take what is his right. The land is patient.' Jardi said the words with a new resolve and in the doing clearly implied that the friendship between Adam and Winston meant nothing to the clan.

Adam had been reared in their ways. He expected nothing less, but the ability of the tribe to wait many years until satisfaction was sought was a chilling reminder of how brutal their traditions could be, and yet across the mountains those who made the law of the land under an English sovereign could lash a man's back to pulp with the cat-o'-nine-tails and then hang him if they wished.

'Colby and Annie are taking the little ones and heading south,' Jardi explained. 'And we must go too. There will be trouble here if we stay.'

Adam agreed. 'If that convict, Donaldson, had not been killed, things may have been different.'

'Bidjia will be blamed for these troubles and not the whites who take our land and our women.'

Adam knew that Winston would report the incident. Besides his father's death, a convict had been murdered and once the police were involved Bidjia and his clan would be wanted for the attack and the matter would be out of Winston's hands. Adam wondered if he would be treated with similar disregard. He would never forget the bitterness in Winston's voice, the venom of his accusation. And now a convict was dead. A white settler. Darel's death was unimportant. There was only one thing that Adam could be sure of. Merindah would be forgotten and Winston would never know, probably never want to know, or even care, that he'd had a child. Merindah was simply a distraction.

'The white soldiers will hunt Bidjia down until he's dead,' Jardi stated gloomily. 'It will be as you said, Bronzewing.'

What could he do? Adam knew that even if he went to the authorities and told his account of events, they wouldn't listen to what he had to say. Bidjia was guilty of the attack. And what of Winston? Was it actually possible that he would lay the blame for his father's death on him? Or had shock and grief temporarily twisted his thoughts. But that was the least of what concerned Adam. He couldn't live with the thought of Bidjia and Jardi being pursued. They were family.

Bidjia sat on the ground among his possessions, a spear, an axe, a throwing stick and his animal-hide cloak. In his hand was a small smooth stick of soft wood, the length of his foot, which he began to carve with a series of symbols. At the top of the stick was a picture of a yam, then a tree. Finally, with a few careful flicks of a knife, Bronzewing was noted with a carving of a pigeon of the same name. Bidjia worked deftly, tiny shavings scattering across his skinny thighs as he described with distinctive marks where they came from and why they had to leave. This message stick was hastily prepared. There had been many message sticks in the past once they'd escaped over the mountains years earlier. Most were intricately carved and painted with decorative designs, but there was no time for such workmanship. This stick was not to be used to announce a ceremony, invitation, meeting, warning or event. It explained that they were in trouble and that they sought safe passage through another tribe's land. 'When my spirit leaves this place, Jardi, you will make a new stick, proclaiming your place in our clan and noting Bronzewing as your accepted white brother. You will do this.' It was not a question. 'Gather your things. We go north.' Bidjia blew at the stick, scattering small slithers of wood and dust.

'But this is not our country,' Jardi argued. 'The northern groups are powerful people, warriors, and the way is unknown.'

His father got to his feet. 'We will follow the songlines, the paths made by the creator ancestors. There are many songs to tell us the way, my son. There will be hills and great valleys, then a mighty mountain that rises from the plains. We will cross this mountain and then the cliffs, which will lead us back to the great waterhole. I know the songs of this land and we will follow the footprints we sing. And in the singing you will learn the dreaming track as well.'

'So we go then.' Adam was ready to move.

Bidjia picked up his belongings. 'You have been with us in this place since the beginning. The land knows you and you it, but now you must think to your life ahead. I must protect Jardi, the last of my line, for there is no other to take my place when my spirit leaves the land. Our journey is far and unknown. This is not your fight, my white son.'

Adam shifted the weight of the musket in his hand. 'It has become so.'

Through leagues of dry distance we came,
Where dust-wreaths, wind-woven, upcurled,
Since Dawn dropped the rails of the east
And let the Day into our world.

Slow-moving we travelled the plains,
Trudging on through the sun and the wind,
Till Day galloped out of the west,
And Night set the sliprails behind.

'The Drover of the Stars'
by Roderic Quinn, 1944

❊ Chapter 11 ❧

1837 September – towards the outer limits

The world was obscured by darkness. Kate rubbed at eyes crusted with sleep and peered across the rumple of blankets. Through the rear opening of the covered wagon, the canopy of trees resembled filigree. Branches wavered slowly in the light breeze and through the woody ceiling a few stars glimmered weakly. There was movement beyond the insubstantial structure, which served as both bedchamber and carriage, a crackle of twigs, leaves and the pre-dawn mutterings of a man well-used to a daily task. The cloth side of the wagon was illuminated as the camp fire flared. Gradually the light grew steady and the many crates piled behind Kate's narrow sleeping space were revealed.

The beginning of the day brought relief. Kate found it strange how quickly one grew accustomed to a new life, to the endless monotony of travelling, and the men about her, but she was not without fear. Night had become a living thing. It moved around her, over and under her, like a wild beast circling. Sounds echoed, things moved and there was no sturdy door between her and it.

With the sun's rising some comfort could be gained. The impenetrable countryside was at least visible and there was movement of man, horse and bullock, a distraction from the images that pursued her when the shadows lengthened.

In the pre-dawn gloom came a shuffling noise. It would be the Major sitting in the dirt pulling on his boots. His sleeplessness, which alternated impressively between grunts and snores, kept Kate firmly aware of his presence throughout each night. The man's nocturnal wanderings involved hefting himself up from the rough ground by hanging onto the wheel of the wagon. This action caused the creaking of wood, which invariably disturbed Mr Southerland, who was quick to reach for his Brown Bess musket. The false alarm brought muttering and oaths aplenty from the two convicts, and relief from Kate, who'd grown used to waking wide-eyed. The fact that the men had taken to sleeping in shifts in order to keep an eye on the camp and that Major Shaw was intent on checking that the man on guard stayed awake, should have allayed any fears. It didn't. The men remained uneasy.

The jangle of iron keys announced that the Londoners, Jim Betts and Harry Gibbs, were being released from their nightly leg-irons. The Major was a stickler for protocol although where he thought these two felons would wander off to remained a mystery. Even Mr Southerland, the expedition leader, thought it an unnecessary precaution, although for the first part of their journey there were villages and shanties along the way. Betts and Gibbs were assigned to the colony for stealing, and with months of provisions packed into the two bullock drays, including muskets and ammunition, Kate believed such caution was needed.

From beyond the wagon came a whistled tune. The presence of the convivial if rough Scotsman, Mr Callahan, was a boon. Grey of hair and beard, no doubt as much from the harshness of his life as age, he'd been granted a ticket-of-leave and from the beginning of the journey had assumed the role of cook. 'Nothing like a good fire. Black as the Earl of Hell's waistcoat it was this morning,' the Scot exclaimed to no-one in particular.

To date their group had travelled together reasonably well. Generally complaints were short-lived for, depending on the perpetrator, punishment could run to the withholding of food from the felons through to the Major's withering gaze, should anyone query the slightest of things. But the final word on nearly everything invariably lay with their designated leader, George Southerland.

The three chickens roosting in the timber cage on the ground squawked on waking and the rooster gave a single call. The Major lifted the birds. 'Miss Carter?'

Kate sat up and wrapped the blanket tightly about her cotton shift.

'I thought you'd be awake.' He pushed the cage into the rear of the wagon, his voice betraying his discomfort at disturbing her. 'I hope you slept well,' he muttered as he turned to walk a short distance from the campsite.

'Yes, thank you,' Kate replied over the noise of the flapping chickens as she reached in the dark for her clothes. It was reassuring to have the Major sleeping next to her wagon, even if he did disturb her during the night and made a point of ensuring she was awake every morning. Kate was not happy that he was soon to depart. The Major's ablutions carried across the shadows, loud and long. None of them were precious about keeping close to the camp's perimeter when nature called. Mr Southerland had been strict in his rules. No walking off, no dawdling and no complaining. Men had wandered into the bush and got lost and he wasn't one for chasing after lunatics.

'There's many a Scot who'd lay claim to a pint of piss on a cold morning, Major Shaw, sir,' Mr Callahan commented when the Major reappeared.

'But then I'm betting you'd be one for pure alcohol,' the Major replied, 'and I can't help you there.'

The Scot gave a throaty laugh. 'Tis true, it's a sad day to be out bush and not even a shanty to be had. When I think of those fine establishments we passed . . .'

The timber boards were pitiless beneath her knees as Kate peered through the wagon's opening. A harder night's sleep she'd never experienced, but it had been at her insistence. The thought of the cold, hard ground held little appeal while they travelled through mountainous country and the heavy dew that covered the land was reason enough to stay in the wagon. It also allowed the removal of the boned bodice she wore and a few hours' respite from the men who surrounded her every day. She'd never been party to such continued male companionship before, to their looks and innuendo, and at times Kate wished she'd given more thought to the irreconcilable decision made some weeks prior.

Kate had decided that if the colony of New South Wales had a creator, then surely it was a man. No woman would conjure brown dirt, patchy grasses and rough ground. No woman would make a sun that dried the land and those that walked upon it, nor create the fractious natives who'd killed one of their own, a harmless girl no less. Kate rubbed her arms and hands briskly, coaxing warmth into stiff limbs, begrudging the men their spots by the fire where, bodies outstretched, they enjoyed the freedom of a warm night's sleep.

Now the men were risen Kate hiked up her skirts and climbed down from the rear of the wagon. There were three men standing near the fire, their dark figures silhouetted by yellow light. The two convicts were waiting for the quart-pots to boil, while Mr Callahan was dolloping spoonfuls of a lumpy mixture – flour, water and salt – onto the griddle. The flat iron disk with its upturned rim was the Scot's favoured cooking item. He'd hung the chain that was attached to the hoop handle from a sturdy bough, supported by two upright branches, and the johnny-cake mixture sizzled as it hit the hot metal.

'That be the only good thing to come out of Scotland,' the convict Betts stated.

'Apart from me,' the Scotsman chuckled.

Kate's stomach growled as she picked her way carefully to the edge of the rim of light and, hiding behind a tree, gathered up her skirts and squatted. It was weeks since the Kable farm had vanished from view. In its place was the rough life of the traveller, with long days of being jolted across uneven ground, limited conversation and the problem of being the only female in a party of eight men, including the Aboriginal, Joe.

Kate tugged at her petticoat, tied the string on her drawers and sniffed the breeze. The smell of smoke, beyond that of the camp fire, hung in the air. At various stages of their passage they'd seen smoke on the horizon or passed through country previously burnt. It was a harsh scent, bitter to the throat and stinging to the eyes. And it rarely dissipated. Mr Southerland told her the natives did it to entice the regrowth of grasses, which in turn brought the animals that were part of their food supply. A less sinister reason could not be devised. A female she may well be, however Kate knew when she was being placated.

She walked back to the wagon. Lieutenant Wilson and Captain Gage were leaving today with the Major. They had already travelled farther than they intended as Maitland was a good three days' ride south. The infantrymen who'd accompanied them from Parramatta and who'd been seconded to join mounted troopers based in Maitland had not journeyed with them further. Their leaving made the reduced party so much the quieter and after this morning their numbers would be smaller still. The horses whinnied and shuffled their feet.

The convicts were grumbling about the cold as Mr Callahan advised them to cheer up, for it would be another perfect day. 'There was a red sky last night. You be forgetting the signs, Betts.'

'You and your signs, old man. I didn't grow up surrounded by fields. It's you who should be the shepherd, not Harry or me. We're not born to it.'

Mr Callahan told them to finish their johnny-cakes and save their talk for those who were interested in hearing it. 'It's not right to force a man to come out here,' Harry Gibbs said woodenly. 'I don't know nothing about nothing out here.'

'Excepting that it's full of blacks,' Betts added, 'and that some men make their fortunes and others lose what little they had and those that do the work are just as likely to be speared in the back as die as paupers.'

'You two will be just fine then, for you've nothing to lose,' Mr Callahan answered brightly. 'Besides, I've heard tell that a convict can do well out here. Put your mind to the task at hand, do what you're told and you'll make a go of things.'

'If a man's not speared.' Gibbs slurped his tea.

Kate had grown used to the comforting crackle of tinder and the black sugary tea which followed, and with the chill wind blowing this morning the hot drink would be doubly welcome. Spring may have been upon them, yet the hills were unkind once the shadows encroached.

'Here you are, Miss Kate.' Mr Callahan deposited a pannikin of tea and a two johnny-cakes in her hands. 'There's sugar in your tea, just how you like it.' He lowered his voice. 'And I sprinkled a bit on the cakes.'

'You're too good to me, Mr Callahan.' She ate quickly, moistening her dry mouth with sips of tea, her eyes still crusty with sleep.

The bullocks were being walked back to the wagons by the convicts, ready to be hitched. Their complaining bellows signalled they would soon be leaving and it paid to be ready on time. Kate rolled up her bedding and, securing it with a leather strap, stowed it safely away, then she set about brushing her hair and gathering it into a bun at the nape of her neck.

Now that the convicts had left to attend to their allotted tasks, the soldiers and Mr Southerland gathered near the fire and broke the night's fast with gulps and belches as they ate, and then they too completed packing up their gear, rolling swags and kicking dirt onto the fire. By the time the bullocks were hitched Lieutenant Wilson was waiting as he did every morning to assist her up into the wagon, where, once seated, Mr Callahan would talk to her from the ground as he walked, barely drawing breath for the entire day. Kate knew the rest of the men thought it a great joke that she'd been lumbered with a man that Mr Southerland said had the vocal constitution of his dead mother-in-law. The comment made her wonder what happened to Mr Southerland's wife.

'I would be pleased to see you again.' Lieutenant Wilson held her hand for longer than necessary as Kate stepped up to her seat, a battered sea-chest. In the half-light the paleness of his skin made the young man appear almost sickly in pallor. He only ever spoke to her at this time. It was as if in the minutes between night and day, when features were partially concealed and the bustle of departure was upon them, that he felt comfortable in conversing with her, away from watchful eyes and the smirks of the men. 'You will take care, Miss Carter.'

Kate clasped the side of the wagon as the bullock team took a few steps forwards in anticipation. 'I fear you worry too much. There are plenty of women settling beyond the mountains.'

'Not so many where you are going. You will be in demand.'

Mr Callahan was at the lead, speaking to the animals as if they were children, reminding them of the cargo they carried and of the miles he expected the team to travel this day.

'Were you able to write to me you could send it care of the barracks at Parramatta.'

Kate should have guessed by the Lieutenant's attentiveness ever since they'd first met that his departure today would not occur without comment. 'You have honoured me with your attention, but

I have no idea how long I shall be away for.' He was a soft-hearted young man and for that quality alone Kate liked him. Over the past weeks she'd learnt a little of his life. The youngest son of a wealthy northern English family, whose father had purchased his commission, the Lieutenant was intent on proving his ability to both his family and himself. He would be a loyal friend, but it was clear that where Kate was concerned, such a relationship was not on his mind.

'Time matters little,' the Lieutenant pursued. 'I have been promised land. You would want for nothing.'

The Major approached on horseback as the faintest touch of colour tinged the sky, a pre-dawn pearling light. 'Lieutenant, if you've finished holding Miss Carter's hand perhaps we could get a move on?' His gaze lingered on Kate as Wilson backed away reluctantly. She busied herself, rearranging the shawl across her shoulders. Kate knew she should have said something, anything, at least thanked the Lieutenant for his interest. His was a fine offer, a far better offer than what may have been available to her if she'd been born in England.

'You will listen to George?' The Major's horse breathed a fine mist. 'He may not have the subtle niceties that you're used to, Kate, but he will keep you alive and you have yet weeks of travelling before you.'

It was the first time that he'd addressed her by her first name. 'Of course, and I wanted to thank you, Major, for staying longer. It has been something of a comfort to –'

'Call me James, Kate.' The mare lifted each leg in turn, shifting the weight on its feet.

Kate wanted to say that she would miss him, that without his solid presence some of the courage within her would depart when he did, but unlike the conversations she'd shared with the Lieutenant, the Major had maintained a level of politeness that until this morning had been difficult to breach.

'Our availability to protect Mr Hardy's expedition while escorting the troops to their next posting was fortuitous, however these extra days were unplanned, Kate. Please keep alert to your surrounds. That is my best advice.' He hesitated. 'The only advice I can give you, apart from wishing you a safe journey.'

'May I ask the cause of your concern?'

James gave the request some brief consideration. 'Where you are headed,' he said, 'there have been problems with the natives.' When this news was not commented upon, he continued, 'And in Maitland I learnt that a respected settler has been killed west of the mountains, his wife went missing and one of his convicts also speared. There are blacks on the run and a renegade white travels with them. No-one wishes to see another uprising.'

'And you think these outlaws are here?' Kate glanced over her shoulder. The memory of a line of natives chained neck to neck and being led down the main street of Maitland came to her.

'Doubtful, but certainly we must, all of us, be on our guard. Heed Mr Southerland's advices and you will do well, I have no doubt of it.'

'A compliment? Such a rare occurrence,' interjected George Southerland. 'You should remember that, Miss Carter, for James's praise is rarely given.' His firearm rested across his saddle as he rode towards them. He wore a kangaroo skin hat and possum hide coat, and blended with their environment like one of the dead animals he wore. 'They've gone west. Joe followed them for six miles.'

'Who has gone west?' Kate queried.

It was the Major who broke the short silence. 'Nothing you need worry about, Kate.'

George Southerland cleared his throat at the familiar use of her name and spat on the ground. 'There's not much point pretending the two of you are in some fancy drawing room in Syd-e-ney, James. Blacks, miss. Troublemakers. They kept their distance while we had the extra soldiers with us, which was just as well.

169

We can't fight them in the hills, they know the terrain too well, and we were real fortunate to have the company of the redcoats up to Maitland. But there's a nice open valley ahead of us and in that country, with our muskets and our horses, we have the advantage. We can chase the bastards down real quick on horseback and the crafty ones know that, so they took off for easier pickings. At least for the time being.'

'But what do they want?' The fact that natives had been following them and Kate had not noticed made her feel foolish.

'To cause trouble mostly, although they don't mind a twist of sugar, and they're right partial to a tomahawk, so pretty much anything that we've got, but usually as long as we keep moving we'll be right.' Mr Southerland's reply didn't comfort Kate. 'It's when we stop,' he continued, 'when the white man stays, that's when the problems start. This is their land, you see, and as far as they're concerned, we're taking it from them, but to travel through it? Well, most of the tribes are real hospitable, they'll show you where the water is, where the best grazing is for the horses and bullocks. Show them a bit of courtesy, be generous in return, give them a bit of tucker and the odd trinket and they'll wave you on your way. But stay put, well, that's when the troubles can begin if a person's not careful. And those that have gone before us haven't always given thought to the fact that the blacks consider this land theirs.'

'But how can they think it their land?' asked Kate, incredulous. 'New South Wales is a British colony.'

The Major crossed his wrists, resting them on the saddle. 'You see, George, *terra nullius*. No-one owned this land before the British Crown took possession of it.'

'Really?' The older man tugged at the brim of his hat. 'A bit of paper drawn to suit another's purpose means nothing to them.'

'For a British subject, George, you are inordinately disloyal.'

'Perhaps, but that doesn't change the facts.' Leaning from his mount Mr Southerland handed Kate a small pistol. It was a beautiful piece with an intricately engraved wooden handle. 'I've been saving this for you.'

'Thank you.'

'Do you know how to shoot?' the expedition leader asked.

'Of course she doesn't,' the Major interrupted.

'Yes, point and shoot.' Kate sounded more confident than she felt.

James's eyebrows lifted in amusement.

Mr Southerland chuckled. 'Close enough.' He beckoned for the flintlock back. 'Watch carefully.' Tipping black powder from a flask into the muzzle end, he then followed this with a round lead ball wrapped in a piece of paper. 'That's your shot. This,' he pulled a short rod from where it was stored on the underside of the barrel, 'is your ramrod and you push it all down hard. Add some powder – a small amount mind – to the flashpan at the top here and then close it up and put the safety on. To fire, undo the catch, cock, point and shoot.' He demonstrated. 'Understand?'

'And try not to shoot yourself or Mr Callahan,' James quipped.

Accepting the pistol, Kate tucked it into her skirt pocket. It was unnerving to think that they thought she may well need to protect herself.

Retrieving a map from his coat, Mr Southerland unfolded the parchment. Lifting the chart he studied the series of lines. The paper was cracked in places and frayed about the edges. The sight of the well-worn chart was comforting until Kate recalled the map that James had shown her prior to their departure. She wondered now if they were nearly beyond the known counties, if the engulfing whiteness which spread upwards from the line that signified the outer limits was close at hand. She couldn't help but feel that they were heading into oblivion. He pointed at a gap through the timber. 'A couple of miles of forest and then we're in open country for a bit. The going should be reasonable across the valley and it will be safer. We've got a good few weeks of wagon tracks to follow before we have to keep a look-out for the blazed trees that mark the trail towards the outer limits. If all else fails, we simply keep going until we reach land that hasn't been eaten out by livestock yet.'

'And the weather?' the Major queried.

'Weather, what weather?' The Englishman looked at his soldier friend as if he were daft. 'Joe tells me that the coming summer will be bad for all concerned. No grass is one thing, but water is life-blood for black and white alike.'

'Well, you'll not have to worry about muddy roads then.' The Major shook hands with his friend.

Mr Southerland lifted a shaggy eyebrow, folded the map and secured it in his pocket. 'Don't give those young troopers of yours too much of a hard time, James.' He touched his hat in deference to Kate. 'We've another solid day of travel, best we get a move on.' With a cluck of his tongue the horse trotted off.

'Callahan, keep an eye on Miss Carter,' the Major instructed the Scot. He nodded in Kate's direction, lingering as if there were words left unsaid.

She too felt compelled to say something, anything, but the Major was already reining his horse clear of the wagon, not waiting for Mr Callahan's reply.

'Aye, I'll do me best, Major Shaw, sir.' Placing his cabbage-tree hat on his head, he winked at Kate and then cracked a long-handled whip. Eight feet of plaited greenhide unfurled to snap at the leading bullocks up front. The wagon began to trundle across the rutted ground as Mr Callahan walked alongside the team of fourteen bullocks, guiding them through the trees, the second wagon following close behind.

James rode briefly beside Kate. 'Goodbye, Kate Carter.' He smiled.

Kate smiled back, but too soon he was tugging on the reins and turning to travel in the opposite direction. She wanted to look back over her shoulder, to crane her neck around the canvas dome of the wagon. Instead she gritted her teeth and focused on the moving animals.

⬥

Once the bullocks were walking at a steady pace, the Scotsman retraced his steps until he was level with Kate.

'Peas in a pod those two, the Major and that leader of ours.' He glanced ahead to where Mr Southerland was just visible. 'Both of them got a hankering for adventure. Had I my druthers over I'd never have done what I did and been forced to leave Scotland. It's bad enough to be branded a felon but to come here, to a land where everything can kill you – snake, spider, the pox, the natives – well, you have to wonder who decided to send a person to New South Wales. Of course it doesn't bother the likes of Southerland, the man's just trying to survive, and by all accounts he never applied to get his wife and child out here, unlike some of us. As for the Major, well, he's here to make his mark before returning to the Mother Country. He's got no interest in land out here. No, he's after a bit of adventure and then it's back to London and the high life. He's a toff and toffs have only ever got one person in mind – themselves. Keep the scum from the toffs' trough. That'd be his thinking.'

Kate didn't share Mr Callahan's opinion. 'You don't like the Major?'

'Miss Kate, the day the man gets off that horse of his to talk to the likes of us, I'll eat my hat.'

'Mr Callahan, I believe you have a problem with figures of authority.'

His grin revealed a missing eye-tooth. 'Aye, you've found me out. I do.' The Scotsman cracked the whip and the team kept plodding along to cries of 'move along there, you buggers', 'find your feet' and 'steady as'. Behind them the wagon load creaked and groaned. The bullocks lumbered onwards and out into a dark avenue of stately

173

trees. Kate tied the shawl securely about her shoulders and licked sun-dry lips.

'We should all have muskets,' Mr Callahan called to her as the bullocks walked on, their sloping shoulders and hefty rumps swaying from side to side as if a galleon upon the sea. 'But I'm glad for your sake that Mr Southerland gave you that fancy little piece. Where we're going, a man would have to be mad not to be able to protect his person. We should all be armed now. As for worrying about them blacks stealing, it's more likely they'd be lifting a spear in our direction.'

Kate huddled on the hard chest. The area they passed through was all woody plants and dense foliage, beyond which lay the unknown. She'd be pleased when they were back in more open country. In such places Kate was content to leave the discomfort of the dray and walk alongside the slow-moving wagon. 'We've not seen many natives,' she replied. 'Well, apart from the ones at Maitland. You'd think we'd see more of them, or at least hear them.'

'They be out there, you can put coin on that. Hiding behind that tree, or that one.'

Kate leant forward, examining the timber lining the track. She almost expected to see yellow eyes peering from between the woody plants. The trees were tall and straight, thick girthed and spaced so close together that it was almost as if they'd been planted.

'They was born out here, Miss Kate. They're like animals – knowledgeable, cunning. They know everything about this place. We know nothing. Best we all keep an eye out, for you never know when they'll come for us.'

It was unlike her companion to voice his concerns. Kate guessed he'd been aware of the blacks that had been tailing them and like the rest of their group had chosen to keep this fact from her, especially while their party was larger. Although she could have been annoyed at such collusion Kate was in fact grateful for their complicity. There had been much to contend with already without being in immediate fear of one's life.

'Maybe when we get to the farm, Mr Hardy will give you a musket,' Kate suggested, the weight of the pistol dragging at the folds of her skirt.

'Me? Not likely. I've only me ticket-of-leave, there's no muskets for the likes of me. I've heard tell some settlers allow it, on account of plain common sense, depending on what you were sent out for, of course. But Hardy? Southerland says he's a stickler for the rules. Which is why I keep me ticket in me pocket.' He rubbed it for luck. 'One day I'll get that pardon. In the meantime I'll work for wages and bide me time, again.'

'Again?'

'I've had the odd problem with authority.' He grinned. 'So there you have it, lass. You and me we're like chalk and cheese.'

'Oh, I don't know. There's not that much difference, Mr Callahan. My father was sent out for stealing.'

'A currency lass, eh? Aye, I heard such a whisper. It took you some time to spit that out. Well, a woman's got to be born with a bit of gumption to do what you're doing, miss. Good luck to you, I say, and if you need a helping hand with anything, I'm your man. Now what was we talking about yesterday?'

The stench of fire was on the wind. The acrid scent seemed to grow more powerful every day. 'The fires.'

'Ah yes.' He cracked the long whip, reminding the bullock team to retain their steady gait. 'The blacks are all about burning, burning, burning. One would think they lived on fire instead of water. They're trying to burn the whites out, Miss Kate. That's what it is, for if they burn the grasses, what will the livestock eat?'

'Mr Southerland told me it was so new grasses would grow, for the animals. The kangaroo and such-like.'

Mr Callahan rolled an aching shoulder. 'I've heard the same. He's got a name he has, our leader, for getting on with both black and white. He pacifies us all with stories tried and true and some-where in the middle is the truth.'

Kate shielded her face with the end of the shawl as the bullocks kicked up dirt and dust. The track they drove along was rutted and dry, the tree branches overlapping so it was as if they moved through a dim tunnel. A few hundred yards on, the pink comfort of dawn greeted them as they left the forest and entered an expanse of open country. She smiled at her companion, but Mr Callahan was focused on the route ahead, on Mr Southerland and his dapple-grey mare and . . . three figures.

Blacks.

The Aboriginals appeared between the wagon and Mr Souther-land, and ran directly towards them, throwing their spears in tandem. Kate screamed as a spear sailed directly at them. The warrior was tall and lean with a mass of dark hair and deep scars etched across his torso. In an instant Mr Callahan reached up, pulling her roughly. Kate fell to the ground with a thud and rolled on her side. The bullocks bellowed, the wagon rocked violently and lurched to a stop. The chickens within screeched as musket shot echoed.

Kate got to her hands and knees. Mr Callahan was running towards the lead of the bullocks, Mr Southerland was at the gallop, his musket directed towards one of the natives. Another shot followed and one of the attackers dropped to the ground. Dazed, Kate retrieved the pistol from the folds of her dress, ran to the edge of the trees and fell to her knees. Her hand trembled violently, the pistol wavered from left to right. With difficulty she removed the safety and tried to steady a raspy breath.

Wrenched to her feet and spun around in one movement, Kate looked up into the eyes of an Aboriginal. His hands were on her shoulders. There was a smell of animal fat, of the earth. A bone pierced his nose. He pushed her hard against a tree so that the scream within her was lost with the winding. His appraisal was brief, interested. Kate cocked the pistol and fired. Sparks flew. A burning sensation struck her hand. The native fell to the ground, clutching his stomach as she took a shocked step backwards. Feet away, the warrior with the matted hair and scars met her gaze. Then he was gone.

The black tracker, Joe, rode past her, his horse jumping the fallen logs amidst the timber, then he too disappeared into the scrub.

George Southerland galloped towards her and dismounted. 'Are you hurt?'

'No.' Kate couldn't take her eyes from the moaning man writhing on the ground before her. His hands clutched at his stomach.

Mr Southerland winced. 'It's a slow painful death you've given him, miss. But a kill is a kill, I suppose.'

'I thought . . . he touched me. I thought . . .'

'Come now.' Taking the pistol from Kate's shaking hand, he led her back to the wagon.

Behind them Betts and Gibbs had left their bullock team and joined Mr Callahan. Mr Southerland handed his musket and shot to the Scotsman. 'You know how to use it?'

'Aye.' The Scotsman took the firearm without further comment.

'Keep a lookout then.' He checked Kate's pistol as she leant against a wagon wheel, reloaded it and handed it back into her care. 'You'll be right. You did good, girl.'

Kate could barely find the pocket amidst the folds of her skirt, her hands shook so badly. As their expedition leader climbed into the rear of the covered wagon to emerge moments later with another musket and extra ammunition, she dry-retched onto the ground.

'Here.' Mr Southerland handed her a bottle.

'No, I'm fine really.'

'Drink it, Kate. It'll fortify you somewhat.'

It was rum. The drink burnt all the way down, but it stayed down and to her surprise Kate took another gulp. Their leader took two big swigs, stuffed the bottle inside a saddle-bag and then, remounting, gave chase to the fleeing black, and Joe.

'Damnation.' The bullocks bellowed and kicked out in fear and then one of the two lead animals fell to the ground. Mr Callahan wrenched the spear free of the animal's mid-section as Mr Southerland galloped past. The Scot studied the spear, which had broken off inside the beast, and threw the weapon away in disgust.

'Will it live?' Kate walked closer, her legs still shaky. The bullock's back legs scraped the dirt as it kicked out.

'No, he's near dead as a saint and just as useless to us out here.' The man shook his head. 'Damn fine beast. It's just a waste, a waste I tell you.'

Betts and Gibbs scanned their surrounds. 'That be a first.' Betts gestured to the musket. 'Maybe we'll be armed as well.'

'And a good thing that would be,' Gibbs decided. 'Even the lass has a pistol.'

Mr Callahan passed Betts the yoke key and ordered them to unhitch the dead bullock, while he stood guard waiting for the Englishman's return. 'They were a well-matched pair, my leaders,' he told Kate as the metal bow that secured each bullock pair to a wooden yoke was undone and the central chain coupling each pair together in tandem was disconnected.

Two shots sounded from the bush and minutes later Mr Southerland reappeared with Joe. They rode swiftly back to the stationary wagons as the two convicts took one of the less experienced bullocks out of the team and tied him to the rear of the wagon, then they backed up the team and re-hitched the old and new leaders.

'Are there enough to pull the load?' asked Kate.

'Aye, lass. We'll be right,' Mr Callahan advised. 'We've brought extra in case of loss.'

'Anymore harmed?' Mr Southerland didn't wait for a reply. He ran an experienced eye over the bullocks and then the dead animal. 'Cut a hind leg off it, wrap it in a blanket and put it in the rear of one of the wagons. We might as well treat ourselves to a bit of beef. Any problems, Mr Callahan?'

'No problems, Mr Southerland. We'll manage with what we've got, though they were a doughty pair, those two.'

'Good as you are then.' He flung a knife in the dirt at Betts' feet and told him to cut the leg and be quick about it. The convict's lip curled. He glanced from their leader to the black tracker on horseback but he did as he was told and, with Gibbs' assistance, carried it to their wagon. 'I'd be keeping a watch on things, Mr Callahan,' their leader suggested.

'Aye, you can be assured of that.' He lifted the musket.

'Keep it.' The men exchanged nods. 'We could be lucky, but I'm expecting we won't. News travels fast out here. The blacks will know we're coming, how many are in our party and what stock we have. And I fear we haven't made a good first impression,' he said sarcastically.

'They be after the muskets then, do you think?' the Scotsman asked.

'Those who have seen them know their limitations. The blacks prefer their spears, they're faster and more accurate, unless you're up close and friendly like Kate was. They'd rather use muskets to shoot birds.'

'Did you get the other one?' asked Kate, hoping so.

'He was long gone.' Mr Southerland trotted away to take up position at the front but this time he stayed closer to the wagons, his musket across his thighs.

Joe reappeared from the timber line to canter his horse across and joined him.

Kate climbed up into the wagon and sat on the chest, her heart still pounding as Mr Callahan enticed the bullocks to movement. The animals were testy. The wagon rolled back and forth unsteadily. She would get off and walk in a few minutes but her legs trembled at the thought of what she'd done. Point and shoot, she'd said earlier that morning.

Ahead, Mr Callahan snapped his whip, once, twice and then resumed his position near the leaders as finally the beasts began to move. The black tracker shared a few words with Mr Southerland and then rode back to Kate's wagon and, taking up a position alongside, kept pace with the bullock team.

Kate felt unnerved by Joe's presence. They'd never spoken directly to each other, which was as it should be, and yet she sensed his dislike, although whether his perceived animosity was for her personally or their expedition it was impossible to tell. 'Can I help you?' Kate asked, her fingers grasping the lid of the chest as the vibrations from the rough ground shook the wagon. Around Joe's neck hung a metal disc with the letter *J* carved into it. Kate wondered at this trinket, looking quickly away when Joe saw her staring at it. In the grass lay the shot man. The team trundled past the killing spot and Kate couldn't help but look. Red blood pooled on luminous skin and flies were settling on the body. Lifting a hand to her mouth, she turned away. For all the danger they'd been in, there seemed to be something terribly wrong with what she'd done.

Joe turned to her. 'You take a good look, Missus.' He stared openly, his eyes hard and bright. 'Welcome to blackfella country. You just done murder.' He twitched the reins and rode away.

❧ Chapter 12 ❧

1837 September – following the songlines

The rifle shots echoed loudly across the countryside. Bidjia lifted a hand to halt their progress and then together the three men began to run down the hill in the direction of the noise to investigate. It was not yet mid-morning but the men were aware that the base of the tree-lined hills that bordered the valley below was a good place for an ambush. They kept their weapons at the ready, alert to anyone who may be escaping up into the safety of the slopes as they descended. They would be the unexpected strangers, once again moving through lands belonging to another tribe. Small stones scattered as they ran, but soon their path was slowed by the steep and rough terrain and by the time they reached the bottom, nearly an hour had passed.

Bidjia, convinced that any blacks in the area would have already moved on, took up position behind a clump of trees, the two younger men flanking him. Jardi's breath came hard and fast.

'You are growing slow, Jardi,' Bidjia complained. 'Soon Bronze-wing will outrun you.'

The younger man grunted as they squatted on the ground, peering through the trees. The squeak of wood and leather carried intermittently on the air.

'Wagons.' Adam leant on his musket, the wooden stock lodged in the dirt. 'Well, I guess if they were attacked, it's over now.' He didn't mean to sound disappointed but it was some weeks since he'd spoken to a white person and, although they were on the run, Adam found himself more than willing to render assistance to his kind if it were needed.

'We will leave this place and cross back to the west,' Bidjia announced.

Since leaving the Lycett farm Bidjia had been most careful in frequently altering the direction they travelled in. Adam knew that the older man was right to do so as the path they now journeyed along was heavily settled. It would be better if they did head west and away from the scattering of farms.

They waited with interest for the wagons to reach them. Their leader came into view first, a straggly-limbed white with a dense beard, dressed in skins. Adam knew his sort, a rough but capable adventurer, undoubtedly vital to the holding to which the wagons travelled. He was accompanied by an Aboriginal. Both were on horseback.

'Guide,' Bidjia said softly.

'And no livestock,' Adam added, 'so they're resupplying a holding with provisions.'

The voice of the teamster, a Scotsman, rang out loud and clear as he called out to the bullocks; the crack of the long rawhide whip snapping smartly in his hands. The wagon drew closer until it was level with their position behind the trees. Adam watched as a woman came into view. She stopped walking and, removing the straw hat she wore, turned in the direction where they hid in the timber. He knew she would not be able to see them, they were well-concealed, and he lifted a leafy branch obstructing his line of sight in order to get a clearer view.

The girl was a dark-haired beauty, slim of figure and of middling height. She appeared to pinch the bridge of her nose as if exhausted. A hand strayed to the skirt she wore and from within the folds of the material a pistol was revealed. She studied the weapon, holding it at arm's length, as if she were considering throwing the firearm away, but eventually she placed it back in her pocket and kept on walking.

They waited as the second wagon lumbered into view. Two rough-looking types clothed in convict garb walked alongside the bullocks. Adam expected more riders, a man suited to being the young woman's husband, brother or father perhaps, but no-one else followed. Her inclusion in the party seemed at odds with the people the girl travelled with and he couldn't help but wonder what or who had led her to travel northwards. Clearly it had been too long since he'd experienced female company and the chances of that happening now were becoming more remote by the day.

'Come.' Bidjia was already moving uphill.

The dust rose as the last wagon trundled past. Adam observed the sway of the girl's skirts and the way her hand lifted to the wide-brimmed hat on her head when a gust of wind threatened to blow it away.

Jardi thumped him on the chest. 'Come, this is not the time to be looking for a woman.'

'No, we are meant to be finding one for you,' Adam countered.

Jardi grinned as they picked their way through the timber.

'You be better with one of ours,' Bidjia told him. 'White woman too much trouble.'

Adam laughed, but quietly he decided that some women were worth a little strife.

❧ Chapter 13 ❧

1837 October — towards the white space
on the map

Mr Southerland had informed the expedition that he believed that there were only ten days to go before they reached their destination. But that was before Mr Callahan's bullock dray became bogged crossing a muddy creek. Kate had been forced to wade through the mud to the bank and it was here she now sat, surrounded by the wagon's contents, which had been removed to lighten the load. Amidst barrels and sacks, trunks and wooden crates she remained, her palms planted firmly on the ground, grateful for the lack of passage. It seemed as if she still moved for the endless momentum of bumpy travel stayed with her even when stationary.

A few hundred yards away the men heaved on thick ropes attached to the lead bullock's yokes. There were yells and curses and the crack of a whip and more than once they halted in their task and surveyed the few inches they'd managed to drag the wagon forward. Kate observed the seemingly useless attempt to recover the dray through eyes half-closed against a too-bright sun. The Major and his men would have added significantly to the manpower required but they were long gone. In their absence, the trip seemed never-ending, the days grew longer and the men edgier. Another bullock had been speared in the past week. The native had run towards them, thrown the spear and disappeared into the scrub. On other occasions the natives followed them at a distance for a whole day and then melted into the landscape. Kate understood now this was not white man's country. She kept the pistol on her person and scanned the surrounding land nervously as everyone else did.

Theirs was a solemn procession. Mr Southerland took the lead, followed by Kate and Mr Callahan, and then the two convicts and the second bullock dray. As they journeyed further northwards, conversation became limited. Even the rooster eventually stopped his daily crowing, a bad sign in Mr Callahan's opinion and silently Kate agreed. It was as if the quiet which they travelled through had invaded their souls. So lonely and desolate had the country become that the call of a crow came to signal despair, an owl, the depth of the unknown surrounding them.

Strangely, sitting on the creek bank, it was heartening to hear the men shout and swear, even though their comments were shockingly unsavoury. It made Kate feel alive, gave hope that even out here they as a group had a voice which might be heard.

They'd seen no-one for weeks, apart from a dilapidated humpy that had housed a man and two native boys. They had come across the dwelling by accident, having taken a detour to bypass some fallen trees. There was no thought of Kate venturing near the dwelling. Ordered to stay with the wagons while Mr Southerland and Joe had spoken to the inhabitant, they returned with little news, other than to say that the man was a loner, a runaway no doubt, who was only interested in tobacco and sugar. The man had watched them as the wagons trundled away.

Picking at the drying mud that encased her feet, Kate bashed the heels of her wrecked shoes together. They would need to be sun-dried before she had any hope of removing the sticky black sludge. She hoped for fresh water before they reached the Hardys' run, to wash her body and hair, to finally eat more than the kangaroo, birds and bread they existed on. Every day she thought of the orchard left behind and of the barrels of preserved oranges and lemons behind the dray's seat. During the long afternoons as their small party travelled onwards, the scent of the fruit tantalised in the heavy air. Kate knew it was just her imagination, that the citrus enticed through its very existence, but it did not stop her thinking of prising the barrels open and stuffing her mouth with the sweetness within.

The dray and its contents were the heart of the venture. Theirs was a travelling store, holding provisions for the Kables and the farm's inhabitants. There would be no more trips south for at least a year once they arrived, Mr Southerland explained in the early days of their journey when Kate had remarked upon the quantity of goods. It seemed that many a settler had been forced to abandon their expeditions to a new run when their provisions were lost or spoilt en route. It was impossible for most to survive without supplies on the frontier and there was also the problem of cost. Kate learnt that goods were extraordinarily expensive and in many cases could not be replaced by those who'd spent their savings. There were those who ran out of supplies before they'd established themselves and, after months of living only on meat, grew grievously ill. Some died. Such stories made all in Kate's party protective of their cargo. For a loss of stores affected everyone – settler and convict alike. There was flour, salt, sugar, tea, tobacco and grain. Apparently the wheat crop had failed and seed was urgently needed for the coming year and that most precious of staples, bread. There were also vegetable seeds and two potted fruit plants, seedlings. Miraculously they were still alive, although watering had been infrequent.

The men heaved. The timber wagon groaned. The bullocks' muscled shoulders rippled as the animals dug their hooves into the swill at their feet. They managed one foot, two and then with a jolt the lumbering animals rushed forward, pulling the wagon free. The men gave a cheer. Nothing was broken. With the wagon checked and double-checked for any damage, the bullock team was led to shade.

'We'll rest here,' Mr Southerland advised as the men fell to the ground exhausted. Overhead the sun grew hot. Sticky black flies antagonised eyes, noses and mouths. In the distance the land grew hazy with heat.

'Is there clean water near, Mr Southerland?' asked Kate, sipping from a waterbag.

'Joe's gone a-looking.' Sinking to the ground he upended a bootful of sloshy water. 'That was lucky. I wouldn't like to have arrived having lost that load.'

It was too hot to sleep in the middle of the day. Kate always felt listless afterwards if she did close her eyes like the others. In spite of her nervousness and the strict rules laid down by Mr Southerland, she'd taken to walking, always keeping in sight of where they camped. Today was no different. As the men drifted off, she left them to skirt the listless creek upstream and down, stooping to collect shiny pebbles, sticks and branches. Most would be thrown away on leaving but the objects gave Kate something to examine while she waited for the trip to recommence. Some items she kept, dropping them onto the dirt from the dray, as if one day she would return this way and her markers would lead her back to Sydney.

Ahead, in their path lay a line of stony hills. Mr Southerland promised that once they reached the other side that they would come upon a well-watered valley, with excellent pasture, bounded on each side by a bold and elevated rocky range. His description was certainly compelling, however, before such a splendid sight was reached there was still a couple of days' travel, and water was vital. A half-empty barrel of water for human consumption was all that remained on one of the drays. Of more concern were the bullocks and horses.

Along the bank the men still dozed. Kate wandered through the trees, dragging a fallen branch behind her in order to find her way back. She'd not gone far and was admiring the lightly timbered country when she came across the skeletal remains of three humans. They lay where they'd fallen. Their clothes tattered by the wind, sun and rain, their swags in the dirt by their sides. It was such a dismal sight to stumble upon that Kate simply stood and stared. It was as if they'd not had the strength to carry on. Maybe they'd died of hunger, or perhaps the same creek that bogged the dray was also dry when they'd walked through here.

So intent were her thoughts that Kate didn't hear the four blacks walk out of the scrub. They were upon her before she had a chance to run. Nervously she began walking backwards, aware they studied every move, conscious of the snapping of twigs as her mud-crusted shoes found purchase on the uneven ground. She reached for the pistol, her progress halted by a tree. She backed hard into the thick trunk, and screamed.

'You alright, Missus? These blackfellas heard your mob is all.'

It was Joe. The guide joined the four blacks. 'They okay. I tell them Mr George not sit down here. We just passing through.'

Her throat was dry and raspy. 'The dray got bogged,' Kate found her voice. 'But it's out now.'

One of the native men, a tall individual with a painted chest and a querying stare, approached her. Kate wanted to run. Instead she pushed her shoulder blades tight against the tree trunk, dug her nails into the bark and, although frightened, held her ground.

'They heard of white man, but this one not seen white man, especially white woman,' Joe explained.

That didn't make Kate feel any safer. The black walked straight up to her and touched her cheek, rubbing her skin. Kate flinched and turned her head.

'He think you spirit from across the sea, that beneath the paleness there will be black, maybe you dead family.'

Kate pushed the man's hand away. 'I don't think so.'

Unperturbed, the Aboriginal ran a hand across her breast and shoulder then he fingered the material of her skirt. Finally he tried to lift her dress to see what was underneath.

She brushed his hand away. 'Stop it.'

'Step away.' George Southerland was at her side, his musket lifted. 'What did I tell you about wandering off?'

The blacks bolted, hiding behind some distant trees.

'They not all see white man but they heard about white man's thunder.' Joe gestured to the musket. 'No harm, Boss. I tell Missus they not see whitefella, they think you come across the sea from the place of the ancestors. They not realise there be more lands beyond the water.'

'How can they not know that?' Kate asked curtly. She suspected that Joe had enjoyed her discomfort.

''Cause they only know this land, they have no sense that there be more. You stay here long enough, Missus, then you too will learn this land enough. We don't want no trouble with another.'

George lowered his firearm and gradually the blacks reappeared. 'Did you find water, Joe?'

'Yes, Boss. Good crick two mile. Rough travelling.'

'Well, we'll have to go slow. What do they want?'

Joe turned to the natives and, in a mixture of pigeon English and a local dialect, repeated the question. The same man who had subjected Kate to such scrutiny responded.

'Tomahawk, Boss. And maybe sugar,' Joe interpreted.

'Very well, and they'll give us safe passage?'

Joe pointed to the stony hills that were knife-edge sharp against the horizon. 'Yes, Boss. Then you be in Mr Stewart's place, big run, big station.'

'Stewart's done well,' he told Kate. 'It was somewhat of a shock for Samuel Hardy to reach the valley ahead only to discover that a Scotsman had already claimed 40,000 acres of it.' On turning to leave, he noticed the remains on the ground. The Englishman kicked one of the bodies. 'Poor blighters.' When he picked up the swags, the material fell apart. 'Ran out of water I reckon, or the sun-sickness got them.' The bush was quiet in the midday heat. Lifting his hat, he wiped at the sweat on his brow. 'No rain since we last came through, Joe.'

'Everything get plenty thirsty soon.' The tracker stared at Kate. 'Whitefella have plenty problem then. Blackfella, cattle and sheep, bush animals, all want water, all want food.'

'One thing you can be assured of in this country is drought, Joe, we're agreed on that. And you, Miss Carter, it's a hard land. If you don't want to end up like them,' he pointed to the bodies, 'I suggest you not go wandering off again.'

'But we cannot leave them, Mr Southerland.'

He didn't give the dead a backward glance. Increasing her pace Kate caught up with him. 'Mr Southerland, we must do something. We must at least bury them and say the proper words out of respect.'

'Respect? They didn't have much respect for the land they found themselves in and I think the time for burial is long over for those men.'

'As Christians, Mr Southerland, it is our duty to ensure that those men are accorded the proper rights. Surely in our leaving of Sydney we have not also left behind the fundamentals of civilised society,' Kate said indignantly.

'You believe in all that, do you? I thought you had more sense. But it's to be expected, I suppose, with you having lived with a Reverend.'

'I-I don't believe. It's just that there are certain practices which mark the civilised from the uncivilised and —'

'Miss Carter, look about you. We are in the middle of nowhere. Outnumbered by blacks though you don't see them all. But I see them. Every day there is some sign that tells me we are travelling across an old land and the people whose territory it is have been here for a very long time. The trees carry their markings, the waterways their camping spots, the smoke you have seen has been caused by them. They're everywhere. You walk into the timber and scream at the sight of them and truly I wonder that you were not speared, for women aren't immune from attacks and few people are lucky twice.' He drew breath and adjusted the musket on his shoulder. 'You were lucky. Joe tells me that the clans in this area are peaceful. And we're lucky we've made it this far with no deaths, excepting two bullocks and a dent to my pride. But it is my task to ensure that this expedition reaches its final destination and having already been delayed for a good part of the day, I will not stop to bury those who, whether it be through their own making or not, have fallen foul of this land. They are dead. They know not whether they are buried or not, miss. This is a harsh place. If you've not the stomach for it, you should not have come.'

Kate clenched her fists together, rushing to think of an appropriate retort. 'You are no Christian, Mr Southerland.'

The man grinned. 'Well, miss, that's one thing I never professed to be.'

Kate's fingernails dug into her hands. Some feet away Joe observed this exchange with a scornful grin. If her mother were still alive, a daughter's letters home would be of little comfort, for surely Kate travelled with the worst of men; convicts, one black and a heathen. Hardly the company Lesley Carter would have hoped for for her only child.

The group continued through the timber and out onto the creek flats. The four Aboriginal men trailed their progress, as Kate tried to keep pace with the quick strides of the tracker and Mr Southerland. The men were busy debating their intended route and, once satisfied as to the distance to water and the next camping ground, they began to discuss the news the tracker had gleaned from their new escorts.

To the north there was fighting between black and white. Shepherds had been murdered while a settler and a convict had been wounded and another convict killed while erecting a hut to the north-west.

'One of the Beeton men?' George picked up a twig from the ground, chewing it thoughtfully between his teeth. 'Shepherds is one thing, but attacking that family won't ease the situation. They'll be onto the troopers about that.'

'This my land. Big tribe. Very powerful.' Joe strung the words out slowly. 'Not all clans sit down and watch whitefella take their land. There is anger.'

'I'd imagine the Beetons feel the same way, Joe. Well, we best be extra careful from now on.'

'Some of the settlers been riding out after the blacks, Boss. Some of them be my mob, they chase, Boss. It don't sound good, Boss.'

The leader of the expedition stopped at the boggy creek. 'It never is. Tell Mr Callahan to supply you with sugar, Joe. The tomahawk they can have when we make it to the stony hills.'

The tracker didn't respond, although it seemed there was more he wanted to say.

'And, Joe, when you've finished, show those two convicts those skeletons. It's been some time since we stopped putting their leg-irons on at night and a bit of a reminder of what can happen to a runaway is always helpful.'

'Can they be trusted?' Kate whispered as Joe and the Aboriginals headed for the wagons. Mr Callahan stood warily on their approach.

'The convicts? They won't last two days out here if they make a run for it, but some try.'

'I meant the natives.'

'As long as we keep our word, give them what they want and move on, but who knows? All we can do is make for Hardy's lands. Once we're there, we'll be safer.'

Kate didn't feel as confident. 'And Joe?'

A look of annoyance crossed the expedition leader's face. 'Joe's been with me many years.'

'I just wonder if it's such a good idea –'

'Don't stir up trouble, Miss Carter. That altercation back there was of your own doing.'

As Mr Southerland began to oversee the reloading of the wagon, Mr Callahan cautiously handed over a small quantity of sugar. This was followed by a pouch of tobacco and two wooden pipes. Joe passed the items onto the blacks, but not before pocketing some of the tobacco for himself. Kate knew that Mr Southerland's opinion of their tracker should be enough, but after so many weeks in the bush she'd developed her own instincts as to who could and couldn't be trusted. Out of their small expedition party, only their leader and Mr Callahan could be relied upon. The Scot had left behind a family on his assignment to the colony and was a lonely man trying to live out his life as best he could. As for the others, Jim Betts and Harry Gibbs were opportunists. They begged for extra food, scrambled for the best spots to unroll their swags each night and slyly watched the camp's undertakings.

After Joe had shown Betts and Gibbs the bodies in the scrub, the four Aboriginals moved off to the shade of a tree. Joe sat cross-legged beside them as the others dug out hollows in the cool sand in which to lie.

Mr Callahan was calling to her to make ready as Betts and Gibbs finished tying the contents of the dray down with ropes. 'Why doesn't the black lend a hand?' Betts tied a secure knot on the last rope. 'It's not right we be working like dogs while he sits.'

'He's got a job,' Mr Callahan reminded them.

'Give him another.' Gibbs wiped sweat from his brow. 'A black shouldn't be working less than the likes of us. It goes against the natural order of things.'

Kate waited until the two convicts were out of earshot. 'I don't trust those two one bit, Mr Callahan. They watch me at times, you know, and they don't mind me knowing that they do.'

'I know, lass.' He tapped the side of his head. 'I'm onto them, but I reckon they're harmless. If the truth be told, both Betts and Gibbs are nervous nellies. They lived their lives in the streets of London. Nothing could have prepared them for this.'

'And what about you, Mr Callahan? Were you prepared?'

The Scot gave a lopsided grin. 'I'm of the country meself, but prepare a man for this? I can't say I had any inkling.' He cleared his throat. 'My lass, Lizzy, well she'd be waggling her finger at me if she were here. Always getting myself in strife, she'd say. But then no matter the troubles, my Lizzy would crinkle up those dark eyes of hers and tell me that even if a person failed, at least he'd been trying. Come now, you'll set me thinking about me bonny wife all the rest of this fine day, Miss Kate, and we can't have that. Me bullocks don't like me maudlin.'

The day grew hotter, a dense heavy heat that pulled and tugged at a person's body. Some days Kate felt as if the land and the heat and the dusty haze would consume their small party. For the hot breath of the bush was remorseless and during each day of their travel the hours stretched on and on like a funeral cortege. At night Kate dreamt of an endless winding road, which eased across the green hills of the coast to merge with the brown plains and hills of a land too vast to comprehend. It was important she remain positive but her thoughts were beginning to turn inwards, and at times when the camp was quiet and the sky star-bright, there were tears. It was a hard thing to be a woman and to be alone in the world. To have no kin. To have murdered a man.

She'd taken to recalling the environs of the Reverend's cottage. In particular, the fig tree at the end of the garden. The trunk was massive, its rough bark grey-brown but it was the leaves that fascinated. They were large and leathery and deep green in colour. A gust of wind lifted the dirt along the drying creek. Her skirts fluttered as the hot blast buffeted her forwards. She lifted a hand to stop the straw hat from being blown away. It hardly afforded any shade. In the mornings the sun slanted from the east as it rose, flushing her cheeks red. In the afternoon it felt as if a thousand needles were attacking her skin. Kate needed no looking-glass to know that, like the land around her, she was burning up as well.

❖

A week or so later, George Southerland let out a loud *coo-ee* and was immediately answered by Joe. The two men met under a stand of trees and spoke animatedly, their horses nickering quietly. The sun was yet to find a position mid-sky and the pearly blue of the heavens betrayed the coming heat. Kate wiped at her forehead, her hand clutching and releasing her skirt as she lifted it free of shrubby bushes and small spikey-leafed trees. Beside her the wagon creaked and groaned, the lumbering bullocks plodding over the faint tracks in the dirt. All waited for the final confirmation that the Hardy farm was within sight.

'There!' The Scotsman pointed to a blazed tree. The axe mark, sure and strong, shone like a beacon. 'Didn't I tell you the Englishman would get us there? And he has.'

Kate recalled no such conversation, but they had put their lives in the care of this leader and the man had apparently delivered them to the promised destination.

'A job well done, aye, very well done,' the Scotsman enthused.

The first of the blazed trees, which marked the final fifteen mile of travel, had been reached yesterday and it was all they could do not to crack the raw-hide whips and rush the bullocks onwards, to journey a little farther in the dark. Mr Southerland, true to the disciplined nature shown throughout the long weeks, was in no rush. *As sure as we move*, he'd told them, *we'll come to grief.* A broken wheel, a bullock gone lame in the night . . . Better to wait until piccaninny dawn and then set out.

Kate began thinking of a warm hip bath, on the surface of which a number of muslin herb bags floated. There was a cosy bed in her imaginings, one with an arrangement of outer curtains, valances and accoutrements, which she was sure Mrs Kable enjoyed. Hers would be of slightly lesser quality to that of Mrs Hardy's, however it was not beyond assumption that a lady's companion would enjoy the trappings of the position for which she was employed. When she thought of the house she would soon enter her mind drew a fancy picture of a dwelling not dissimilar to the Kables' home. The thought of female companionship also bolstered her thoughts.

'You keep that smile, Miss Kate, for I reckon it's a sign of better things.'

'I do believe you're right, Mr Callahan.' Kate rubbed the small of her back and began to hum a tune.

'You make sure you come and say hello once we're settled, Miss Kate. I know you'll be at the big house and all, but it would make me right happy to see you now and then. I imagine my girl would be about your age now. Tubby little thing she was, took after me.' He sniffed and wiped his nose on a dirty shirt-sleeve. Kate reached to pat his arm, but thought better of it, her own eyes damp. They'd been travelling for over seven weeks. The sense of relief at nearing the end of the trip, the creep of exhaustion, of gratefulness, threatened to turn her weepy and Kate forced herself to concentrate on the path ahead. The dray passed through a dense stand of trees, the branches filtering the sun's rays and throwing patches of light and shade on the lumbering beasts ahead. The rooster let out a weak crow.

'Well, I'll be,' the Scotsman exclaimed. They shared a laugh.

They trailed Mr Southerland and Joe for a number of miles. The riders merged with the bush frequently, managing to reappear just when confirmation was required as to the direction to head. But Mr Callahan grew surer with every mile travelled and soon he was counting the axe marks in the trees and not bothering with the location of their guides. It was some time before Kate realised that the agitation that had crept upon her was not due to the antici- pation of finally nearing their destination.

The first native stood some distance from the trail. The second, a little closer. Kate's stomach lurched.

'I see them.' Mr Callahan reached into the moving wagon for his loaded musket and then let out a *coo-ee*. 'You'll be right, lass. Don't be a-feared.'

It was as if the bush came alive. Trees grew extra limbs, stubby bushes moved. The natives came from all directions, mainly old men, women and children. They kept to the sides of the track, like spectators watching a street parade. The women were bare- breasted with barely a skirret of clothing to cover their private areas, while the little ones were naked. Kate blushed to be in the company of men as the two convicts in the second wagon called out to the women in a rush of enthusiasm. She moved closer to the moving wagon.

'They be God's creatures,' Mr Callahan enthused. 'God's creatures.'

Kate was not so taken with the gathered natives, not after the attack and the subsequent fear they'd all lived with, although she had to admit they were certainly a fine looking people; a marked contrast to the wretched souls wandering around Sydney. These people were tall and lean, the women and men handsome and proud. A wide-eyed child stared at Kate from its mother's arms and then pressed its face against the woman's shoulder.

Ahead, Mr Southerland came into view. He lifted a hand in greeting. 'You'll be right,' he shouted. 'This mob lives on the Hardy farm. Through the trees apiece, you'll come to a ridge. You can see the huts from there.' Dismounting, he stood talking to a number of the natives. As the wagons moved closer it was clear that one of the Aboriginals was a favourite, for Mr Southerland was petting her face and hair and giving the young woman a trinket from his pocket, a beaded necklace. Kate could only guess at their relationship and it made her more than uncomfortable.

'There be no women up here, miss.' The Scotsman seemed to have read her thoughts. 'And men have needs, after all.'

Kate's cheeks grew hot. The bullocks walked through the next clump of trees and then traversed a slight ridge. Kate kept close to the teamsters as they passed the Englishman and the native girl. Old men and women joined the couple and patted Mr Southerland's arms and back. Despite the strangeness of this welcome, Kate thought the scene resembled a man returning to dear friends and family.

The bible lessons Kate had endured taught that the Lord God had made all creatures but the natives were a people apart, unknowable. Fraternisation between black and white was wrong and Mr Southerland – as a civilised Englishman, a subject of the crown – should have known better. What their black guide thought about this greeting was unknown. Joe sat astride his horse, speaking to the gathered people in their tongue, pointing and gesturing to the wagons as if a minister of the cloth advising his congregation. On passing, he caught Kate's attention. His look was undecipherable.

From the top of the rise directly before them was a small valley and, on the other side, a wind-blown hill. A curl of smoke drew the eye and on closer inspection two huts could be seen framed by trees on the western side. It was a desolate spot but the position afforded a clear view of part of the valley. Mr Callahan kept a firm hand on the dray's brake as the bullocks lurched down the slope. A small group of cattle were feeding into a westerly wind, while mobs of sheep were being herded to the east by a single shepherd. The Scot was moved by the sight. 'Could almost be home.' 'Course the hills would be bigger and it'd be colder and greener and there'd be trickling streams and deer, and less trees, and there'd be cairns to mark the trail, but it could nearly be home.'

Kate suppressed a laugh. She would miss seeing Mr Callahan.

On reaching the flats, Mr Southerland, devoid of his admirers, galloped through the trees and drew level with them. 'As good a sight as a man could wish for.' He reined his horse in, keeping pace with the wagon. 'I reckon the Hardys will be pleased to see us. Be prepared for days of questioning, Miss Carter. I doubt they've seen anybody else since I left months ago.'

'And the main house, Mr Southerland, is it behind those trees?' Kate strained to be polite after what she'd just witnessed, although her own enthusiasm at nearing the end of their journey fought for release.

The Englishman lifted a shaggy eyebrow. 'That is the house. The smaller hut is the kitchen. Behind it a quarter-mile is the men's hut.'

Kate looked at the distant buildings and looked again. Surely it wasn't possible. The structures were partially circled on the north and western side by trees. While behind them, the steep hill rose to a timbered peak. The two buildings jutted out from the side of the mound in precarious fashion, and it appeared as if at any moment both huts could slide down the side of the hill.

'If you were expecting the likes of the Kable farm, I fear you'll be disappointed. Best you forget the comforts of Syd-e-ney, Miss Carter, and any expectations that might be filling your head. Here we only have what we bring with us, or what we can grow or make ourselves.'

She'd travelled for weeks on end, very nearly been speared by natives, *for this*? The thought of Reverend Horsley with his comfortable cottage and ordered life made Kate momentarily stop mid-stride. She thought she would sick up the knob of bread and black tea eaten hours previously.

'You best rest the bullocks a mile further on, Mr Callahan, no more than a half hour. We want to have these supplies unloaded and the bullocks unharnessed before dark.'

'As you say, Mr Southerland.'

'And the musket, if you please.'

With reluctance Mr Callahan passed the rifle back to the Englishman and their expedition leader rode away. 'Mr Southerland will do right by us. He'll speak to this Hardy and tell 'em what's what.' The Scot displayed his missing tooth in a wide-lipped grin. 'Come on, lass,' he encouraged, although his enthusiasm had diminished somewhat, 'there's houses and people and a new life to reckon with. We must all make the best of things and remember, you can leave eventually.'

Kate thought of the return trip and gave a wan smile. What lay behind her was little better than the alternative ahead. Dispirited, she placed one foot in front of the other. They made their way across the narrow valley, following the ruts of previous wagon tracks. The bullock teams were left to meander slowly as the Englishman rode on ahead.

Mr Callahan and Kate walked side by side. 'You'll get used to it, Miss Kate, we all will.'

Kate doubted it. Behind them, the natives followed at a short distance, while in front rode Joe. Kate couldn't help but think of the Pied Piper. When they stopped to rest she remained close to the wagons and Mr Callahan, for the natives were curious. They stopped as well, pointing and chatting and sitting in groups nearby.

'Mr Southerland will be cooling his heels with a drop of tea, I'd reckon.' Mr Callahan waved at the flies about his face, which quickly resettled, despite his attempt to shoo them away. 'By the time we arrive at the run he'll have handed over the bill of sale for the wool. I heard that they overlanded the sheep with seven months' worth of wool, shore them a scant three months later and then returned the fleeces to Syd-e-ney so the lease could be obtained and the first clip delivered, simultaneous like. So the monies will be in and spent on these here supplies, I reckon. Of course Southerland will have us lot summed up nicely.' He noticed Kate's startled face. 'That's his job, lass. Get the supplies and the help safely to their destination and then make his report.'

'Blind leading the blind, settling out here,' Betts commented, 'and they won't get me living out in the bush by meself with all them blacks around. A person can't be expected to give up life and limb for a sheep.'

'Shepherding sheep is what we've been told we'll be doing,' his companion replied.

'They've cattle, haven't they?' He pointed to where cows grazed. 'That's what I'll be angling for, a horse and a musket and the task of looking after a few cows.'

'There won't be no muskets for the likes of you two.' Mr Callahan sat fanning his face with his hat by the wheel of the wagon. He'd removed his blucher boots and the raw scent of his feet was rank in the hot air. 'You might be free of irons but you're here to do what you're told, just like me. Mr Southerland told me there's a dearth of cattle up here and this lot is kept in sight of the house.'

Betts threw a stone into the dirt. 'We'll see. This place is the ends of the earth.'

His mate scoffed. 'You said that when we got off that hulk in the harbour. Bet you're wishing you didn't steal that bread now.'

'Shut your trap,' Betts growled.

≪ Chapter 14 ≫

1837 October – The Rocks, Sydney

Georgina Lycett was seated by the window, her gaze fixed on some point beyond the tall masted ships moored in the harbour. The view across the water to the heavily timbered foreshore was breathtaking. The ocean glimmered. Vessels plied the calm surface leaving tiny streamer-like trails in their wake. Winston could have watched the activity for hours. It was a scene so different from the brown-green stillness of the farm that he found himself wondering why his father hadn't chosen a merchant's life, or at least some employ associated with the riches that the ocean could provide. There was also the intriguing enjoyment of being in Sydney, where women, wine and song were available any hour of the day, if one had the coin to pay for it. Which he now did.

It was a clear, sunny morning and fashionable Princes Street was abuzz with activity. Men and women strolled casually, stopping to talk to friends, their voices carrying upwards to the second storey of the townhouse owned by a family friend. The friend in question, Mrs Annabel Beuth, sat on the opposite side of the room, her fingers rarely faltering in the cross-stitch she was absorbed in. Her merchant husband had been one of the first to see the benefit of building in this particular section of The Rocks and Annabel, now fifty years old, was at long last enjoying the life that years of toil had rewarded. It was true that their locale was bordered by minor streets with less than desirable occupants, however, in only a matter of years the wealthy had made Princes Street a coveted address.

Although pleased to see his mother, Winston wished to be anywhere but here. Georgina Lycett had not shifted in her chair, her profile, with its patrician nose and stubborn chin, thrown into relief by the brightness of the day. Mrs Beuth had rung for tea and an assigned servant had delivered the hot drink. Small talk had been made and still his mother remained silent. A carriage clock ticked. From the street below came the sound of a woman laughing. There was to be a hanging this morning and the crowds on Gallows Hill were already thick.

'I must thank you for the care you have shown my mother, Mrs Beuth,' Winston began, noticing not for the first time the fineness of the furniture in the room; the chairs with their brightly upholstered seat cushions, the matching window dressing and the gleaming breakfast table, an environment that was in stark contrast to the Lycett farmhouse. 'Is she sufficiently recovered?' He was inclined to reach for the fruit bowl where grapes, nectarines and plums enticed. The quality and cheapness of the food in the city was quite remarkable.

The heavily built woman lifted her cap-covered head. 'I wonder you have not been to visit sooner. It is past a month since her arrival.' Mrs Beuth's grey eyes were reproving.

Draining his tea cup Winston sat the service on a side table. 'There were things that needed to be attended to.' What was he meant to say to a mute woman? He assumed that his mother would regain her speech when her strength returned. In the meantime there were too many sights and sounds drawing him. He'd spent the early morning walking about the foreshore. The area was crowded with merchants and chandlers, hardware shops, taverns and bond stores. This was a place of smells and sights such as he'd never imagined.

The woman returned to her sewing. 'Your mother has expressed a desire to return to London. I have written on her behalf to your father's sister informing Mrs Farrah of her imminent return. You will make the necessary arrangements for her passage.'

His mother remained expressionless.

'Of course.' Winston tried not to show his surprise. Mrs Beuth was a right old boiler, but then what could one expect of the merchant class. 'I did not think, however, that she would wish to leave here. There is our farm, after all, the family business, and my father's will stipulates that my mother remain in my care.'

Mrs Beuth held the cross-stitch aloft and studied it critically. 'You can hardly expect your mother to return to those wilds. My husband, may he rest in peace, always maintained that the lands beyond the mountains were no place for an English woman.' Satisfied with her handiwork, she placed it aside. 'Ridiculous. Still, your land cannot founder and sink to the bottom of the ocean,' she concluded, referencing the loss of a whaling ship acquired and equipped by her husband for £10,000. 'Your mother wishes to sell your father's acreage. She will need monies of her own, else she'll be at the mercy of her sister-in-law.'

Winston turned to his mother. He would never forget searching for her those many days, only to find her three nights after her husband's death curled up by the creek. He had nursed her at the farm and then, once capable of travel, taken her to Sydney Town and Mrs Beuth's home. In all that time she'd never uttered one word to him. Food and drink had passed her lips, indeed she'd been a most dutiful patient, but she never spoke to him, not once. Not even his father's grave, placed with care amongst the smaller remembrances of Winston's siblings, encouraged her to speak.

'My father's property has been bequeathed to me. I will not be selling the farm,' Winston stated flatly. 'I thank you for your interest in my mother's situation, Mrs Beuth, but these matters are not of your concern.' He wanted to add that Mrs Beuth should attend to her sewing and not meddle in the affairs of men, but for the moment the woman was providing his mother with all the necessary comforts appropriate to her station. 'It is only right and proper that my aunt offer my mother hearth and home, if that truly is her choice, but I'm sure you will understand that I would like to hear such sentiments from her own lips.'

'There is nothing for me here.' His mother's voice was soft, broken. It quavered like an unfinished musical note. 'Annabel, you will excuse us, my dear. I need to have a few minutes alone with my son.'

Their hostess was slow to move. 'You are sure?' When there were no words spoken to the contrary, Mrs Beuth placed her sewing down. 'Do not upset your mother, Winston. She has been through more than a person ought.'

Winston rose. 'We both have.'

'Really?' Mrs Beuth regarded him coolly before leaving the room. The door closed with a sharp click.

Through the window a convict hulk and deep sea whalers sat stationary as a fleet of other vessels navigated between them. For the briefest of moments Winston wished he was aboard one of the boats moving men and equipment to whaling stations scattered along the coast. He focused on the activity. Sailors were busy loading barrels of salted meat, bales of wool and a supply of empty wooden casks to store whale oil.

'The police paid me the compliment of a visit.'

'The police,' Winston repeated.

'Have you become like one of the caged birds that your father kept?'

His mother rose, steadying herself on the windowsill. On facing him her eyes were puffy, her face blank. But it was the disappear-ance of her ready smile, a constant in his life, that struck him.

'They wanted to confirm events on the day . . . the day of your father's death.'

'I see.' This was unexpected. Winston had described the incident fully to the local police, the report of which was forwarded to the sheriff of New South Wales. He'd thought a warrant to have already been issued.

'They wanted to confirm that it was indeed Adam who shot and killed your father.' She paused as if to gauge his reaction. 'I did not realise the regard in which Adam was held by some, although we knew his many attributes, didn't we?' Again she waited. 'After the shooting was reported in the newspaper, apparently a number of people came forward attesting to his character.'

Winston said nothing. He'd been given no sign previously as to his mother's recollections from that day, believing that the shock of his father's death had obliterated the details.

'It is a sorry thing that has happened.'

'Indeed. Father's death is a great loss to us both.' In his own way, Winston wanted to honour his father's life and dream. To that extent he intended to employ a manager to run the farm instead of selling it, and purchase a townhouse in one of the more fashionable areas of Sydney as his main residence. There was no point acquiring more land. Winston knew his father wouldn't approve, but it was the best he could do. He wasn't living out in the wilds a minute longer.

His mother began to pace the room, the dark taffeta of her skirt rustling as she moved. 'If it was not Adam, the young boy who sat beneath the schooling tree, your friend, a man which your own father held with some regard, if it was another,' her eyes grew glassy, 'you, perhaps . . .'

Winston swallowed.

'Then there might still be some form of punishment allotted to you. Someone must be held accountable for your father's death, for the death of the shepherd, kin or not, accidental or not. Who knows what the verdict might be, or the sentence handed down, especially after the stories in the paper, after your rendition of that day. If the truth were to come out it may look as if you tried to mislead. If gaol was involved, there would be no-one to manage the farm and I will not waste money on a manager nor ever set foot on that property again. There is the possibility the holding would have to be sold.'

'What are you trying to say, Mother?'

'I told the police that I agreed with your *version*' – she said the word slowly, deliberately – 'of events. Though it went against my conscience, against my religion, against everything I was brought up to believe in. Do you want to know why I did this?'

Winston shoved his hands in his trouser pockets. 'Firstly because it was a terrible accident and secondly, I'm your son, your only surviving child.'

'The gossipmongers have filled the papers with stories, fact and fiction, about your father's death. And thanks to you, Adam has already been tried by the press and found guilty. Do you know that the description of your friend was very detailed? Every item of clothing, the way he wore his shoulder-length hair, the darkness of his eyes, down to the shells he wore about his wrist were listed for all to read. But you are not surprised, are you, my son? For it was you who gave these details.' Georgina brushed her hands together as if wiping away dirt. 'In the end my current situation needed to be considered,' she finished tiredly.

'I don't understand.'

'I'm sure you do, Winston. As you already mentioned, your father left everything to you in his will with a small stipend for myself. But firstly let me confirm that a warrant has been issued. Adam is wanted for your father's murder, along with the natives involved.'

'You have done the right thing, Mother,' Winston replied. What else could he say? It was too late to recant his story. The events surrounding the attack on the Lycett farm had grown out of all proportion and spread like one of the many fires across the colony.

'Tell me this, why Adam? He was your friend. If you really were too scared to take responsibility for your own actions, why not blame one of the natives? Heaven knows there are plenty of them in the area and they were there that day. They started it.'

'It happened so quickly. Adam arrived and he found me and Father and,' he took a breath, 'he just stood there with this horrified, disbelieving look on his face.'

'The use of a musket would be a last resort for Adam,' his mother concluded.

Winston hesitated. His childhood friend had grown to be a reminder of the type of person that he could never be. If his father hadn't offered Adam management of the prospective holding at Bathurst, if Adam hadn't told the blacks about Merindah, if that convict had not arrived as Adam had left that day . . . Winston had been in shock. He'd been angry, at life, at his father, at Adam. Grief and resentment and fury had led him to blame Adam for his father's death. He'd told the convict, Chaffy Hall, that Adam was responsible, and then the constabulary. By the time Winston realised the enormity of what he'd done, it was too late. He couldn't go back on his word, wouldn't change his story, couldn't risk smearing the Lycett name. It was all too late. And as his mother rightly insinuated, there could be consequences if he admitted his deception. 'Adam was raised by blacks, Mother. There are things you don't know about him.'

His mother had a stony look about her. 'Clearly there are things I didn't know about you either. Adam was your friend. You have shown yourself in a most despicable light. The farm is to be sold. We will share the proceeds equally.' Moving to the bell pull, she tugged at the length of material that fed down from the picture rail.

'I will never agree to it. That property is mine by right.'

'Do not think, Winston, that I will return to England a pauper, not having buried your little brothers and sisters, not after having been subjected to the loneliness and discomfort of your father's dream, though I loved him dearly.' She gritted her teeth, her words leaden. 'And do not think that I would hesitate in changing my story, in sullying the Lycett name with the truth, that you shot your father because you were terrified, a grown man cowering behind the door. You shot him in your cowardice even though I told you I could see him running towards the house.' Her breath grew irregular. 'I only agreed to your story because I will not return to London penniless, and in spite of what you have done I would not see you in trouble with the law. You have your conscience to answer to and the loss of the livelihood that you expected. You may consider the punishment in the extreme but it will never atone for the death of my husband or the noose that you have surely placed around Adam's neck. Yes, the land is rightfully yours but you will sell it, my boy, or risk an uncertain future.'

'You would reveal me if I don't agree? But I'm your son.'

'The pity of it is that you are my only child.'

The door opened. A servant bobbed a curtsey.

'You will show my son out, Susannah, and then I would like you to accompany me up George Street. I wish to purchase some silk and lace for a new gown and I'm unsure of the best place to obtain these goods.'

'Of course, Mrs Lycett.' The girl waited for Winston.

'I do miss him, Mother, and I'm sorry.'

A single tear was the only response Winston received as his mother turned away.

'You will return Tuesday week, Winston. By that time I will have had the necessary papers drawn up for you to peruse. I already have an interested party.'

'But, Mother, what do you expect me to do? I will have to work. I will have no income. I intended to pursue my studies, to purchase a residence in town and find a suitable wife. Please, you must forgive me. I too suffer. I wake up in a cold sweat at night thinking on what I've done. I have cried for my father, until I can cry no more.'

His mother returned to the seat by the window. 'You are lucky. I am yet to reach that point. If I ever will.'

Winston shooed the maid from the room and took a step forwards. 'As for Adam, please don't think I don't regret what I have done. I was just so angry. It was because of him that the blacks attacked.'

His mother spun in her seat to face him. 'How is that possible?'

Winston was lost for words. How could he admit his fraternisation with Merindah? 'I will spare you the details, Mother, but believe me when I say that it was Adam's fault. I am only sorry that in my anger I accused him of Father's death. It was a most terrible thing to do and I regret it.' His hands dropped to his sides. The wickedness of what he'd done would stay with Winston forever.

'We will say no more about this matter.' Georgina Lycett turned back towards the window and the harbour beyond. 'You are my son and I love you, but I don't like you. Not after everything you have done. As for your future, you will have funds enough to afford decent lodging and you are a learned man, Winston. It is time to put your mental faculties to use, perhaps as a clerk, or a book-keeper or a journalist – it seems you have a penchant for stories.'

'Yes, Mother.' Winston could think of no retaliatory argument that would restore her favour. Georgina Lycett was a grieving widow intent on ensuring her future comfort and meting out punishment along the way. 'Goodbye, Mother.'

She didn't respond as he left the room.

Outside, Winston blinked at the glare and, head down, began to walk. The street was busy with people, horses and drays and he found himself yearning for the quiet of the bush as he aimlessly turned down one street and then another. When he finally stopped to check his bearings Winston realised he had no idea where he was. The sun was at its highest point and he was hot and thirsty. The street housed a number of taverns and was close to the harbour, and unlike the area where his mother currently lived, it was certainly not a place for the upper classes.

Inside one of the taverns, Winston ordered a rum and sat at a corner table. The room held an assortment of men, rough sailor types from whaling ships and other undesirables. In hindsight it was not the best of hostelries to stop in for he was immediately the subject of unwanted stares, although the innkeeper was happy to keep his glass full, and by his fourth rum Winston was feeling a little better.

'You want some company then?' The girl was young and full-breasted, a feature enhanced by the unlaced bodice which gave a tantalising glimpse of pale skin. She straddled a chair, hiking the skirt up to her thighs. There were pox marks on her face, but not enough to mar the thought of bedding her and it only took a nod and she was leading Winston up narrow stairs, to the approving nod of the innkeeper.

In a tiny room with a crumpled cot and a washstand, Winston sat on the bed and told the girl to undress. She obliged, defrocking in an instant to stand naked before him as he quickly removed his jacket and shoes.

'How do you like it then?' she asked, giving him a coy smile.

'Without any talk.' He hated these women with their knowing smiles. 'Turn around.' Winston examined her body for any lesions. 'Clean yourself.'

The girl gave a scowl. She couldn't have been more than four-teen, although her breasts compensated for the slimness of her body. 'I usually do it after.'

'That's no good to me. I don't know where you've been.'

Obediently she began to wash, wringing a cloth in the bowl and wiping at herself disinterestedly. When she was finished, Winston pointed to the bed. He was loath to lie on the filthy cover, but his need outweighed the grimy environs and he pushed her face down.

The sting to the middle of his back a moment later bit deep and he fell sideways as the girl squirrelled out from under him.

'Be quick about it.' The man's voice was gruff. Winston opened his eyes. The girl was riffling through his clothes. Coins clattered as the man counted notes and then he was coming at Winston again, punching him hard in the nose.

'You said no more murder,' the girl complained in a high-pitched tone.

'He'll live.' The man gave a chuckle. 'I think.'

'What about my share? Give me my share!'

The man lunged. Slamming the girl hard against the wall, he lifted her up by the throat until her feet no longer touched the floor. She fought and kicked for a few moments and then he dropped the lifeless body and left the room.

Winston guessed he'd been knifed in the back. He lay on the bed feeling the wetness of his own blood. He could have staggered downstairs. The rough-looking patrons may well have given assistance. Instead, as his mind began to waft in and out of consciousness, he couldn't help but think how very different their lives may have been if Bidjia had not walked through their farm all those years ago with Adam in tow.

❧ Chapter 15 ❧

*1837 October – beyond the outer limits,
the Hardy farm*

The wagons crossed powdery ground, throwing up dust and dirt. A billowing haze hovered above the bullocks as Mr Callahan coerced the animals around a long, curving corner. It was then Kate saw them again. The huts on the hill. They huddled together as if derelict, fringed by a half-circle of bush on the western side and the bleak hill they clung to. There was no neat fence, white-washed walls or dappled orchard. No tapestry of fields with swaying wheat or corn, no mill rising proudly in the distance.

Mr Callahan, at the lead of the team, looked back towards her. Kate stumbled on the rough ground and resumed walking. What had she done in deciding to travel to this place?

A curl of smoke streamed into the air from one of the huts. Empty ground fanned out in a half-mile perimeter, affording a clear view across treeless dirt to the timbered foothill. A creek appeared to weave towards this timber, while in the foreground sheep fed into the westerly wind.

Their arrival was greeted with a single wave. Red-bearded Samuel Hardy, his five-foot-nothing wife Sarah and a young girl stood out the front of the hut as they approached. Mr Southerland was with them, drinking from a pannikin and smoking a pipe, and by the look of satisfaction on his face, pleased to be at journey's end. The Aboriginals kept a good distance from the huts and slowly dispersed to sit in a group to watch proceedings.

'Go greet them, lass. Go on, don't look so poorly. You didn't come all this way to be a-feared of them.' Mr Callahan gestured towards the waiting group.

With a determination she didn't feel, Kate walked up the incline towards the huts, tucking a strand of hair behind her ear. She was terribly hot, thirsty and tired. Her dress was dirty and she'd not bathed properly for ages. Her last attempt was three days ago with a cloth and a half-bucket of muddy creek water in the back of the wagon. She was hardly at her presentable best.

The two timber and bark huts, which formed the Hardys' home and the kitchen, were roughly constructed, although the house had the benefit of its eastern wall being partially built into the hill. Its verandah jutted out on spindly legs, the stone and timber fireplace and chimney rising at an angle. At the skew-whiff porch where the assembled group waited, all Kate could think of was what she'd had to contend with to get here. *Here* was the blank space on Major Shaw's map.

Mr Southerland made the introductions. The Hardy family were berry-brown from the sun, however the child's eyes were tinged yellow, while Mrs Hardy's face, partially obscured by a hat, was disfigured by a large boil low on one cheek. All three were hollow-eyed, dull of skin, with the barest of smiles between them, but Mrs Hardy and her daughter Sophie exchanged pleasantries, clearly pleased at the arrival of the wagons. The woman spoke with the clipped pronunciation of the well-educated, as the child bit at

214

a thick bottom lip, her gaze fixed on the laden wagons. It was not the welcome greeting Kate had expected.

Mr Hardy talked of their scant supplies all the while pushing the brim of his hat back and forth as if he weren't sure if he were coming or going. 'But you're a welcome sight I tell you, George. Most welcome.' Samuel Hardy was not unlike his cousin in build, although broad-faced and big-boned rather than fat, with orange whiskers and small round eyes, which blinked continuously. 'Course I knew you'd make it. If anyone could without hindrance, I knew it would be you, although as I said, you were expected a week ago and we've been waiting.' The man was appreciative, Mr Hardy said as much, but the tone was accusing.

'Every morning, noon and night for a fortnight and a half, we've been gazing down the valley and across to the hills,' Mrs Hardy agreed. 'We were beginning to think you weren't coming.'

'Will there be the food you said, Mama? Will there be fruit for puddings and the makings for jelly and will there be a new book for me?' Sophie's words tumbled into each other.

Mrs Hardy told her daughter to shush and not disturb the adults' talk as her attention drifted to the wagons as well. Did the chickens survive? Were there preserves? Did they remember to pack more reading material? Was everything in quite sound condition? Mr Southerland answered each question slowly and patiently and then, to Kate's astonishment, the expedition leader began remarking on the consistency of her character throughout the journey. His comments were complimentary and he concluded his brief assessment by suggesting that Kate fared better than expected, having shot a native and escaped injury.

Mrs Hardy's mouth opened and stayed that way for long seconds.

'Well, it's just as well you can take care of yourself, miss,' Mr Hardy answered evenly. 'She has a pistol?'

'A flintlock,' Mr Southerland advised.

'Good. Keep it with you at all times. If you can protect yourself, miss, it'll be one less to worry about.'

'Mama has a pistol under her pillow,' Sophie told Kate, 'but she's never used it. If the blacks come I'm to crawl under my bed.'

'And what of the men on the farm? We heard at Maitland that the blacks were not behaving themselves up here.' Mr Southerland said. 'There are extra muskets, powder and shot, enough for all the labour.'

'Yes, there have been problems in the north-west, which we'll discuss later, George, but give a weapon to a convict?' Mr Hardy pulled the straw brim forward and gave it a tug. 'I'll not be trusting my soul and that of my family's to the criminals. Besides, it's against the law.'

'Many a settler's entrusted their men with the right to be armed, especially in these outer areas,' Mr Southerland said pointedly.

Mr Hardy pushed his hat so far back that it hung on the back of his head like a bird about to slip from its perch. 'We've enough concern without adding to it.' Turning his attention to Kate, he gave her a fleeting appraisal from head to toe, and asked what skills she brought with her for his cousin had promised her a fine penny and he hoped Jonas had not been turned by a pretty face.

'Skills, sir?' All she wanted was to sit down, to be offered a cool drink of water.

'Yes, what can you do? Apart from cooking, cleaning and sewing?'

The convicts were beginning to unload the wagons. A wide-hipped woman, undoubtedly the cook, trundled downhill from the kitchen hut and, taking sight of Mr Callahan, began to tell the Scotsman where the goods were to be deposited.

'I have been a housekeeper of sorts for the Reverend Horsley, Mr Hardy.' She thought of the expected role on the Hardy farm. 'A companion and teacher.'

Her new employer withdrew a crumpled letter from his coat pocket and waved it in the air. 'I have here your letter of introduction from my cousin.'

Kate was not aware one had been written, nor that Mr Southerland had been its keeper. Perspiration soaked her dress, it ran down her thighs to the backs of her knees.

'For the exorbitant sum mentioned in this letter, I expected a little more.'

'As did I,' Kate carelessly replied. She couldn't help it. Never in her wildest imaginings had she expected to be delivered to a place like this.

The silence that followed was made more obvious by Mr Callahan, who was currently abusing Betts for his slowness.

George Southerland removed the pipe clenched between his lips and scratched at the mat of beard on his face.

Mr Hardy lifted the letter in the air, crumpling the piece of paper in his fist. A ropey vein beat in his neck. 'We've been a year in this place, Mr Southerland. There's been scant rain since your leaving.'

Mrs Hardy, freckled and half-hidden beneath the wide-brimmed hat, clasped her hands together somewhat nervously. 'Progress has been slow.'

'You've proceeded at a fair pace,' Mr Southerland drawled, tapping out the pipe and sticking it in his shirt pocket. 'The verandah has come along well.'

The child, barefoot and restless, pushed at a timber board with her toes. It rose an inch at the opposite end.

'And you've begun construction on a fence, I see,' he persevered.

'Half of it has been built. This side and at the rear.' Samuel rubbed his furry chin. He was dirty in appearance. When he took his hat off to brush at the grit layering the crown, it was difficult to determine if the line resembling a tidal mark on his forehead was from dirt or the sun. 'We needed that labour.' Replacing the hat, his voice steadied. 'Why the Governor plies that Agricultural Company with men instead of looking after those of us who are opening up these lands is beyond me. But he must look after his kind, I suppose.'

'With Members of Parliament and eminent men from both the Bank of England and the British East India Company involved, those like us are the last to be considered,' Mrs Hardy stated.

'They're milking the convicts to make a profit,' Mr Southerland stated.

'And I'm left with a slip of a girl with a pretty face.' Kate's new employer dropped the crumpled letter on the ground. A light breeze blew the missive downhill. 'I can't pay what my cousin suggests.'

Kate was stunned. 'It was not a suggestion, sir.' A bitter taste grew in her mouth. She had not come this far to be so poorly treated. 'Terms were agreed.'

Sophie began to run up and down the verandah. A yellow dog appeared and chased the girl from the dirt below. Up and down child and dog ran. One laughing, the other barking.

'Terms? With a woman?' Mr Hardy gave a sour laugh.

'He said you would be agreeable,' Kate began. 'He said –'

'Do you see my cousin standing here afore you, girl? Do you think it is him riding off to watch my sheep and check on my shepherds and hope to God no stock have been run off, the labour been speared, or his family attacked while he's been away?'

Kate's eyes began to water. She wiped angrily at the tears. 'I would not have come otherwise,' she replied weakly. 'What other reason would I come out here for, if not for money?'

'One thousand head of ewes have disappeared off Stewart's run since you left, George. Gone, just like that. Rushed by the blacks, to be sure. It's a dent for him but he's land and stock enough to weather such a loss. But us,' Mr Hardy looked meaningfully at his wife, 'we'd be ruined. We'd have to walk away.'

'Mr Hardy, please,' Kate begged.

'Make the best of things is my advice,' Mr Hardy replied. 'That's an end to it.' The two men turned their attention to the unloading of the wagons and walked away.

Mrs Hardy suggested that Kate sit and they did so at a rickety table that appeared to have been nailed to the floor. Two large tree trunks served as chairs beneath the extended roof, above which a bush spider had spun a thick web in the bark. Dog and child stopped their playing, the animal sitting in the dirt at the end of the verandah.

'Does she have my seat now?'

Mrs Hardy told her daughter to shush. 'This place is not what anyone expected.'

'I came all this way,' Kate said to the older woman. 'Mr Kable promised me.'

Mrs Hardy ran her hand across a book that sat on the table. It appeared to be a sketch book of sorts. On closer inspection a title had been written on the front cover, *Native plants existing on the property as collected by Mrs Samuel Hardy.*

'Well, let's put all that behind us, shall we?'

'But surely if terms were agreed to they should be honoured?' Kate challenged.

'They were Mr Hardy's cousin's terms,' the woman replied, 'not my husband's. That's one of the difficulties of living out here, my dear. There is no opportunity of writing a letter in advance when it comes to business.' She gestured at their surrounds. 'How would we receive it?'

Kate felt what remaining energy was left within her begin to dissipate like a rat departing a sinking ship.

Mrs Hardy's voice was too bright, too eager as she began to ask for news, first of the Kables and their health, then of life in the heart of the colony, followed by any titbit of gossip Kate could possibly think of.

'Nothing is too small for my ears. Fashion, food, whom the Governor and his lady have been entertaining, what grand parties they've attended.' She clasped her hands together. 'And what foods did you bring? Sheep meat and bread have been our main fare these many months. The potatoes did not flourish as we'd hoped. As for my Sophie, she is not growing as she should either. Did you bring preserves? For we shall eat them tonight. And the fashions, what of the latest fashions?' She gave Kate's dusty dress a cursory glance. 'We've always been a good season behind England, however, up here,' Mrs Hardy gave a tight laugh, 'we are far more than that. And then of course you must regale me with some morsel of scandal –'

As the woman continued Kate tried to listen, tried to calm down, to content herself with the knowledge of what the Kables had achieved and that it stood to reason that the same could be expected of their cousins, eventually. And when it looked like a profit was to be turned, that the farm had gone beyond the measly venture that currently surrounded them, then she'd demand payment. Kate had little choice. The cook strode past carrying the caged chickens and the rooster, who crowed as if he was heading for the slaughterhouse.

'Might I have a glass of water?'

Mrs Hardy removed her hat, revealing gold hair streaked with grey and a round, bland face that fell to a receding chin. She'd once been pretty, undoubtedly with a peaches-and-cream complexion, but her skin was now dry and red. She'd been ruined by the sun. 'Of course. I am sorry. Here I am breathless and questioning in anticipation, having had no news for months and you are no doubt exhausted.'

The ill-fitting boards of the verandah groaned as Sophie hovered at her mother's side, jumping from one foot to the next. 'You're pretty. We didn't think you'd be pretty, did we, Mama?'

'No indeed.' The older woman studied Kate carefully and smoothed her own hair with a freckled hand.

Kate guessed Mrs Hardy to be in her early forties, although she appeared older.

'Did you bring pretty things with you? Did you bring things for me? She would have pretty things, Mama, because she is pretty and I would like to see them.'

'Such looks will be wasted up here.' Mrs Hardy's tone was dismissive. 'I wonder at your coming. I wonder at your need for money. Pretty is trouble, my husband tells me, especially with so few of us womenfolk in these outer areas. Best you stick to your tasks and not draw attention to yourself. We don't want any trouble. We've had trouble enough.' She tugged at a frayed cuff and a pale pink slip of material appeared. She dabbed the square of silk, no doubt cut down from a dress, at her perspiring brow.

'What trouble?' Kate interrupted, noting Mrs Hardy's changeable temperament.

'The natives do not all tend towards peace. The ones here are generally amenable, but there have been incidents along the river.'

'Such as?' After the journey Kate had just endured, she'd actually prefer not to know.

'Stockmen have been killed, stealing, the rushing of stock, the odd spearing of shepherds. Either they have no concept of property or they are simply intent on causing trouble. We can't afford losses. It's cost us our savings to settle up here. Mr Southerland's return and those of the assigned convicts is doubly welcome. And it's a boon that you carry a pistol. Yes, it'll make me feel a lot better when Sophie is in your care.' Mrs Hardy rubbed tiredly at an eye. 'It is so difficult. How does one tell between the good and the bad? How do we know that one we feed today on our land will not spear a cow in the morning? But enough of this talk. I'm told you are against marriage and turned down a respectable position with a man of the cloth?'

Mrs Hardy told Sophie to fetch a pitcher of water. The girl dragged her feet on leaving. 'You will understand my intrigue.'

Glancing in the direction her daughter had just taken, she lowered her voice. 'If you are running away from some disgrace,' she leant forward, clearly eager, 'I would share your concerns.'

'There is no disgrace,' Kate replied brusquely. 'I simply believe that a woman should be allowed to make her own choices in life and not be dictated to.'

Mrs Hardy fanned her face with her hat. The cabbage-tree fronds in the crown were partially worn and had been lined with a piece of old newspaper. 'My, my, I see why Mrs Kable did not offer you some form of employ.' There was a tinge of amusement. 'My daughter is my salvation in these wilds my husband has set us in and she needs schooling and discipline. I'm afraid, however, I am much remiss in these two fields.' She looked out across the bush. The sun was tipping the trees to the west. 'There is much to do here and although the days are long, too long, they are not long enough. I shall place her in your hands.'

Kate frowned. 'It was my understanding I was employed in the capacity of companion to you, Mrs Hardy.'

'Good gracious,' the older woman let out a chuckle, 'my husband's cousins have indeed sent us a gentlewoman.' She turned at the approach of her husband and waited for him to deposit a trunk in their dwelling. 'Mr Hardy, your cousins have fulfilled my original request.'

'How so?' Behind him Betts and Gibbs were lugging a large sea-chest, while Mr Callahan carried a hip bath. Kate could have cried as the items were transported into the house. She had no idea a bath was stored within the goods they'd transported northwards.

'Miss Carter thinks to be my companion.'

There were two perpendicular lines above Mr Hardy's nose. Combined with his impressive frown he appeared almost beakish. 'You will find, Miss Carter, that your role here will consist of anything that is required of you, especially now we are without the labour I requested. As a currency lass you should be fit for most tasks.'

'Heavens.' Mrs Hardy stopped fanning her face and placed the hat on the table. 'A currency lass? Native born. Please don't tell me that your parents were convicts. Are you a convict?' She looked aghast at her husband. 'I did say I wanted no woman with the stain. You did tell Jonas that, Mr Hardy? For we are surrounded by these infernal offenders and I so wanted some semblance of normality, someone at least –'

'They have done their best to find us someone suitable,' her husband placated as he followed the men back to the bullock drays.

Sophie returned with a single pannikin of water. 'Mrs Ovens says that she's no time to be fetching pitchers of water for the servants.' She sat the cup on the table. 'She says she needs help in the kitchen. Do we call her Jelly-belly?'

Kate looked at the pale brown water and cautiously took a sip. It tasted of bark and dust.

'Jelly-belly. Jelly-belly.'

Kate looked furiously at Sophie. 'My father was assigned to the colony, my mother was born of free settlers.' Kate spoke over the chanting child and, finishing the water gratefully, was careful not to wipe her mouth on her sleeve as she'd become accustomed to doing over the weeks of travel.

Mrs Hardy composed herself with some effort. 'Dear me, your grandparents must have been most disappointed by your mother's union.'

'I believe they placed happiness above the constraints of society.'

'A supposed luxury undoubtedly much admired by the lower classes but hardly appropriate in civilised society,' was Mrs Hardy's response. 'I have learnt that there is a place in the world for everybody, and that everybody has their place.'

'They have my trunk,' Kate pointed out. Betts and Gibbs were stumbling across the uneven ground carrying her mother's chest. 'Where am I to be lodged?' She was eager to escape both child and mother.

'With the cook,' Mrs Hardy informed her. 'Her room adjoins the kitchen.'

There was little point arguing with this arrangement, so Kate excused herself and followed the men towards the other hut.

'And make yourself helpful in the kitchen,' Mrs Hardy called after her.

Kate's legs felt like lumps of wood as she trailed the convicts. It appeared her new accommodation was not much different from that she'd left behind when a child in the Reverend's kitchen. She had come full circle.

'What did you expect?' Kate overheard Mr Hardy speaking to his wife. 'A gentlewoman would hardly journey to the outer limits.' He did not bother to lower his voice.

'I did,' Sarah sighed.

'She is presentable and speaks passable English.'

Mrs Hardy rubbed her hands on her skirt. 'You are right of course, my husband. And the girl is educated, a boon for young Sophie, but unmarried. With those looks, I thought there was some shame there that we were yet to discover. Having spoken with her, however, I believe her character is such that she would need a strong husband. She was most outspoken to you on arrival.'

'Yes, Jonas implied that there were certain inconsistencies in the girl's nature. Considering her background I suppose one should not be shocked at her trying to negotiate the terms of engagement, but really, whoever heard of such a thing?'

'A daughter of an emancipist. They think they are the same as everyone else.'

Kate halted and turned back towards the couple. The Hardys noticed that she had stopped and was listening in, but they kept on talking.

'Well, they aren't, wife, so keep your eye on the girl and keep her busy. Regardless of the young woman's opinionated nature, a few months up here will soon rid her of the pretensions that are so endemic among the native born. You'll see, she shall be of some benefit to you.'

Kate wanted to scream.

⊰◈⊱

The kitchen hut, a mere ten feet from the Hardys' dwelling, had a woodpile and chopping block near the door, while a dray held a number of wooden water-barrels.

The kitchen was empty. Betts and Gibbs carried the trunk around to the rear and dropped it in the dirt where a lean-to at the back served as the cook's sleeping quarters. Exchanging sly grins, they walked back around to the front.

Kate knew what they were thinking. If she'd thought herself better than the likes of them it appeared that they were now all on the same level. 'I hope things go well for the both of you,' she said politely. Now they were here it was best she made a point of being cordial. Who knew when she may need to call on them for assistance?

The convicts were rendered dumb. Betts took interest in an ant tracing the toe of his boot, while Gibbs stared at the kitchen hut. It was an airless box. Each wall had an airhole the size of a small fist.

'Musket holes,' he said quietly, disbelief creeping into his tone.

Betts' eyes widened.

Kate digested this sobering news, noting that there wasn't even a covered walkway between the house and the kitchen, which would make for a wet passage when it rained.

'You need a hand,' Betts mumbled, 'let one of us know, eh? I'm a fair judge of a person and Hardy has the look of a hard man.'

Kate was surprised but very grateful. 'Thank you, I will.'

'"Need a hand"?' Gibbs bandied his friend as they walked away. 'She's up here to hold the Missus's hand and wipe the arse of that toffee-haired brat of theirs while we'll likely be sleeping rough, under the stars, watching our backs of a night, and you're offering to help the likes of her?'

'You be forgetting she's like us now. Besides, I don't like the look of 'im.' Betts spat in the dirt as they walked back towards the wagon. 'Nor those musket holes in that hut.'

The screeching of chickens led Kate uphill. The cook sat cross-legged in the dirt, poking at the caged birds with a stick. Cut lengths of timber lay side by side on the ground, walls for a building perhaps, laid out and yet to be constructed. The woman kept trying to stick the chickens, and the hens pecked angrily at the twig as the rooster attempted to spread his wings in the close confines. In return the woman muttered back, complaining that there had been no eggs for the past month, despite the rich scraps they'd been given.

Kate cleared her throat. She may well have been a ghost for all the notice the woman paid her. The poking continued. The birds screeched. 'Stop it.' Kate reached out a hand and made a grab for the offending piece of wood. She considered it a miracle the hens had survived the journey.

The woman clutched her chest. 'Jelly-belly, you pointy-nosed wrench, you gave me a fright, you did. What are you doing sneaking up on a person like that? I thought I told you to peel those tatties. You know Mr Kable likes 'em roasted a dark brown and they'll not be ready when they ring the bell for tea.'

Kate squatted by the thin-haired woman. 'I'm Kate Carter, Mrs . . . ?'

'Mrs Ovens. The cook.'

'That's not your real name,' Kate said softly. 'What is it?'

The woman seemed momentarily unaware of her surroundings. 'Mary Horton, I be Mary Horton, cook and housekeeper to Mr Jonas Kable.' She clambered to her feet. 'And housekeeper to Mr Kable senior afore him. No-one told me to expect another maid.' She rubbed at the pink scalp visible above her ear.

226

A kindly smile and a soft voice were the only things that Kate could think of to bring Mrs Horton back to the present. 'And you're now cook and housekeeper to Mr Samuel Hardy.' Kate could see the cook's mind working overtime in her rheumy eyes. 'Jelly-belly is still with Mr Kable at Parramatta, Mrs Horton. I'm newly arrived with Mr Southerland.' It was almost impossible to believe that Mr Kable would have sent this old woman on such a journey northwards.

'It's the heat, you see. It comes at you like a blanket and tightens itself about your neck until your lungs dry and crack and your throat closes over. Affects a person's head, it does. Makes you remember things you don't want to and forget the things that you shouldn't. Just look at the land if you don't believe me. Hard and dry and endless, and not a bit of green to soothe a person. I only just survived it last year I tell you, lass. I had a terrible thirst the whole summer long and it was only when the rain came that I was better. 'Course now there's been no rain again, not a skirret for months.'

'It will rain soon,' Kate promised, knowing no such thing.

The cook shook her head and sat heavily on the timber boards. 'It won't, you'll see. I ain't got no feeling in me bones. So then, you've just arrived with the wagons?'

Kate told the older woman a little of the journey, omitting the engagements they'd had with the Aboriginals and saying she was hopeful that the stores had all arrived in good condition. The news was greeted warmly.

'It was the same last summer,' Mrs Horton explained. 'It's a task just to keep the water up. I've two orange trees down the hill apiece which are still alive, but we're living on bread and kangaroo, although there's sheep meat when Mr Hardy decides to kill one. And then there's the rabbits. Got eight he has now and right proud of them he is. Brought a breeding pair from Sydney. Kept them alive all that way. Mark of a gentleman that, keeping rabbits for the table. Mr Kable senior was like that. Oh, he kept a fine table. But Mr Hardy, well, he's hard with the rations. Wants to keep his sheep for wool he does. For the money. I'm right glad you made it through. Real glad.'

'Well, I've two more plants for the orchard.'

The cook rolled her eyes.

'And apart from the other stores there's preserved fruit. Oranges and lemons.'

The older woman's face brightened. 'They've not gone bad?'

'They smell fine,' Kate told her.

'You poke your finger in them, did you?'

Kate laughed. 'No, but I thought of it.'

The cook pointed to a wooden door that was partially concealed in the side of the hill ten feet further up from where they sat. 'That's where they'll be going.'

'And the holes in the kitchen wall?' Kate had to know. 'Has there been cause to use them?'

'Frightened you, did they? Well, you best get used to them, girl. That's our lot. An airless box. But if they attack us again, it's a comfort to have them there.'

'Again?' Kate repeated.

'It weren't the mob what live here. No. Some mad black came through these parts the first few months we was here. Tall he was and scarred something terrible with a mass of dark hair. Held us up in there for half a day. Luckily it weren't real hot or we all would have been asphyxiated. 'Course that's how the Missus lost the baby. The shock of it. But Mr Southerland killed a couple of the men who were with that black bastard. They pinched some sheep and then they was gone. Since then we've had cattle rushed, but no more attacks. That black-loving Englishman has seen to that. Talks to the mob on Mr Hardy's land, he does, treats 'em as equals. Keeps them happy. They hunt and fish and the women go a-digging and the rest of us keep out of their way.'

'How old was the baby?'

'Born too soon, it was. I birthed it meself in that very room on the kitchen table while the men fired their muskets and yelled at the blacks. It were a terrible day. Now tell me, who's with you? Any likely lads? My eyesight's not what it used to be but I can appreciate a fine description.'

Kate found herself liking the muddle-headed cook, and she did her best to satisfy the woman's demands, Mr Callahan becoming something of a Scottish dandy with a strong gait and intelligent forehead while Betts and Gibbs were described in terms that made them twice the men that they actually were.

'Convicts, eh? If you ask me we didn't want anymore, but I heard Mr Hardy himself complaining about the shortage of staff. Can't blame the immigrants for staying in the city. No, if I had me druthers, I'd never have come.'

'Why did you?'

The cook wrinkled her nose. 'I was getting forgetful and what with my eyesight, well, Mrs Kable she wanted someone younger. Got tendencies to greatness the Kables have. Not that a person can blame them. Anyways, I had a choice: come north with the Hardys or end up on the streets of Parramatta to spend me days down-at-heel. Not much of a decision in the end,' she sniffed.

'It's a long journey,' Kate agreed, marvelling at the cook's hardiness.

'Aye, and this lot complain about being surrounded by convicts but one thing's for sure, there's hardly a free man who wants to come this far north to work for another.' She hugged her arms, as the sun began to set. 'And a person doesn't have to worry too much about runaways up here. Bleached bones is all that's at the end of an escape – bleached bones and crows. 'Course, occasionally I'd like one of them to try it. It'd give us something to think about. It's not like Syd-e-ney Town with the goings-on down there. There's always someone with their tongue a-wagging. When I was younger, maybe twenty years ago or more, two convicts ran away from Syd-e-ney. Oh they gave the redcoats a merry chase they did. Man and woman they were, with a boy child. It weren't unusual back then for the men to risk the cat-o'-nine-tails, or the noose. Come to think of it, it still isn't. But for a woman to run, well, it was news. The gossips said it was true love. That the pair of them would die if they couldn't be together. Had the kitchen in the big house in raptures, it did. We sat around the table late into the night talking about them: where they were, the new life they were living. We were proud of them, and just a bit jealous for they'd risked their lives to be together. Ain't never been such a love story, never will be again.' The corners of the cook's mouth lifted in memory. 'We wrote our own penny-dreadful novel that year we did. Lived out their love into the wee hours and dragged ourselves ragged around the kitchen during the day. It was the best of times.'

'What happened to them?'

'They died,' the old woman replied simply. 'The redcoats caught up with the man, Fossey his name was, and flogged his back and rump to jelly until he told 'em where his lover was. Then they hung him dead. Watched him swing, I did, from Gallows Hill.' She nodded sagely. 'It were a ghastly thing to see, but a body had to be there for it were something of an event after all the gossip. Afterwards some of us walked down to the water's edge and shared a pipe between us. It were a beautiful day.'

'And the woman?' Kate asked.

'They found her body in the mountains. At least they thought it was her. Those of us what worked in the big house moped about for days. Of course, I was younger then and yet to realise that a man don't want love, he wants a mother to care for him by day and a rutting partner at night.' Her eyes were distant.

'And the boy? What happened to the boy?' Kate asked, mesmerised by the story.

'They never found him. Lost to the wilds, I suppose.'

They never feel the breezes blow
And never see the stars;
They never hear in blossomed trees
The music low and sweet
Of wild birds making melodies,
Nor catch the little laughing breeze
That whispers in the wheat.

'Old Australian Ways'
by A.B. Paterson, 1902

⪻ Chapter 16 ⪼

They had left the sandstone outcrops in the south, cutting through the western edge of a great forest that was dominated by the sandy wash of past flooding creeks and ancient empty waterways. All manner of creatures existed here and they grew fond of eating the small furry tree climbers that were easy to catch. They camped in shallow caves during the hottest part of the day or buried themselves in the cool wet sand that bordered calm water. With time, Adam became less troubled. He hoped they were clear of the authorities. Certainly Bidjia had led them a distance, arcing far to the west before heading north-east and to the security of the great forest. But he would not consider camping here through winter in the shade of the tall pines and instead they had crossed the harsh, hot flatness of the plains and headed for the tallest mountain that rose prominently from the surrounding land.

The north-west side of the mountain was dense with timber and it had taken a half-day of solid walking and climbing to find a path that circled around this barrier. Having reached the leeward side, the setting sun was now masked by the mountain and a haze of dust hung, suspended in shafts of tawny brown light. Adam waited silently with Bidjia and Jardi, his musket at the ready.

The kangaroos hopped slowly to a patch of springy grass. The largest, a male, had red-brown fur, fading to pale buff below and on the limbs. This was the one they wanted. The females would be left alone to breed. Jardi lifted his spear, aimed and threw it in one fluid movement, but the big red had already sensed them and darted away, scattering the rest of the mob.

The men gave chase. Jardi ran through the clearing, collecting the spear on the run and rejoined Adam. They passed rough-barked trees and ones of silver-white, all the while descending across gullies and narrow ravines. Through the vegetation the three men caught sight of the edge of the heavily timbered area. Patches of open land beckoned, only to become littered by woody plants and bushes as they got nearer. They were running hard now, their breath coming in gulps as they rushed through the timber. They jumped fallen logs and skirted scrubby bushes, twisting around saplings in pursuit of their prey. Occasional flashes of red fur were glimpsed but the animal was canny and fast. It ducked and darted, leading the men on a downhill chase.

Adam knew the red kangaroo was probably long gone but the rush of blood spurred them on. Landing on a stony outcrop, the musket clasped firmly, he jumped from one ledge to another, angling downwind of the animal, just in case it had halted its escape. He had left the older man behind, but Jardi still followed. The younger man's steps were fast and sure across the leaf litter but there was also another noise, the dull thud of the kangaroo.

At the bottom, where the land spread outwards from the folds of the mountain and the trees grew thinner, the red kangaroo reappeared. The animal stopped abruptly and in that instant

Adam lifted the musket and fired. The kangaroo dropped to the ground. Startled birds flew from nearby trees then all was quiet.

Bidjia ran from the timber, his breath catching in his throat, and together the three men made their way to where the animal lay breathing its last breath.

'A good kill, brother,' Jardi said quietly. He knelt by the kangaroo, leaning on his spear.

Bidjia touched the animal's body, stroked the furry pelt, muttered something undecipherable and then, unsheathing his knife, slit the kangaroo's throat. A moment's silence drew attention to the cooling breeze and the distant scent of fire.

'The animals are easily alarmed.' Adam used his knife to cut through the thick fur of the hind leg. He sliced the flesh down to the bone and, with the whiteness of the limb exposed, twisted the bone in its socket until it snapped, and then hefted it over his shoulder.

'The kangaroo is made flighty by others. Come.' Bidjia led them away from the mountain. 'This is big tribe land. The Big River country.' Since their wanderings had begun they had crossed lands belonging to many different tribes. The message stick had been well-used.

'Are they still following us?' Jardi asked. 'I haven't seen them.' The further north they'd ventured, seemingly, the more empty the land grew, although everywhere they went there were signs of other tribes. Some, like the warriors who'd been watching their progress from a distance, simply waited to ensure that they moved on. Others expected the laws to be respected and for Bidjia to ask permission to pass through lands belonging to others.

'They have gone,' Jardi's father confirmed. 'We have passed through their country. We have not seen so many wagon tracks, and the grasses beaten by the overlanding of sheep have grown less.'

'We journey a way unknown to the whites,' Adam explained.

The countryside was a patchwork of pale greens and browns in the fading light. 'Perhaps, but maybe there are not so many of them that they fill this land. It is too big, even for them,' Bidjia replied.

Adam was aware that men were settling beyond the defined counties, the imaginary line of British rule. Archibald Lycett had spoken of new and displaced settlers and their need for land, but Bidjia remained deaf to his warnings. The Elder grew more certain with each day that they could out-walk those who followed behind; that unspoilt earth could be found by the great waterhole further to the east, that another tribe would welcome them, they, the dispossessed; that his son, Jardi, would find a woman so that their line would not die out. Adam only knew one thing. That they had kept moving until they were beyond the stretch of the law.

'We should stop and make camp before darkness comes,' Jardi suggested. Their attention was drawn to a large carcass on the ground. A cow had been killed. Its hide pierced by a spear, two legs roughly hacked off. Placing a hand on the animal, Bidjia looked from the dead beast across the darkening countryside. The kill was a day old. The whites did not take kindly to such losses. They knew from bitter experience that there would be retribution.

'It's best if we keep moving. We want no trouble.' Bidjia increased their pace and soon the three men were walking quickly northeast, picking their way across unfamiliar ground, the kangaroo leg growing heavy on Adam's shoulder. Above them the sky grew blueblack, the air chilled. The coldness from the earth rose steadily and they picked up their pace, trotting across a land of deepening shadows.

⊰◈⊱

A few days later Bidjia sniffed the air. The scent of smoke was bitter and close. It was not the dense smell of burning bush but something contained, manmade with pieces of dead timber and gathered kindling. Here in this place where they intended to camp during the hottest part of the day, there was the smell of a cooking fire and the outline of a rough dwelling through the trees ahead.

Although the sun woman was fierce, Jardi decided they must leave this place and move on quickly. Adam was in agreement.

'No.' Bidjia sat heavily in the dirt beneath a thickly branched tree.

Adam dropped to his knees by the older man's side. 'Are you ill?'

Bidjia patted Adam's shoulder. 'It is a long time since I found you, Bronzewing,' he looked up at Jardi, 'and it is many seasons since I chose your mother and whispered your name so that you would come. I grow old and tired.'

'We have wandered too long,' Jardi complained.

The soil was cool in the shade of the intertwining branches. It was a good place to rest. Adam looked at the hut. 'I will go. I doubt whoever lives within will be too pleased to see the likes of you knocking on their door.'

Jardi nodded reluctantly, but he crept forward and took up a position some yards from the building, spear at the ready.

'Be careful, my white son,' Bidjia cautioned.

Musket in hand, Adam approached the dwelling. '*Coo-ee.* Anyone within?'

In reply came the sound of something being overturned, the scuffle of movement. 'Who wants to know?' a rough voice answered.

'A traveller.'

The bark door barely opened and a wedge of yellow light glimmered weakly. 'Who you be then? Friend or foe? I've got nothing worth thieving.'

'Friend. I'm alone.'

'Show yourself.'

Adam stepped towards the dim light.

The man within was sun-cracked and stoop-shouldered, but he grasped a wooden club and looked capable of wielding it. He stared at Adam, from his blucher boots and coarse cotton trousers to the cream shirt he wore, blinking as if the man before him was an apparition. 'I've got nothing worth stealing so you can put the musket down.'

He scratched at a grey beard and mumbled something about not having seen a white man for a few months. His Irish accent was thick and he spoke with a slur. 'A few months,' he repeated. 'It's been more than a few months. But there was a woman. Dark-haired thing. They were travelling onwards, before the massacre. Two wagons, loaded to the hilt they were, but not much for company. You'd think they would have stayed a bit, being how a man doesn't get much of a chance for a good yack, and a woman, well, I couldn't tell you the last time I saw a white woman. Only saw her from a distance, mind. But I can still smell her. You know how a woman smells? Rich with promise.' He gave what passed for a wink. 'Well, come in.'

Adam stepped inside. The hut was small, well-built and hot. There were two young black boys curled on the ground near the fire, who sat up rubbing their eyes and proceeded to stare suspiciously at him. Behind them the fire crackled, the smoke spiralling through a hole in the ceiling. A rough shelf held two tin plates and a pannikin, while a cast-iron pan and quart pot were suspended from hooks above the fire. Against one of the mud-plastered walls a number of spears rested while a stump passed for a chair. The rickety table made up the extent of the furnishings. The man complained of the draft and Adam pulled the door shut, but not before noting Jardi, who stood flattened against the outside wall. Immediately the tiny space became acrid with smoke, cooking smells and the long unwashed.

'Not many visitors. You want a feed?' The pot he sat on the table smelt of boiled kangaroo meat. There was a bald patch on the side of the man's head and a mess of scarred flesh suggestive of a brutal accident or fight. 'There's salt and bread.' The blackened dough was unwrapped from a piece of cloth and placed on the table beside a chipped bowl of salt. 'I had a woman but she gone and died a while back.' He ruffled the hair of one of the native boys. They were not pure of blood. They sat cross-legged and waited patiently as the food was ladled onto a plate and held out their hands for the chunks of bread, which were torn from the tough loaf with some effort. The boys scoffed the meal down and then proceeded to wipe the vessels clean with fingers and bread. Adam declined the meat but accepted a piece of the bread and an old jam tin filled with hot water.

'No sugar, but I keep a store of berries, better than nothing.' The old man tipped a wooden vessel onto the table and Adam recognised the small dried fruit of the wild plum and, selecting one, dropped it in the water. 'I had tea once. You don't got any, I suppose? No? Ain't nobody around here to get anything, excepting those people that came through. They gave me a bit of tobaccy. Since then I've only had the Superintendent from the station.' The man served up the watery kangaroo on a tin plate and ate it between bites of bread and sips of sweetened hot water. With no other seat in the room, Adam sat on the dirt floor. 'The young'uns stayed. Not much choice in it for them. Their lot didn't want them back, but I reckon one day they'll come for them. Still, while they're here, they're a bit of company. What you doing here then?'

'Heading east towards the coast.' The bread was made of ground native millet. The Irishman owed his survival to the ways of his dead Aboriginal woman and the two boys, who Adam guessed were his sons.

'Bit late to be travelling. Where you come from then? Seen anyone?' He watched Adam as he slurped the water.

'Only a few blacks.'

The man tapped his head. 'So you being alone, you'd be on the run? Convict or bushranger, it makes no difference to me.'

'Something like that.'

'Man's a right fool to be travelling about in this weather, so they must be on your tracks. Summer's settled in for a bit, but when she breaks the cold will hit you like a stab in the chest. Still, there's plenty to burn. Ain't been much rain so the going will be easy. Find yourself a good camp near water's my advice, be cold in the mountains already if you're heading east. You be right careful though, lad. The blacks have always been a bit uppity around these parts, but things are worse now. Times were when they'd spear a cow or a sheep, maybe even the odd shepherd, but not now. Last year there were white men murdered, stockmen.' The old man rose and Adam noticed for the first time dozens of knife-carved notches on the wall. 'Caused a real commotion in these parts. Not least of all because good workers are hard to come by.' A filthy finger counted the marks backwards. 'But the big ruckus,' he tapped the wall, 'that was,' he began to count, 'near two months past.'

'January,' Adam offered.

'Aye, January.' He returned to his stump and sat. 'The settlers complained about there being no law and order after them men were murdered the year afore, so the troopers appeared they did, arrested some blacks and then kept on the tail of the main mob. Well, the blacks attacked them, as you'd expect them to do, and then they fled so the troopers rounded up a whole lot of the buggers. Killed them they did. Massacred them. Called the place Waterloo Creek, on account of that general, Napoleon. Nice touch.' He grunted a laugh. 'So the blacks are uppity again.' His smile turned to a grimace.

On the dirt floor directly beneath the rough calendar were two perforated human skulls. The bone was smooth and shiny as if they received the benefit of regular polishing. The old man noted Adam's interest.

'Those there heads belonged to my woman's kin,' he explained. Selecting one of the skulls he picked it up and, rubbing it briefly with a shirtsleeve, placed it on the floor again. 'She be traded fair, but then when the sugar and the tobaccy ran out they wanted her back. Seems the terms were meant to be ongoing, so I shot 'em one night and the next week others near bashed me head in. Well, fair is fair, I thought. Anyway, after that I reckon they decided to leave things be. But eventually they came for her. She's dead now, so we're square. You got grog, tobaccy?'

'Nothing.' Adam finished the sweetened drink.

'And not likely you be getting your hands on some neither unless you work for one of them squatters.' Returning the blackened pot to the fire, he patted one of the boys on the head. 'The Lago Station Superintendent wanted me to be a hutkeeper, on account of this here hut sitting square on the station's boundary. Be damned, I told him. Risk getting speared to look after another's sheep?' A gnarled finger tapped his forehead. 'I been around. You know what I'm saying? I been around. Finally he offered me some rations just to keep my eye out, you know, let him know of any goings on. In return he reckoned he'd keep quiet about me being a runner. 'Course I said yes. I took his sugar and flour, but ain't nobody comes through here. Only the black-haired woman and them settlers last year. Imagine settling up here? Desperate they must be. This is the blacks' land, they should leave 'em to it. At least there's no cat-o'-nine-tails here. I do alright. I'm a-living.' Dipping the ladle in the cooking pot, he scooped up the scant remains and sucked the spoon clean.

'But he came back again, the Superintendent did. A while ago it was. A month past. All riled up and ready for a fight. Asked me if I wanted to come hunting. He wasn't talking about no wallaby neither.' The man sat the pot on the fire and added a drop of water. It sizzled loudly. 'He told me that them that keep the law weren't much interested in sending troopers north to these areas. That if man and beast wanted to settle beyond the counties then they had to look after their own troubles. And there's trouble a-plenty up here.' The old man tilted his head and narrowed his eyes. 'What you here for then? Are you one of them riders out on the hunt? I don't want no troubles with the blacks. I keep to meself and they leave me alone. We've an understanding.'

'Just passing through.' Adam thanked the man and opened the bark door.

'No point leaving now, stay awhile. It be a hot one. Talk some more.'

'I best keep moving.'

'Suit yerself. I know what it's like, being on the hop. Stay low then, lad, stay low.'

The man was still muttering as Adam walked away from the hut. He headed east a bit and then circled back through the scrub, Jardi tailing him to ensure they weren't followed.

'You on for a talk then?' Jardi chided.

'Just passing the time of day.'

Bidjia was waiting for them. The men hunkered down among the trees as Adam repeated what he'd heard. 'So we best keep our wits about us,' he told them. 'By the sounds of things some of these settlers will be shooting first and not bothering to ask questions.'

'This is bad business.' Bidjia poked at the dirt absently. 'No good comes of settlers left alone to resolve disputes . . .' He looked up through the leaves sheltering them. 'There are good and bad whites, we know this. Your people have renegades as we do, but what little hope I had in your white brothers, Bronzewing, has dried like a caked riverbed.'

Adam thought of Winston. 'The settlers are scared and angry. They don't understand our ways.'

'They wish we were like the grains of sand that could be blown away with the wind,' Jardi concluded, lying down to rest next to his father. 'I wish the same of them.'

Adam checked the ammunition pouch tied to the belt about his waist. He hoped Bidjia only needed rest and that nothing else ailed him for there was still much travelling ahead. In the midday heat his thoughts drifted to that of the settlers and the woman the old man had mentioned. It had to be the same girl he'd seen last year. The chances of it being another female were slight. But there was little point thinking about her, although the thought of that dark-haired beauty was a pleasant diversion. He sighed and, closing his eyes, conjured up the songlines that Bidjia had taught both him and Jardi. Hopefully the ancestor's footprints would lead them safely to the sea.

≪ Chapter 17 ≫

1838 May — the Hardy farm

K ate woke to the sound of scratching. Daylight was yet to arrive but the weak paleness that preceded dawn crept through the rough wall boards, layering the dim room in a pasty light. Level with her nose, only four feet away, was the outline of something against the wall. Rubbing at the crusty sleep in her eyes, the blurry shape grew clear. It was a spiky-looking animal in the corner of the narrow room.

Rising on her elbow she watched as the creature continued snuffling along the wall. Her shoe was the closest object. Reaching for it, she flung it as hard as possible in the direction of the animal. The leather made a loud thud as it hit the timber and fell to the dirt floor. The thing appeared to curl itself into a prickly ball.

'What is it? Who's there?' The cook sat up, the wooden frame and sagging canvas of the cot creaking dangerously.

'I'll get rid of it, Mrs Horton, don't you worry.' Kate stepped into a long beige cotton skirt, tugging it over the thin drawers and shift she wore and, slipping her arms into the matching boned bodice,

244

positioned the hem neatly over the skirt's waistband. A shawl completed her dress.

The cook swung her legs out of the cot with a pained slowness. 'You'll do no such thing. You'll leave my Henry exactly where he is.'

'Henry? It has a name?' she replied, tucking her hair beneath the straw hat.

'Henry's been with me from the beginning. It's been a while since he's visited. Show'd up he did a month or so after we came here. Followed the ants what came in for the sugar he did, has 'imself a nice burrow under this hut. 'Course that mangy yellow mutt scares him off occasionally but he always comes back. Summer's his favourite weather, but he don't mind it when the leaves fall and the air gets chilled. Be a bit warmer today, Henry. You keep out of sight of Mrs Kable and later we'll walk down to the orchard. It's a fine sight, what with the windmill and the fields and the smokehouse in the distance.'

'We're not on the Kable farm anymore, Mrs Horton,' Kate reminded the older woman gently. She had good days and bad, both with memory and sight. Yesterday Kate stopped her just in time from mixing sugar and salt together instead of flour for the bread.

Brown-coloured Henry was uncurling himself to reveal short limbs with claws and a long sticky tongue, which protruded from its snout.

'There, you see, sees you as a friend he does. He's timid, Henry is, not like most men, so don't be scaring 'im.'

Kate scanned the room. Although roughly built against the wall of the kitchen, there didn't appear to be a gap big enough for the creature to have got in. The door had been kept shut during the night on account of the cold wind and the tiny window, a hole with its scrap of Indian cotton, was the only other entry point. The spiny creature waddled past Kate's chest to where Mrs Horton's few possessions sat on an upturned crate, walked behind it and disappeared.

'Made a little hole for him, I did. Comes and goes as he pleases.' The cook picked up Kate's shoe and tossed it across to her.

Kate wondered what else could come and go from their room. Unlike the cook she was yet to be provided with a cot. With the heat of summer past, the earth was already cold. The chill travelled through the rough bedding to eat at one's bones, making her weary before the day began, but she could be grateful for the change in the seasons for there were no longer slithering, scuttling creatures entering their room, until Henry. Unchanged were the days of work, which could lead to despair, such was the isolation and monotony, and yet she worked constantly, almost grateful for the distraction. Exhaustion helped sleep, helped Kate to forget where she was, why she had come, what she'd left behind, and the native who lay dead by her hand. Most of all it helped ease her anger at the coin that should have been hers. She thought of Madge often. Wondered how the woman was. *Better the devil you know*, she'd advised. A convict knew better than her.

'Well, don't dawdle, girl. It's gone daylight already and them will be wanting their tea and honey. Them natives will have to go searching for more. Nearly out of it, we are. I don't touch it. Scoop it out with their bare hands I reckon, but the Missus loves it. Go on then, get the fire good and hot.'

'Do you want me to warm the –'

Mary Horton let out a gaseous explosion, the noise of which matched the putrid stench. 'I don't want you to do nothing for nobody excepting what I tell you. Do that and then go down and pick some more of those wild peaches near the creek. I've bread to warm and a rabbit to roast.'

Fine, Kate thought, you cranky old woman. Lacing her shoes, Kate tied a length of twine around one flapping sole and slipped the pistol and shot into her skirt pocket. Outside, one of the men was unloading lengths of timber and stacking them in a pile at the rear of the Hardys' dwelling. Additions to the homestead were

246

in the process of being pegged out, although from what Sophie revealed, the building of the 'gracious homestead' – the girl's words not hers – was dependent on Mr Southerland's availability, for Mr Hardy was loath to start the project himself without the overseer's knowledge regarding the erection of joints, trusses and ceilings.

The woodpile was getting low. Soon they'd be calling on the men to drag a new log through the hole in the kitchen wall and into the hearth, but in the meantime there was a handful of split timber remaining. Cradling two pieces, Kate used her elbow to lift the latch and entered the cook's domain. It was smoky, dark and hot. Ducking her head beneath the bags that were suspended from the ceiling to keep ants from the sugar and the like, Kate quickly poked the lengths of timber into place on top of the smouldering log, enticing the glowing embers by blowing softly until the flames caught. The soot-black kettle was already hot but she wedged it closer to the heat and selected a tin pannikin from the shelf.

'Slept in, I did,' the cook announced grumpily behind her. 'Half the day's gone. I told you to wake me up, girl. Why, the birds are out and the sun's near up.' Sitting a blackened cast-iron pot on the table, she lifted the lid and poked the rabbit carcass that had been left to soak overnight in salt and water. The animal was scraggly and with Mr Hardy doubtful that it would survive the winter, it had been placed on the menu. 'That'll do.'

Quite often the four women were left alone while the men camped out for weeks on end, tending to the business of farming. But Mr Hardy and the overseer were home at the moment, which made Kate and the cook busy with cooking and washing, but their presence also left them feeling safer.

'If I be home in England, we would have had the day off, we would.' The cook scratched a mark on the wall beside rows of similar scratches. 'I'm sure it's May. When I was a girl I danced around the May Pole, had ribbons in me hair and all. 'Course there's not much need for a pole here. Everything's backwards. We ain't heading towards summer but leaving her behind, and thank heavens for that.'

'I'll fetch the fruit, then water the orchard and tend the vegetable garden.' Kate couldn't wait to have some time to herself.

'Don't you wander off. There's them sheets to be washed in the copper.'

Outside the stuffy kitchen, dawn turned the sky white. Kate took a gulp of the chill air and steeled herself mentally for the day ahead. The land seemed caught between the vast shadows of night and the endless haze of a too bright sky. It was difficult not to feel as if she'd been tossed into a great void. The country stretched forever in all directions, across tree-spotted hills and shadowy valleys, and somewhere out there other settlers were trying to carve a place for themselves and their families with their bare hands. It was a mighty undertaking, and almost presumptuous to think that the untameable could be brought to heel. In Kate's mind if ever there was a place that should be left alone, it was here.

A horse whinnied. Down in the valley a line of moving shapes travelled towards the huts on the hill. Kate watched fascinated and scared, ready to let out a warning cry as she'd been told to do. The shapes grew legs and arms. The natives carried spears. The warriors walked at a brisk pace across the surface of the land and kept on moving to the east. Kate let out a breath. White men had been murdered last year and mounted police had chased the perpetrators down after Christmas. Mr Southerland said it was a massacre. Mr Hardy announced it to be a pleasing result.

From inside the kitchen came the clang of pots and pans. Mary Horton cursed in a sailor's tongue. The yellow dog barked in response to the ruckus, ambling into view to urinate in the dirt.

'Mama, don't!'

Young Sophie was awake, her irritated voice clear and loud. The door to the Hardys' hut squeaked open. Instead of the listless child who'd grown troublesome over summer, her father appeared on the verandah. Sliding the lid across one of the rainwater barrels, Kate dipped the pannikin into the bark-tinted liquid and drank thirstily.

'Is my tea ready?' Mr Hardy was smoking on the verandah as she passed, basket in hand. 'I told Cook I wanted it early today, before they arrived.'

'It'll be served directly, Mr Hardy.' *They* were the Aboriginals. Most mornings they came a little after dawn to sit cross-legged in the dirt opposite the verandah.

'Ridiculous, a man never has a moment's peace.'

The cook arrived, mumbling apologies. Heaving herself up the short height to the verandah, she passed her employer a pannikin of hot black tea and then from a basket began to set the table, white tablecloth, matching napkins and assorted cutlery. There were only three sets of tableware and Mrs Horton guarded the implements with her life.

'And Mrs Hardy is not feeling her best. She'd like to take a bath. You will see to it that there's water by mid-morning, Kate.'

Kate assured him that she would and continued walking downhill towards the creek. To her left was the valley and through the trees a five-acre field was being hoed by Mr Callahan. He worked there every day, sometimes with another man, sometimes alone. In the preceding months he'd burnt off timber to turn ashes into rich potash, and then hoed the ground thoroughly. When grass and weeds grew these were dug in as well so that the sod became rich with plant matter. Soon it would be time to sow the wheat. There was a hand-made plough sitting out on the flat, ready to be pulled by bullocks for this very purpose.

The young orchard struggled. The saplings were still alive but it was left to Kate to bucket water onto them; a chore that had become a welcome undertaking. Out here no-one told her what to do. Beyond the bleakness of the huts on the side of the hill, the land fanned out gently. Tussocky grass matted the earth, growing knee-high in places. Her palm brushed the tips of the pasture, her footfall disturbing small brown ground-birds who fluttered away to land nearby.

Back on the hill the regular audience were arriving in twos and threes. Mrs Hardy had made this first meal of the day with her daughter somewhat of a spectacle, and this morning there was a half-circle of native women and children sitting down to watch them. The Hardy women dined and chatted together as if they were quite alone, silver cutlery clattering, warm bread served wrapped in a white napkin, and a pot of wild honey. A silver teapot with sage green tea cups and saucers completed the table. From a distance it was quite a sight. The poorly built hut, mother and child sipping tea as if they were in a breakfast room with a crumb cloth beneath their feet, and the row of natives, silently watching.

The fruit the cook wanted grew on a small tree near the creek. Kate turned from the crooked hut on the hill and headed northwards. The pale green leaves and reddish fruit were easy to spot among the shrubs and trees, and she headed directly to the plant and began to pluck a quantity of the ripe berries, placing them in the small basket. With luck she could dip her feet in the creek and massage her aching calves before returning to the kitchen. Kate ate as she worked, nibbling at the white tart flesh.

'You eat plenty.'

Kate started at the voice. A group of young women and children stood nearby, giggling. She hadn't heard them approach and it wasn't the first time they'd snuck up on her. It was a trait Kate would never get used to. Most of the group were naked, although some of the women were wearing skin cloaks against the morning chill. Wiping her mouth, Kate checked the amount of fruit already picked. The tree was nearly bare. The basket only half-full. The girl was right – Kate had consumed more than she'd realised.

'Hungry?'

The girl who spoke was named Sally. Slender, with a smile that could make a person grin, Kate knew she was George Southerland's woman. Sally wore the beaded necklace that he'd given her on the day of their arrival at the farm. Kate noticed the swell of her stomach. She was with child. 'Do you want something?' Kate asked cautiously. Although these women were part of the tribe that lived on the farm, Kate remained wary of striking up any form of friendship with them. The murder of the girl at the Kable property and her own experience still haunted; only the weight of the pistol comforted her.

The girl crinkled her nose. 'Hello.'

'Hello.'

'You come dig with us.' It wasn't a question, more a matter of fact.

'Dig what?'

The women carried sturdy sticks with a pointed end.

Sally walked a few feet away to a clump of low-growing plants with oval leaves. Positioning the stick, she dug the plant out in three quick movements. It had a large pale tap-root. 'Wudhugaa.'

'Wudhugaa,' Kate repeated, her efforts drawing more giggles. 'Do you eat this?'

'Eat, cook. You come dig?'

It was not the first time Kate had been approached to join them. She lifted the basket. 'I can't. I have to leave.'

'You not be friend?' Sally appeared disappointed. The other women turned away and muttered as if they expected a refusal. They moved in the direction of the creek, their children running ahead, laughing and calling to each other. 'This our home too,' Sally added quietly.

The girl was right. Her tribe were welcomed here and existed happily under the terms of the agreement that George Southerland had brokered on their behalf with their Elder. Kate wondered if she'd been too quick to keep her distance from Sally and the other women. Admittedly, it had taken some time to get used to their living in such close proximity to the house grounds, yet this wasn't the Kable farm and there was no reason to suspect that any members of the tribe were disgruntled enough to hurt one of their own through association with the whites.

'Maybe one day you can show me what you dig?'

'Maybe,' Sally agreed.

Both of them smiled and as Kate walked away, she couldn't help but think that she'd made a friend. It struck her that she'd never really had one, at least not since before her father had died and she'd played regularly with Henrietta McKemey after lessons. Swinging the basket back and forth, she moved through the trees. Sally's people were healthy and happy. The young men barked trees and occasionally worked as shepherds, helping to bring in mobs of sheep from further afield when required, and in return the tribe stayed on their native lands, hunted and fished as normal and were given rations. Blankets and sugar were particularly well-received.

'You shouldn't be out here.'

Kate turned on her heel. Betts may have been speaking to her but his attention was drawn to where Sally walked through the trees.

'They're not like us,' he said slowly. 'You watch yourself, miss. Thinking you can be friends with them will only bring you trouble.'

Kate hugged the basket to her chest. Sally faded from view. They were quite alone.

'Heading out again, we are,' Betts stated with reluctance. 'He's sending us miles south to watch his bloody sheep. Reckon I'm lucky to have survived this long.'

'Well, don't let me keep you.' A knot of anxiety grew in her chest. There were a number of men, convict and pardoned, working on the property, but most were usually watching over the livestock miles away. When they were back for chores that didn't involve camping out, they left before dawn and returned at dusk, spending their nights in the men's hut. It was rare for Kate to be alone with one of them. She didn't like it.

Betts barred her path. Yellow teeth contrasted with sun-reddened skin. He was almost beyond bathing such was the dirt ingrained in the large pores on his nose and cheeks. 'They'll smile at you, tell you to follow them and then –' He made a slicing motion across his throat. 'I'm just saying, watch yourself, lass. Mr Callahan's right, he is. A musket a-piece is his advice. Putting the word out, he is. Trying to make that toffy-nosed squatter see sense. There's sheep been rushed and a fire was lit yesterday on the western end. I'd bolt I would, but I know they'd get me, probably skewer me good and proper, put me in one of their fire pits, cover me with dirt and cook me with me skin on like they do everything else.'

Kate began to back away. There was a strange look on the convict's face. It was more than fear. 'I don't want to go out there. Put in a word for me, will you, girl? I've done you no harm. Did me best I have. Nearly served me time and all. It's not right to send a body,' he looked beyond Kate, into the scrub that fringed the creek, 'out there. By himself.'

'Betts, what are you bloody well doing?'

The convict shuddered. George Southerland, on horseback with a musket in hand, lifted his weapon and aimed it at Betts. The man dropped to his knees.

'Leave him alone, Mr Southerland,' Kate cried out. 'We were only talking.'

'Talking? He's keen to be our first runaway, that's what he is. Aren't you, Betts?'

The convict remained mute.

'Look at him,' Kate argued. 'Can't you tell he doesn't want to go out there? He's afraid.'

Mr Southerland rested the musket across his thighs and walked his horse forward. Kate would have stood her ground had horse and rider not kept coming, but they did, forcing her to move swiftly out of the way. She tripped and fell heavily on her bottom, losing fruit from the basket that tumbled across the ground.

'Get moving, Betts.'

The convict remained cowering. Jumping from his horse, the overseer lifted the butt of the rifle, jabbing it viciously into Betts' face. The man fell sideways, howling in pain. 'Get up and get moving. Now.'

The man rose shakily, holding a hand to his cheek, and began to walk in the direction of the valley, head bowed.

'I'll not tolerate meddling in the running of this property.' Mr Southerland remounted his horse as Kate gathered the spilt fruit.

'But he's scared of the land, of being out there alone, of the natives,' Kate replied. She couldn't blame him. The idea of being left alone to watch sheep in the middle of the bush would scare anyone.

The former expedition leader holstered the musket and pushed his wide-brimmed hat back on his head. 'He should be and so should you. Look, there ain't nobody without problems here, Kate,' he said a little less roughly. 'There's some blacks that aren't taking kindly to their land being overrun in these parts and some hot-headed young bloods and assigned men that are hell-bent on teaching them a lesson. But the mob on this land are glad to be here. And I'm pleased to have 'em. Most of them are good people.' He tugged on the horse's reins. 'Most.'

'Where are you going?' Kate was suddenly afraid to be left alone.

'I've got Hardy fighting with one of his neighbours over a boundary, I don't have time for whining labour, man or woman,' he said pointedly as horse and rider began to walk away. 'We're riding out now to sort the southern border once and for all,' he called over his shoulder. 'We can't have Stewart's sheep eating the grasses we're leasing. So stay close to the huts with the other women.'

'But why are you leaving if there's trouble?' Kate had begun to run after him.

'Does a man no good to sit around and wait for it.' He spurred the mare and rode away.

At the kitchen hut, Kate upended the fruit on the table. Breathless and unnerved by the altercation with Betts and what she'd learnt from Mr Southerland, she approached the cook, hoping for a friendly ear, *needing* a friendly ear. 'Mrs Horton, I just saw –'

'What's the matter with you then and where have you been? Lift your chin, girl. I don't have time for your worries. I've plenty of me own.' The cook was quick to complain about the length of time Kate had been away, about the Missus needing water for a bath and the fact that there was barely enough fruit to fill the corner of her eye. 'Where's the rest of the fruit? Eat it, did you? Haven't I told you to eat a morsel before sun-up? Always you're shaking your head when I pass you a bit of bread. Saying the heat's too much. That you can only eat in the cool of a night. Then you go gobbling up the Missus's jam. You'll get in plenty trouble for that. Stealing, it is. Taking what isn't yours.'

'Maybe the blacks ate the fruit. I got what I could,' Kate replied stiffly. She couldn't deal with the cook's niggling. Not this morning.

'Maybe they did. Wouldn't be the first time. What are you looking so wan about, eh, Jelly-belly? It's not as if you've been in here, a-stoking the fire.' Roughly chopping two irregularly shaped onions, the cook dropped them in the iron pot over the cut rabbit pieces and added some dried herbs. 'Well, don't mind me. Get that fruit in a pot, add a handful of mixed peel from the herb shelf along with two cups of water. Put it on to simmer. Don't add the sugar yet, girl. I'll do that. It's the Missus's birthday today so I don't want any tongue-wagging from you. And don't forget to fetch the glass covers for the candles from the Missus's rooms. Them smelly tallow candles smoke more than a chimney, they do, and filth, well, I wash more cleaning rags here than me own clothes. Come on, hurry up. Sometimes I don't know why the Kables haven't sent you to the Female Factory, I really don't. You're more curse than blessing, more hindrance than help, more –'

'Stop it! Just stop it, Mrs Horton.' Kate's voice trembled. She closed her eyes tightly.

The older woman was breaking up day-old bread to make crumbs for the rabbit dish. 'It's the heat in here. Makes a person giddy, it does.' She pointed a grubby finger at Kate's bodice. 'Cut them bones out of your bodice, lass. There's not much needs holding in and you'll take the air a lot better. Cut me own bones out years ago, I did. What's the point, I thought, killing a great bloody fish to keep a woman's innards tight?' Mrs Horton sprinkled the crumbs over the rabbit and added a cup of water. 'It's the men what did it. Stop us from running about too much. Keep us meek, pliable. Well, I was onto them. 'Course the swells don't agree. Saw the Missus's catalogue from London what came with you. They got boned stays that you're laced into now. Truss you up like a turkey. The Missus is ordering two, one for her and one for young Sophie. The menfolk will be liking it. Lace 'em tight and keep 'em quiet. That's what they'll be saying.' The cook tucked a thin strand of hair underneath her mob cap and with a large wooden spoon scraped out two servings of rendered sheep fat from a ceramic dish and dolloped the lard onto the rabbit. 'Well, go on. Mr Callahan fetched a barrel of water from the creek. There's buckets outside. The Missus is waiting.'

With the buckets filled, Kate carried them to the Hardys' house. The door was open.

'Where have you been, Jelly-belly?' Sophie chastised. 'Mother's been waiting.'

'Good morning, Mrs Hardy.'

Kate emptied the water into the hip bath that had been set up in the middle of the room, which served as drawing, breakfast and dining room. The bath was placed on a brightly coloured rug and beside it sat Mrs Hardy, fanning herself with an old newspaper. The older woman didn't speak, electing instead to watch as Kate trundled back and forth across the tamped dirt floor, carting enough water so that she could bathe. By the time Kate had finished and the bath was full there was a trail of mud across the room where she'd slopped the water.

Mrs Hardy nodded to Sophie. The girl dropped two herb sachets in the water.

Kate drew a chair to the open door and sat down to a wintery view of the valley. Her role in these proceedings was to stand guard in case Mrs Hardy's ablutions were unwantedly disturbed, and the quiet allowed Kate the luxury of daydreams. Last night she'd dreamt of Major James Shaw, and his blond-headed presence had been a most welcome distraction. Kate wondered what he was doing and if he ever thought of her. Probably not. It was easy to be friendly towards a currency lass when the likelihood of seeing her again was slight.

'The water's a dreadful murky colour and it smells. You should have added a little rainwater.'

Kate swivelled in her chair. 'The creek is low, I think, and our water is down to four barrels, Mrs Hardy. We can't spare it for such –'

'Indulgences?' The woman finished the sentence and with her daughter's assistance removed her shift and stepped into the hip bath. Sophie began to soap her mother's shoulders, rubbing her neck with a flannel. 'Sophie, I would like to talk to Kate alone.'

'But I always –'

'Go.'

The girl left the hut, each step a stamp on the verandah floorboards that vibrated throughout the dwelling. She poked out her tongue at Kate on the way.

'If the wind changes it will stay like that,' Kate said softly.

Sophie scowled. 'You don't know anything, Jelly-belly.'

'I know you have lessons soon. Best you ready for them.'

'Bring your chair over here, Kate.'

Kate wondered if the woman expected her to take up where her daughter had left off. If so, she would be disappointed. The last person Kate had washed was her mother's body after she'd died, and Kate wasn't inclined to wash anyone, dead or alive, again.

'For one so outspoken you are prim,' Mrs Hardy commented as Kate positioned her chair at a slight angle, facing away from the bath and its occupant. The level of the brown water sat at the woman's waist, her knees protruding. A piece of wet muslin was draped across Mrs Hardy's chest for propriety's sake. 'I wasn't always so useless.' Her breasts wobbled as she searched for the dropped soap.

Kate did her best to keep her eyes averted although she couldn't help but notice that the woman looked ill.

'When we first arrived I did everything that you do now. It was difficult. Very difficult. It is not what I imagined. To work like a scullery maid. To dig holes into an unyielding ground. I have done my best. But it is too much, I have not the strength. My health is not as it was and so I contain myself to keeping an observant eye on the rabbit hutch, on the health of the vegetables, on my small family.' The woman looked at her nails. 'I'd thought once of growing vines.' She wiped the flannel across the wedge of homemade soap and delicately rubbed her neck. 'I find the heat quite suffocating. I'm glad for the winter. A cold bath is far more invigorating.'

In spite of the loneliness she was sure Mrs Hardy experienced as well, the woman was at pains to keep Kate at arm's length. She'd not been asked to sit at the rickety table and share conversation since the day of her arrival. Although, in fairness, there was little time to be idle. The closest Kate came to familiarity was at bathtime, as designated water carrier and guardian, then

Mrs Hardy talked. Otherwise the hut was quite out of bounds unless Kate was serving at table, cleaning the house or the silver. Both of which were done every second day, such was the dust.

A carriage clock ticked on the stone mantelpiece, the bath water splashed as the bather washed a leg, resting a cream thigh over the edge of the bath. The timber walls of the three-roomed hut had been plastered with a thin layer of mud and then newspapers. Needlework, images of flowers, were tacked onto the walls for decoration and the shelves held a mismatch of things: candles, glasses, books and a teapot. Swatches of material curtained windows that were mere holes with wooded shutters. Mrs Hardy had done her best to bring a touch of the feminine to the wilds.

'Some nights I dream of London, the foggy mists, the cool, cool air and the green, the grass is a true green, not this washed-out version. My sons are over there, studying. One day they will be great men. Look at my hands, ruined, my face ruined. Truly this land has the most abominable weather.

'My mother cleansed her face morning and night with equal parts Milk of Magnesia, paraffin oil and witch-hazel. It's very refreshing and fortifying for the skin, she –'

Mrs Hardy turned her head ever so slowly to stare at Kate. 'I should order some perhaps. Will you run to the store?' She gave a brief laugh. 'I have a list of things to be ordered. Such huge quantities I brought with me on arrival. It wasn't enough. Everything ran out. Six months, seven months and still I think of things that would make life easier: correspondence, a glass of milk, the newspapers. I wish the sheep would grow their wool faster for then Mr Southerland would journey southwards with my list. You should make one too, Kate. Things you need. It's all about need here, not want. I wonder how I used to fret over a pretty hat or a piece of lace.' She looked upwards. A length of canvas was swathed across the bark roof from corner to corner. A ceiling of sorts. 'I'd like a decent house with glass windows. Mr Hardy promises to secure the necessary materials, but he's no craftsman.' There'd been little progress made on the additions to the house although the fence was now completed and floorboards had been put down in the Hardys' bedroom.

Withdrawing her leg from the bath's edge, Mrs Hardy stuck out the other. Kate noticed the limb was swollen from the knee down. It was as if the pustular boil, having left the woman's face, had travelled south.

'When will the wool be ready for market?' It was difficult not to stare at Mrs Hardy's toenails, which were long and yellow.

'July or August. Mr Southerland is in charge of such things.'

A return to Sydney more than tempted. The hardships of the journey north were all but forgotten, save the killing of the native. That would never leave her. Kate thought of the fig tree in the Reverend's garden, of scowling Madge. Certainly there would be other schools requiring teachers, and employers that would pay her.

'I envy you. As a currency lass you are bred of this land and are naturally used to its demands. Hard work never hurt a person, Kate, though I know you resent it.'

'It's not what I expected.'

'You hoped for better things.' Mrs Hardy nodded in understanding. 'I thought I knew where I was travelling to, but self-sufficiency does not come easily to everyone. My one consolation is that the evenings do bring simple pleasures. To sit and sew, my daughter at my side while Mr Hardy reads by the light of his brass candlesticks, well, it is difficult to explain.'

'I shared such a childhood with my own parents,' Kate replied. 'Novels, books of travel and history.' It was a pleasure to talk of these things again.

The older woman wrung out the wash cloth and dabbed the material across her face and neck. 'Really? You are quite learned, aren't you? And what of the bible?'

'I am not a reader of it, no. I fail to see the devotion to one who has made the world a misery for so many. If God did create the world, and man and woman, why did he then create illness, snakes and spiders? Why do some people starve and children die young?'

'Enough, Kate.' The woman dropped her hand in the water irritably. 'Your Reverend certainly achieved very little in enlightenment where you are concerned. I would suggest not speaking this blasphemy in front of my husband. We are a God-fearing family and suffer daily from the lack of ministrations from a goodly servant of Our Lord.'

There was little point in quarrelling on the subject. The need to believe in something larger than one's life provided guidance and support for many, although Kate imagined most prayers went unanswered.

'Among all of us you look the better since your arrival. You have lost the puppy fat you carried and are far more amenable, or perhaps I have been too self-absorbed. In any case you know how much work is required of you. There is scant time for anything else.' Mrs Hardy rested her back against the bath, her eyes becoming heavy-lidded. 'You don't like me, do you? Don't answer that. If we were in Sydney I would simply expect my due deference. But it takes time to understand that things are different out here.'

There were plenty of things that Kate could have said in response as to why she had every right to dislike the Hardys. 'You forget, Mrs Hardy, I am the daughter of a free settler. And I am not used to this place either, nor its hardships. I still sleep on the floor.'

The woman sat upright, revealing sagging breasts beneath the sheer cloth. She grimaced as if in pain. 'Yes, you have complained often enough. Well then, you should have a bed at least. I shall speak to my husband about the building of one for you. Tell me,' she asked thoughtfully, 'where do your thoughts on marriage stand now?'

'You are here through marriage, I here for the lack of it. I could ask you the same thing,' Kate answered quietly.

'You are a most exasperating young woman. I didn't send Sophie away so that you and I could argue. I am ill. It has been a gradual thing, starting with some pain but it grows worse by the day. I wanted to know if you had any skill with healing, if your mother had been so inclined.'

'Only the barest, I'm sorry to say. It is your leg? May I?'

The older woman nodded and Kate pushed the skin in a number of spots on the swollen limb. The mark of her finger remained, an indentation in the puffy flesh.

'It's dropsy, isn't it?'

'I believe so. I have seen it a number of times but never treated it,' she hastened to add. 'Rest, I believe, and raising the leg may help drain the fluid.'

'Yes, I have a medicinal and pharmacological tome that suggests it is indeed dropsy, but my leg is not the only part affected. My stomach grows distended.'

'Perhaps you are with child?' Kate suggested.

'My courses ceased last year.' Mrs Hardy placed her leg back within the confines of the hip bath. 'The blacks killed my baby through fright and made me barren.' Her voice drifted. 'Dropsy can be fatal?'

How should she reply? People did die of dropsy, but whether it was the actual swelling of the limb or some other unrecognised problem was beyond Kate. 'I really don't know. Have you had the ailment long?'

'Long enough. I grow breathless and exhausted whether doing the simplest of tasks or in bed at night.'

They were beyond the ministrations of a doctor, of a hospital, although the limited exposure Kate had with these institutions suggested that more people went in than came out. In spite of Mrs Hardy's condescension, Kate felt sorry for her.

'Mr Hardy expects me to sit down to a feast of rabbit for my name day.' Her words trailed. 'We have had a shabby beginning, you and I, Kate Carter, but I would ask you not to tell a soul of this.'

'Surely your husband should be informed? I know he would want you to seek advice. To return to Sydney.'

'Perhaps, but no-one will be journeying south until the sheep are shorn and the wool is ready for market. It will be a chance to recoup some of the monies outlaid on this venture. This is a vital time for us, Kate. For all of us, and he can't spare men to take me to Sydney, not now, especially with the current problems.'

'The natives.'

She nodded somberly. 'Mr Southerland arrived with news last night that there are continued small uprisings. The mounted troops will not be coming to our aid this time. It seems that although we have leased acreage, and used our savings to settle in this unfathomable land, having gone beyond the designated nineteen counties we must look to our own to protect us. Imagine. Men were killed last year and they leave us on our own.'

'But haven't some of the natives been killed as well?'

Their conversation was interrupted by the sounds of approaching horses. Mrs Hardy sat upright, the water sloshing. Kate's hand felt for the pistol in her skirt pocket as she ran to the open door. 'It's Mr Hardy. Mr Southerland rides with him and another. A man I have not seen before.'

'A visitor? Heavens, and here am I bathing.' Her voice trembled with excitement. 'We've not had a visitor since, well, we never have. Fetch my robe, Kate, and help me out of this infernal contraption, then run and tell Cook we have a guest. She must do her best to provide.'

Kate placed the robe around Mrs Hardy's shoulders as she rose and assisted her from the hip bath, then walked outside to the verandah, closing the door firmly behind her. She too was excited to see who had arrived. The men drew up abruptly, their coat-tails dragging across their horses' rumps as they dismounted. The animals nickered softly, dropping their heads to feed.

'I will show you the map.' Mr Hardy stomped up onto the verandah. Ignoring Kate he kicked the door open and went inside.

Kate retreated to the side of the hut. Inside fervent whispering could be heard between husband and wife. By the looks on the faces of the waiting men they wouldn't be sitting down to enjoy tea and johnny-cakes. Mr Southerland was stuffing his pipe intently, while the other man's hands were placed firmly on wide hips. He was tall and solid with a flintlock pistol holstered at his waist and a ragged beard that matched the overseer's in length and breadth. A deep frown line, crevice-like, ran between his brows. Considering this was the first visitor to the Hardy farm since Kate's arrival seven months earlier, it was not an auspicious start.

'Here, Stewart.' Mr Hardy reappeared, waving two sheaths of paper. 'Lease agreement and farm boundaries,' he stated, spreading the documents on the verandah table.

'You should have sought me out before you began blazing trees to suit yourself.' Stewart joined him on the porch and studied the separate parchments for long minutes.

'I've been here for near two years. The most I knew of you was a name on a map.'

'Fetch me a light, girl,' Mr Southerland told her.

Kate rushed to the kitchen hut, returning with a lighted twig, young Sophie following and Mrs Horton yelling at her to attend to her chores.

The overseer held the burning stick to the pipe as his gaze met Kate's. He sucked hard on the tobacco until the leaves lit, a puff of smoke coming from his nose and mouth. 'Best you take the girl away, Kate,' he warned. 'These two have been arguing for the last five mile.'

Sophie remained mute as Kate dragged the girl to her side, but they moved only a few feet away, Kate holding a finger to her lips to ensure the child remained quiet. The air was thick with expectation. Kate drew on the atmosphere, aware that their droll life made a major problem between neighbours a welcome diversion for onlookers.

'See,' Mr Hardy announced with obvious satisfaction, 'it's as I told you. The tree with the markings is on my land, not yours. I'd appreciate it if you could move your sheep. I've had problem enough with the blacks burning out sections. I can't afford to be losing more feed.'

Retrieving his own map from a coat pocket, Stewart unfolded the paper and pressed a thumb on the area in question. 'Aye, well, not by my reckoning, nor the date of this map,' he replied. 'I was here eighteen months afore you. The right to that land is mine.'

Mr Hardy waved an impatient hand at the overseer.

'Even if that be true, you'll have to redraw the boundary so that it's fair to both parties,' Mr Southerland advised. 'Once it's done the agreement can be signed and dated.'

'I'm not giving away land I claimed and paid for by the right of law.' Refolding the map, Stewart replaced it in his coat pocket. The same hand slid towards the flintlock at his waist.

'And you think I should, Scotsman?' Mr Hardy's voice rose. 'You think I should give way to you?'

'Aye, I've fought blacks, whites, fire and fever.' Don't think I'll fold to the first new-comer land-grabbing Englishman. You're not in your Mother Country now, Hardy. This is a new land, new rules. You'll not be lording it over me. If you've a problem with the bound-aries,' Stewart told them, his fingers closing on the pistol's hilt, 'then get on your horses and ride to Sydney, sort it out with the Colonial Secretary, but I tell you now I'll not give up one bit of –'

Mr Southerland extracted a musket from his horse and levelled it at the landowner. 'As I said, we'll be working this out amicably ourselves, Mr Stewart, sir. If the people in Syd-e-ney Town ain't interested in our problems with the blacks then they rightly aren't going to be concerned over a boundary dispute. Besides, do you think the likes of them will ride all this way to see who's right or wrong?' He cocked the trigger. 'We're the ones who must come to an understanding. I thought you'd be amicable with that, especially since it was the Australian Agricultural Company that pushed you off the land you were squatting on, down south.'

'How the hell did you know that?'

The door to the house opened. Mrs Hardy, dressed in a cream and lace gown more suitable for a reception room in a grand Sydney townhouse than a bush hut, gave a sunny smile. 'Mr Stewart, is it? Wonderful. You're married, I hope? I would be delighted to make your wife's acquaintance. Perhaps when the current difficulties with the natives are behind us we can meet at some midpoint between our respective farms. A picnic of sorts.' She noticed Kate and her daughter. 'Kate, dear, do ask Cook to make tea for us. We'll take it here on the verandah.'

A flummoxed Mr Stewart removed his hat and mumbled a hello.

'Come now. Join us at the table.' She linked an arm through that of the Scotsman and the man found himself escorting the lady of the house to a chair at the table. 'You too, Mr Southerland. Those of us living in these parts must do our best to come to terms. There are so few of us, after all, and one day either of us may call on the other for assistance. Don't you agree?'

Kate watched in admiration as Mrs Hardy's gracious tone eased the tense standoff. Mr Southerland lowered his musket, although the two men on the porch didn't rush to speak. Sophie ran barefoot to her mother's side.

'There's good grass in that area.' Having seated Mrs Hardy, Mr Stewart began to pace the unstable verandah. 'But I suppose we could mark out the area together. Then a fence of sorts could be constructed perhaps. As long as it's fair, mind. I'll not put up with any shenanigans.'

'We'll be cutting timber for the rest of our days,' Mr Hardy complained.

'A brush fence would do,' the overseer suggested. 'Pile branches and cut scrub to make a barrier.'

'Better to use cut poles,' Mr Stewart decided. 'Forked sticks driven into the ground, and saplings or young trees laid across them.'

'It would stop further boundary problems with other settlers,' Mr Hardy agreed.

'Aye, it would do that. If we had the labour we could add a second, shorter row. A two-railed fence.' The Scotsman scratched at his beard. 'It might ease the straying of sheep as well.'

'We'll use the blacks. The tribe here would do it.' Samuel Hardy waited for the overseer to answer. 'Well, wouldn't they, George? You keep telling me they're harmless, that they'll do as they're bid. Mind you, that doesn't stop them from firing the land or that tracker of yours, Joe, from taking off and not returning. How long's he been gone for now?'

'They can be persuaded, but you'll have to make it worth their while,' the overseer replied.

Mr Stewart also agreed to send men from his farm to assist in the building of the fence. 'We just need to agree on the date.'

'George will oversee the construction for me. We need someone armed, after all.'

'All my shepherds are armed, so there's no problems there,' Mr Stewart told them, 'and in truth we've had few problems with the blacks.'

Mr Hardy nearly choked. 'Convicts, armed? You must be daft, man.'

'Not at all. I can't afford to lose labour. I had one man run off six months ago or more but he came back, sad and sorry and more frightened than a child without a candle on a dark night. He's a willing worker now he has a musket. But another, a half-caste, has been and gone twice now, without arms. I'd lay odds on his death.'

Kate left the group to their discussions and went in search of the cook. Mary Horton was sitting in the dirt next to the hole in the hill where their stores were kept. As she moved closer Kate saw at once that the wooden door was ajar and a trail of flour leading to the north suggested robbery. The cook merely pointed on her arrival and Kate walked into the space of hollowed-out dirt. The storehouse was the cook's domain and only she and Mr Hardy had a key to the heavy padlock. Kate never could have imagined that so much was stored within. Goods were piled high to the rafters. Bags of flour, drums of tobacco, barrels of preserved fruit and one apiece of middling sugar and the cheap black ration kind, shared space with pairs of shearing shears, quart pots, tomahawks, iron nails, a large chest of tea and another filled with clay pipes. There were piles of men's clothing, blue blankets, a bolt of women's dress material and any number of bottles holding potions. Kate saw that a portion of the flour was gone, some of the sugar and half of the tobacco and the men's clothing had been rifled through. Only the cook and Mr Hardy would know exactly what had been taken. The markings on the wooden door suggested an axe was used. Kate guessed the thievery was done this morning after the men had left and she'd headed to the creek.

'Blacks,' Mrs Horton mumbled. 'We give them blankets and sugar, flour and the like and still the ungrateful sods take what's ours. We'll be on rations now until the next trip to Syd-e-ney or when the crop comes in. Whatever's first. You'll be busy the next few days, girl, so no lay-abouting. I'll have to do an inventory. Mrs Kable will have the book. She always has the book.'

'You mean Mr Hardy,' Kate corrected.

'I mean whatever I say.'

Kate didn't argue. 'Mrs Horton, Mrs Hardy would like tea made and –'

'Tea? They want tea when the blacks have done this?'

'Would our blacks have done it?'

268

'Our blacks.' The cook spat in the dirt. 'Jelly-belly, you sound like George Southerland. He thinks by bedding the women he can keep them in line. Throw them a few stores, pass out a handful of trinkets. In Syd-e-ney there are enough of us to push the natives over the hills, to keep us safe, but out here, well it's them that will be doing the pushing. If we run out of food we're not like them. We can't scratch around in the dirt to get a feed.'

The wheat crop was still to be planted. There'd not been enough rain and the little moisture stored from March's showers had quickly dried. 'We must hope for rain, Mrs Horton.'

'Pray on it, lass, if you're a believer, for we'll be out of rainwater in a few weeks and then we'll be drinking from the creek. Eh, where are you going?'

'To tell Mr Hardy that we've been robbed. That door needs to be mended.'

'Best be on your guard.' The woman scrambled to her feet and hurried after Kate. 'For now we know.'

'What do we know?'

The cook looked at Kate as if she were foolish. 'That they've been watching us.'

⚜ Chapter 18 ⚜

1838 June — near the Big River

They were camped in a valley near pointy-topped hills. Behind them lay the mountain in whose shadow they had met the old man in the hut. The giant monolith with its forests and low-scrubbed heathlands was now invisible, hidden behind a line of stony hills, while in the east the sun was yet to rise, the land cast in tones of pinks and purple. Adam shrugged off the kangaroo hide cloak; beside him Bidjia stirred. The head of their clan had been quiet the last few days but they had kept up a reasonable pace, although their midday rests had lengthened. Jardi had risen to explore their surrounds and would soon return. Light seeped across country captured by the chill of winter. They'd covered a mosaic of landscapes over the previous months but the valley they were in now held the promise of glistening life come spring. Here there would be good grasses and animals in abundance. Only water and warmth were needed to bring this land to life.

In the west where the countryside lay in shadows, a line of thin smoke appeared to form a bridge between land and sky. Blacks were burning the terrain. Fire-stick farming had made the land plentiful. There would be many tubers and fibrous roots for the eating in this peaceful place. The whites were not yet here in great numbers and Adam and Jardi both thought Bidjia would be tempted to stop, for they had already travelled far and the great hills which they headed for and that existed as a barrier between land and water were not yet visible. They had been on the run for nearly nine months. It was time to stop moving, but Bidjia grew more adamant with every passing day. He wished to follow the gathering creeks and rivers, to trace these life-giving waterways to the mountains and beyond to the sea.

'Are you sure you don't wish to stay here? The nights grow frosty and this would be a good place to camp for the winter.'

Bidjia blew on the pile of twigs and leaves, gradually feeding the fire so that it grew hot. 'We have already spent too long here and my bones grow weary. With my lands gone they draw me to the great waters. To a place like that I knew as a child.' He laid a larger branch on the growing flames. 'I would have our blood continue. I would have Jardi find himself a woman so our clan goes on, so that we are not lost. So that our people and our stories survive. To do so we must find a compatible tribe.'

'We're safe here,' Adam argued.

'We are not free of the white settlers,' Bidjia countered. 'I fear this place we have entered. It is like the placid river. Here the surface appears still, suggesting good fishing but beneath, the currents boil and rage. The fish in their confusion swim in all directions and eat each other in bewilderment.'

'You sense all this?' Adam wished he had such foresight.

Bidjia shrugged. 'Some I sense, some I see, some you learnt from the old man in the hut, the rest I know from what we have left behind. The white man who has a cow killed will kill a black in vengeance. It may not be the black that speared it, nor may the white man kill just one of us. In truth he does not care. We are nothing to him. He has no respect for our way of life and we do not understand his. We live from and with the land, they seek to own it, control it. And here,' he spread his arms wide, 'it is worse, for the whites are not yet everywhere and so they are scared of our kind. They hate what they do not understand. They wish we would go away, or at least take the sugar and blankets that they offer and in return see us toil for them.'

Adam unwrapped the remaining black duck left from the three he'd snared the previous evening. He'd stuffed its beak with pepper and wrapped the bird in damp grasses so the night's fast would be broken by more than a mouthful of water and some tuberous roots. They were good eating, although Bidjia laughed at his white-man preparation.

'They are like meat-ants, the settlers. They build their nests and then pick the bones clean of each place they come to.' Bidjia stopped speaking, lifted a leg until his foot rested in the crook of his knee and leant on his spear. 'They know we are here.'

It was not the whites the old man spoke of. Adam threaded a stick through the small carcass and held it above the fire. Close by lay his musket.

'The musket is no good here.' Bidjia spoke as if he read Adam's mind. 'The spear and the boomerang are quiet, like the rustle of grasses. Remember that as we move through this place.'

Adam rotated the duck carefully as the flames licked the feathers burning the plumage. Once the body was blackened he rested the ends of the threaded stick on the forked branches that made a makeshift spit.

Jardi appeared from the trees with two quart pots filled with water. He'd taken to wearing a cotton shirt with the onset of colder weather. Squatting by the fire he wedged the vessels in the embers. 'There are signs, but I saw no-one.'

'They will come,' their father said with confidence. 'They always come.'

Yesterday morning they had awoken to the sound of musket fire. The younger men had been keen to investigate but Bidjia had been adamant. They were moving forwards, not back, and he had no wish to interfere in another's fight. They'd already been involved in enough skirmishes.

'We have no clan ties to these people,' the old man reminded them. 'They will not like us being here.'

Adam rotated the spit. 'I wouldn't have expected them to be any different than the rest.' The moment they had left their lands it had begun. They'd soon discovered that they were not always welcome when they crossed into new lands. There was always a small group of warriors ready to attack without provocation. All three of them had the scars to prove it.

Jardi poured sugar into each of the quart pots. 'To the west along the water there were women's things scattered nearby, baskets, cooking tools. The camp appeared seasonal. It looked like a raiding party perhaps two, three nights ago. They are ahead of us.'

'White?' Adam asked.

'There was one with boots, the others blacks. Eight including a woman, have headed east, another five, old people and children, escaped north.'

'I have seen enough fighting.' Bidjia turned to his white son. 'Now do you understand why I tell you not to use the musket? It is best that we pass through here quietly.'

Jardi turned to his father and laughed. 'My white brother is no good with the spear. He has not the muscle for the throwing stick. The musket is easier for him.'

Adam charged Jardi, knocking him into the dirt. They rolled and tumbled across the ground, strong hands clutching at taut bare skin. They laughed and shouted abuse at the other before stopping, their bodies crusted in dirt. Finally Adam extended a hand and helped Jardi to his feet.

They ate quickly, crunching the soft bones of the bird between their teeth and sharing out the tea. By the time the sun was warming their skin they were ready to move. Jardi doused the fire with dirt and the three men set off on foot.

◈

The country was sparsely timbered in places and they made easy going of the gullies and small rises that threaded the valley. Over the previous months they'd been watchful, tentative, but as they'd headed north the white man's settlements grew fewer and today the men felt a sense of exhilaration. They'd kept away from the dirt tracks, avoiding shanties and stockmen. It almost seemed as if they'd walked free of the settlers' boundaries and come to untouched country. But in truth they knew better.

At noon they were stopped by a river. Kangaroos and wallabies startled by their approach lifted their heads tentatively from where they nibbled grasses on the sandy bank. They hopped away cautiously to hide among the timber as the three men walked down the steep bank. The river moved sluggishly, waiting to be topped up with rain from the mountains to the east. Jardi wanted to build a canoe, to speed down the waterway to the west until the land flattened out and he could see the setting sun. There was logic to this. The days were cool. The nights grew long. A warm place to wait out winter appealed. Such a thought was not welcomed by Bidjia though, who'd grown up in the shadow of cliffs and fished in the great waters.

Bidjia waded into the water, testing the depth. It was too deep to cross.

'We'll go further, find a narrower point.' Adam remained mindful of what the old man in the hut had told him. He shared his thoughts with the men, that this must be the Big River. 'Best we be on guard.'

There was a waterhole not far from where they stood. The older man walked to the edge where great trees hugged the moist edges, their massive roots exposed like skeletons. The blue-brown stillness of the pool of water suggested depth and good fishing but although the day had grown warm the place felt cold. There were scarred trees on both sides of the waterhole. Some of the markings were indistinguishable, their shapes obscured by a lack of light due to the thick canopy, others were recent and clearly defined. One tree was scored in the shape of a shield, another trunk bore an outline that resembled a spear thrower. The two younger men clambered up the steep bank and walked out into the timber. A tree with a large trunk and thick, fibrous bark had recently had an outline cut into it. Stone wedges had been inserted around the edges to loosen the bark.

Adam ran his hand across the rough surface. 'A canoe. This bark is ready to be pulled free.'

Musket shots sounded. At the river they joined Bidjia and then ran into the bush. They headed west following the water-course, running through trees and bushes, spears at the ready, Adam with the musket. In the distance came the unmistakeable sound of musket fire. The shots carried on the breeze, but with a northerly wind they couldn't be sure from how far away the noise had carried. At the top of a rise they stopped. They could smell smoke and the tang of sheep. They'd hoped for land untouched, unsullied by strangers.

'They have already settled north of here.' Jardi stuck his spear in the dirt, his anger evident. 'Did you not once tell us, brother, that there were nineteen counties? That the settlers were to stay in these areas governed by their white king?'

'I also mentioned the Governor is finding it impossible to control his people and has changed the laws. Land outside the boundary can be leased now.'

Bidjia looked askance. 'So they go anywhere? They squat on

land and make it their own? What of the white king, Bronzewing? Does he not know of us?'

'There is no king,' Adam explained. 'A woman now sits upon the English throne.'

'A woman.' Bidjia shook his head. 'All will be lost.'

Jardi pointed to where a wisp of smoke was visible through the trees. 'I think there is trouble ahead.'

Turning back in the direction of the river, Bidjia pointed to the scarred trees. Fresh imprints marked the passage of men in the soft river sand. He ran a finger in the dirt, tracing the heel and the spreading toes and then slowly lifted his head.

At the top of the riverbank five men waited, shields and spears at the ready. Painted with ochre and animal fat, all had bones through their noses, their arms and wrists decorated with bracelets of fur and hide. Only one wore the trousers of a white man. This man, their leader, walked a few paces towards them. A luminous oval shell, engraved with tiny figures, hung from the centre of his string belt. Adam lifted his musket, Jardi his spear, but Bidjia was quick to raise a hand.

'Listen first,' he commanded.

The warrior rested his spear in the sand. The stone tip was barbed, a weapon for fighting as it could not be withdrawn from flesh. Although his companions were dark skinned, this man was slightly paler. He talked quickly at first in a strange tongue but gradually it became apparent that he spoke in a mix of his own dialect and English. The warriors had been following them for two days. Bidjia and his party were in the heart of their lands and they were not welcome at this special place.

When the warrior had completed his address, Bidjia handed over the message stick. As the man studied it, Bidjia introduced them and, announcing his clan name, pointed south to their lands. The stick was well-used. Each new tribal territory demanded introduction and then the granting of permission to pass through it. The message stick seemed to appease the warrior for he handed it back to Bidjia and beckoned the other warriors forward. The leader had a mass of long hair. He was tall with deep scars etched across his torso, his body hairless. He called himself Mundara and gestured to Adam as if it were better he was not present.

'I have raised him since this high.' Bidjia lifted his hand to indicate that the white man had been a child when he'd found him.

The warrior pointed his spear. 'You raise a white and yet they take our lands and kill our people.'

'He is of my clan,' Bidjia replied calmly.

The warrior spent long minutes studying Adam, as if sizing him up for a fight. 'I am a descendant of a great warrior.'

Bidjia was silent. The names of the dead were not talked of.

'Where do you travel, Bidjia?'

'Across the mountains to the great waterhole.'

'The cold has come. You best move fast. You are far from home.'

'There is no place for us in the lands of our people. The whites have claimed it. My clan is no longer and so we wander.'

This response seemed to satisfy the warriors for they formed a circle and, as one, sat on the ground cross-legged, leaving spaces for Bidjia, Jardi and Adam. Overhead the sky was a wedge of blue fringed by tawny leaves. Elongated shadows reached across the swirl of water to where the men sat.

Mundara gestured to the musket. 'Trade.'

'There is no trade worth the gun,' Bidjia countered.

The warrior snarled but knew Bidjia's words to be true. Instead he pointed to the shell bracelet on Adam's wrist, offering a cuff of fur from his arm. When this was refused he grew displeased. 'I have no quarrel. Bronzewing, trade?'

'No trade.'

Mundara frowned. 'Across the mountains, by the waters, you will find more.'

Untying a pouch at his waist Bidjia pulled out a plug of tobacco, sitting the piece in the middle of the circle. He explained that the whites used it as payment along with their version of honey, a grainy substance called sugar. Breaking off a piece of the plug he placed it in his mouth and chewed carefully, the tobacco balling in the side of his cheek. He gestured for Mundara to try some and the warrior snatched it up.

'You tell me nothing I don't already know. I have worked for a white.' He gnawed at the knob for some seconds and then offered Bidjia the fur bracelet. This was accepted. The trade was complete.

The warriors muttered among themselves. 'You will join our fight,' Mundara stated. 'Our lands are rich, we protect them.'

'How do you protect them?' Adam argued. 'The whites have muskets and horses. The more you attack, the more they will come, we have seen this. It is better to sit down and make terms for peace.'

'Peace?' Mundara scowled. 'When our ancestor, the Sky Father, came down from the sky to the land he created the rivers, the mountains and the forests. He gave us our laws and our songs, he did not do this for the white man, he did it for his people, us. This is what we fight for, what the whites would try to steal. You do not understand because you are white.'

'I understand plenty, and so should you.' Adam frowned. 'I can see by your skin that you have the blood of the white man in you.'

'It does not rule me,' Mundara scowled.

'In this place,' Bidjia warned, 'we talk only.'

'So you will fight,' the warrior stated.

'We wish to move through your lands peacefully. We want no war,' Bidjia answered.

'Such a word does not exist here.'

'We heard whites have been murdered,' Jardi said carefully.

'They stole women. Took what is not theirs to take. This was their payback, but the white man can never be bested. He must

278

show that he is stronger. Soon after the whitefellas sent men on horses to kill those of our people who were responsible. Hundreds were slaughtered. They named this place of victory in honour of a Great White Chief.'

Bidjia offered his sympathies for the tragedy. 'We have heard of the sorry business. It is a bad thing.'

'If you do not want to fight you should not have come here,' Mundara said simply. 'We are at war.'

'Then we will go.' Bidjia stood.

'Follow the water,' Mundara directed. 'There is a crossing place nearby. You will see it. The rains have been slow to come and the river is not full. Go north, then head towards the mountains. Do not come back.'

From the depth of the timber came a scream. A young black woman appeared, naked except for a strip of hide which hid her woman's parts from the world. She skirted the edge of the bank as a piece of wood sailed through the air. The throwing stick hit the female in the back and she fell, tumbling down the sandy slope to lay sprawled near the water's edge.

The man in pursuit collected the stick he'd used to bring her down and, without slowing his stride, reached the woman and pulled her upright by the hair. She was young, with plump features and large frightened eyes.

Adam and Jardi got to their feet.

'This is not our business,' Bidjia cautioned.

The girl stretched out her hand to them. She was covered in sand, pale crystals against jet black skin. She called to the men on the riverbank and then, on seeing Mundara, fell silent. The warrior spoke and the man who held the girl replied in apologetic tones. Taking her by the arm he began to drag her away.

'The whites displace the natural order of things.' Bidjia spoke to placate Mundara as well as Adam, but it was Jardi who grew anxious.

The younger man recalled the scattered cooking items that he'd come across at dawn. It was possible that the girl had been abducted from that very spot. 'We should do something.'

'Do nothing,' his father said quietly. 'This is not our fight. Her clan will decide what is to become of her.'

'And you think they will sit down with these men to get her back?' Jardi's statement hung. 'You see the scars, the weapons.'

'Does the white man stop another from beating a wife? No,' Bidjia replied angrily.

'He's a renegade. Worse, there is white blood within him. This Mundara may speak like a black but the two parts within him means he fights himself.' Black warriors had crossed Adam's path over the years. Desperate men who'd left their tribe, some simply intent on causing trouble, others keen to avenge the wrongdoings of the whites. Some were banished by their Elders, others were quietly revered, but those of mixed blood were harder to gauge.

As the girl was dragged along the riverbank, Jardi followed their progress. She was slim, with shoulder-length hair, and she fought her abductor at every step, digging her heels in the dirt and straining against his grasp. He hit the girl in the face and flung her over his shoulder. Her arms hung lifelessly down his back as he stalked up the bank.

'You leave this place,' Mundara ordered. His men followed him silently up the incline of the riverbank to disperse into the bush.

'What of the girl?' Jardi queried. 'If what you say is true, we should go after her.'

Bidjia trudged ahead. 'There will be other women. Ones that don't come with blood-letting.'

They followed the river as instructed. The crossing place was indeed close by and they waded through the waist-deep water holding their weapons aloft and filling waterbags. They were soon climbing up the sandy bank on the other side. Bidjia led them cautiously through the dense timber, walking steadily for the remainder of the day and into the next, until the river lay far behind them.

They came upon the bodies at mid-morning. There had been rain overnight and few tracks were visible. Birds scattered on their arrival and a wild dog growled and ran off into the bush as the three men approached the grisly sight. The first thing Adam noticed were the large number of human heads. These lay separate to a pile of bodies that had been burnt and partly consumed by fire.

Jardi bent over and sicked up his breakfast. Bidjia was too shocked to speak. The majority of the dead Aboriginals were women and children as well as some old men. It was clear that they'd been either hacked to death, shot or both, and had then been set alight.

Adam could only guess at the people who'd committed these terrible murders. 'My god,' he said loudly. He turned to Bidjia. 'Women and children? Decapitated?' There must have been at least thirty dead Aboriginals.

'Whitefellas.' Bidjia squatted, scraping up some sand and letting the grains trickle through his fingers. Very slowly he let out a low moan. None of them could believe what they were seeing.

'What do you want to do, Bidjia? Bury them?'

'Their essence has already gone, as we should go. Come.'

Jardi and Bidjia remained quiet for the rest of the day. Adam followed the two men, equally subdued. It seemed that they had unwittingly entered a land at war.

'We make camp here,' Bidjia told Jardi, stopping in a sheltered clearing. 'I must rest for a time.' They had walked a day only.

Adam thought of Mundara's warning and the carnage of the previous day. 'We should go further, Bidjia.'

'I cannot.' Resting his spear against a tree trunk he surveyed the campsite, nodding as if pleased with the selection. 'I have seen too much. Jardi will stay with me, you, Bronzewing, will go walkabout. I know you, my son. You will not sit down for a few days while I rest. Go.'

Adam looked from Bidjia to Jardi. The younger man was clearly not impressed to be left behind, but he didn't argue. Someone had to care for Bidjia while he regained his strength and Jardi was a capable hunter.

'Go,' Bidjia urged. 'On your return we will continue.'

Adam didn't know if he should leave them or not. There were white murderers around. But perhaps Bidjia and Jardi were safer without him. Mundara had taken an instant dislike to Adam and his white presence invited trouble for all. Adam guessed that Bidjia had weighed his decision carefully.

'Be safe,' Jardi warned.

Adam adjusted the leather strapping of the musket across his shoulder. He guessed that if he came across any farms over the next couple of days that he could warn the occupants about Mundara and tell them of the slaughter. In return he might well learn whether their proposed track to the east was safe. Adam said his goodbyes and walked off into the scrub.

Thus passed the time, until the moon serene
Stood over high dominion like a dream
Of peace: within the white transfigured woods;
And o'er the vast dew-dripping wilderness
Of slopes illumined with her silent fires.

'The Glen of Arrawatta'
by Henry Kendall, 1869

❦ Chapter 19 ❧

1838 June – the Hardy farm

The edge of the spade hit the ground and vibrated in Kate's hand. Lifting the implement she struck the frosty soil again and again until the butt of the small tree was ringed with dirt. Into this slight depression she slowly tipped the bucket of water, watching as the liquid was gradually absorbed into the ground. The two plants they'd brought from the Kable farm had survived the hot summer. She was almost proud of their tenacity. When she left this place, with luck they would still be here, standing as a testament to endurance, both theirs and hers. From another bucket Kate scooped out some sheep manure and spread it around the plants. She was due back at the house within the hour. Mrs Hardy wanted the hut swept, the washing completed and hung to dry and was keen to have the curtains in her room altered. Then there were Sophie's lessons, in between the demands of the kitchen.

There was movement from the direction of the creek. Kate reached automatically for the pistol and then silently chastised herself. Sally appeared out of the scrub, a baby on one hip and a basket in hand. She'd not seen the girl since the day by the creek, since the storeroom had been raided. The tribe's absence during this time suggested guilt, but there was no proof of Sally's people being responsible, although Mr Hardy had condemned them from the first. The robbery had made everyone nervous. Mrs Horton refused to venture further than two hundred yards from the kitchen hut. That was the distance to the privy, a roofless bark structure with a hole in the ground where one had to squat to do one's business.

'Orange.' Sally pointed at the sapling, displaying perfectly white teeth.

The girl was quick to pick up vowels and consonants and imitated Mr Southerland's phrases with striking accuracy and understanding. Kate was less than adept at learning Sally's language, and the girl often laughed at her mistakes. 'Yes, orange. Well, at least one day it may bear fruit.' Although bare-breasted, Sally had taken to wearing a long skirt, a cast-off of Mrs Hardy's.

She held her chubby child out for inspection. 'I name her Kate,' she announced.

'You called her Kate after me?' What should have been an honour was beyond uncomfortable.

'Yes. Kate,' Sally repeated.

When the baby was born Kate expected it would have the look of Mr Southerland about it and she'd been right in this suspicion. She took the child in her arms and tickled the baby under the chin. The child was a healthy, creamy half-caste.

'You come and dig with us today?'

'I can't.' She handed the child back.

'That Missus she all work, work, work.'

'I know,' Kate agreed, 'but I would like to come and learn more about your medicine. Maybe on Sunday.'

'You come find me after the Boss reads from his book.'

Mr Hardy was strict with his Sunday service. All those on the farm, except for those shepherds tending sheep and Mr Southerland, were required to sit in the dirt in front of the main dwelling while Mr Hardy read passages from the bible.

Sally held out the basket. 'Warringaay.'

'Warringaay,' Kate repeated with difficulty, lifting a bunch of the long-stemmed grass from the basket.

The girl laughed.

Grass-like leaves sprouted from the base of the plant and Kate recognised it as one of a number of sedges that grew near the creek. She knew the plants as nut grass and bush onion. Sally's tribe dug up and ate the small pale tubers and wove the leaves together to make mats, baskets and fish nets.

The girl jiggled the baby on her hip. 'You mix up and it fix plenty.' Sally gestured to her throat and stomach, to the slight graze on her arm.

Placing the grasses back in Sally's basket, Kate touched the baby's downy head. 'Sally, did your people take flour and sugar from the store room?' It was an awkward question to ask but one that Kate hoped their friendship would bridge.

'Did you take our land?' The young mother left, singing softly to her child, the folds of her skirt swaying gently.

Kate was left standing alone. The blatant response was not what she'd expected. In fact, Kate had hoped that the tribe was not responsible. She glanced up at the house. A whiff of smoke curled from the chimney. Sally's confession should be reported but she worried about Mr Hardy's response. Initially her employer wanted to make an example of one of the male natives after the theft, a public flogging was even discussed. Mrs Hardy was against it and thankfully Mr Southerland interceded and a loss of two months' stores was the penalty. Not that there was anything to give the tribe now. Everyone was on restricted rations. No, it would be better to say nothing, Kate decided. To go on as they were, two peoples doing their best to live together. Such an arrangement had worked for the Hardy farm and apparently also for the Scotsman to the south thus far. With the boundary dispute resolved, a reasonable friendship had developed between Mr Stewart and Mr Hardy. It seemed that the Scotsman had forged a strong relationship with the different tribes across his vast acreage, with some of the men becoming stockmen. It was proof that they could all live in harmony, and yet Sally's parting words made Kate uneasy.

Mrs Hardy appeared outside the hut, slowly limped the length of the lopsided verandah, passed the kitchen and, lowering the hurdles, entered the vegetable garden slightly downhill of where the cook was washing in the copper. Neither woman acknowledged each other. One bowed low over a steaming cauldron, the other, basket in hand, selecting something from the garden. Mrs Hardy's sickness had become impossible to conceal. Everyone knew she was ill. She spent most days resting, and even then she could be sitting on the stump chair at the table pressing native specimens for her sample book and suddenly fall sideways as if knocked unconscious.

Sophie appeared as the sun breached the hills to the east. The child was calling her. Gathering up the buckets and spade, Kate moved quickly from the fledgling orchard and ran towards a tree. The girl appeared from around the corner of the kitchen and began to skip down the hill, her mother waving to her as she passed. Kate ran further afield to where three close-grown trees stood. Sitting the buckets and spade on the ground, she hid from the girl. Kate really didn't want to see her. Not yet.

'Jelly-belly, Jelly-belly!' Sophie yelled. 'You're meant to come when you're called. Mama says you must.'

Does she now? Kate muttered. Lifting her skirts she made a dash for the next grouping of timber some twenty feet away.

The girl reached the orchard and walked around the plants examining them. 'I know you're here, Jelly-belly. You're always here in the morning.' Leaning down she snapped a branch from the freshly tended sapling. 'Oh look, it's broken.'

Kate gritted her teeth, but didn't move. Pressing her shoulders against the rough bark, she looked down the short distance to the valley flats. A shepherd was opening the hurdles where the sheep had been contained overnight. There had been attacks by native dogs with the arrival of winter and Mr Southerland had enlarged the hurdles to hold five hundred head, thereby ensuring that there were enough shepherds to watch the sheep overnight. Between the animals and her position were two men on horseback and the yellow dog. Mr Hardy and Mr Southerland were inseparable. Were it not for the constraints of social hierarchy imposed by Mrs Hardy, Kate thought the two men would dine together every night, perhaps sleep under the same roof if possible. Such were their fortunes tied to the other.

'Found you!'

Kate tied the shawl in a knot about her shoulders and continued staring ahead.

'What are you doing, Jelly-belly?'

The time had long past for reprimanding the girl. The child was hardly going to address Kate properly when the mother still absently used the same moniker at times.

'Jelly-belly?'

'Go away,' Kate scowled.

'You can't talk to me like that.'

'You can pout and stomp your feet as much as you like, Sophie Hardy.'

The child was adept at turning on the waterworks, especially since she'd become aware of her mother's illness. Kate couldn't help that she'd never taken to the girl. As she moved away she slumped to the ground, her fists balling her eyes.

In the distance the two men continued surveying the bringing in of the sheep. The animals were soon to be shorn and then the wool would be headed south to market. The arrival of this first mob was like a beacon of hope, for Kate was determined to be with the valuable commodity when it finally left the property. She'd not discussed her leaving. Kate thought it best to announce her intentions when she was assured of escape. For that was what it amounted to.

'Her ladyship has her nose out of joint.' Mr Callahan and the convict, Gibbs, were walking towards the creek, but he dawdled to speak to Kate, the two of them watching as Sophie finally clambered to her feet and began to walk back towards the homestead. 'There'll be trouble at the big house.' He gave a wry smile as he joked about the impressive homestead that they'd expected to see on their arrival.

'There's always trouble with that one,' Kate replied.

The Scotsman waited until the other man walked on. 'They found Betts. Mr Southerland rode out again yesterday.'

'I didn't know he was missing,' replied Kate, surprised.

'I reckon they thought he'd done a runner, but the poor bastard was dead as a doorknob with his head bashed in.'

Kate lifted a hand to her mouth. 'Oh heavens, no. Natives?'

The Scotsman lifted an eyebrow.

'He didn't want to go back out there, Mr Callahan. He told me as much. He was very frightened.'

'Well, I reckon the poor bastard's dreaming of the Mother Country now. You know another mob of blacks have been massacred. Hunted down they were on a station to the south-west, a place called Myall Creek. The word is they was harmless, women and children and old men.'

Kate was shocked. 'Who did it?'

'Landowners, stockmen, convicts, who knows? Word is they went out hunting with muskets and swords. Settled a few scores they did.'

'But why? Why kill innocents?'

'"Cause them that own this land are sick of their meddling ways. The thieving, the burning. And there was whites killed just last year and now Betts. People don't forget. Not when there's money at stake. They needed to be taught a lesson.'

'Murder isn't the way.'

Mr Callahan rolled his mouth around like a cow chewing its cud. 'What is then? For it's them against us. This might not be much of a life but as I cannot be assured of what's on the other side of it, I'd like to be here a wee bit longer. I'm getting meself a musket. Keeping it close. Have you still got that fancy pistol, girl?'

Kate patted the folds of the brown skirt she wore.

'Good lass. Keep it ready.' He looked heavenward into a cold blue sky. 'They be washing the sheep. Too cold, it is. Aye, far too cold. They'll die if there's a frost in the morn.'

'What do you mean by washing?'

Mr Callahan laughed. 'They'll not be boiling them up in a copper if that's what you're thinking, lass. No, it's to the creek they're going. Can't have dirty wool being shipped to London. The buyers won't have it.'

'If you think they'll die you should say something,' Kate urged. 'Tell Mr Southerland, at least.'

The Scotsman grunted. 'They know everything, lass. Everything. If I weren't who I was and they weren't who they were, well, I'd slap them both in the listener.' He doffed his cap and grinned his fatherly smile.

Kate noticed he'd lost another tooth.

'I better go. Come down to the creek, lass, and have a look-see. The Missus will only yell at you half the day for being tardy.' The man left with a wink and began to traipse after the other convict, who had already broken into a run. Mr Callahan increased his pace, a stumbling gait that was more limp than lope.

Kate's shoes slipped on the frosty ground as she followed the Scotsman. The sheep formed an arrow-head formation, a convict flanking each side and the two horsemen bringing up the rear. They were large animals with coarse wool and she knew from overheard conversations that the Hardys hoped to purchase Saxon merino rams from Mr Stewart to improve the bloodline when funds allowed.

Losing sight of the mob briefly in the trees, the rhythmic calls of the animals grew steadily louder. Kate reached the sandy creek bank just as the lead of the mob appeared on the opposite side. On seeing the water they began to circle back.

'Keep 'em ringing, keep 'em ringing!' Mr Southerland yelled. He cracked a whip, cracked it again, forcing the mob in an ever-tightening circle. Finally a sheep stopped, sniffed the air, gazed across the stretch of brownness and walked in. The rest of the mob soon followed suit, urged on by a shepherd, the whistling and *coo-eeing* by Mr Southerland and the Hardys' yelping yellow mutt.

In the middle of this disorder Mr Callahan and another convict stood waist deep in the middle of the creek, doing their best to dunk each animal as it swam past.

The sheep emerged in twos and threes, most thoroughly soaked. Finally, with the process finished, the men escaped the freezing water and Mr Southerland walked his mare across the creek. On seeing Kate he headed towards her. 'What do you think of our methods, Kate?'

'I wonder they do not freeze to death. What if there's a frost in the morn?'

The man gave a chuckle. 'Well, you've been keeping your ears open. I'm glad someone has.' His gaze flickered towards Mr Hardy, who waited for his man at a distance. 'It may frost, it's true, but with luck it'll be a good drying day.'

'After the wool's shorn, how long before it's loaded for market?'

The older man cocked his head sideways. 'Thinking of greener pastures, Jelly-belly?'

She didn't answer.

'I'll be delivering it so you'll know in good time, Kate.' He pushed his hat back on his head and gave her a cool appraising gaze. 'I might be inclined to settle down. Find me a few acres in the Cowpastures. I've got coin enough for it. You might be interested in joining me. I could teach you a few things that I've no doubt you've been missing out on to date. Things that I doubt that Reverend of yours could.'

Kate tried to answer but found her tongue all tied and twisted.

Mr Southerland burst out laughing. 'Don't worry, lass, I'm not the marrying kind. I'll not besmirch your honour, although you could do with a good besmirching.'

'Come on, Southerland,' Mr Hardy called. 'You as well, girl, you're not paid to do nothing.'

The shepherds were following the sodden sheep back down towards the valley. Through the timber, glimpses of Mr Callahan's blue twill trousers and check shirt moved in and out of the brush, the tail of the mob with their bulky grey-white bodies gradually disappearing from view. With their departure, the area grew quiet. There was not a breath of wind, not even a zephyr, to stir the leaves.

Kate walked to the water's edge and sat on an upturned log. She knew she should be rushing back to the huts but the thought of leaving this place when the wool went to market was more than distracting. The piece of leather holding together the sole of her shoe had come loose. Untying it, she rested her bare feet in the water, wiggling her toes in the cold stream. It felt wonderful to have a moment's peace even if her feet were verging on freezing. Cupping the water, Kate splashed her ankles. When she looked up there was a man standing on the opposite bank. For a second she was too shocked to move. Kate sat very still, thinking of the twenty feet that needed to be crossed before the safety of the timber behind was reached. The stranger guessed what she was thinking for he instantly held up a hand to stop her, slowly laying the musket he carried on the ground.

'Who are you?' Kate called, fumbling in her pocket for the pistol.

293

'I don't mean any harm, miss.' He took a step closer. 'I'm travelling through. I came to warn you that blacks have been slaughtered. There'll be trouble.'

Kate's fingers closed around the hilt of the gun in her pocket. 'Have you spoken to anyone else?'

'Yes, the Superintendent at Lago Station, but as I said I'm not from these parts and he wasn't too forthcoming on giving directions to other settlers, except for this place, the Hardys' farm, am I right? I saw the sheep being walked in and then sighted the chimney smoke so I figure I'm in the right place.'

'You are.' Kate relaxed her grip on the flintlock. 'You best come with me up to the house. Mr Hardy will want to speak to you.'

As he crossed the creek, Kate quickly brushed sand and water from her feet and began to put on her shoes. The man was already in front of her as she struggled to straighten the flapping sole. She tugged at her skirt so that her knees were covered.

'Here.'

To her amazement, the stranger knelt on the ground, examining the shoe. 'You'll have to get this mended, or you'll go lame.'

His hair was dark, burnished with glints of copper. Lifting her foot he slipped the shoe on and, positioning the leather sole, tied it securely in place with the length of leather.

'Better?' He smiled up at her.

'Better,' she nodded. Whoever had heard of a man helping a woman dress? He wore a bracelet of shells around his wrist and smelt of grass and herbage. Kate smoothed her skirt more than was necessary. She could still feel the touch of his skin on hers. It had been a long time since someone had been so gentle. 'Thank you.'

He smiled crookedly, one corner of his mouth lifting slightly more than the other. 'We best find this Mr Hardy then, miss.' His hand was extended.

Kate allowed the man to help her up and then together they walked towards the huts.

'I've seen you before,' he admitted, as the trees thinned and the dwellings on the hill became visible.

'How? Where?' Kate exclaimed, for if she'd laid eyes on this man before she would remember.

'It was from a distance. Last year when you travelled with the wagons. My party heard musket fire so we went to investigate but by the time we got there you were already passing through.'

'And you didn't make yourselves known? If we were travelling in the same direction we would have done better to join up.' Kate was quite taken aback by the thought of this man having seen her from a distance and remembering her.

'We weren't, so we kept on going.'

'But, you're here now,' Kate pointed out, wondering at her boldness.

'Yes,' the man smiled, 'I am. What's your name?'

'Kate Carter. What's yours?'

He ignored her question. 'And what's a woman like you doing in these untamed lands?'

Kate looked across at her companion and liked what she saw. He was softly spoken with the speech of the educated and he seemed genuinely interested. 'Surviving,' she finally replied. 'And you?'

'Pretty much the same, although I'd not expected to meet a girl like you out here.'

'Maybe I could say the same of you?' Kate countered playfully. They had slowed in their walk, although Kate was unsure who'd done so first.

'Maybe.'

Heavens, Kate thought, what had come over her? What would this man think of her, dallying as she was with a stranger? She'd never dallied with anyone, ever, except for maybe Major Shaw, and she didn't know if that was the same as this. It didn't feel the same. This is ridiculous, she decided. 'It's not far now,' she told her companion, increasing her pace.

Mr Hardy was sitting on the verandah, drinking tea. On seeing Kate and the stranger, he stuck his hat on his head and stomped down the length of floorboards, a pistol in his hand.

'This man's come to warn us about the natives, Mr Hardy,' Kate explained, realising that he hadn't given his name.

'Who are you?'

Kate looked apologetically at the man by her side. One could always rely on Mr Hardy to be blunt.

He wiped at the sheen of perspiration on his brow. 'I'm travelling through. Blacks have been slaughtered, women and children, to the south and I heard word that a half-caste by the name of Mundara is itching for trouble.'

'We heard about the killings.' Mr Hardy wrinkled his nose and spat on the ground. 'But I haven't heard of this Mundara. Anyway, he's the least of our problems. There's fighting going on everywhere and it'll only get worse now.'

'The Superintendent at Lago didn't seem too interested in spreading the word to others. Yours is the only place he mentioned.'

'That's because everyone knows the blacks are uppity and no-one's sure who led the last attack but they stirred the blacks up good and proper, so any man in his right mind is keeping 'imself to 'imself.'

The two men eyeballed each other.

'Perhaps you'd like some tea,' Kate offered. It was not her place to do so, but fortunately neither Mrs Hardy nor the child had appeared to commandeer the conversation and surely a hot drink on a cold day should be extended to a traveller. 'I'll fetch a cup,' she said and walked quickly towards the kitchen hut.

On return the two men were still standing where Kate had left them. She poured tea from the pot on the rickety table and topped up Mr Hardy's drink before carrying the pannikins out onto the flat where the men stood.

'So why don't you have a horse then?'

The stranger thanked Kate for the tea and took a sip. 'Snake bite. It happened some miles back.'

'And your companions?'

'Resting. I'm travelling with an older man in our party. We'd hoped to cross the mountains to the sea before winter set in, but were delayed.'

Mr Hardy took a sip of the tea before tossing the remnants on the ground. 'The sea? There ain't nothing up this way. You've come too far north. You best turn back and make your way to Port Macquarie if it's the sea air you're after. It's the closest settlement on the coast. You did lose your way.'

'Yes,' the man agreed, warming his hands on the tin cup while looking at Kate. 'I reckon we did.'

'I can't offer you much in the way of stores.' Mr Hardy wiped his nose on the back of his hand. 'The blacks raided us some weeks back, near cleaned us out.'

'Thanks for the offer, Mr Hardy, but we're pretty self-sufficient.'

'Really?' His brow wrinkled. 'Well, that's more than I can say for most of us. You better stay for a feed then. Mrs Horton isn't the best in the kitchen but she can turn out something that will fill a man up.'

'Thanks, but I can't. I have to get back to my party. They'll be wondering where I am and I don't want them wandering off.'

'No, indeed,' the older man agreed. 'I've heard tell plenty of stories of men who've got lost in the bush. You know the way then?'

'I do.' He passed his empty pannikin to Kate, holding her gaze for longer than necessary. 'Thank you.'

Kate wanted to say something, but she was at a loss for words. He was a stranger after all.

'Keep an eye out for blacks,' Mr Hardy warned.

Adam dipped his chin to Kate. 'I will. Take care, miss.'

'And you,' she replied, clutching the warm pannikin.

'Who was that man?' Mrs Hardy limped out onto the verandah as the stranger walked away. 'I heard voices but I didn't realise we had a visitor. You should have said something, Samuel, offered him a bed for the night, to dine with us, to –'

'I did that but he had to be on his way, Sarah. He only came to warn us that the blacks were uppity.' Mr Hardy resumed his seat at the verandah table. 'Everyone knows that.'

Kate watched as the man walked swiftly downhill past the fledgling orchard and began to head across the valley.

'But who is he? Where is he from? What's his name?' Mrs Hardy was curious.

'He's a fool that's lost, Sarah. He was trying to make his way to the sea. *The sea*. Port Macquarie is miles to the south.'

'Oh dear,' his wife answered.

'Exactly.'

Outside the kitchen Kate waited for the man to fade to a distant speck on the far side of the valley. Even when he'd finally disappeared she kept watching, as if expecting him to reappear. It was only a little later, in the midst of rendering sheep fat for the lamps, that Kate discovered that the feeling of distraction she'd felt earlier had left her. For the first time in weeks she felt calm.

❧ Chapter 20 ❧

1838 June – the Hardy farm

The potatoes were brown with dirt. Selecting one of the larger ones Kate wiped the earth free, watching as it fell in little clumps, the table growing messy with soil. Brushing the earth aside, she washed the potato in a bowl of water. As the cleaned spuds began to form a pile, Mr Callahan could be heard yelling out in pain. Through the slab walls of the kitchen, his voice merged with the crack of the whip. With each lash stroke Kate shuddered. Mr Hardy may have been a hard person but she'd never believed him capable of such a terrible sentence, especially one he had to carry out himself. Her employer was nothing like his cousin Mr Kable. In fact, in Kate's eyes he was less than half the man.

'He shouldn't have done it. Thieving is thieving. Then he made things worse by not keeping his mouth shut.' The thin-haired cook entered the kitchen holding a large bush turkey, shot by Mr Hardy and partially mauled by the dog. Dropping it on the table with a thud, she poked at the burning log in the fireplace. 'Damn bird. Peppered with shot and all chewed up.' A steady stream of smoke wafted up through the hole in the bark ceiling. A line of sweat striped the back of the cook's dress from neck to waistband, where a roll of fat bulged comfortably on either side of her apron ties. Pulling up a chair made out of candle boxes, she began plucking the bird. "Course, it'll be a change for them having a bit of bird for dinner, if they don't bust their teeth on the shot inside. I ain't got the time to be a-digging for it. But there'll be a bit left over for a tasty soup for the two of us. I'll boil the bones down good.'

The whip cracked again. Then there was silence.

Kate prayed that Mr Callahan's punishment had ended.

As the cook worked, sweat dripped from her brow onto the turkey. 'He knows what Mr Hardy is like,' she began. 'He's a fair man if firm, but you can't be expecting him to put up with the likes of Mr Callahan, not out here, not after what's been going on. Everyone's talking about settling scores.' She gave a huff. 'Gone too far those men did, killing those black women and children. And then ride on and kill more? You can't tell me someone from their lot won't want revenge. An eye for an eye.'

'But you've never cared for the natives, Mrs Horton,' Kate replied stiffly. The cook could make all the excuses she liked but flogging Mr Callahan was wrong.

'Make me right frightened, they do. Nothing wrong with that. Don't you be forgetting they attacked us once, afore your time. Holed us up in here. In this very kitchen and they stole my stores. I can't forgive 'em for that. They ain't like us, but what those white men did, stirring up trouble for the sake of it.' She shook her head. 'Daft. Just daft. I'm not one for the killing of women and children. Bit of give and take is what's needed, but now everyone's looking over their shoulder.'

Kate dropped the peeled potatoes into an iron pot and sat it next to where the cook worked. 'It's because of what's been happening that Mr Callahan stole that musket. Surely he shouldn't be punished for wanting to protect himself? And even then it doesn't call for a flogging. And where's the law? Have they been notified?'

'The law? You best have a look about you, girl, and remind yourself of where we are. Anyway, Callahan knew what would happen if he were caught. He's a ticket-of-leave man, second time lucky. He didn't tell you that, did he? Thought not. By rights he should have been hung by the neck until he was dead, but the man's got more lives than a cat he has.'

'Whatever he may of done, Mr Southerland trusted Mr Callahan enough to give him a musket when we were attacked travelling from Sydney. And there are other stockmen with muskets, men who were once convicts too.' Kate mopped the table free of dirt with brisk movements.

'They've earned the right. Callahan hasn't. So you best keep your opinions to yourself.'

'But he's an old man.' Kate knew there was no point arguing but she felt so useless.

The cook lifted the roughly plucked bird and flipped it over on its other side. The bird hit the table with a dull thump, rattling a bowl that held an assortment of unwashed carrots.

Kate peered through the fist-sized air-hole in the wall. Outside the chooks ambled across the dirt, pecking half-heartedly. 'We're entitled to our opinions,' she said bitterly, her breath appeared as puffs of steam in the morning air.

The plucking finished, the cook wiped the bird down with a damp cloth and then sat it in the pot with the potatoes. Into it she poured water and added a pinch apiece of salt and pepper. A good dollop of rendered mutton fat completed the ingredients. 'Keep quiet's my advice. They say one of the landholders has ridden to Syd-e-ney to report the slaughter. Everyone's got the willies, Kate. Who's to say the blacks don't come after us?' The lid of the pot clanged over the meat and potatoes. Lifting the camp oven Mrs Horton sat it amongst the coals. 'We don't need the likes of a hardened man like Callahan carrying a musket. I don't trust any of that lot. If there's an advantage to be had he'll take it. What if a bushranger showed looking for food and horses?' Mrs Horton continued. 'Do you think Callahan would defend us with his life or join 'em? Do you think if the blacks rose against us that he'd stay and fight to protect the Hardys or us?' She glanced over her shoulder and, assured they were alone, lowered her voice. 'This is a hard place we've come to. Keep your nose clean, that's my advice.'

Mrs Hardy appeared in the kitchen doorway, Sophie clutching her mother's hand, the mongrel dog by her side. 'Are there many potatoes left, Cook?'

'A month's worth at best, Missus.'

'Not enough. I wonder what we will be eating in two months. Kangaroo and bread, no doubt.'

'I'll do me best, Missus.'

'I thought we'd left such punishment behind us,' Mrs Hardy began. 'That was one of the few consolations of journeying here. Was your father ever flogged, Kate?'

'No, Mrs Hardy,' Kate answered curtly.

The lady of the house frowned. 'And what about you, Cook?'

'I came across with my parents, Mrs Hardy. We was immigrants. There isn't any convict blood in my kin.'

'Of course. I forgot. It looks a dreadful thing to be flogged. And one's marked for life. I can't understand it. We've had little problems with the assigned men.' She grew breathless.

'Everyone's uppity, Missus.' The cook stoked the fire.

'Yes, yes they are. Well, Mr Hardy would like you both to leave your duties and join him outside. Come on, now.'

Kate didn't move. She had a terrible feeling that Mr Hardy wanted to show them his handiwork, and she just couldn't bear to see poor Mr Callahan suffering.

Mrs Horton wiped her hands on her apron. 'Begging your

pardon, Missus, but I need to keep an eye on this bird. I don't want you chewing on boot strap.'

'Now.' Selecting a pannikin from the shelving on the wall, Mrs Hardy limped from the kitchen hut. Outside she dunked it into one of the wooden barrels filled with the last of the rainwater. 'Follow me.'

They passed the woodheap and copper. Young Sophie ran ahead, the dog by her side. Child and dog gave chase to the chickens and immediately the air was filled with squawking and the flapping of wings. Mrs Hardy yelled at the dog to sit down and then reprimanded Sophie. A rare event. When the scuffle finally ended Kate shooed the chickens back to their pen with a handful of potato peel.

Mrs Hardy and the cook waited quietly and then the three women circled the two huts, and began to walk along the track that led towards the men's quarters. Mrs Hardy limped along slowly, stopping to catch her breath frequently. Ahead a tripod of wooden beams had been erected.

'Jesus, Mary and Joseph,' the cook whispered, 'it looks like a crucifix.' She duly crossed herself.

It was here that Mr Callahan was bound. His wrists and feet tied to the timber so that he was spread-eagled, his body stretched tight so that the taut skin would increase the damage done by the whip. The two women waited at a distance and tried not to stare at the bloody mess that was once a man's back, as Mrs Hardy limped on ahead.

'Is he alive?' Kate whispered, horrified by the sight of her friend.

The cook grimaced in response and looked at the ground. A trail of red meat-ants were making their way towards the whipping place.

Mrs Hardy was deep in conversation with her husband, her back turned firmly against the wretched man behind her. He listened intently and sipped the water she'd brought him as little Sophie and the dog ran around the bleeding figure.

'People shouldn't be treated like that,' Kate whispered. She felt sick to the stomach.

'Well, then you've come to see Mr Callahan.' Mr Hardy wiped his beard with the back of his hand and passed the cup back to his wife. 'He's alive, aren't you, Callahan?' The man didn't respond. 'Come closer, Kate, you too, Mrs Horton. Have a good hard look at what happens to rabble-rousers and thieves.'

The two women did as they were told, although their feet dragged and they kept their heads bowed until the very last moment. When they were still some feet away they lifted their eyes reluctantly. Mr Callahan's back was latticed with deep cuts. His head sagged. Small black flies were gathering. Kate dry-retched at the sight.

Mr Hardy waited for Kate to compose herself. 'Of course it's to be expected. Once a convict, always a convict.' Mr Hardy flicked sweat from his brow. 'He was sent over for stealing and then in Sydney Town he did it again, didn't you, Callahan?'

'I told you he couldn't be trusted,' the cook hissed at Kate.

Mr Hardy turned to the flogged man. 'We housed him, fed him and gave him an honest job and after less than a year in my employ he becomes a troublemaker. Well, we don't want troublemakers. We don't need thieves or liars. Not out here. This country's on the brink of war. Whites being murdered. Blacks being massacred. You women take heed of that for I'll not be swayed by your sex. Understand?'

Kate and the cook bobbed their heads in unison.

'Off you go.' Mrs Hardy attempted to sound lighthearted but her voice was strained, though whether from the morning's events or her illness, Kate was uncertain.

'I don't blame Mr Hardy for the flogging he gave Callahan,' Mrs Horton mused as they returned to the kitchen hut. 'We can thank the agitators and the do-gooders for leaving us with ticket-of-leave men. Emancipation ruined New South Wales. We'd all be better off having convicts who could be locked in their huts every night. Chained like the dogs they are.' The glance she shot at Kate suggested that the woman was keen for an argument.

In the kitchen Kate angrily spooned leaves from a tea-caddy into the teapot, added water and sat it in front of the cook along with the chipped cup that she liked the most. Was she really the only one who thought that the Scotsman's punishment was too harsh? 'I should take Mr Callahan some water.'

'You'll do no such thing,' the older woman snapped. 'We come into this world by ourselves and we leave the same way. If the Scotsman dies from thirst, through folly, instead of going peaceful like, that's of his choosing. He don't need no friend.'

Kate walked outside and stared across at the valley. The sadness and anger welled up uncontrollably until large tears slid down her cheeks. If she could leave the farm this instant she would. The lands beyond the outer limits were not the place for her.

It was late afternoon by the time the men came in from the paddock. The sun was dipping through the trees, turning the hills blue-black against a pale sky and it seemed to Kate that she was never further from civilisation than at that moment. The horse's hooves and the faint call of pigeons echoed as sweat patched her dress, running in rivulets from her hairline. Although it was cold outdoors the kitchen was hot and stuffy with the heat of the fire. She'd spent the hours since midday trying not to think about poor Mr Callahan. Kate had darned the Hardys' clothes and then rendered down fat for soap. The dough for the next day's bread was the last of her chores. With that task completed Kate picked at the drying water and flour lodged beneath her fingernails, thinking of a time when she had watched Madge doing the exact same thing in another kitchen far away. She pressed her forehead against the rough timber of the doorway, relishing the coming of evening.

Behind her the cook snored at the table. Outside the yellow dog lay sprawled in the shade of the water dray, one of the wooden barrels dripping into a bucket beneath.

The lead horse came into view, emerging from the thick bush on the narrow creek track. Mr Hardy rode straight-backed, his coat-tails flapping over his mount's rump, Mr Southerland close behind. Two unknown riders trailed him, and a man on foot. One of the shepherds. For a moment Kate wondered if the dark-eyed stranger had returned and with the thought she felt a twinge of anticipation. She focused on the approaching group. Two of the riders wore red tunics. The military. In the kitchen she scrubbed the dough from her hands and then washed her face briskly, exchanging her filthy apron for a clean one. It may not have been the man she'd thought, but any visitor was welcome. Quickly re-pinning her hair, Kate shoved unruly tendrils beneath a straw hat, picked up an empty bucket and walked outside.

The riders bypassed the huts and headed directly towards the flogging post and Mr Callahan, the yellow dog straggling behind. In comparison to the soldiers, the other two men appeared rough. They wore their beards long and kept their reins tight, and were it not for the fact she knew her employer and the overseer they looked the type that at any moment might bolt into the scrub.

Kate moved a little closer to loiter behind the Hardys' hut, seemingly to pick up something from the ground. The animals' rumps were glossy with sweat, the men's backs a wall of haphazard proportions. Although the grouping of men around the post were at least two hundred yards from the buildings, one of the figures was familiar. The taller of the soldiers was wide-shouldered and slim-hipped. For an instant he was blocked by the ring of men and then Mr Hardy stepped aside. Kate did indeed know the man. It was Major Shaw. And he had seen her.

'What are you doing, Jelly-belly?' Sophie unfurled Kate's fingers. 'Why are you collecting pebbles?'

'Shush, child,' she replied. The sight of the Major was quite unexpected. Kate's mind raced at his reason for being there.

The Major had turned away.

'What do you want?' Kate said curtly. 'Why must you always be following me? I'm sick of it, do you hear?'

The girl kicked at the bucket. 'Look, they're cutting him down.'

Kate sighed. 'Thank heavens.'

'Mama, Mama,' Sophie called out, skipping towards the hut.

The convict, Gibbs, walked slowly up the track. Kate ran to him. 'Why are they here?'

'They're with the coppers what came north,' the convict replied. 'The Major says that we're to be armed, that many a convict on runs further out have firearms. Hardy, well he's none too happy, but the officer said that convicts have been carrying muskets and pistols out Bathurst way since the '20s, probably afore the '20s. 'Course it's been on the quiet, though them that make the law know. You can just see the looks on the swells if they all knew that us convicts were armed.'

George Southerland cut the ropes binding Mr Callahan and then together with the unknown soldier the two of them half carried and half dragged the older man towards one of the horses and hefted him onto the animal. Kate couldn't believe it. If only the Scotsman had waited another couple of days.

'You best tend to his wounds, Kate,' called out Mrs Hardy from the rear window of her house.

'Of course. Perhaps Mrs Horton can make up a salve to apply.'

'No,' Mrs Hardy replied. 'Rinse the wounds with brine, that will do. Mr Hardy would want it so. Once a convict, always a convict. And don't dally over at the men's quarters, Kate. They'll be testy, the lot of them. It only takes one person to put everyone out,' she said pointedly. 'One of them will have to take on that man's tasks. Mr Callahan won't be anyone's friend by the end of this.'

'If he survives,' Kate countered, hoping against hope that he would recover.

'That kind always do.'

In the kitchen Kate waited for the cook to mix up salt and water in an iron bucket. It was a crude and painful disinfectant, but neither woman suggested going against their employer and taking something more soothing. Once the concoction was ready Mrs Horton handed Kate the bucket along with some clean rags. 'Don't dally, girl.'

'I won't,' Kate assured her, although if the chance came to speak with the Major, she would risk an ear-bashing for the opportunity. Never would she have imagined that James would turn up at the Hardys' farm.

The men's hut sat downhill less than half a mile away and was ringed by lightly timbered country thinned by the daily need for wood. In the distance, men's voices could be heard. Kate rounded a corner and saw the building. Next to it was a rough lean-to that served as stables for the horses, although they currently wandered freely to graze, their progress limited by the leather hobbles they wore. There was a fire burning. The smell of roasting meat and smoke grew strong. Men's voices rose and fell like the rumbling ocean. Overhead the sky turned a reddish pink, the change in light creating a moment of enchantment as a cascade of colour spread through the bush. The men's voices grew angrier.

At the door to the hut Kate announced her arrival, hesitated and then called again that she was there to tend to Mr Callahan's wounds. A nervousness turned her stomach.

'Brine.' Gibbs' disgust showed itself in flaring nostrils as he met her at the door. 'Come in, I've cleaned him up as best I could.'

'I better not,' she replied. She'd never taken to Gibbs. A guffaw of crude laughter sounded.

'The rest of them are out back, eating.' He leant close. 'That fancy Major and the others 'ave ridden down to the creek. There's fifty or more sheep 'cross the other side, some speared, others with their hind legs broken. Seen it before, Southerland has, a handful

308

maimed, says they do it so they can find a feed real easy. Sheep can't move too fast with a broken leg. But fifty? It's a sign.'

Kate followed the convict down the length of the narrow room lined with sagging beds. Although she didn't say it aloud Kate agreed with Gibbs. It sounded like the blacks were looking for trouble by causing it. Or was it revenge? A prone body lay on a cot at the far end beneath a shuttered window. Fading light seeped through the ill-fitting timber boards, something scuttled across the bark roof.

'A man should never have come up here. You best keep your eye out, girl, for not all of us will be staying to fight for the likes of him.'

Mr Callahan lay on his stomach moaning, his forearms and hands resting on the dirt floor.

'If you run, they'll go after you, Gibbs.' Kate sat the bucket on the ground and squatted until she was almost level with the injured Scotsman. His breath was raspy.

'Maybe, but we'll take our chances,' the convict replied.

Kate couldn't blame the man. 'I've only got salt and water, Mr Callahan.' The long, dark room smelt stale. There was a trickle of liquid as Kate dunked a cloth in the brine and then wrung some of the fluid out. The waistband of the Scotsman's trousers was crusted with blood. His back, red raw. Kate was revolted by the messy wound, but she swallowed her disgust as the meaty scent of the injury began to fill her nostrils. She repeatedly soaked the material in the brine and squeezed the mixture carefully across the ravaged back. Her patient groaned loudly, flinching with every drop to his skin. 'I'm sorry, Mr Callahan. It's the best I can do.' He lifted a hand and she took the sweaty skin in her grasp, squeezing gently. 'I'm here.' Her eyes grew moist.

'A man has the right to arm himself,' Gibbs said righteously.

Kate completed her ministrations and dropped the bloody cloth in the bucket. 'I best go before it gets dark,' she told the convict, wiping at her damp eyes. 'Take care, Mr Callahan.' The old man didn't answer.

'And this, flogging a man till he's near death, I'll not stomach it no more.'

'It's a bad thing,' Kate agreed. 'I thought Mr Hardy better than this.'

'No, you didn't.'

Kate waited until Gibbs left and then with a final check on Mr Callahan, she too went outside. The air was chilly as she tossed the bloody water from the bucket. She could hear a horse approaching along the track and she moved to the side lest the rider round the corner and knock her over. But the rider, a soldier, had seen her and he drew his mount up hard and fast.

'Miss Carter.'

'Major Shaw.' She grew almost breathless at the sight of him.

'You are well, I hope?'

'Well enough,' she replied cordially, trying to stem her delight at seeing him.

He looked down at her, his mount shuffling its legs back and forth impatiently.

'I didn't expect to see you here,' Kate told him.

'Then I have the advantage.' His voice grew soft. 'You shouldn't be out here, Kate, it will be dark soon.'

'There is trouble?'

'Enough, to the south and west,' he told her.

'Why are there not more of you then?'

The Major crossed one hand over the other and leant forward in the saddle. 'There are, to the east. We're scouting, meeting with settlers. You best get indoors.'

The echo of another rider galloping towards them caused a shiver to run down Kate's spine. The Major dismounted quickly and, pulling Kate behind him, drew his pistol. Horse and rider came from the south-west, from across the creek, cutting between the huts on the hill and heading along the rough track towards them. The unknown man, a youth, yanked on the reins on seeing them, stirring dirt and gravel. He muttered a string of garbled words.

'Steady, boy,' the Major soothed, holstering the pistol he'd drawn and taking hold of the boy's bridle.

Kate moved to stand by the Major's side, grateful for his protection.

The lad was wide-eyed. He tightened his grip on the reins and appeared as if he were about to bolt for the safety of the scrub. 'The blacks have risen up,' he began with the breathless tone of a frightened woman. 'There's smoke rising from the Stewarts' run. You all best arm yourselves.' He noticed Kate. 'And lock your womenfolk up for protection.'

'When?' the Major asked.

'Today, yesterday, who knows when it began.'

'By the sounds of it,' Major Shaw interrupted, 'it's never stopped.'

'I heard it from one of the shepherds, who'd heard from another. They say the Lago Superintendent has been missing more than a week. They told me to spread the word.' The boy was white with terror and tiredness. 'I ain't staying out there watching sheep no more. I don't care if they put me in a chain gang.'

'Go around the back of the men's hut, ask for Gibbs.' Kate pointed in the direction of the convict and the other men, whose fire was visible from the smoke that rose behind the building. 'Tell him I sent you. They'll look after you.'

'Will it be safe here?' The boy peered into the timber anxiously.

'Yes, off you go,' the Major commanded.

'Bless you, lady, bless you.'

As he rode away Kate repeated the question. 'Is it safe?'

'Let's just see you back to the house and once you're there, stay inside, Kate.' Remounting he extended an arm to her. Kate dropped the bucket.

'Tuck your skirts up, Kate.'

311

She did so, swinging up onto the horse's back with difficulty. 'You've never ridden before?'

'No,' she replied.

'Well, put your arms about my waist. Tighter. Tighter. Right, hang on.'

The animal took off at the gallop. Kate, afraid of falling, drew her arms tightly against the Major, pressing her cheek against the width of his shoulder. She'd never been so pleased to see someone in her entire life.

≪ Chapter 21 ≫

1838 June — to the south-east
of the Hardy farm

The smoke was acrid. Adam crawled on his stomach below the tainted air, which rose gradually on a rising wind. Carefully he reached out a hand to lift sticks and branches from his path, anything that might make a noise. Snaking his body across a log, the edge of the burnt-out grass appeared through the dense smoke. The fire was creeping to the south, coerced by the northerly breeze. Jardi tapped his shoulder, gesturing that all was clear. Bidjia was already padding across the smoldering ground. The two men rolled their eyes and rose as one.

The white man lay on his back near a camp fire, a spear protruding from his chest. The remains of a haunch of meat suggested he'd been cooking at the time of the attack. He was young, perhaps twenty, with stubbly growth on his chin. Adam closed the dead man's eyes and then, placing his boot on the man's ribcage, pulled at the spear. The spike caught on a rib. There was a cracking sound and then the weapon came free. The point of it was barbed.

The hut behind the dead youth was partially collapsed and still burning. It was this dark smoke that they'd seen in the distance. The building had been torched, which in turn started the grass fire. They walked around the dwelling. It had been one-roomed with a stone fireplace that still stood. A few pots lay on the ground, next to a blanket and some stores. A small book, partially blackened, was the only other thing not totally destroyed.

Bidjia and Jardi examined the footprints left in the ash. 'It could be any number of warriors seeking payback.' Bidjia contemplated.

'But it's not, is it? You think it's him? You think it's Mundara?' Adam asked.

'I cannot be certain.'

'The girl would be with them.' Jardi referred to the captured woman on the riverbank the day they met Mundara. It was not the first time he'd mentioned her.

'Forget about her.' The light finally dwindled to nothingness. 'The moon grows fat tonight and we must move on, as others will be moving.' Bidjia pointed to boot marks in the ash and led them away from the isolated hut to the north-east.

'The spear was barbed,' Adam reminded the older man, 'and the stores have not been taken.'

'There will be many spears now and more muskets loaded with shot.'

Yesterday they'd come across a well-built homestead. The three men had run under cover, seeking shelter behind trees and logs in order to get closer without being seen. There were grape vines and roaming chickens, a separate building for the smoking of meat and a handsome set of yards near what remained of the stables. Two of the outbuildings were torched and still burning, the occupants of the farm holed up inside the house. Planks of wood had been nailed over some of the windows and muskets could be seen poking out through sections of shutters. There'd been little point in stopping.

'Now what?' Jardi grew moody. He pointed out the footprints belonging to the attackers. They led to the north. 'Bronzewing, we must do something. There are only four of them.'

'This is not our fight. You forget why we came to these lands and why we must keep moving.' Bidjia walked on, padding across the ground at a steady pace, spear at the ready. He'd recovered much of his strength after a few days' rest.

'I remember everything,' Jardi complained to Adam. 'The loss of my clan, our lands. The women and children dying from disease, the old people melting away as they grieved for their country. And now us, running, always running. Would my father have another clan destroyed? Would he see that girl used as a man uses a waterbag? Would he see her dead?'

They caught up with Bidjia near a stand of wilga trees. One of their kind was propped up against a knobby trunk. Legs splayed and arms lank, the man's breath was ragged. It came in gasps that produced small bubbles of blood that sat on his top lip like gathering flies. The men squatted next to the stranger. His shirt-front was glossy with blood. Fully clothed, a musket and pistol lay within reach although he would not have use for these weapons again. The blucher boots he wore were near new, a sure sign he was hired labour.

'Maybe stockman,' Jardi suggested.

Bidjia prodded the wound to the man's chest, carefully prising the shirt free of the injury to check the colour of the blood. 'Musket shot. He will not survive.'

'I wonder if he gave chase to those that attacked the boy,' Adam pondered, 'or if he was one of the attackers and the boy shot him?'

Eyelids fluttered open, a hand scrabbled uselessly in the dirt for a weapon.

'You're amongst friends.' The look of doubt in the man's eyes was strong. 'Are you with one of the settlers?' Adam searched the blackfella, turning out his empty pockets as the stranger scrutinised every movement. 'What's your name?' A metal disc with the initial *J* roughly etched on it was tied to a piece of leather cord about his neck. 'We came across a burnt-out hut back a bit; a man had been speared. Do you know anything about that? About the big run a bit further to the south?'

'Whitefella dead?' The black's breath was shallow.

'Yes,' Bidjia answered.

The man gave the slightest of nods. 'Good.' His head slumped to his chest.

The three men looked at each other.

Untying a powder pouch and one of shot from the man's waist, Adam gathered the weapons. 'He must have joined with Mundara.'

Jardi took the musket, Bidjia a pistol. 'This is an impossible war.' Jardi shoved the pistol in the waistband of his trousers. 'Who is friend and who is enemy?'

Adam found himself thinking of Winston Lycett and then of the dark-haired girl on the Hardys' farm. He'd not mentioned her to his companions for although he could do nothing else, it felt wrong to have left her there. Trouble was brewing.

The moon was beginning to appear, a slither of light rimming the earth's crust, eating away at the shadows and casting the land in a soft glow.

'Come,' Bidjia urged.

≪ Chapter 22 ≫

1838 June — the Hardy farm

The moon rose quickly. It clipped the trees to hang hard and bright, dulling the stars and casting elongated shadows across the ground. Major Shaw linked an arm through Kate's and she slid awkwardly to the ground with a thud. 'Stay inside.' His tone, although firm, was kind.

Her heart beat quickly. The ride from the men's hut had been delayed by the arrival of Mr Southerland, who'd stopped them midway seeking the youth who'd ridden in. Kate spent the time the two men conversed doubled-up behind James, wishing for George Southerland's departure. Kate was desperate to know of the Major's moves, if he was heading south, and if so, if he would help her return to Sydney, but the chance for such questioning never came. The convict, Gibbs, was the next to delay them, seeking further information and now they were already returned to the kitchen hut, and Kate was feeling helpless, scared and very much alone. There was something solid and familiar about the presence of this man. Kate didn't want him to leave.

'Major Shaw? James?'

'This isn't the time, Kate.' His attention was already drawn to the Hardys' hut. The overseer and the other soldier who'd arrived earlier were on the verandah speaking with Mr Hardy.

Kate rested a hand on the warmth of the horse's neck.

'Everything will be alright.' James surveyed the musket holes in the kitchen wall. 'Don't forget what you've already endured. Few women would have made the decision you did, Kate Carter. Truly, everything will be fine.'

That was the second time he'd said as much. Once was a comfort, Kate thought, twice was not. 'How do you know?'

'Go inside and stay there.' Then, as an afterthought, 'Are you armed?'

Kate drew the flintlock pistol from the folds of her skirt. He smiled. 'Point and shoot.'

'Point and shoot.' She felt a blush come to her windblown cheeks.

'You'll be safe here.' His mount took a few steps back and forth, the horse nickering in the cold of the night air.

The thought of him leaving sat badly with her. 'Will I see you in the morning?'

'Go.' He watched her retreat towards the kitchen hut, pulled on the reins and was about to steer his horse away when he turned back. 'Yes, I'll see you in the morning, Kate. Keep the door shut and that pistol loaded.' His boots touched the mare's flanks, and they trotted away, disappearing around the corner of the building.

In the empty kitchen, Kate surveyed the mess. A rushed supper had been served in her absence and the dirty plates and platters sat untidily on the table. There was a stench of rancid fat from the slush lamp, around which varying sized insects flew. Pouring hot water from the fire-blackened kettle into a large basin, she began scrubbing the crockery with a brush, intent on keeping her thoughts from that of the Major, from what may be out lurking beyond.

'There you are.' Mrs Horton arrived carrying an empty tray. 'And haven't I had a to-do of things tonight what with Mr Hardy calling everyone a bastard after what happened to his sheep and the Missus too ill to leave her bed and then them two soldiers appearing like wraiths. I had a time scratching up food for them, I tell you. Bread and soup was the best I could do. Left it for them, I did. I ain't going outside again this night. It's enough to give a woman a fit of the vapours, it is.' Dumping the tray on the table she sat heavily on a candle-box. 'Blacks and full moons, gives me the willies. And that lean-to of ours, I never liked the place. Walls as thin as parchment, might as well be half open to the wilds. Not that it matters. I lie awake most of the night wherever I am. But after what happened to them poor sheep, well, I ain't leaving here. Besides the moon's full and I ain't lying outside to be touched by it. There's plenty a person who's gone to sleep under a full moon and woken up a lunatic. And it goes without saying that it'd be worse out here. This moon, well, it's nothing like an English moon. A person can't escape from it here.' The cook scraped the box across the dirt floor closer to the table, one eye fixed on a hole in the wall, as if a moonbeam could strike her at any moment. 'Well, serve us up a bit of that watery soup and cut us some bread, Kate. Good, now that rendered fat. After what I've been through I don't mind gobbling down more than my share.' Dipping a spoon into the bowl of dripping, she smeared the bread with it and then pushed the bowl towards Kate. 'Get it into you, girl.' The cook raised an eyebrow. 'What else do you know? For a chatterer like you, you're being too quiet. You best tell me.'

Where should she begin? It had been a terrible day. 'Settlers have been attacked and the Superintendent at Lago Station is missing.'

'It's the moon. Bad things always happen when the moon's fit to bursting, for that's when people move about and the bad ones, well, they don't need no almanac to tell 'em when the moon's on its way.'

An hour or so after they'd eaten, the cook fell asleep, her head lolling back against the wall. Some of the pieces of mud sealing the cracks in the ill-fitting timber had come loose and a cold draught wafted through the stuffy room, stirring the woman's hair as she snored. Outside the brightness of the night unsettled Kate. Deciding against the walk to the privy, she took a few steps from the hut and, lifting her skirts, squatted on the ground. The warmth splashed her shins and she scuffed clean damp shoes, noticing a weak light in the main room of the Hardys' hut. The shuttered window was open and the outline of four men could be seen. The presence of the soldiers was a consolation, especially that of Major Shaw, but it was difficult not to feel abandoned in this place. Betts was right. They shouldn't have come here. This land belonged to others while in contrast the settlers tried to impose their will on a mysterious place and its people. No good could come of such behaviour.

Away from the dwellings the landscape was haloed by light. The familiar call of an owl broke the silence. Movement in the air and the whoosh of wings drew Kate to a scurrying creature on the ground. The owl swooped and then flew off, clutching something between its claws. Trembling, she retreated to the hut, closed the door and drew the latch. Mrs Horton gave a snort in her sleep, as Kate took up a position at the table opposite the door, the loaded pistol before her. Stroking the prettily engraved stock, she began polishing the barrel with a cloth, humming under her breath. *Point and shoot*, she whispered. She'd done murder once, surely, Kate thought, she could again. Eventually she rested her arms on the table and slept.

The slush lamp flickered. The fire spat.

The door creaked.

Kate blinked away sleep as a shaft of moonlight angled onto the dirt floor. She ducked beneath the table, remembering too late that the pistol was on the table where she'd left it. The slush lamp had burnt itself out, however the moon's glow combined with the flickering fire filled the hut's interior with a hazy light. Her breath caught. A wash of fresh air eddied around the room, displacing the sour scents of the day and lifting the dust. After a minute or so, Kate scolded herself. It was only a welcoming breeze. She must have forgotten to latch the door properly. Gripping the edge of the table she was about to pull herself up when the door swung open.

A black man stood on the threshold, the moonlight accentuating a scarred torso and matted hair, holding a long spear. He wore trousers and an open-checked shirt and a hide cloak. Surveying the room, his gaze fell on the sleeping cook and he muttered a few words in his native tongue, which seemed to be directed towards Mrs Horton. The older woman awoke with a start as the savage lifted his spear. For a moment Kate thought the man only meant to frighten them but as the older woman screamed the spear was aimed and flung in a single movement. The point struck the cook in the chest, slamming the woman against the wall with a deadening thud. As blood gushed from the wound, the cook gave a weak cry. Kate gasped in horror. The black saw her, overturned the table and was on Kate immediately, tugging at her hair, pulling her upwards until his stern face was inches from hers.

'Please,' she begged.

The savage yanked her outdoors by the hair and began to drag her away from the huts, up the hill. Kate wrapped shaking hands over his, trying to ease the pain of scalp and hair being pulled by the roots. Shots, screaming and the yelp of a dog followed their progress; still the man pulled at her, jerking Kate's body so violently that she tripped and stumbled and fell again and again, and every time she staggered he pulled her upwards, intent on leading her away.

'Help!' she cried. 'Help me!'

Further down the hill James and a native were fighting. The Major shot the black and then, although dead, began pounding his head in with the butt of his rifle.

A chorus of yells chased them up the hill. Musket shots rang out. The native halted, swung Kate about as if she were a shield and lifted a throwing stick at the Major and George Southerland, who pursued them. Both men trained their muskets, but neither fired. They couldn't risk hitting Kate. The black began to lead her away again, backwards over the rough ground, the men stalking behind in their wake.

They were past the store shed in the side of the hill, past the halfway mark to where spiky-topped timber crowned the peak. There was such a small space left between the moonlit ground ahead of them and the dark of the trees that Kate realised there was little time for anyone to save her.

'Stop!'

The voice was loud, firm. Two black men and one white stood between Kate and certain oblivion. The eldest native held a spear aloft, the youngest a pistol and the white . . . the white lifted his musket and dropped to his knees.

'Don't move, miss.'

His voice was firm. Kate recognised him immediately as the stranger who'd visited the farm.

Mundara snarled. 'This is not your fight, Bronzewing. Tell him, Bidjia.'

'There has been much death already,' the Elder replied.

'Did you hear me, miss?' the white man called. 'Don't move an inch.'

Kate gave a shocked nod. She couldn't move, the black had his arm tight about her.

'You'll never get away, Mundara.'

'You will be my enemy, Bronzewing,' Mundara shouted. 'Forever. I will hunt you down like the white dog you are.'

'Let the woman go,' Bidjia countered.

'Does the white man let the black woman go?' Kate's captor replied.

Bidjia moved quickly to the left. His younger companion to the right. Their sudden movement distracted Mundara and the instant Kate felt his grip lessen she stomped hard on his foot. The action unbalanced her abductor. Musket fire sounded and the next moment Kate was falling to the ground. She sat up quickly, her fingernails clawing the dirt as she scrambled backwards. When Kate finally looked over her shoulder the black had gone, disappearing into the night. In his place was James Shaw, his hand outstretched. She took it gratefully and huddled against his body as the other men ensured all the attackers had left.

'Much obliged.' George Southerland was the first to speak as the Major assured himself that Kate was unharmed. 'What are you men doing here?'

'Heading north-east.' Adam casually reloaded the musket. 'Across the mountains to the sea. Are you alright, miss?' He rammed the shot down the barrel.

'Yes, yes, thank you,' Kate replied shakily, staring at the three men as if they'd appeared in a dream. She'd thought the native would kill her.

'We've got problems up here, as you can see,' Mr Southerland told them. 'We could do with a hand.'

Although keen to keep to their own agenda, Mundara's trail had been obvious. The renegade had moved ahead of them and was swift and direct in the path he and his men chose. Had Adam and the others not seen the huts in the distance with their curl of chimney smoke, they never would have diverted from their intended direction but Mundara clearly planned on wreaking more havoc. And knowing the girl may be in danger only hardened Adam's resolve. He spoke quickly with Bidjia and Jardi and then asked the two strangers to step to one side so he could speak to them out of the woman's hearing. 'What did the girl do to cause offence?'

Mr Southerland frowned. 'Offence?'

'A slight of some sort? A wrongdoing?' Adam persevered.

'There's nothing that I know of. Why?'

'I'm Major James Shaw and this is George Southerland. Miss Kate Carter's was here as a companion to Mrs Hardy. There can be no offence.'

'In that you are wrong,' Bidjia muttered.

'What did that black say?' the Major asked.

'Nothing, he said nothing,' Adam replied testily. They'd been right to track Mundara but now they had an officious soldier with an Englishman in tow to contend with. He looked at the girl. She was pale with fright.

A strong smell of smoke carried up the hill. Two buildings below crackled and popped as angry plumes of fire ate at the timber, collapsing a wall as they watched. Part of the Hardy house still stood but the kitchen had caved in on itself and continued to burn. There was no movement below. No people, no yellow dog and no pecking chickens. Only the scaffolding erected to punish Mr Callahan remained untouched, highlighted by the moon's glow.

'Come, we're walking out of here now,' Adam told them.

'But it's pitch black,' the Major disagreed. 'Best we make camp in the timber and let Miss Carter rest.'

'Stay if you like,' Adam glanced around the open position where they argued, 'but I'd not risk it, not with a renegade on the loose.'

Mr Southerland rubbed at his beard and looked skyward. 'A renegade. Do you know that for certain?'

This time Jardi spoke. 'Yes.'

'The bastard. It's not the time to be standing out here then. Come on, Major, he's right,' Mr Southerland admitted. 'Best we keep moving.'

'We can't leave Mrs Horton, we can't just walk away.' Kate turned to George Southerland and James, imploring them to stop. 'And what of Sophie?' She gave a sob. 'What happened to Sophie and Mr and Mrs Hardy?'

James drew her away, leading Kate roughly over the uneven ground. 'They were inside the house when it caught alight. I saw them through the window. Sophie wouldn't leave her mother's side. George and I tried to get to them . . .'

Kate bit her knuckles to stem the horror. Behind them the fires crackled and roared. 'He killed Mrs Horton!'

'I know, Kate,' James took her arm more firmly, 'and the young officer travelling with me. There were four of them, Kate, and they knew what they were doing. Come, you must keep up.' He was practically dragging her towards the timber, his arm moving to her waist, so that he half-carried her uphill. Kate willed her feet to keep walking.

Ahead, the two natives and the dark-haired man led them into the night.

≪ Chapter 23 ≫

1838 June — on the run

Through the tangle of brush, daylight beckoned. Twigs and leaves caught in Kate's hair and clothes as she pushed and pulled at the cocoon of a nest that seemed to have been erected around her. With difficulty she crawled free of the hiding spot, brushing dirt away. The sleeping place where she'd collapsed a few hours ago had been made invisible by the careful placement of plants. Her legs were aching and her head and neck pained from last night's ordeal. Exhausted and thirsty, Kate scanned the area, and realising that she was alone, peered through the woody plants encircling the sheltered spot for any sign of life. To her relief James and Mr Southerland were standing a short distance away. They turned at her approach and then wordlessly resumed their stare. Kate joined the silent companions and followed their line of sight.

Kate didn't recognise the land they'd come to. To the east there were strange hills that crisscrossed each other like bell-shaped skirts and forested areas interspersed with open areas. They were in a valley inhabited by kangaroos and a flock of birds who flew overhead in an arrow formation. Smoke hung in the air to the south and south-west. In places it appeared to ring the dense bushland. Kate thought of the Hardys, of all they'd hoped to achieve. A dull pain settled within her. 'What happened to the other men? To Mr Callahan?'

'They set the men's hut alight.' George Southerland passed her a waterbag and Kate drank gratefully. 'Maybe the others cleared off before the attack. I don't know.'

Kate was glad for Gibbs and the rest of the men. 'And Mr Callahan?' She handed the water back.

The overseer shook his head. 'Unless he managed to crawl out of there.'

'You mean, he's dead too?' Mr Southerland didn't reply. Kate stood quite still, her mind trying to absorb the deaths of the people she'd lived and worked with for nearly a year. Mr Callahan in particular had been so kind to her. 'He, he was a friend,' she said quietly. If the old Scotsman had not been so desperate to arm himself and if Mr Hardy were not so intent on instilling order, Mr Callahan might yet be alive. Kate thought of him lying in the hut unable to defend himself. It was too much. All of it was too much.

'With luck the smoke may have got him first,' the overseer suggested as if reading her mind.

The thought gave her little comfort. Kate watched numbly as the two blacks and the white man who'd saved her the previous night appeared through the timber and jogged towards them. They moved effortlessly as if at one with the land, small ground-birds fluttering from the grasses as they approached. Kate recalled the stranger she'd met by the creek, his gentle touch and the ease she'd felt in his presence. But when he'd talked of his companions to Mr Hardy, he'd never mentioned that they were natives. 'Can they be trusted?'

327

'They saved you, Kate, didn't they?' In daylight, the Hardys' overseer was covered with soot and a nasty burn, red and bubbly, marked one side of his face. 'And at this point we don't have much choice.'

'You're injured, Mr Southerland,' Kate noted.

'It'll heal.' He waved away her concern.

'He followed Mr Hardy into the house to help save the man's wife and child,' James explained.

'The bloody building collapsed like a deck of cards.'

Kate saw the overseer in a new light.

'Nothing,' Adam shared on arrival. 'And the horses have been run off.'

'Damn.' Mr Southerland itched his hairline. 'Well, there's still the sheep and the cattle, if they haven't been rushed.'

'You can't seriously be thinking of going back?'

'James, I ain't been paid and I'm not likely to be if I don't return and see what's what. If I can get to Stewart's farm and borrow a horse and some men, I can muster what's left of the Hardys' sheep and then walk them to his farm, shear them and get the wool to market. There's also Kate to be considered. She'd be safe there.'

'But weren't they one of the places attacked?' James queried.

'So we were told, but the Stewarts have a big spread and if it's the same mob of blacks that attacked us last night, then on my reckoning there's only three of them. Stewart's got enough men to hold that number at bay.' He turned to Adam. 'It's due south from here, maybe thirty miles. I'd appreciate having you with us as a guide. I'm figuring you know this part of the country, while I don't.' He contemplated their surroundings. 'Nothing's recognisable to me, and if you're right about a renegade being involved, we'll do better if you lot are with us.'

Kate stared at the white man as he considered Mr Southerland's request. They didn't even know his real name although the old black man addressed him as Bronzewing. Kate wondered if she should mention that he'd been to the Hardys' farm; that Mr Hardy had spoken with him and that the unknown man had never mentioned that he was travelling with natives. It struck her as odd that their fate rested with this man who was named after a pigeon. He didn't answer Mr Southerland immediately, turning instead to consult with the two blacks as if they were equal.

The older of the blacks, Bidjia, was unimpressed. 'We should leave them, walk away from their troubles, they are not ours.'

'We'd be indebted,' James announced. 'I gather you're trackers or stockmen. Who do you work for?'

'No-one,' Adam answered a little too quickly. He should have known the questioning would begin eventually.

'Where have you come from then?' the soldier persevered.

'Nowhere in particular.' Adam dismissed the querying and lowering his voice turned once again to discuss their options with Bidjia and Jardi. He'd made their new friends wary, especially the officer, however they hadn't journeyed this far to be caught up with a redcoat, not after everything that had occurred.

Bidjia wanted to go on and leave these people to make their own way south, but Jardi agreed that it was wrong to leave the white woman, especially if safety was close by.

'But I don't like the redcoat,' Jardi spoke quietly, his voice barely a whisper.

'I'd not lend him a knife to cut up a plug of tobacco,' Adam replied, 'but I agree the woman should be taken to safety. Mundara seeks revenge for some wrongdoing and she's his target.'

'You like this woman?' Jardi asked.

'She's a darn sight prettier than you.'

'He came to the farm,' Kate spoke quickly to Major Shaw and Mr Southerland. She was unnerved by these strange men whispering among themselves. 'The morning the sheep were washed he spoke to Mr Hardy, warning us about the natives. He said he'd spoken with the Superintendent at Lago Station and that his party was on their way to the coast.'

'Is that so?' Mr Southerland tugged thoughtfully at a wispy bit of beard that appeared to have been singed.

'What's your name?' The Major studied the three men, then, as if seized by a revelation, he walked forward and grabbed Adam by the wrist. 'A shell bracelet, a white man travelling with blacks, one of them named Bidjia? I'll ask you again, where have you come from? What is your name?'

'Bronzewing,' Adam answered, reefing his arm away. Was the soldier stupid? In such close proximity Bidjia would spear him through before he could lift a weapon.

'What sort of name is that? What's your real name?' James demanded. 'Tell me.'

'Leave them be, James,' Mr Southerland said curtly. 'We need them.' He held up his hand for emphasis. 'Well, will you help us?'

'They can't be trusted,' James answered with conviction. 'That man is –'

'The best hope of getting the lady out of here.' Adam completed the sentence and lifted an eyebrow mischievously at Kate. She didn't know where to look.

The overseer flattened his lips together. 'Well, at the moment,' he said testily, 'they're all we've got, James. So, Bronzewing, what do you think, head straight for Stewart's run? It's due south.'

'It wouldn't be safe,' Adam replied.

'Safe? Why, do you think those warriors will come after us?'

Adam glanced fleetingly at Kate. 'It's not the time to be talking, put it that way. We came across a dead white yesterday and another farm had its outbuildings burnt. A big place with a smokehouse and stables. The homestead was still standing.'

'That's the Stewart place,' George confirmed. 'Did you see any of the men?'

'Holed up inside, I reckon. By the tracks it appears that Mundara and his followers kept going,' Adam told him. 'They killed the lad and then saw your farm. Either they reckoned it would be easier pickings or they had a reason to go there. I can't be sure which, but he sure knew what he was after when he got there.' He looked at Kate, who was sitting on a log retying the twine around the sole of her shoe.

'Come.' Bidjia began to lead them away, then turned to Adam. 'The redcoat knows us,' he muttered. 'This is what happens of trying to do good.'

'There's no point heading east,' the Major exclaimed. 'We need to travel south as George told you.'

Adam drew their attention to the line of smoke on the horizon. 'Good luck with that.' Hitching the strap of his musket across a shoulder, he too began to walk. 'We go to the east first and then we'll circle back when we're clear of this. I'm not walking into trouble. Once we get to the Stewart land you're on your own.'

'Now wait just a minute,' James shouted, 'there are five men here. We've got muskets and pistols. I said wait. You, sir, are a British subject and I'm ordering you and your men to turn around this instant and take us south directly.'

'Actually,' Adam replied, stopping to wipe sweat from his brow, 'I don't call myself subject to much at all.'

Jardi sniggered.

The Major lifted his musket. Adam moved swiftly, knocking the firearm from his grip and grabbing him by the front of his tunic. 'Don't worry,' he brushed at the material, 'I won't dirty your fancy uniform.' He pushed the soldier away from him.

'We'll do it your way,' George said calmly, stepping between the two of them and breaking the stare that threatened to lead to a fist-fight. 'We've more chance of getting safely out of here together than splitting up.' He turned to his friend. 'Don't we, James?'

'This isn't finished,' James told Adam, stooping to collect his rifle.

He gave a laugh in reply. 'With your lot, it rarely is.'

'Wait,' Kate called after them. 'What about the Hardys? What about Mr Callahan?'

'There's nothing we can do for them, miss,' Adam advised. 'The farmhouse is a good ten mile behind us now. Best we move on and leave them be.'

Lifting her skirts Kate stormed after him. 'Leave them be? The Hardys were doing their best to carve themselves a home out of the wilderness. They were good people. They deserve to be buried. They deserve to be treated with respect. Your, your indifference, sir, startles me.'

Adam turned on Kate, walking towards her so that she backed away under his fierce stare. 'It is not indifference, *miss*, and they stay where they lay.'

❦ Chapter 24 ❧

1838 July – heading east

Kate wasn't sure when the exhaustion ebbing at her bones gave way to numbness. At some stage the feeling simply dissipated into something dazed and unknowable. Perhaps it was the speckled light shining through the leaves of the timber they walked through or the enticing glimpses of a watchful sky that drew thoughts away from the most immediate of concerns. But gradually the placing of one foot after the other, the constant caution of watching where one trod and the never-ending breathlessness of keeping pace with the others overtook all else.

In an attempt to block out the awful images of the previous night, the memory of the Reverend intruded, making Kate ponder on the possibility of a God. For years she'd been a non-believer, never even considering the concept of faith except in terms of the authorities using the church as a way of keeping the masses at bay, curtailing them into righteousness with the threat of fire and brimstone. Kate knew now that she'd been right. Out here, beyond the outer limits, where there was no threat of religion, no pretend salve for the needy, the weak and the lost, only the misguided attempts of settlers trying to recreate pastoral life on Sundays, life existed at the most basic level. Men, women and children were left to rot where they fell. Convicts ran away, the natives rose up against the whites, the whites against the natives and the haves still suppressed the have-nots. If ever a body needed proof that there was no great and almighty God, the far-flung reaches of the colony of New South Wales had shown as much.

On only one point could Kate ever find herself in agreement with the Reverend Horsley – there was indeed a hell, and it was here.

At a small creek Kate drank greedily. She desperately wanted to dangle her aching feet in the cool water that fed down from the mountains, but their escorts were determined to press on.

'Miss Carter needs to rest,' James called out for the second time that day.

Ahead, Bidjia and Jardi slowed. Adam grimaced at the thought of a delay, but aware that the girl would be refreshed by even a short break, he reluctantly agreed. It would be in everyone's best interest. He quickly set all the men on guard at each point of the compass. The Major complained about being dictated to, intent on staying by the girl's side, until Mr Southerland approved of their guide's caution.

When the men had merged with the trees and Adam had checked their surroundings and been assured of their safety, he returned to where the girl sat by the trickling creek. She was fiddling with a shoe again, retying the leather strap and flexing her foot to ensure it was good and tight. He knew he shouldn't stare from afar but he couldn't help but notice that most of her dark hair had come loose from the bun at the nape of her neck to hang in curly tendrils in the middle of her back. She moved to kneel at the water's edge and, cupping her hands, began to wash her face and neck. Kate Carter was as pretty as he remembered.

'You should have had that shoe mended.'

Kate started at his approach and jumped up quickly. Beads of water trickled down her skin as she did her best to brush the moisture from her face. 'I've not the skill, and the man who might have repaired it for me is now dead.'

'A friend?' Adam asked.

'Yes, and a good man.' She dabbed at damp skin with her sleeve.

'Then I am sorry for your loss.' He sat down on the ground and stared at the water. 'True friends are hard to come by.'

Kate wondered if he too had lost a friend. She stood awkwardly for a moment and then joined him on the ground. 'Why didn't you tell Mr Hardy that you were travelling with natives the day you came to the farm?'

'You know the answer to that.' Adam picked up a pebble and skipped it across the surface of the water. 'Some whites are not so welcoming where blacks are concerned.'

'You speak as if you were one of them.'

Adam didn't respond. He wanted to know how she'd got the scar that cradled one eye like a question mark. Instead he asked why she had journeyed so far.

Kate removed the few hairpins left holding her hair and let it fall around her shoulders. There weren't enough left to secure it properly so she threw the useless pins in the water. 'There are few opportunities available to women. I came where I was wanted.'

'It is a fair journey for a woman.'

'It is a fair journey for anyone, man and beast alike.'

Adam chuckled.

Kate turned to him. 'Are you laughing at me, sir?'

He lifted his hands in mock defence. 'Not at all, it's just some time since I've been in the company of a woman who speaks her mind.'

Kate sighed. 'Well, it will not be the first time that I've been accused of outspokenness.'

'On the contrary,' Adam argued, 'you have a brain and an opinion, why shouldn't you share it with others?'

Kate didn't know what to say. This man was unlike any she'd ever met. They sat quietly, companionably. He selected stones to skip across the water, while Kate thought of all the things she wanted to question him about. Specifically, she wanted to ask why he'd left the Hardy family without giving them a proper burial, but she had not the strength to argue and, although she'd wondered initially if he and his companions could be trusted, it now seemed wrong to query a man's actions when he was trying to help. She recalled his conversation with Mr Hardy. 'And you, are you really travelling to the coast?'

'Yes, we are.'

'Can I ask why?'

He flicked at the sand between his boots. 'To start a new life.'

That was a reason Kate could understand.

'We have to keep moving.' Taking a knife from his belt, he trimmed a length of leather from the musket strapping crossing his chest and gestured to her foot. 'Can I?'

Kate watched as he deftly wound the leather around the broken shoe, tying it firmly. 'That should keep it secure for a while.' Extending a hand he helped Kate to her feet.

'Thank you. It seems that you are always coming to my assistance.'

Adam didn't answer. He adjusted the musket on his shoulder and, cupping a hand around his mouth, made a series of birdlike noises. A few moments later Bidjia and Jardi appeared with James and Mr Southerland. All of the men drank from the creek, filling the waterbags they carried.

'You think that man is after me, don't you?' Kate hadn't wanted to ask the obvious, but it was clear from the earlier glances and innuendos that Bronzewing thought as much.

'Come on then,' George Southerland finished splashing water on his face, 'let's keep moving.'

James cleared his throat as he moved to Kate's side. Taking her by the arm he led her away.

≪ Chapter 25 ≫

*1838 July — heading towards
the Stewart farm*

'I think a hot bath and something warm to drink is in order, Kate.' James did his best to cheer her. It had been some hours since they'd rested and, in spite of her best efforts, Kate knew she was tiring.

'Soon you'll be resting under the protection of the Stewarts.'

'And you?' Kate asked. Her skirt was damp where she clutched at the material as they stepped over fallen timber. 'Will you go directly back to Sydney?'

James kept a watchful eye on her, assisting Kate over the some-times steep and rocky ground as they continued to weave up and down and around unfamiliar foothills.

'Eventually.' He took her hand once again as they crossed a dry gully. 'But when I do, you'll be coming with me.'

The feeling of relief was indescribable as she felt the brief touch of the Major's hand on the small of her back. There would be soldiers, of course. A rider would be sent south and troops would be mustered to quell the bloody skirmishes. Then once peace was restored, Kate would be escorted back to Sydney by the military. A spurt of energy enticed her onwards. Nothing would stop Kate from leaving this place. Since her arrival there'd been little reason to stay.

'You should never have left Sydney. I told you as much then.'

She wouldn't admit that he'd been correct. 'I did what I thought was right at the time.'

'And in the doing made me understand the benefit of resilience. You have shown yourself capable of enduring more than some of the men under my command, Kate. A man needs more than a pretty face in this colony, and you have been graced with beauty and more. I have given the matter some thought,' he continued, offering his arm for support as Kate stepped over a large log. 'A well-born girl may not take to life out here. For it is here in the colony that I intend to stay. Granted, there has been little discourse between us, but I sensed a growing friendship while escorting your expedition north and I believe you were quite glad on my arrival at the Hardys' farm. Am I wrong in my assumption?'

'Yes, no, that is to say, it has been difficult, and a friendly face is always welcome.' Kate wondered where the conversation was heading, for she was beginning to feel uncomfortable.

James gave her a smile that suggested he did not quite believe her. 'It has come as somewhat of a shock to myself as well, Kate, what with my position in society, but the dangers of the past day have made me understand much about my own, shall we say, desires, and I am not immune to the mutual benefits that would stem from our union. People have married on less. And a lifetime is ample enough for the knowing of another, don't you think?'

Kate was sure her lips opened, but no words came forth.

'I have witnessed firsthand how this journey of yours started and I hope to see it through until the end.' James halted, so that his meaning was understood. 'The very end.'

'James, I really don't know if –'

'Think on it, Kate.'

He said no more, but slowing his pace, drew level with George Southerland. The two men began to speak in whispers, as Kate increased each stride. Major James Shaw and Kate Carter . . . she could not see it. He was right in that she had been incredibly relieved and pleased when he'd arrived at the Hardy farm, and Kate was flattered and liked his attention, but his wife? His declaration was so unexpected, so beyond the daydreaming of a lonely, scared woman, that Kate didn't know what she should think or how she should reply. Only one thing came to mind. If her mother were alive she would tell her daughter to seize the opportunity with both hands. It was, for a girl of Kate's background, the very best of offers.

Some time later, James was at Kate's side again. The two natives, Bidjia and Jardi, changed positions frequently, sometimes leading, or moving to the left or right, at others slowing so that it appeared they barely moved at all. Behind her, George Southerland kept up with the rhythmic pace of the group, his musket loaded and ready for action. Initially every time Kate glanced over her shoulder, the man who'd delivered her safely to the Hardys' holding was also looking behind, as if he expected the arrival of an unwanted visitor. As the day drew on, however, and Kate became attuned to the overseer's footfall, she knew that Mr Southerland concentrated more and more on the business of walking, although he still stopped occasionally to ensure they were not being followed.

James extended a hand, assisting her over a rocky outcrop and down the other side. Her shoes slipped and slid on the loose gravel, but Kate held her footing, pushing off a tree-trunk and speeding her descent so that level ground was quickly reached. The concern on the Major's face was obvious.

'We will discuss things further once we reach Sydney, Kate.'

'I am flattered, James, but we barely know each other.'

'But we are friends, yes?' he urged.

'Of course we are.'

340

'Well then, isn't that a good enough place to start?'

Kate gave an awkward smile. What was wrong with her? Any other woman in her position would be accepting his offer of marriage with open arms.

A single raised hand from the man known as Bronzewing brought their party to a sudden standstill. They were entering a heavily wooded area. Ridged and knotted, the great woody plants extended upwards to where their branches met, thickly intertwining to form a dense canopy.

On command they silently dropped to their knees. Kate was sure her heart grew as noisy as a beating drum.

James released the safety on his musket and, turning to the right, wedged the stock against his shoulder and looked down the length of the barrel to scan the dim spaces between the trees.

Kate's hand went to the waist of the dress she wore, to the constrictive bodice with its boning. Trembling fingers reached for the folds of the skirt, but the flintlock was not there. The pistol was where she'd left it, on the table, in the burnt-out kitchen hut.

Ahead in the timber Bronzewing kept perfectly still, a single shaft of sunlight accentuating the dense black of his hair. Kate observed the man, poised like a cat, ready to spring. Outwardly he appeared to be quite the opposite of the Major. James's steadfast solidness, the appeal and security of his rank, the allure of uniform, hid an outwardly aloof man difficult to understand and, as of today, more than surprising. But was this stranger, this man who would guide them to safety, any different? Both men shared strength and exerted authority. And their guide could indeed be a stripped-down version of James Shaw. Lithe and lean, quick to anger and even quicker to a fight, based on this morning's altercation with the Major, he ran easily and nimbly over and through the terrain he was clearly at one with.

Bronzewing aimed his musket for long seconds. The seconds became minutes. Kate was beginning to feel sick with fright. The stillness emphasised the slightest of noises: a fluttering bird, the snap of a twig, the rustle of leaves high above them. She sat carefully on the ground as a leaf spiralled to the earth, coming to rest near her hand. The movement diverted her line of sight. Opposite to where she crouched, the bark of a tree had been scarred. Only yards away another trunk was similarly disfigured. Feet away a large bush spider was scuttling towards her. Kate searched for something to throw at the creature. She had to move. She had to get away from it.

'Come.'

Kate ignored James's outstretched hand. She was already on her feet and moving away from the spider. 'The danger has passed?'

The Major shrugged. 'I saw nothing.'

Bronzewing gestured animatedly to the two natives. The younger of the group, Jardi, padded towards Kate and the Major.

'It is dark soon, we rest here.' The area Jardi directed them to was slightly uphill, across a narrow open space to where trees grouped as if planted. 'Stay, all of you.'

James and Mr Southerland led Kate to the stand of trees.

'Who do you think that man is, James? You know this Bronzewing, don't you?' It was not the first time the overseer had asked the question.

'I know of him, yes, but as you said earlier, George, for the moment he is someone in whom we must place our safety until such a time as his service is no longer required,' James replied stiffly.

Kate squirrelled her eyebrows together. 'That is too cryptic.'

'He's on the run then?' George Southerland queried, as Kate sat tiredly within the naturally curved ring of timber. 'I'm not surprised. Only convicts or those of mixed blood take to the bush. Still, we've got nothing worth the taking and he didn't have to help us.'

They passed a waterbag back and forth. Kate wanted more of the liquid gold. She could have drunk a river. But the overseer was adamant that the precious water be conserved and so she contented herself with the bark-tinted residue that laced her tongue.

'How far is it to Mr Stewart's run?' asked Kate. Her tiredness was making her head ache.

'I don't know, Kate.' Mr Southerland rested the stock of his musket in the dirt between his legs. 'Rest now while you've the chance.'

Kate awoke, teeth chattering. Something hard and cold pressed against her skin. She scrabbled in the gloom, rubbed at her eyes, wondering where she was. She had no sense of time or place, no recall as to location. The dark was an unending blackness. The earth freezing and the air beyond cold. But there was something . . . soft snoring, and it came from nearby. The noise eased Kate's mind, turning the pitch-black familiar. Mrs Horton was not a quiet sleeper. The woman was worse than Madge if that were possible, the way she tossed and turned. And her bowels? Kate would never understand how a woman's body could turn food so sour. She sat up, wiping a thin line of saliva from her cheek, brushing at the dirt that had stuck to the drool. The scratchy blanket must be somewhere on the floor. She reached out a hand, searching for the covering, but all that she found was a handful of dirt and leaves.

It wasn't the cook snoring next to her. It was James. And no blanket had slipped from the bed. The acknowledgment of where Kate was and why struck her forcefully.

A murky light began to stream through the dense timber, throwing into relief the straight-sided trees that towered all around. A little further downhill the figure of their guide, Bronzewing, was visible. He lay on his stomach. The moon rose gradually, tinting their surrounds in a sepia light, sending beams of paleness to coax away distant shadows. It was as if the man who lived on the bright

343

orb had come down to earth and was busily pulling at branches and shrubs so that the light could inch its way into the very worst of places.

A few feet away from Kate, James coughed and sat up, stretching out his legs. 'You should be sleeping,' he told her. 'I'll change watch with George.' Bent low to the ground the Major moved inconspicuously, the crushing of leaves and twigs the only sign of the direction he travelled.

The moon lifted above the ridge of trees in the distance, rimming the jagged skyline. Bronzewing hadn't moved. The man's long legs were slightly apart, the toes of his boots braced by the ground. He angled a musket in the direction of the moonlight and was partially concealed by brush to any that may approach. There was no sign of his native companions.

Getting carefully to her feet Kate travelled the short distance downhill. She was only a few yards from her destination when Adam heard her. He moved swiftly, reaching up to grab hold of an arm and pulling her roughly to the ground. He flipped her onto her back and covered her mouth with a hand. Kate bit down hard and stared up at him, her chest heaving.

'Quiet,' he murmured.

His attention remained on the area in front of them. Kate released his hand, the taste of blood in her mouth. She could feel the heat of his body, the weight of his arm on her shoulder and still he hadn't freed her. Then, very slowly, he turned back to where she lay. He studied her almost lazily, as if it were not impolite to do so, as if they had all the time in the world. Then with deliberate slowness, he withdrew his hand and resumed his sentry duty. Kate lay quite still. In the moonlight the muscles in his forearm strained against the cream of his shirt. A vein pulsed in his neck. When he caught her staring Kate rolled onto her stomach.

Briefly examining the bloody bite mark on the soft fleshy part of his palm, Adam pushed a pistol across the dirt towards Kate, along with an ammunition pouch. Swiftly unplugging the stopper from the powder bag, he passed it across as well. Kate carefully loaded the weapon and then pointed it out into the semi-darkness, although she had no idea at what.

Slowly three figures emerged. Dark shapes that moved soundlessly towards them, the tips of long spears glinting in the light of the rising moon. One of the men Kate recognised. She'd not soon forget that mass of hair or the scarred torso, nor his murder of Mrs Horton.

Kate took a long, slow breath. Bronzewing's finger rested on the musket's trigger. The men trod noiselessly towards them, stealthy, and then just as abruptly they became unsettled. They backed away to merge once again with the dark.

Adam relaxed as he leant the musket on the shrubby barrier between their attackers.

'Why have they left?' Kate whispered.

Turning so that he lay side-on to Kate and, resting on his arm, Adam drew her attention to the trees underneath which Kate had slept. In the moonlight one of the upper branches seemed to hold something. There was a lone, narrow silhouette that stretched the length of the timber some fifteen feet from the ground.

'Burial ground,' he told her.

Kate's eyes grew round. 'Are we safe?'

Adam turned to her. 'It seems so,' his eyes studied her, 'at least for tonight.'

Kate considered his words. 'Why did you refuse to return and bury the Hardys? They were good people.'

'It may have placed you and the others in danger. It was best that we leave that place and head for safety,' he replied simply. 'This land is at war with itself, miss. There is no point courting trouble.'

Kate plied the soft dirt with hesitant fingers. 'I thought ill of you.'

'It's to be expected.'

'Expected?' Kate repeated indignantly.

'Keep your voice down.' He peered over the top of the branches concealing them and, satisfied they were alone, continued, 'I don't expect you to understand, miss. In my experience all are quick to judge and slow to see reason. The Major said you were a lady's companion. Why would you travel to such a remote place? Did no-one advise you of the dangers?'

'Dangers, yes.' But the rest of his queries Kate couldn't answer, not anymore. Her reasons for leaving the environs of Sydney seemed ridiculous now. 'Why are you with those natives?'

'When my mother died Bidjia took me in, adopted me if you like, and raised me as part of his clan.'

'And your English? Did a missionary teach you?'

'There was a settler family nearby, the Lycetts. They had a boy my age. They were good to me.'

'What about your father? Are none of your family alive?'

'No,' Adam said adamantly, 'none.'

'I'm sorry.'

'Don't be.' He fingered the shell bracelet around his wrist. 'Bidjia's people believe that the spirits of the dead travel to the sky, remaining with the creator beings for all eternity. The old become young and the sick are healed. It's a nice thought.'

They both turned their faces heavenwards. There were scant stars with a bright moon illuminating the sky but those that could be seen appeared fragile and so very far away.

'I think of my mother when the morning star rises,' Adam said, his voice soft. 'The Yolngu people say that the star draws a rope behind her on rising that's attached to the earth and that through her people are able to communicate with their dead loved ones.'

'So we remember them always.' Kate thought of her parents.

'At least it will be clear going over the next few days,' Adam said, changing the subject.

'How do you know?'

'Look at the moon, there's no ring circling it, so we can be assured

346

of dry weather, and he sits a little to one side, so there'll be a wind coming – a westerly, I'd imagine, the way it's angled. Generally the weather's always calm about a full moon in the colder months but all you have to do is look to the sky to check.'

Kate thought of the leech in the Reverend's jar. While he'd been watching a creature through glass, this man had been observing the heavens. 'What else is up there?'

'The emu in the sky – that's the Milky Way. You can see the long, stretched-out shape of the bird but it changes through the seasons. Come August it will look like an emu egg, ready to hatch. That's the month when I was initiated into the tribe.'

'What did they do?' Kate had never had such a conversation, especially with a white man brought up by Aboriginals, who chose to roam the wilds. She wondered where he truly felt at home – in her world or that of the natives.

Adam chuckled. 'I can't tell you that, miss. It's man's business, as women have their business.'

'Why do men always think they know best where women are concerned?' Kate didn't mean to sound huffy, but it was always the same.

'I'd imagine that most of us don't, miss, but perhaps it's expected that we should.'

Kate didn't anticipate such an answer. 'Mr Southerland and the Major think you're a convict or runaway. Is that true?'

'What do you think?' The contours of his jaw hardened.

'I think,' Kate answered carefully, 'that it takes a lot for a person to leave civilisation and want to live out here.' She moistened her lips. 'What's your real name?'

'Does it matter?'

It was obvious that he didn't feel comfortable telling her. More than anything Kate knew what it meant to place one's faith in someone and have that trust destroyed. 'You don't have to tell me, I understand.'

347

'Adam,' he finally responded. 'Now, go and rest, miss. No, keep it,' he told her when Kate offered the flintlock pistol back. 'We leave before first light. And take this.' Reaching into his pocket he retrieved a handful of native seeds. 'Chew slowly. You'll be less tired in the morning.'

'I'm s-sorry about your hand.'

He examined the bite mark. 'No, you're not,' he replied.

Kate knew he watched her as she returned to the cluster of trees and settled back down in the dirt. The bark was rough against her shoulders but Kate stayed upright, resting the pistol in her lap and cradling the cold metal. The moon glowed brightly, filling the sky. Two small furry animals scampered across the ground as if chasing their moon-shadows and disappeared into a hollow log. Adam had not asked if she knew how to fire the pistol, if she could point and shoot, he'd simply assumed that she could.

'Probably not the time to be wandering about, Kate.' Mr Souther-land stepped out from between the trees.

She wondered how long the overseer had been standing there. He moved to sit not far away, leaning his musket against a tree.

'I wasn't wandering.'

Kate shifted a little closer to the tree, rubbing her arms to entice warmth. The desire to remain awake, to observe the man below who kept guard for all of them, was strong, but Kate knew that tiredness would soon overtake her and sleep was needed if she was going to keep pace with the men in the morning. She ate the offered seeds slowly, quietly, licking her palm until they were gone, grateful for the simple act of sharing and the kindness behind the deed.

Her thoughts drifted. Above them, high in the branches, some ten feet or more, another watched over them. A native person from this very land but of an unidentified time. In the moonlight the form grew definition. Long and lean, the deceased was laid out along the length of a branch, as if cradled in midair. The tangled foliage dangling down and around rustled in the light breeze, wrapping the body in a delicate shroud as the glow from the moon descended through the highest branches. Arching her neck, Kate stared at the form that hung above her. How could she be unnerved by the presence of this person? Whomever it was who had been laid to rest with the caress of a soft wind and a coverlet of stars had protected them this night.

⫷ Chapter 26 ⫸

1838 July – en route to
the Stewart farm

Adam and Jardi paused between two trees. A long cobweb strung between branches was broken.

'They are ahead of us,' Bidjia stated, allowing his palm to hover above the footprints, 'no more than half a day. The spider has not rebuilt.'

'They know where we're going,' Adam decided. The hill that lay before them was steep. It would be hard going for all.

'We should have walked away from this,' Bidjia told them. 'No good can come of our being here.'

Behind them the others followed. The red coat of the officer was obvious in the timber.

'But we're close, yes?' Jardi asked.

'Close enough.' There was the hill to climb and then, they hoped, the valley that led to the Stewart farm would come into view. 'To leave now would be wrong,' Adam told them. 'Mundara would have the advantage. Southerland would put up a fair fight, as would the Major, I've no doubt of that, but I can't walk away.'

Bidjia muttered something in his native tongue, and then, 'You have too much white in you, Bronzewing.'

'They would not save us,' Jardi argued, 'you know this.'

'But I'm not them and we have given our word to get them safely to the Stewart property,' Adam countered. The rest of their party drew closer. The group had slowed over the last few hours. 'They need food and rest before we continue on.'

Overhead the sun grew warm. 'Camp here, then,' Bidjia ordered. Promptly moving a few feet from their path, he sat cross-legged at the base of a tree. 'The sun-woman nears the midpoint.'

'It is the girl,' Jardi mocked. 'If not for her we would be free of this place.'

Adam didn't want to venture into a discussion about Kate Carter. He liked her, that much was true, and although he thought of her often, observing her graceful movements, he also chided himself for his stupidity. How could there be a future in such thoughts. When the others arrived he gave orders to rest while he and Jardi gathered food.

'I can help,' Kate offered, 'I know some of the native plants.'

The whites of Jardi's eyes grew large. Shrugging, he headed slightly downhill.

'You should sit and rest,' James argued.

'I will be fine. I'm not some helpless female, James.' Kate followed Adam and Jardi, her shoes slipping on the thick grasses as they made their way to where rich herbage grew. Instantly recognising some of the plants that Sally had taught her about, Kate searched the area until she found a stick. Breaking it off so that it was slightly pointed, she squatted and began to dig.

'Maybe she's not so bad,' Jardi conceded, watching as the woman tucked her skirts between her knees and concentrated on the task of digging up food. 'Maybe she be a good woman for you, Bronzewing.'

'*Maybe* you should look for food instead of watching her,' Adam replied.

Jardi smiled. '*Maybe* I leave so you can talk whitefella things.'

'*Maybe* that would be a good idea,' Adam admitted. He grinned in return at the younger man and walked to where Kate was flicking up dirt as she dug for the tuberous roots.

'Who taught you this?'

Kate paused. Sweeping away the earth that had collected on her skirt, she twisted her hair so that it fell over one shoulder. 'One of the natives at the Hardys' farm. I would have learnt more if I'd had the time.'

There was a small pile of plants by her side. Adam poked through the selection. 'They're better boiled but we can't risk a fire so it will have to do.'

'We need more than this.' There had been little opportunity to speak with Adam over the past day. Kate found herself trying to prolong the conversation. 'Maybe if we searched over there.' She pointed to an area some feet away.

'Jardi will find more,' Adam replied. 'You go and rest.' He nodded towards the mount before them. 'We must climb it this afternoon.'

'Oh.' The sight of the steep hill and Adam's disinterest deflated her. Kate got tiredly to her feet.

Helping to gather the plants she'd collected, Adam accompanied Kate back in the direction of the waiting men. She slipped in the grass as he steered her towards the timber and immediately his arm was about her waist, supporting her until she regained her balance. For a brief moment they stood looking at each other and then Kate busied herself with the plants and continued on alone, confused.

≼ Chapter 27 ≽

1838 July – the Stewart farm

The Stewart homestead and outbuildings sat in the middle of the valley. The farm dwellings were mere specks from this distance, but on first sight it was a serene view. Trees appeared to have been cleared in a circle from the site, extending a half-mile to where the natural surrounds, lightly timbered country interspersed with pale green fields, resumed. The landscape was similar to some of the country Kate had journeyed through since leaving Sydney. It was like an English country estate, such as one saw in picture books. She almost expected to see a group of well-dressed men on horseback readying for a hunt.

James pointed out a gully that led from the eastern foothills across the valley floor. A narrow creek which no doubt would have to be crossed before they reached the Scotsman's run.

The house appeared expansive in proportion and the numerous outbuildings and series of yards suggested a profitable business had taken root. It was only after scrutiny that the tell-tale signs of recent trouble became apparent. The crops in the ground bore the scars of recent firing and smoke drifted from a number of spots close to the main house. A large number of sheep grazed in close proximity and Kate commented that one mob in particular were very white. George Southerland informed her that they'd been recently shorn.

From the vantage point of the hill, the surrounding country appeared quiet although Kate was now aware of how deceptive the outer limits could be. Adam expected to reach the property by nightfall; indeed all hoped that would be the case for none were partial to spending another sleepless night outdoors and the party had been on the move since before daybreak. But the timing of their arrival, Adam explained, was based on walking straight downhill, veering westward and ensuring they kept to the open country afforded by the valley floor. The plan was not greeted favourably for along this path there would be few places to seek cover, a route that did not appeal to George Southerland.

'I know this land now. I recognise the lay of it.' The overseer drew an outline of the undulating horizon with his finger in the air, turning on his heel towards the north-west. 'The Hardys' farm is that way. Surely we're better off hugging the hills, keeping to the edge of the timber. That way has served us well so far and it will be quicker than your suggestion.'

'We only travelled through that area because there was little choice,' Adam explained irritably. He was also trying to placate Bidjia by keeping Jardi away from the eastern foothills. The old man sensed trouble and not just from the renegade tracking them. Jardi had traced Mundara's camp and although the warrior was not present, he'd caught sight of the girl they'd seen at the river weeks previously. Once they'd reached the white man's run, Jardi intended to return to the camp and take the girl.

'You were the one who suggested we head east first,' James reminded him. 'You're meant to be our guide and what have you done but had us walking for nearly four days traversing ridges and gullies. We could have been at the farm by now.'

Bidjia interrupted his conversation with Jardi. He stared hard at the Major and then, turning his back on the group, walked down the slope a little to lean on his spear, one foot resting in the crook of his knee. His son joined him and soon the pair began to argue again.

'You're still alive, aren't you?' Adam countered. They'd been on the move for too long. Now the group wasted time with their complaining while he sensed that Bidjia grew tired again.

'Normally I'd be in agreement with you,' George Southerland consented. 'It is always best to stay in open country, to see what's coming.' A stubby finger inched its way into his thick beard. 'It's a pity we've no horses. We can't chase the bastards down if we're attacked.'

'A quick hit with the stirrup-iron, eh?' Adam was finding it difficult to control his temper.

Kate felt ill at the thought of what Adam implied.

'But we haven't seen a black in three days, nothing,' Mr Southerland continued as if Adam had not spoken. 'These things always come in runs. The trouble's died down now. I reckon it's safe to walk on directly.'

'I agree with you, George. If something happens and we're delayed,' James added, 'there's scarcely anywhere to mount a decent stand.'

'A decent stand?' George laughed. 'Look, James, the blacks are uppity. They've been riled to melting point with what's been happening up here, but they're not like us. If they do come at us again it will be a quick skirmish. They'll run out, throw their spears and be gone again. I'm not saying it will happen, no, sir. I think we're safe, but the timber affords the quickest route making us assured of reaching the farm before dark. There's no fat moon to light our way tonight.'

'So you would give them the advantage,' Adam complained. 'We're dealing with a renegade half-caste and we've seen what he's capable of.' He wiped sweat from his brow with a shirtsleeve. 'And as for your thoughts on their ability to mount an attack, Southerland, I've seen it before west of Sydney, over the mountains. Small raiding parties are an effective means of –'

The Major bristled. 'And you'd know about that, wouldn't you? In fact I'm thinking you'd know a lot about the area west of the mountains that edges into the Bathurst Plains.'

'Stop it, the two of you,' Kate said loudly. 'We are so close and yet you stand there arguing like children.'

The Major looked past Adam as if he didn't exist. 'I wish the blacks would realise that if they don't measure up to what's expected of them they'll have no place in this country.'

'They're not like us,' Adam responded. 'They don't believe a person has the right to come onto their land and steal it away. They don't think it's fair that waterholes should be fouled by livestock, or that their women should be stolen, that their traditions should be destroyed. They don't care for money or progress, power or prestige, they think only of and for the land and the continuation of their way of life.' He paused, as if exhausted by the futility of his words. 'They have chiefs but as for designated leaders to rally and lead their people into battle,' he shook his head, 'their society is not organised that way. But they do have warriors, and some seek payback for the violations done to them.'

'You should be shot for such talk.' James balled his fists. 'You make them sound like damn patriots.'

Adam drew so close to the officer that their chests almost touched. 'And isn't that what you call a people when their land is invaded and they are prepared to fight for the country they love?'

'I will see you hang.' The words were strung out through gritted teeth.

'But not before I get you to safety, eh, Major?' Adam stepped away.

There was no final decision. Kate simply took up a position

between James and Mr Southerland and silently they headed down towards the valley floor. Once out in the open they walked in an arrow formation – Adam at point and the two natives flanking the sides. It was mid-afternoon and the going was easy. The muscles in Kate's calves and thighs, well-worked from the hilly terrain they'd already crossed, gradually relaxed. She brushed the tops of the tall grass with her palms as they passed, trying to blot out James's harsh words.

As they crossed the valley floor the Major attempted to engage Kate in discussions pertaining to life in Sydney but she found her thoughts revisiting Adam's earlier remarks, particularly his use of the word 'patriot'. She understood what was implied, indeed the man's words were clear enough, but to view the Aborigines as such flouted established thought, that the natives were a breed apart, savages that rightly should be contained, constrained, subjugated. Yet here were two natives leading them to safety.

Kate plucked at a piece of grass, twirling the pale length of it between her fingers. If the natives had been dispossessed of their lands, if the British settlers were in fact invaders and the British Government's declaration of *terra nullius* – that no-one had owned this land before the British Crown took possession of it – was simply enacted to ensure a convenient and therefore righteous excuse to subjugate a native peoples, then Adam was right and James was wrong. And hadn't George Southerland once said a similar thing on the journey north?

'Your mind is on other things, Kate.'

'I'm sorry, James. I was thinking about the natives, about what they must think of us.'

'I doubt they think much at all, Kate. Some people say that they may well be linked back to the very first type of human. Accordingly there is much learned study being undertaken.'

'Of what? The measurement of skulls and bones? Murder for rational understanding?'

'I am amazed you could make such a comment after the slaughter of the Hardys!'

Kate could see his point and yet Adam had presented a compelling argument. 'But do we not have criminals as well in our society?'

James gave a choked laugh. 'Hardly a comparison.'

'Why not? Why can't these things be compared?' Kate argued.

'I have always doubted the appropriateness of a woman's education. Too much information can be detrimental and confusing, which is not your fault, Kate, but that of those who believe a necessity for such teachings in a modern age.'

'Please, James, I have lived with a tribe on the Hardy farm. I have seen firsthand that they have the ability to learn English and their plant knowledge in regard to both foods and healing remedies is extensive. We talk of them being savages but did you not fell a native on request so that a skull could be sent to England for study? Did not Jonas Kable speak of his fine collection of native curiosities? If the natives are savages, then surely we are barbarians.'

'I think you have had your head turned by our guide, Kate.' The Major's blue eyes were accusatory. 'He is little more than a savage himself and you can be assured that his rebellious days will soon be over.'

The possibility of a response was not given for the Major was already dropping back to walk side by side with the overseer. Although disappointed, Kate knew she should not be surprised by James's comments. He was not alone in his beliefs. As a child she'd thought she would grow old with two cats for company. Such a life remained a possibility for there were few men in the world who gave women their due. Kate looked ahead to where Adam walked . . . very few.

The afternoon sun was slowly wreathed in patchy cloud. Intricate patterns appeared across the hills, which edged prettily away to the west. It was like watching a moving tapestry, as varied cloud shadows slid across the surface of the land, tipping trees and slopes, ridges and gullies, gliding across grasses thick and lush. At some point an understanding came to her as she watched the countryside transform beneath a changing sky. Money and supplies, the establishment of homes and businesses, labour, families, none of it was possible without the land, and here it was in its pristine state. Kate could see and feel it; an all-encompassing beauty, that in this place, for the briefest of moments, made her consider that if there was a God then maybe he dwelt here, in this land.

'Do you think he knows what he's doing?' The overseer had exchanged places, coming to walk by Kate's side.

'Sorry, I was lost in my own thoughts,' Kate admitted.

'I was talking about him.' Mr Southerland gestured ahead to where Adam maintained a steady gait. 'I hope he knows what he's doing.'

'You're following him,' Kate pointed out. 'We all are.'

'Well, we're nearly there. A couple more hours and you'll have a roof over your head again.' He slung the musket he carried over a shoulder. 'You've been talking to him. What's he told you?'

'Why?' The comment was said lightly but Kate knew from experience that Mr Southerland never did or said anything without a reason.

'He's from Sydney originally,' he began, 'born there, like you, but convict blood on both sides.'

'How do you know that?' Kate was intrigued.

'He told me.'

She couldn't recall the two men talking beyond the necessary, but by nightfall Kate was invariably so tired that it was possible the two men had struck up conversation.

'He's had a hard life, abandoned, reared by blacks,' the overseer continued. 'They say there's a few like him roaming the country, but there's more of them that are of mixed-blood than pure white.'

Kate thought of her namesake, Sally's child. 'Will Sally and the others still be at the farm when you go back?'

'Who knows? Most likely they will have moved on by now, considering the troubles.' The overseer coughed, wiping his nose on the arm of his shirt, and briefly studied what had been deposited. 'But you know it's a grand thing for a man to be educated. I wonder how our guide managed his letters out in the bush.'

'He said a settler family schooled him.'

'Ah, I would have thought some God-fearing missionary got his hands on him,' he replied conversationally. 'The Lycetts?' the overseer probed. 'Was that their name?'

'Yes, I think so.' Kate turned towards him. 'If you didn't know how he was educated, where did you hear of the name Lycett?'

The man squinted into the sun. 'He's not who you think he is, Kate.' Mr Southerland nodded over his shoulder at the Major.

The exchange unnerved Kate. 'And do you know who he is?'

'We do now. We just needed to have a few facts confirmed before we arrived at Stewart's place. Best to know what's what, eh?'

Ahead, Adam slowed his pace to talk to his two friends. The elder of the natives was arguing with the younger, who, lifting his spear, pointed to the east. A thin stream of smoke was just visible in the distance. Was it the warrior who'd attacked the Hardys? Kate wondered. She dearly wanted to ask but felt unsure after what had just transpired. Adam had entrusted her with certain personal information and Kate had naively shared it with George Southerland, who in turn appeared complicit with the Major. Whatever their guide may or may not have done, Kate had unwittingly assisted in their investigations.

⋙ Chapter 28 ⋘

1838 July – the Stewart farm

The Stewart farm came into view gradually. It was another hour before the speck became a distinct mass, and still the farm flickered in and out of sight, as if playing hide-and-seek among the scattered stands of timber. At one point Kate imagined that she could almost make out the clutch of bark and wood outbuildings, which sat low to the ground, in the middle of the narrowing valley. The main homestead was not yet visible, but twirls of smoke drifted in the dying daylight hours. It was as if they approached a small village for Kate counted five smoky streamers high in the cooling air. Such signs of civilisation were a welcome sight and the tiredness seeping through her limbs dissipated a little. There was not much further to go. They would rest and make plans.

She'd not noticed before how the sweep of timber on the distant sides of the valley had grown in thickness, nor how the trees now collared the edges of the tapering flat. The simple process of continuing to place one foot in front of the other had consumed Kate's thoughts but now she found the dense foliage and the closeness of this forested area disconcerting. Was it her imagination or had their small party increased their pace? Don't be silly, she mumbled quietly, calm yourself, soon their labours would be rewarded and they would arrive at Mr Stewart's farm. The Scotsman had visited the Hardys' property once only, the day of the argument regarding the boundary between the two runs. Kate remembered the man as one who could be reasoned with and hoped his wife was equally affable. She'd had her fill of puffed-up settlers' wives.

Their escorts still flanked them. Bidjia was on the eastern edge, a quarter-mile away, his son a little closer on the opposite side, while Adam's position remained unaltered. Kate thought of what she'd told the overseer and then considered what the man ahead of them may have been guilty of. James's attitude towards Adam had been fractious from the beginning and yet here they all were, depending on him for their very survival. Kate observed Adam's steady stride, the continual turn of his head from left to right as he scanned the surrounds, the way he held the musket at the ready. But she saw other things as well. The thickness of the man's dark shoulder-length hair, the taut pull of material across the width of his shoulders, the leanness of a body honed by rough living. This man was a breed apart.

The sound of barking dogs, intermittent in the air, carried across the grassland, drawing everyone's attention to the great sweep of movement that appeared in the south-east and headed steadily towards them. At first Kate couldn't make out what approached from afar but it soon became obvious. A big mob of sheep were being driven over and down an embankment like a cascade of bubbling white-water, spilling outwards across the land.

'Now that's a welcome sight,' the overseer commented, 'especially with the sun close to setting.'

To the west the rim of the sun was indeed not far from touching the tops of the soft peaks. With the earlier cloud having grown streaky and insubstantial, a halo of golden light stretched out towards them, gilding the swaying grasses and infusing the treetops with vibrant colours of russet brown and green.

Lifting a hand, Adam halted their small party as Bidjia stood motionless, directing his attention to the timber that was less than a half-mile away. James and Mr Southerland urged Kate onwards.

'If they're going to attack there's little point standing here and waiting for the bastards,' James muttered, pointing to a gully ahead of them.

'Take cover!' Adam yelled.

The Aboriginal rose from the tall pasture like some mythological being from the underworld.

Adam dropped to one knee, aimed and fired, but the native's spear had already been thrown and the shot missed. The target, Bidjia, turned swiftly to avoid being hit but the barb found its mark, striking the old man in the side of the ribs, the impact throwing him to the ground. Another native rushed George Southerland. The overseer responded with fire, wounding the man, who barely faltered in his attack. Black and white fell to the ground fighting, as Jardi sped across the grassy plain towards his fallen father.

James pushed Kate forwards and she ran towards the narrow gully, tumbling down the steep short sides. Her feet touched water, a thin brown-green excuse for a stream. She stepped away from the muddy edge to peer over the top of the ravine. Shots were being fired, precious seconds were now needed for the men to reload. Kate fumbled for the pistol in the folds of her skirt. The light was beginning to fail them. She had no extra powder and what was in the pistol had been placed there three nights ago when they'd hidden in the burial ground. If the powder had become damp, Kate couldn't be certain that the flintlock would still fire. Pointing the weapon over the embankment, she watched. James was running back to where Mr Southerland was fighting his attacker in the grass. Adam ran towards Jardi, who in turn pursued the man who'd speared his father.

The bash to Kate's head came from nowhere. One minute her heart was pounding, her fingers curled around the useless pistol, waiting for the attack to be over, and the next she was upside down, the blood roaring through her brain, the ground a moving, murky blur of sand, mud and water. Her arms were hanging uselessly and her head . . . the pain was shocking. The ground shifted. Something peppered her face and arms, pinpricks of grit and dirt. She spat out soil. The pain grew worse. Kate was sure she would be ill, then a creeping blackness began to descend. Death, the oblivion of it, the nothingness that awaited, scared her more thoroughly than she could have imagined. The threat of it forced her to focus.

The warmth of another human being; she could feel it now. Someone carried her, she'd been flung over a shoulder, and they moved quickly. Twisting her neck, Kate caught sight of a brown arm. It swung back and forth holding a wooden club. Summoning all her strength, she screamed. The next moment she was spinning through the air and landing with a thud on the hard earth. Someone or something had collided with them.

Adam. Kate heard his voice, low and threatening, like a growl. He said the warrior's name, Mundara.

The sides of the gully were steep as Kate grabbed at the shifting dirt, scrambling awkwardly up and away from the narrow waterway where the two men now faced each other. Her head spun. Adam dropped his musket and unsheathed a knife. His attacker leant forward, tossing the club from one hand to another. The native was tall and wiry. It was not a body or face one would soon forget, especially if you'd been dragged by the hair, certain of death or, she suddenly comprehended, had been attacked while journeying northwards to the Hardy farm. This was the third time that Kate had seen this savage, but the man was not as dark as she'd supposed; up close there was a lightness to his skin.

The two men rushed at each other.

The black struck out with the club, hitting Adam on the side of the head. The blow pushed him slightly from his path, momentarily dazed, but he gathered himself and wielded the blade swiftly, slicing through Mundara's bicep and, instantly spinning on his heel so that the knife was driven forwards with the full force of his body, cutting through the shirt the black wore and finding flesh. The man retaliated by diving forward, forcing Adam to the ground and straddling him. He gripped Adam's knife hand and the two men locked eyes.

Adam lifted a knee and the impact of bone against Mundara's back unbalanced him, jolting the attacker forwards and forcing the loosening of his grip. Instantly Adam plunged the blade upwards and the knife lodged deep in the man's chest. Mundara fell lifelessly to the ground.

Pulling the blade free, Adam wiped the blade on his trousers and went to Kate's side. 'Come now,' he said gently. Helping Kate to stand, he wrapped an arm about her for support. She pressed her cheek against his shoulder.

'Are you alright?' he asked softly.

Kate probed tentatively at the growing lump.

'Here, let me see.' Very gently Adam examined the wound, before brushing away the long strands of dark hair from Kate's eyes, and resting his palm against the soft contours of her face.

Kate lifted a hand, partially encircling his wrist with her fingers. 'Don't.' She was breathless and shaken, so why was she saying no to this man's touch when all Kate really wanted was for Adam to hold her.

'Why not?' Adam asked.

A click sounded. Major Shaw aimed a musket at them, as George Southerland limped towards them. The overseer was bashed and cut up about the cheeks and eyes and a bloody wound to his thigh had turned his trousers wet with blood.

'Step aside, Kate,' James ordered.

'What do you think you're doing?' Kate replied angrily.

'Give me the knife, Adam.' James beckoned with his hand.

Kate moved to stand a few feet away. Adam gave the officer a hard look but dropped the blade in the dirt, the point lodging in the soil.

'You're under arrest for the murder of Archibald Lycett.'

'Who?' Kate queried, confused. 'Who is Archibald Lycett?' And then she remembered, they were a settler family, friends of the man who'd just saved her life for a second time.

Adam was mute. He couldn't believe what he'd just heard. Winston had accused him of his father's murder? From the direction of the Stewart property three men on horseback were approaching at the gallop.

George Southerland bent over the dead black's body. 'Well, we've seen him before. He was part of a group that attacked our wagons. Bloody half-castes.' He spat in the dirt.

'What are you doing, James?' asked Kate, outraged. 'He just saved my life.'

'As any man should, Kate.' He gestured for his captive to turn and Adam did so as the overseer tied his hands behind his back with a short piece of leather.

The Major pressed the end of the barrel into Adam's back. 'Walk.'

'James, please?'

Kate's plea was ignored. The men's attention had been diverted by the arrival of Jardi. He stopped ten feet short of the group and, lifting his musket, aimed it at the Major.

'Leave him be,' Jardi ordered.

The Major remained steady. 'George, you take aim between his eyes and if the boy makes one move, shoot him.'

The overseer levelled his weapon reluctantly. 'I've got no quarrel with you, lad.'

'This is not your fight, Jardi,' Adam told him, 'you know this. Leave me. Tend to Bidjia.'

The boy was outnumbered.

'Musket first,' James demanded.

Adam nodded for Jardi to comply. He did so unwillingly, dropping the musket on the ground, his upper lip curling. The officer picked it up, handing it to the overseer.

Jardi, clearly unsure what he should do, looked to Adam for help. 'Bronzewing?'

'Bidjia? How is he?'

'My father says the spirits call him, my white brother.' Jardi's skin glistened with sweat in the remnants of the sun's light. 'It is his time, for the moon is dying and the darkness is coming.'

'Get on with you,' James gestured to Jardi to move away, 'lest you want to be locked up as well.'

'Leave, Jardi,' Adam told him, 'you cannot help me. This is white man's business.'

Jardi began to back away. 'I must sing the songs. I must tell the spirits that Bidjia comes.'

A shiver ran down Kate's spine.

'Tell him. Tell Bidjia . . .' Adam searched for the right word. In the end, no matter what he said, it would never be enough. 'Tell him thank you.'

'You are his son, you are of the clan.' Jardi backed away reluctantly before returning to his dying father.

'He helped us,' Kate argued, 'you must go and fetch Bidjia, James. We must tend to his wounds at least.'

'No,' Adam replied, 'leave them be.'

The pound of hooves grew louder. They waited for the approaching horsemen, who rode towards them across the wavering grass, kangaroo-hide coats flapping in the air. The men tugged on long reins and drew up in a spatter of dirt and gravel. The horses snuffled and whinnied as they came to a stop. The grit carried forward, coating those standing in wait with dust and bringing with it the scent of horse flesh and saddle-grease, sweat and tobacco.

'George Southerland? What in the name of Mary Queen of Scots are you doing here?' Mr Stewart ran an observant eye over the ragged group and dismounted. His men were wary. They were bearded, stocky types who surveyed the surrounding land with suspicion.

'The Hardys have been murdered, Mr Stewart. I've brought Kate Carter here for safety and this is Major James Shaw. And that there' – the overseer pointed to where Mundara lay dead – 'is the bringer of the troubles.'

Mr Stewart tipped his hat back on his head with the flick of a finger. 'Mundara.' He examined the body as his mare whinnied and backed away to nibble at herbage. 'That's his native name, we know him as Kent Harris. His mother was part white. He worked here for a time but took off a year or so ago.' His boot pushed at the prone body. 'He was running with some blacks further south, rushing cattle and eating the fattest. Built himself a set of cattle-yards he did. Aye, Kent was a sly one, but he came back before the end of last year, right melancholy and talking about some dark-haired woman who'd murdered his half-brother. I put him back to work and then after a month or so he'd gone again.'

Adam and George Southerland looked at Kate, Mundara's reason for vengeance becoming clear.

'I thought he'd come back, but . . .' He didn't bother finishing the sentence. 'I'm sorry for the Hardys, real sorry. And the little girl?'

The overseer shook his head. 'There were no survivors that we know of. The place was burnt to the ground and what men weren't killed probably ran off. I could use some help to get their sheep mustered, shorn and the fleeces to market.'

'It doesn't look like you'll be sitting on a horse anytime soon, George.' Mr Stewart clucked his tongue thoughtfully, eyeing the wound to the man's leg. 'But no doubt we can come to some arrangement that's beneficial to all. Well, we best get you lot back to the house. The dark's setting in and although we've had no raids or attacks for a week, it's best not to tempt fortune.' The Scotsman turned towards Adam. He placed his hands on his hips, the action pushed aside the brown skin coat he wore, revealing a brace of pistols. 'And who is this?'

'This man is under arrest for the murder of a settler west of the mountains near Bathurst.' James pushed the end of the barrel roughly into Adam's back, jolting him forwards.

'He saved our lives,' Kate countered, taking a step towards Mr Stewart. 'He should not be arrested.'

'You've been fully occupied, Major,' Mr Stewart commented dryly, looking from the officer to Adam and then Kate. He whistled for his horse and the animal came immediately, although the mare shuffled slightly back and forth as he remounted. 'Well, come on, lass. You best give me an arm,' Mr Stewart told Kate. 'You look as if you could faint at any moment.' He extended a hand to her.

Kate glanced at Adam. She didn't want to leave him. James was wrong.

'Go,' Adam told her.

Reluctantly, Kate walked towards Mr Stewart and was heaved up roughly behind the Scotsman onto his horse. She rubbed at her shoulder. It felt as if her arm had been pulled out of its socket.

'Marcus and Riley, stay with this lot and I'll return with a couple of horses.'

'There's one thing,' Adam finally spoke, 'a man's dying out there, a friend, his son is with him.'

With the setting sun the expanse of pasture was made dark and impenetrable.

'Blacks,' James explained. 'I'm pretty sure one of them was involved in the same attack as this man,' he pointed to Adam, 'but by the sounds of it he won't last the night. As for the younger one we've no quarrel with him and he's not armed.'

'Fair enough, I'll let them be for now, however, just in case you can put the prisoner in the smokehouse. He'll be secure there.' Mr Stewart gathered the reins and turned his horse homewards. 'Hang on, girl.'

Kate did as she was told, wrapping her arms around the barrel-chested Scotsman as the horse changed effortlessly from a trot to a canter. Mr Stewart was soon commenting on the murder of the Hardys, on how lucky the group had been to make it through unscathed. That his wife Nettie would be pleased to have a bit of company. Kate knew she shouldn't do it, that she daren't glance behind as they rode away. But she did. Adam's silhouette was unmistakeable in the twilight.

Across the country came a terrible wail. A moaning cry that grew thick with pain. The sound never varied, never weakened or grew stronger, but remained constant, throbbing. The noise echoed across the grassy plains, hovering among trees and spiky-headed grass. It was all around them as Kate rode on, away from the dreadful declaration of death. Her cheek was pressed firmly against the Scotsman's broad back as tears streamed down her face. She thought of the Morning Star Adam spoke of and Kate wept for all of them, dead and alive, friend or foe. She wept for the land that black and white bled for and the life that fate had given her.

I have seen
Your rays grow dim upon the horizon's edge
And sink behind the mountains. I have seen
The great Orion, with his jewelled belt,
That large-limbed warrior of the skies,
Go down into the gloom.

'The Constellations' by William Cullen Bryant
(1794–1878)

≈ Chapter 29 ≈

1838 July – the Stewart farm

It was dawn when Kate woke. A pale light revealed a chair and washstand. The light increased, sliding up close-fitting timber walls and into well-crafted corners. The night had been filled with dreams that Kate couldn't recall, only the memory of a constant wailing came with her into this new day and a fiery glow out beyond the buildings, on the grassy plain. This hadn't been some fantasy of her imaginings. Kate had watched as the red-gold reached up towards the sky.

She blinked and yawned, blinked again, wondering if it was Jardi who'd lit the fire and whether the old man, his father, was dead. Rubbing at sleep-crusted eyes, she realised that she was propped up by numerous pillows in an actual bed with thick blankets and a pale coverlet. She was thirsty and on the wash-stand she could see a pale pink pitcher with a glass next to it. Kate really didn't want to move. Didn't think she could. The dull ache that had lodged in her brain after the attack yesterday remained constant.

She stretched out her legs and wriggled her toes. The sheets were intact, without holes or sprouting ticking and the scent of lavender pervaded the bedchamber. Leaving the bed, with its four posters rising to the timber ceiling and the thick mattress, was the last thing that appealed but finally Kate gingerly turned back the coverlet, swinging her legs over the side of the bed. A dizziness slowed her movements, but the light-headedness and accompanying ache did not detract from the amazement Kate experienced at her surrounds: a brightly coloured mat, floorboards and a round mirror hanging on the wall directly above a plain wood dresser. The cabinet held a matching bone-handled brush and comb, a number of glass bottles with stoppers and on the chair there was a clean skirt and bodice. Kate swallowed. Tears welled.

There was a tap on the door and Nettie Stewart entered with a tray. 'Good. I was hoping you'd be awake with the birds, for the noise this household makes doesn't suit those who need rest. Now, I've brought you hot tea with a bit of sugar, Kate, and bread warm from the oven. Major Shaw told us that none of you had eaten much so we don't want to tempt chance by stuffing you like a bush turkey.'

Kate clutched at the high-necked nightgown that she could barely recall dressing in the previous evening. Was it true? Was this petite woman in her plaid skirt and dark bodice, with the laughing eyes and sun-creased skin, the same kindly woman who'd greeted her last night? 'M-Mrs Stewart, please. You don't have to wait on me. If you point me in the direction of the kitchen, I'll make myself useful. I'm sure the cook –'

'Nettie, lass. My name is Nettie. We didn't come all this way to live the way we had in the past. This is a new world and a new world deserves new rules, don't you think?' She didn't wait for a reply. 'As for a cook?' The older woman gave a lilting laugh, her cheeks turning a pretty pink. She continued chuckling as the tray was placed on the dresser. 'We've no cook, dear. I've three daughters aged fifteen to twelve and a right terror of a ten-year-old son and, believe me, they cause enough of a commotion without paying good wages for more trouble. So I can't be responsible if the tea's stewed or the bread's as hard as riding tack.'

A cloth was lifted from the tray and the sweet smell of bread and tea was enough to make Kate swoon.

'This morning, however, there's a semblance of quiet for my eldest are setting the fire to get the copper in readiness for the laundry while the younger two have already scampered off to the huts with their father. The shearing of the sheep is only part-way through.'

'Thank you.' Kate accepted the tea and bread and sipped at the hot drink. She wanted to gulp and gobble down the offering in one go, but Mrs Stewart was right. Her stomach was barely used to food.

'Of course they were up half the night, what with that black terrorising them with his melancholy whining. Just like a dog it was, but twice as frightening for the little ones, especially in the dark of the moon. Why they let him be,' she gave a dramatic sigh, 'well, I can't say I share my husband's thoughts on the establishment of beneficial relations. Not after what's been happening lately. And I doubt the blacks are too fond of the pretension either.'

'I can't thank you enough, Mrs Stewart.'

'Nettie, Kate. Now my eldest Joanna is about your size.' Mrs Stewart held up a dark blue skirt with a faint pattern running through it and a similarly coloured long-sleeved bodice. The colours of the garments were bold. 'But I'm afraid there's nought we could do about shoes. Yours are close to ruined but we mended them a little so they're wearable.' She lifted Kate's shoes up that had been left near the door and turned them over – one of the soles had been replaced with new leather. 'I'm surprised you could walk at all with that foot. Red raw and blistered it is.'

Kate looked down and saw with some surprise that her left foot was bandaged from the toes to the instep.

'Now let's have a look at that head of yours.' Nettie opened the internal shutters on the window.

A single pane of glass, although cracked from corner to corner, made Kate feel that more than ever she had indeed returned to civilisation. Her spirits lifted in spite of her aches and pains.

'On the bed, lass.'

Perching on the edge of the cot, Kate ate hungrily as Mrs Stewart wrung water from a cloth in the basin on the washstand and dabbed at the injury. 'You've a nasty bump and a bit of a gash and a bruise any prize-fighter would be proud to claim. There'll be a scar, I'm afraid, but it will be close to your hairline. How do you feel?'

Kate swallowed. 'Fine.' Her voice remained croaky and tight, but with the bread and tea already settling her stomach, she did feel better.

'Fine? Well, you're a bonny lass if ever I've met one. The poor Hardys dead in their sleep and you dragged halfway across the country.' Her tongue made a tsking noise. 'Of course I never met them. It was intended after the boundary dispute was resolved but, well, it's not like it's a doddle across hill and dale. Now off with that gown and we'll finish washing you proper like and then get you dressed.'

'What?'

'Don't be bashful, Kate. I cleaned you up as best I could last night but there's a smell about you, my dear, which suggests attention is needed.' Nettie took the empty teacup from her hands.

'I'm sorry, I didn't realise.' Kate brushed absently at the breadcrumbs on her lap and then watched with horror as they scattered on the floor.

'I'd not be expecting you to. You've had enough to contend with.' Kate found her arms lifted and the nightgown tugged over her head. She stood naked and shivering in the weak morning light as Nettie began to scrub at her as if she were intent on removing

Kate's skin. Water sloshed in the basin, more was added to the bowl from a rose-coloured pitcher and the homemade lye soap was used liberally, time and again. 'Here you go, lass.' Nettie passed Kate the wash-cloth and made a gesture to her breasts and private parts. 'Heavens, you're a slight thing.'

Kate accepted the cloth and, aware that the determined woman had no intention of leaving the room, turned side on and quickly dabbed at the areas instructed.

'Good. Now dry yourself with this and then it's a quick splash of lavender water and we're done.'

Kate rubbed her body with a dry cloth as the fragrant water was selected from one of the glass bottles on the dresser and poured into Kate's cupped palms. She splashed it on her face and neck. The scent was sublime. Next Kate was dressed in a clean pair of drawers and a warm shift, woollen stockings were tugged to her thighs, the skirt tied firmly about her waist and the tight-fitting bodice done up. A square piece of tartan resembling a shawl, but smaller, was the last addition, placed around Kate's shoulders and fastened with a silver brooch at the front. Nettie touched the ornament, smiling softly. 'It was my sister's and her husband's mother's afore that. She'd no children of her own.'

'I'll keep good care of it, Nettie. Thank you.' Kate began brushing her hair.

'One hundred strokes, Kate.'

'My mother used to say that.'

'Did she now? Well she's a woman after my own heart for there's nothing so attractive to a man as a sweet-smelling lass with well-kept hair, after food of course.' Nettie giggled. 'In a few days, when that wound's healed, you'll be able to wash it. There's a ribbon on the table.'

'Thank you.' Movement drew Kate to the window as she continued to run the bristles through her hair. An icy mantle criss-crossed the grass, plants and trees.

'A frosty start today,' Nettie remarked, 'but it will be a fine one in an hour or so.'

A number of low fences some ten feet in length and placed like a series of obstacles for a steeple-chase were set back from the homestead. Vines grew up and across the top palings, which were positioned adjacent to a large garden flush with vegetables and herbs. Beyond, a half-mile away, was the woolly traffic that had first caught Kate's attention. Sheep were being driven by men on foot towards a bark hut.

'Major Shaw asked after you, Kate.'

Returning to the dresser, Kate gathered her hair and tied a ribbon around it.

'He's a fine catch,' Nettie smiled.

Kate studied her reflection in the mirror. There were dark smudges under her eyes and her once pale skin was tinged brown by the months working outdoors. She would have two scars now, one on either side. 'For a girl like me?'

'For any girl, although for myself any Highlander is far too uppity for his own good. They always have been.' Nettie peered over Kate's shoulder so that two images stared back. 'But I don't think that an officer in Her Majesty's Regiment at Foot would go by the name of Bronzewing. Don't look like that. I came and checked on you last night after you'd gone to bed and it wasn't the Major's name that you called out in your sleep.'

'I-I don't know what you mean.' Kate fussed with the wrap. She couldn't recall dreaming about Adam. She wished she could.

Nettie patted Kate's shoulder and adjusted the tartan wrap so it sat evenly across her back. 'I know who he is and why he's locked in my smokehouse, Kate. Of course, I've not laid eyes on him but adventurers are such romantic figures, are they not?' Mrs Stewart turned Kate around to face her. 'He's also a criminal, while Major Shaw is a rather dashing gentleman. You mentioned your mother before, Kate. I'm assuming that she would think the same as me, yes?'

Kate felt like a naughty schoolgirl. This was a woman experienced at ferreting out issues and solving them, as a mother should, before they became a problem. She busied herself putting on the repaired shoes, leaving the laces loose on the foot that was bandaged. Kate wanted to ask how Adam was but instead said, 'How is Mr Southerland?'

'He's in the men's quarters with a deep wound to his thigh. We hope for the best. Although I fear poisoning of the blood may occur.' Mrs Stewart gathered the washcloth and the basin of dirty water and sat it on the tray.

'Can I see him?' Kate hoped the overseer would be able to explain if what Adam stood accused of was indeed correct. She just couldn't believe a man like that had murdered anyone, not after the way he'd spoken of the Lycetts that night in the burial ground.

'I think it's best if Mr Southerland rest. For now I'd like you to join me in the kitchen. It's some time since I had female company closer to my own age, Kate, and I'm sure you'd have a tale to tell and I would be interested in hearing it.'

The Stewarts' home was exactly what Kate had expected to find upon arrival at the Hardys' run last year. The original hut stood at the centre of the house from which two square wings had been constructed. Nettie Stewart was rightly proud of her domain and she showed Kate every room, including the pantry, waiting patiently as her guest limped after her. Kate noted how each glass window gave a pleasing view of the surrounds. There were still musket-sized holes in the walls and two of the windows at the front of the house had been broken in the recent troubles but it was a sizeable building.

The kitchen was spacious but cosy. Kate drew up a chair at the kitchen table as Mrs Stewart placed a large blackened kettle on the coals and sat down in front of a spinning wheel close to the fire. The stone fireplace was almost large enough to stand up in. Bread was being baked, a joint of meat was roasting and any number of pots, pans and griddles hung down from hooks in and around the great hearth. They were soon discussing the price of linen and cotton and the flax which Mr Stewart hoped to grow but had not as yet tried his hand at. Kate did her best to talk along, to be politely interested, but she stopped short at sharing her past life, or that of her parents, other than admitting that they too were settlers but were now dead. No good had come from speaking of her birthright before.

'Weaving's not in my blood, although my eldest is markedly skilled with the loom. Self-taught is my Joanna, with the help of kin before we left Sydney. I was of a mind to ask your Major this morning if he'd teach me, but I doubt a Highlander would see the humour in such a remark.' Nettie laughed. 'Honourable man the officer is, although I mark he secretly still follows the Catholic faith and if not he'll be a believer of the fairy folk or some such nonsense. Thank heavens for the union and the end of the Jacobites.'

The fire in the hearth crackled and spat, the room grew warm.

'Come,' she urged, 'do you spin?'

Kate moved to the wheel, shaking her head. 'I used to make cabbage-tree hats.'

'Did you now? Well that's a pretty craft. We could use a maker of hats out here. My husband says I'm a spinner of yarns, a trouble-maker of the worst sort. It's the Irish in me. I tell him it's only a quarter if that, but in fact it's a good half. Now place your hand on the wheel, that's right.'

Kate was soon rotating the wooden wheel at a steady pace while Mrs Stewart held the wool, walking it out as the yarn was spun. The momentary quiet of the kitchen interspersed with the soft whine of the spinning wheel and the creaking timber was almost like a lullaby. It should have been calming, healing, but all Kate could think of was the man locked in the smokehouse.

'If the wool prices are good, which they should be, Mr Stewart has promised me a little wheel. It's operated by a pedal, which means the twisting and winding of the yarn can be done in one step.' Nettie tugged at the yarn. 'I'm not a believer in the buying of things, not if you can make your own, and the only thing I lack is dye. I've only a few cakes of indigo remaining but I'm assured that if the plant can be established here the process is reasonably simple. One must soak the leaves until they are well agitated and then the liquid is mixed with lye and dried.'

'Mrs Stewart, I'm sorry but I need some air.' Kate left the surprised woman, the spinning wheel coming to a squeaky stop. The passageway was chilly and as Kate limped outside, she was grateful for the plaid wrap. She was sorry to be impolite after Nettie's many kindnesses but it was simply too much. To have endured the last few days and then find herself relegated to the kitchen and women's talk? Kate needed fresh air and time to think.

The air was thick with cold. The grass wet underfoot. It was colder here in the valley compared to the Hardy farm. The breeze nipped at her skin, reminding Kate of the last winter she'd experienced, a year ago at the Reverend's farm. No doubt he would be quite pleased to hear of Kate's suffering, considering it God's punishment for her ingratitude and stubbornness. For this was Reversend Horsley's God, a vengeful being. As her head began to throb anew, Kate rubbed her hands together, blowing on the tips of her fingers for warmth.

Around one corner of the house Nettie's two eldest girls were poking disinterestedly at the contents of the boiling copper. Brown of hair in matching blue dresses with red and green tartan about their shoulders, the sisters were a pigeon-pair intent on doing as little work as possible. A set of sheets were strung across a fence upon which small birds perched. They flew off at the girls' cries but not before soiling the clean cotton.

Kate retreated as the screeches of the two young women turned to an argument as to who would wash the bedlinen. She followed the edge of the building in the opposite direction. A wide verandah with a low-slung bark roof encircled three sides. There were roses planted at varying intervals along the edges of the porch and to the west, where the valley began to widen, cattle grazed. The sound of voices drew Kate onwards. It appeared that the noise came from around the corner of the homestead and she soon deciphered the Major's formal tones and that of Mr Stewart. Kate really didn't want to speak to either of them, not at the moment, and yet she couldn't help stepping back up onto the verandah, her breath coming as tiny puffs of whiteness as she tiptoed carefully across to the wall. If she peered around the corner of the porch they would be there. A waft of pipe smoke drifted on the air, a boot scraped on the edge of the porch.

'Well, of course you're right. Both the constabulary and my regiment may very well believe that I've met my end, however, by journeying direct I can report to the authorities at Maitland and hand over the criminal. But, all that being said, I have to ask if I could impose on your hospitality, Mr Stewart, in regards to Miss Carter. I would feel a lot more comfortable with the enterprise if I could escort the brigand back to Maitland and then, with that duty accomplished, return for her at a later date.'

'Why of course, Major. My wife will be quite content to have an educated female for company. Indeed, if you tarry too long, Mrs Stewart may well be inclined to entice Miss Carter to stay. My children could use a governess and Mrs Stewart a companion.'

'I have other plans for Kate and they don't involve such domesticities. I'll be back for her as soon as I'm able, you may depend on it.'

Mr Stewart chuckled. 'Yes, one mustn't wait too long to pick a pretty flower. And what of this Adam, Bronzewing, whatever his name is? You are quite sure he is who you say?'

Kate held her breath. Their footsteps were loud on the wooden floor. Craning her neck, she peered cautiously from around the corner of the building.

'Undoubtedly. There was a detailed description in the Sydney papers, right down to the shell necklace he wears on his wrist. An affectation if ever there was one, and then of course Kate assisted in the final establishment of facts. This colony has enough issues without settlers fearing the likes of him. You can be assured that the murderer will hang by the neck until he is quite dead. And that will be an end to the matter.'

Kate's mouth went dry.

'One wonders at this lawless element,' Mr Stewart replied as they stepped from the verandah. 'They should all be hanged, lest we become a place of overcrowded gaols like England.'

'Yes, hang them or shoot them, but be done with them. This is a land built on the unruly, on the ungovernable. We will never be rid of their kind unless we take a firmer stand and we've enough to contend with here what with the blacks, without ill-bred whites running amok as well. Execution has always been the easiest and cleanest of solutions.'

How was it possible for people to consider themselves so far above others? To actually believe that they had the right to such opinions. Mr Stewart's convictions were certainly at odds with his wife's fine words of being in a new world, with new rules. Kate was about to interrupt the men to argue for the rights of others. The right to life. Adam's life. But it was then that she noticed a man sitting outside a building, a musket across his knees. The structure was squat and round, with stone walls, a single door and a bark roof with a hole in the top. The smokehouse.

'I'll leave on the morrow,' James continued. 'Another day and night without bread or water should make the prisoner a little more amenable.'

'You must carry on as you wish, Major. There was no sign of the black last night although he kept up a din that would have woken half the country. Sitting out there in the middle of the flat with a fire burning.' Mr Stewart kicked at the ground, dislodging small pebbles. 'I expected half the field to be burnt out, but he kept the embers contained and my man on watch last night said he saw the native early this morning carrying the old man away to the east. You let him go last night when we both know he may well be back to try and free his friend.'

'Probably, but he's a fool if he thinks he can walk in here and remain alive.'

The men resumed walking towards a hitching post where horses were tethered near the rear of a building. Kate ran from the verandah, mindful of the many aches in her body, and quietly slipped behind a tree.

'And what of George Southerland?' the Major enquired. 'It will be some time before he is well enough to be of service to anyone. If he survives.'

'He looks to me to be the resilient type and I could use him here, if he's of a mind. You will give a full report to the authorities,' Mr Stewart paused, 'informing them that in all likelihood what livestock the Hardys had have all but been run off by the blacks.'

'But you will send a party to be sure?' the Major asked.

They had reached the horses and their voices were becoming harder to hear. With the men busying themselves with their rides, Kate took the opportunity to move closer, hiding behind one of the trellised vines.

'The Hardys' cousin Jonas Kable was a financial backer in the enterprise, and I am well acquainted with the family.'

'Of course, of course,' Mr Stewart answered quickly. 'From what I've heard, Mr Kable is in a better position than most to withstand the vagaries of settlement, however, you can tell the Englishman I will do my very best to ensure his livestock are found and, if possible, eventually returned. I'll ensure all will be square.'

Kate very much doubted that. Every man in the colony appeared to be looking for an advantage, and the Scotsman was no different. Who would know if one thousand head or two hundred head were walked to the Stewarts' run? Who would know if they were stolen from the murdered Hardys or not? Only their overseer would and Kate was sure Mr Stewart would have the Hardys' run mustered and what livestock were found mixed with his own mob before George Southerland was able to sit in a saddle.

The Major tightened the girth strap on his horse as Mr Stewart lifted a hoof to check the iron shoe. The horses, small geldings that snorted and whinnied in the morning chill, quickly backed away from the hitching post as their reins were untied. The men's conversation changed to the problem of labour in the bush as Mr Stewart threw himself up and into the saddle. The Major, rather more dignified in his mounting, turned the gelding quietly, tweaking the horse's ear and settling the animal with long, rhythmic pats to the neck. His behaviour seemed at odds with the officer who was intent on hanging the man that led them to safety. Kate wondered if James ever questioned the bind of authority that governed his every move or if man and duty had become one. If so, she would have liked to have known the person and not the office.

'Where's your man gone?' The Major's interest was directed towards the smokehouse and the now unguarded door.

'He'll be back directly,' the Scotsman assured him as they rode away.

Whether she was right or wrong, Kate didn't know, but the sentry was indeed missing as she ran to the smokehouse and, lifting the heavy wooden latch, stepped inside and quickly shut the door behind her. Chest heaving with anticipation, she swallowed

385

nervously waiting for her sight to become accustomed to the gloom. It was freezing in the confined space. There was no window and the only light came from an overhead vent that illuminated the shelves lining the circular stone walls. Great cuts of meat – hunks of beef, mutton and kangaroo – sat on the ledges. In the centre of the building was a pile of ash on a stone hearth. The slow drying of the meats ensured the preservation of these foods but now it was winter the area had become a cold storage of sorts.

Adam stood near the far wall, his wrists tethered to an iron ring lodged in stone. It was only when he took a step forward into the wedge of light that Kate saw him.

'You shouldn't have come, miss.'

'I . . .' How should she begin? Now she was here Kate felt unsure in his company. 'You saved us, and you saved my life.'

'Anyone else would have done the same.'

'No, they wouldn't, especially if they were wanted for murder.' The question hung. Kate didn't dare ask if he was indeed responsible. She didn't want to know. 'James is taking you tomorrow. He intends riding to Maitland. He says you will hang.'

'I'm sure he wishes it.'

Kate took a step towards him. 'I can't let you hang. You saved my life. It's not right.'

Adam held out his hands and she walked quickly across the tampered earth floor and tried to undo the rope binding him. Her fingers fumbled with the thick twine, his warm breath on her skin. He was leaning forwards, smelling her.

'Lavender water.' He looked at her.

Kate's cheeks grew warm. 'Yes,' she mumbled.

'Over there,' he gestured. 'There's a file on the shelf.'

Kate fetched the tool and began to saw at the ropes. Her heart was beating faster with every second and she knew it wasn't just from the fear of being caught.

'How did you get in?'

'There was a guard. He'll be back.' The rope was tough. Kate angled the file until the raspy edge began to bite at the twine.

'And horses?'

The grating noise continued as the twine began to give way, strand by strand. Kate was growing more anxious by the minute. 'To the left of the smokehouse I think, behind the vines, but I don't know if there is anything stabled. James and Mr Stewart have just ridden off together.'

Adam tugged at the partially cut binds and, finally free of the rope, touched Kate's hair. 'If I kiss you will you scream?'

Kate stiffened. 'Yes.'

He kissed her anyway, flinging Kate around so that her slight frame was compressed between the cold of the stone and the warm length of his body. The sensation of Adam's lips on hers was beguiling, strange and tingling. Arms held her, protectively, possessively. Kate was both scared and enlivened. When he finally released her she felt like a child, wanting to ask for more yet afraid of the response. She'd never been kissed before.

'I've been wanting to do that for a while,' Adam grinned. 'Come.' Taking her hand they moved to the door. Sunlight slid into the room as he peered outside. 'Do you want me to tie you up to make it look like an escape?'

Kate shook her head. Her thoughts were spinning, whether from the bash she'd sustained or his attentions she couldn't be sure.

He lingered a moment. 'I must find Jardi.'

'And then?' The question was tinged with expectation. She wished she'd said nothing.

'You understand that I have nothing to offer you, Kate Carter?'

She nodded, but she didn't, not really. They barely knew each other and yet a sense of loss was already spreading within her. 'I . . .' What could she say? That she missed him already, although they stood so close as to suggest indecency. Was it possible that a liking for a person could form so quickly or was it because Adam had shown her kindness and saved her life in a wild, lonely land?

The door swung open and a grey-bearded man lifted his musket. Adam knocked the weapon from his grip and, punching the sentry in the face, caught him as he fell. Dragging the unconscious man indoors, he took the musket and ammunition and closed the door quietly. 'You go first,' Adam suggested as they followed the curved wall of the smokehouse. 'Head straight for the house.'

Kate hesitated. 'But what will you do? Where will you run to?'

'Go,' he urged. 'There'll only be trouble if you're caught with me, you know that.'

Reluctantly Kate moved clear of the stone wall, intending to walk directly back towards the homestead, but two of Nettie's children, the girls who'd been washing, were approaching from the far side of the house to sit on the verandah, and they had seen not only Kate but her companion as well. The taller of the two, undoubtedly Joanna, pointed an accusing finger at Kate, while the younger yelled for their mother.

'I should have tied you up,' Adam complained. Taking Kate by the hand, they ran towards the stables.

Kate stumbled after him. She sensed movement to her left. Jardi was running towards them.

'You're injured?' Adam cried as they weaved through the vines.

'My foot, I can't run,' Kate gasped. Her head pounded with the movement.

'White brother?' Jardi yelled. He too ran towards the stables.

A pot was being banged with something metallic and the warning clang was loud and clear.

'Where have you been?' Adam complained, though he slapped Jardi on the arm in greeting.

'Not talking with pretty girls,' Jardi chided. 'I've been crawling through the grass since daylight.'

The yarded horses inside the stables grew restless as they ran into the oblong building.

'Load this for me.'

Kate took the stolen musket Adam handed her and, loading it, rammed the shot down hard before adding the powder. Jardi threw Adam a bridle from a selection hanging from hooks on the wall and he fitted one to a horse. There was no time for a saddle and Adam sprang onto the animal bareback, pulling Jardi up behind him.

'Come,' Jardi pressed, 'we have to leave.'

'Kate.' Adam held out his hand for the firearm. The Major, Mr Stewart and another man were riding hard towards the stables. 'Kate, give me the musket, lass, now.'

But she didn't. Instead Kate stepped away from the two men doubling on the bay mare. What if Adam was a murderer? she mused. What if the kiss had been a ploy to trick her and James was right and she was wrong and Adam really was a criminal? A woman simply couldn't trust men, not in this world. Besides, if Adam was guilty then she too would be punished for helping him to get away. And yet . . . doubt gnawed at Kate. She could still feel his mouth on hers.

A low cloud of dust preceded the approaching men as they drew hard on the reins to halt abruptly at the entrance to the stables. The Major dismounted immediately.

Mr Stewart cocked his musket and pointed it from where he sat on his horse. 'Get down off that horse of mine or I'll blow your head off, son.'

Adam glanced at Kate, his eyes dark with disappointment. He slid from the horse in one fluid movement, Jardi followed suit.

Mr Stewart called out to the eight or so convicts and freed men who came running in from varying directions, informing them to go about their tasks and to be quick about it. These men loitered about before slowly peeling off one by one when it appeared that the action was over.

'You should just hang him here, Major.' Mr Stewart tilted his head towards the single beam that ran the length of the stables. 'Save everybody a heap of trouble. And what about you, lass? Were you staying or going?' he asked. The meaning was clear.

'Are you alright, Kate?' James asked.

'Yes, yes, I'm fine.' She lowered the musket.

'It seems to me that you were about to put yourself on the wrong side of the law.' A deep line etched its way across Mr Stewart's forehead as he addressed Kate. 'And what on earth do we do with the black?' he continued. 'Hanging a murderer's one thing, but . . .'

The Major lifted his own weapon, levelling it at Jardi. 'He's just helped a murderer escape. The two of them can go back in the smokehouse and they can both stand trial for their crimes.'

'Well, it's of no concern to me, and the law must come first, of course.' Mr Stewart sniffed.

'The law?' Kate spat the word out. 'What law, sir? You who sit there passing judgement will soon ride out to steal what sheep are left of the Hardys' flock, while their overseer clings to life under your care quite unaware of your deceit.'

'That is quite enough, Kate,' the Major ordered. 'You are over-wrought and should return to the house immediately.'

'No, it is *not* enough. It is by far *not* enough. I have witnessed more hardship, more fighting, and more death than a person should during a lifetime and you, James, you who saw this man save my life, twice no less, and who guided us to this very farm, remain intent on fulfilling your obligation to Queen and Country out here.' Kate gestured around them. 'Out *here*,' she repeated. 'Do you not see where we are? Do you not know the difference between good and evil? Is it not hard enough for all to survive out here that you must then turn on those who have done you service? You have no real proof as to this man's identity other than similarities and supposition, and yet you would forget all that he has done in order to do your "duty". It is a poor man who thinks so highly of his office, of himself, that he cannot see the difference between right and wrong.'

'I will forget that you have spoken to me in this manner, Kate. It is clear that you have become enamoured with this man and have lost sight of reason.'

Kate frowned. 'And in hindsight I was wrong to think highly of you,' she retaliated.

'Kate,' Adam's voice was tight, 'enough. The Major has his duty to do, as is his right.'

Very slowly Kate lifted the musket, the barrel wavered slightly from left to right as she cocked the weapon and pointed it, at Adam.

'Kate, this is not the way,' James told her. 'Please, put the musket down and leave us. This is men's business.'

Mr Stewart laughed. 'Let her pull the trigger, Major, then the task will be done and we can go about our business.'

Adam looked down the length of the barrel. Kate gave him the softest of smiles.

'I am sorry.' Pivoting on her injured foot, Kate pointed the barrel at James and Mr Stewart. The men paled with disbelief.

'Think what you're doing, Kate,' James pleaded. 'You are choosing a criminal over justice, the civilised over the uncivilised world.'

'For a long time now the two have been blurred to me.' Kate held the musket straight and tight. Her finger rested lightly on the trigger, her breath stilled.

Adam and Jardi were quick to disarm the men. They took one horse only, hit the others on the rump so that they galloped off into the scrub and readied to leave. Adam stood before Kate, aware of the observant ears and sight of the men who, under Jardi's instructions, were now removing their boots. Turning his hand over, Adam showed Kate the mark on his palm where she'd bit him the night they'd sought cover in the burial ground.

'It is a deep wound,' he told her, 'and may never heal.'

Kate traced the injury with a fingertip. 'I cannot stay in this place,' she whispered.

'The Major will not take lightly to your interference.'

'I know,' Kate replied.

Jardi was busy tying the men, back-to-back, with rope.

'I will come for you, Kate Carter. At the next full moon. If I see you walking around the yard without that fancy tartan wrap then I'll know that you are ready, and I will come.'

Kate dropped the musket on the ground as they rode away.

❈ Chapter 30 ❈

Two months later
1838 September – the Stewart farm

George Southerland limped into the parlour. On seeing him, Kate dropped the hem of the skirt she'd been stitching and rose. The overseer had been bedridden for two months and she'd been forbidden to visit him while he convalesced. But the wiry Englishman was made of stouter stuff than most and now managed to walk with the aid of a sturdy branch.

'Mr Southerland, I'm so glad to see you. They would not let me visit you.' The man looked pale and his clothes hung from him but Kate was pleased to see a friendly face. 'Are you fully recovered?'

'When my leg regains its strength.' He sat on the opposite end of the long sofa, resting the stick against a leg. The room was pleasantly but sparsely furnished with a polished wooden table and a number of carved chairs placed about the room. Kate knew the area intimately having recently been given the task of sewing hangings for the window. In fact the room, like the rest of the homestead, had become somewhat of a gaol since Adam's escape.

'It's time you called me George.' His beard was thicker and longer than Kate remembered. 'I can't say whether you did the right thing or not, Kate, but I admire your spirit.'

'So, you know the worst of what I have done.' Kate wondered what Mr Southerland would think of her actions; strangely, his good opinion was important to her. Biting the sewing thread with her teeth, Kate placed the cotton reel in a basket and folded the skirt. 'My deed was far from appreciated. They feed me and house me and I work in return but there is no friendship here.' She looked about the room. 'This is a fine house, with a fine family under its roof, and I have no doubt that Mr Stewart is a capable manager. But for all Nettie's talk of this being a new world with new rules, they have brought the old ones with them like a well-travelled sea-chest.'

'They are afraid,' George replied. 'Scared of where they live, of who they share the land with, afraid of its lawlessness, of the blacks, of the isolation, the hardships. You cannot blame them for clinging to the old ways, Kate. They have moved here carrying their dreams and hopes with them. You and I, we bring nothing but grit and determination. We have nothing and so we have nothing to lose.'

'You are right, of course. I hadn't thought of things that way, but I still can't agree with their beliefs.' And it was true that whether Kate believed her actions were right or not she had gone against the law and set Adam and Jardi free, and the Major still chased them. 'James continues to search for them, you know. He returns here every few days, as I'm sure you are aware, but he must leave very soon to rejoin his regiment.'

The overseer leant back into the couch. 'And you? Will you journey with him?'

Kate tucked a strand of hair behind an ear. The injury to her head was healed, but the wooden club had left a reddish bump.

'He would still take you as his wife,' Mr Southerland told her.

'Please don't tell me that you have come here to act as his broker in the matter.' She began to tidy the reels of cotton in the round basket, standing the spools on their ends and ensuring that the needles were safely back inside the thick card folder.

George gave a slight cough and stretched out his wounded leg, his eyes narrowing with the effort. 'Hardly. I only know by what he doesn't say that his interest is still there.'

Kate sat the lid on the box and placed it beside her on the sofa. 'Interest? That is not enough for a marriage.'

'After all you have been through, Kate Carter,' George shook his head, 'and still you bridle against the accepted standards of society. I would marry you myself if I were so inclined but I fear you would be like a headstrong racehorse, difficult to break in and impossible to control.'

Kate laughed. 'Well, we will never know, for I am not the marrying kind. Best you tell the Major that, lest he pine away.' She shook out the skirt and then refolded the material. Kate was flattered by the Major's interest, particularly after everything that had transpired, but if she ever had fancied him it had been the briefest of thoughts in a moment of need.

'You are a hard woman.' George stood awkwardly, leaning heavily on the stick. 'I can't sit or stand for long and the Stewarts don't offer enough rum to help with the pain, but I come with news for you.'

'Good, I hope?'

He began to walk slowly across the room, the foot of his injured leg dragging along the floorboards. 'With the wages due to you, I imagine you'd be able to set yourself up back in Syd-e-ney.'

'Wages? How? No sheep have been brought in to my knowledge.'

'James tells me that he solicited Mr Stewart to ensure that those sheep remaining from the Hardys would be mustered, counted and eventually shorn. There are six hundred currently being walked back to this run.'

Kate thought of the coin due her and clapped her hands together, before slowly dropping them to her sides.

George stroked his beard, which was longer and greyer since his injury. 'Whatever is the matter, Kate?'

She waved away his concern. 'Nothing.' In his own way Major James Shaw was an honourable man.

'That's the reason why James returns every few days, to ensure the Hardys are not stolen from in death as their lives were stolen from them. Sarah Hardy's sons are in England. They should benefit from what is left of the estate, after the labour has been duly paid of course,' George said. 'What will you do with the monies owed you?'

'I'd once thought of a school,' Kate answered dreamily, 'my own school. Must I go back to Sydney with the Major as he wishes?' Kate grew anxious. 'Could I not stay here until after the Hardys' sheep are shorn and travel with you when the wool goes to market?'

The Englishman rubbed at his leg and grimaced. 'I don't see why not, but it will be another month before we leave. And you must make your peace with James and tell him that you have no interest. Think on it, Kate. His offer of marriage should not be thrown away lightly.'

'I know, and I am not ungrateful.'

George looked out the window to where cattle grazed in the hills. 'If you turn him down, Kate, make sure it's for the right reason. He won't come back,' he finished pointedly.

'I know that.'

George turned towards her, the walking stick scraping on the floorboards. 'I don't mean James, Kate, I'm talking of Bronzewing. No matter your opinion, no matter how you feel, he cannot. Bronzewing will forever be on the run from the law.'

'I don't know what you mean.' Kate gathered the skirt and sewing basket in her hands as George crossed the room and made to leave.

'I have seen you outside looking to the land beyond.'

Kate stiffened. 'As we all do.'

He merely nodded. 'Every night? When the moon is full? You have been through much, Kate, think hard about your future.'

When he'd left her alone, Kate wandered absently about the room, dragging a hand along the back of the sofa, across the chairs, until she returned to the spot where she found herself every day. Before the window, waiting.

Kate had done as Adam said. She had spent the days and the early evening of the full moon outside, without the plaid wrap, but he had not come. And now another month had come and gone. Another full moon. And still she had waited and once again there had been no sign of him. Kate now knew that Adam wasn't coming. That she couldn't expect him to. What man would risk death for a woman? Hers was an infatuation, a daydream. One born of danger and loneliness, one that couldn't come true. How would they live, how would they survive? If the truth be told Kate hated this wild place she'd come to and as a child she'd been determined to grow old with only cats for company. Now she didn't want that at all. A month, George had told her. A month and then they would head south with the wool clip. One more full moon.

≪ Chapter 31 ≫

One month later
1838 October — at the great waterhole

He was buried sitting up, facing the east, his possessions interred in the grave with him. Adam ran a finger along the healed slices on his forearm and thought of the man who had been as a father to him, of the clan he'd tried to keep alive and of his own friendship with the Lycetts, which had been the undoing of them all. But in truth it had started long before that, with the coming of the settlers, with the desire for land, with ignorance and misunderstanding, with people like him, who, through fault or fate, had tried to straddle two worlds.

And now this.

It was a difficult thing not to belong. Especially now when Winston's words came back to haunt him:

You will need your signature to sign the deed to the land you will one day own, and your sums will help you count your coin, while the skills we learnt in map reading could lead you to your wife.

Below, the sea crashed against the rocks, the foamy crests spurting into the air. The beach was long and deep as if a bite had been taken from the coastline. There were shellfish along the rocks and the fishing was good, although Jardi was yet to wade into the thrashing waves. Having finally reached their destination, Adam was tired. Another full moon had come and gone and still he thought of the girl with the long dark hair.

'She is with you again.' Jardi stood next to him in the faint light of predawn.

'Yes,' he admitted.

A little farther away, the young girl they'd seen captured by the river with Mundara lay asleep under the lip of a cave. 'We could go back?' Jardi offered.

Adam clasped his shoulder and then they climbed up the cliff face, their fingers grasping the slippery rock as they worked their way to the top. There, they watched and waited for the Morning Star.

'We still have the horse. You could be there by the next moon,' Jardi suggested.

Adam looked doubtful as they sat together on a flat rock.

'She risked much to set you free and did you not tell her that you would return?'

He ran fingers through his hair. 'Yes I did. But look at us, Jardi. On the run, camping out. I have nothing to offer her. And besides, we barely know each other.'

'This is a big country, Bronzewing. There are many places to make a life.'

'But what sort of life would it be?' Below them the dull crash of waves enticed a flock of seagulls. The birds circled overhead before drawing closer to the ocean's surface. 'I don't even know if she's interested in me.' Adam gave a wan smile. 'When I said I'd return at the next full moon, she didn't reply,' he turned to his old friend, 'she said nothing.'

Jardi tilted his head to one side. 'We jumped on a horse and rode away. When did the woman have time to speak?'

'Either way,' Adam argued, 'two months have gone by. It's unlikely she'd still be with the Stewarts.'

'Excuses. Is that not the word the whites use?'

Adam rolled his eyes. 'You've learnt too well, Jardi.'

The younger man unsheathed his knife and began to whittle a stick. 'Why didn't you just take her when we escaped?'

Adam laughed. 'Because she's not the type of woman that's for the taking. Kate Carter would be more trouble than good if it was against her will.'

'My woman said no, but then by nightfall she was happy.'

'Well, you were lucky,' Adam admitted. 'You two are well-matched.'

Jardi grinned and then grew serious. 'You are not scared of her saying no.' He pointed to Adam's heart. 'You are scared of that.'

'Probably. I have been alone for too many years, Jardi.' Adam walked over to the edge of the cliff. 'But I still can't give her a white woman's life. You know that.'

'What is a white woman's life, what is a black woman's life? This place is like a bird's egg dropped on the ground.' Walking to Adam's side he jabbed him in the chest with a finger. 'And you who have fought for everybody, why do you not fight for yourself? Go to the whitefella's farm. See if she is there. Speak. Then you will know. If she does not want you then you can let the woman go, like a handful of earth scattered in the wind. But if she is there . . .'

Adam gazed out over the ocean.

'Either way, come back, my white brother, even if it's to say goodbye.'

<hr>

Kate stepped out onto the verandah. With the arrival of spring, the nights were kinder. She'd taken to sitting on the porch until bedtime while the rest of the household came together in the kitchen to listen to Mr Stewart reading aloud. Kate's inclusion in their family gathering was clearly never considered and in the months since her arrival on the property she'd grown used to her own company. Kate leant against one of the timber pillars. The Major had left a fortnight previously without a final goodbye. She did not expect such a courtesy having turned down his offer of marriage, but the difficulty of their parting troubled her. They had been through much together and Kate would have preferred to remain friends, especially knowing the unlikelihood of ever seeing him again, but it was not to be. She waited and pondered on the future, counting down the days until her own leaving. The shearing of the Hardys' wool was done and tomorrow the bales would be loaded onto the wagons for the transportation to Sydney. Very soon, Kate too would be gone from here.

Having reached its brilliance last night, the full moon illuminated the land in a pure white light. The countryside beckoned with its stillness and, tugging at the wrap about her shoulders, Kate moved from the porch to pick a rose from the bushes edging the verandah.

'You're wearing the shawl.'

The flower fell to the ground. He was standing some feet away between trees, his outline barely visible. Kate looked towards the sound of his voice as he stepped from the shadows into the light. It was Adam. She couldn't believe he was standing before her. It had been nearly three months since she'd last seen him, since he'd promised to return. 'I . . . I never thought I would see you again.'

'I'm sorry,' Adam replied.

It was a simple response considering the time that had elapsed, his broken promise. Kate hugged her arms. It grew cool. Part of her wanted to turn on this man. To walk indoors and away from the embarrassment of what Adam had made her endure. 'You said you would come and you didn't. You made a vow to return . . .' Kate would never tell Adam how she'd wept with the passing of that first full moon, never reveal that with the coming of the second that she'd still hoped.

'You never answered me that day,' Adam reminded her. 'I said I would come and you said nothing.'

'Oh.' The word sounded very small.

'After Jardi and I escaped and made it to the coast, I thought about that. I wasn't convinced that you wanted . . .' His words grew faint. 'Anyway, it's no small thing for a woman to run away with a man such as me.' Adam looked up at the moon hanging low and bright. 'I don't know you, Kate Carter, I only understand what I feel. So I stayed away and in the doing the more convinced I became that you would have left this place by now.'

Kate took a step forward. 'I'm supposed to leave with Mr Southerland when the wool's ready for market.'

'I see.'

Although she wanted to remain angry and hurt, Kate understood Adam's reluctance. It was true that they didn't know each other, but a bond had been forged between them and seeing him standing before her, Kate was beginning to grow more certain that if there was a choice to be made between a life with or without Adam, she would take her chances with him. Her voice softened. 'So why have you come, Adam? After all this time?'

'In the end I could not stay away. And it is a full moon.' He smiled.

Voices from the building behind carried out into the spring air. Kate glanced back towards the house. 'Major Shaw has left, but it's still not safe for you here.'

They looked at each other.

Kate thought of the one kiss they'd shared. 'I never thought I'd see you again.' A queasy sensation had lodged itself in the pit of her stomach.

'You don't belong in the bush,' Adam said honestly. 'You should be in Sydney, you know that.'

'What if I don't want Sydney? What if I want another life? A different kind of life?'

The man opposite appeared uncertain.

For God's sake, Kate chastised herself, this wasn't the time to be timid. She knew what she'd lived through and what Sydney offered and the truth of the matter was that she had nothing to lose. Unclipping the brooch, Kate removed the tartan wrap and dropped it on the ground.

Adam was by her side instantly. Taking her hand they ran through the trees, beyond the garden to where a horse grazed nearby.

'You're sure?'

Kate nodded in response.

Adam lifted her onto the animal's bare back and, springing onto the horse, gave the animal's flanks a jab with the heel of his boots. Kate wrapped her arms around Adam's waist, and together they rode into the night.

Reading Group Questions

1. What is the common bond that brings Kate and Adam together?
2. Who is your favourite character and why?
3. Displacement and dispossession are major themes in the novel. Discuss how this relates to Bidjia and his clan.
4. Raised in two worlds and yet belonging to neither, Adam is untouched by white man's materialism and attuned to the natural world. Discuss his strengths and weaknesses.
5. As a female Kate is hampered by her sex and curtailed by the prevailing attitudes of the time. What is the driving force behind the major decisions that she makes? Survival or independence?
6. Winston Lycett's single, shocking lie changes Adam's life forever. Discuss the importance of trust in the narrative.
7. Compare and contrast the beliefs of the Indigenous Australian Aboriginals with regards to land management techniques and ownership to that of the white settlers of the period.
8. Kate's journey into the wild lands of Australia's frontier country is also a journey of self-discovery. Discuss.
9. George Southerland, Samuel Hardy and Major Shaw are all adventurers of a sort, but each is driven by different needs. Of these three who is the more complicated character?
10. Isolation and deprivation in the lands beyond the outer limits made for a difficult life. Do you think Mrs Hardy could have been kinder towards Kate or was her adherence to class hierarchy a way of preserving some semblance of normality?
11. The Australian landscape, its beauty and harshness, is an integral part of *Wild Lands*. How well has the author succeeded in capturing both time and place?

THE BARK CUTTERS
Nicole Alexander

Sarah Gordon knows what she wants: the family property, Wangallon. When it comes to working the land she's a natural but, as a woman, it's not her birthright. Even when her beloved older brother is killed in a tragic accident, nobody looks to Sarah to inherit.

Instead her grandfather passes management to Anthony Carrington, who was once Wangallon's jackeroo.

Feeling betrayed, Sarah escapes to Sydney to try to put Wangallon behind her. But her heart is pulled in two directions: Sydney with its cafes and social life, her blossoming career as a photographer, and her accountant boyfriend, Jeremy. Or the property that has been in her family for over 120 years, with its floods, its droughts, the ghosts of generations past, and Anthony . . .

Past and present interweave in a story that traces the Gordon family from the arrival of Scottish immigrant Hamish Gordon in Australia in the 1850s to the life of his great-granddaughter, Sarah.

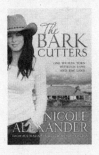

A CHANGING LAND
Nicole Alexander

It's the early 1900s and Hamish Gordon has a massive rural holding, Wangallon, built on stock theft. Embarking on a ruthless plan to buy out his neighbours, Hamish's actions test the loyalties of his family and will have serious repercussions for generations to come.

In the late 1980s, Sarah Gordon now runs Wangallon with her fiancé, Anthony. Their relationship begins to deteriorate when a power struggle develops between them and escalates with the arrival of Sarah's Scottish half-brother, Jim Macken, who is intent on receiving his inheritance . . .

Unable to buy Jim out and with the possibility of losing part of Wangallon, Sarah finds herself fighting the law, her half-brother and Anthony.

Will she jeopardise her own happiness to keep the Gordon legacy alive?

ABSOLUTION CREEK
Nicole Alexander

In 1923 nineteen-year-old Jack Manning watches the construction of the mighty Harbour Bridge and dreams of being more than just a grocer's son. So when he's offered the chance to manage Absolution Creek, a sheep property 800 miles from Sydney, he seizes the opportunity.

But outback life is tough, particularly if you're young, inexperienced and have only a few textbooks to guide you. Then a thirteen-year-old girl, Squib Hamilton, quite literally washes up on his doorstep – setting in motion a devastating chain of events . . .

Forty years later and Cora Hamilton is waging a constant battle to keep Absolution Creek in business. She's ostracized by the local community and hindered by her inability to move on from the terrible events of her past, which haunt her both physically and emotionally.

Only one man knows what really happened in 1923. A dying man who is riding towards Absolution Creek, seeking his own salvation . . .

From the gleaming foreshores of Sydney Harbour to the vast Australian outback, this is a story of betrayal and redemption and of an enduring love which defies even death.

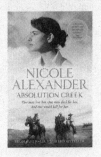

SUNSET RIDGE

Nicole Alexander

Although Madeleine has grown up in the shadow of her grandfather, the renowned artist David Harrow, she knows little about him. For David died long before she was born, and his paintings sold off to save the family property, Sunset Ridge.

Now, decades on, with the possibility of a retrospective of David's work, Madeleine races to unravel the remarkable life of her grandfather, a veteran of the Great War, unaware that his legacy extends far beyond the boundaries of the family property . . .

It's 1916, and as Europe descends further into bloodshed, three Queensland brothers – Thaddeus, Luther and David Harrow – choose freedom over their restricted lives at Sunset Ridge. A 'freedom' that sees them bound for the hell of the trenches.

With the world on fire around them, the brothers bear witness to both remarkable courage and shocking carnage. But they also come to understand the healing power of love – love for their comrades, love for each other, and love for the young, highly spirited girl they left back home . . .

***Sunset Ridge* is a story of bravery and misadventure, of intolerance and friendship, most of all it is the story of three young men who went to war and fought for love.**

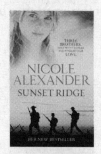

THE GREAT PLAINS
Nicole Alexander

It is Dallas 1886, and the Wade Family is going from strength to strength: from a thriving newspaper and retail business in Texas to a sprawling sheep station half a world away in Queensland.

Yet money and power cannot compensate for the tragedy that struck twenty-three years ago, when Joseph Wade was slaughtered and his seven-year-old daughter Philomena abducted by Apache Indians.

Only her uncle, Aloysius, remains convinced that one day Philomena will return. So when news reaches him that the legendary Geronimo has been captured, and a beautiful white woman discovered with him, he believes his prayers have been answered.

Little does he know that the seeds of disaster have just been sown.

Over the coming years three generations of Wade men will succumb to an obsession with three generations of mixed-blood Wade women: the courageous Philomena, her hot-headed granddaughter Serena, and her gutsy great-granddaughter Abelena – a young woman destined for freedom in a distant red land. But at what price . . .?

A captivating journey from the American Wild West to the wilds of outback Queensland, from the Civil War to the Great Depression, in an epic novel tracing one powerful but divided family.

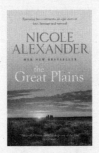